I could touch her. . . . She would accept my touch. . . .

Sebastian had suffered centuries without contact with others, much less touch, yet now a hauntingly lovely female stood just inches from him, open and unafraid.

He raised his shaking hands to her waist, dragging her to him. He barely stifled a shudder when her lush breasts pressed against him. "Tell me your name."

"My name . . . ?" she murmured absently. "My name is Kaderin." Her voice was sensual, a voice from dreams. It seemed to rub him from the inside.

"Kaderin," he repeated, but it didn't fit her. As he stared down into her dark eyes, he realized the name was too cold, too formal, for the creature in his arms. *"Katja,"* he rasped, surprised to find that his thumb was brushing slowly over her bottom lip. The urge to kiss her was overwhelming. "Katja, I . . ."—he began in a rough, breaking voice— "must . . . I must kiss you."

At his words, the dark hazel of her eyes turned completely silver. "I used to love being kissed," she whispered in a dazed tone. Her delicate arms laced up his chest, and she clutched his shoulders desperately. "Vampire, please"—she stared up at his lips and licked her own—*"make it worth it. . . ."*

No Rest for the Wicked is also available as an eBook

"[A] classic romantic adventure that will leave you breathless!"

—*New York Times* bestselling author Julia Quinn

THE PRICE OF PLEASURE

"A splendid read! The sexual tension grips you from beginning to end."

—*New York Times* bestselling author Virginia Henley

"Sexy and original! Sensual island heat that is not to be missed."

—*New York Times* bestselling author Heather Graham

"Savor this marvelous, unforgettable, highly romantic novel by a fresh voice." —*Romantic Times* (Top Pick)

THE CAPTAIN OF ALL PLEASURES

"An exciting, sensuous story that will thrill you at every turn of the page." —*Reader to Reader Reviews*

"Electrifying. . . . Kresley Cole captures the danger and passion of the high seas."

—*New York Times* bestselling author Joan Johnston

"Fast-paced action, heady sexual tension, steamy passion. . . . Exhilarating energy emanates from the pages of this very smart and sassy debut."

—*Romantic Times* (Reviewers' Choice Award Winner)

"Kresley Cole takes readers on the adventure of a lifetime. . . ."
—*New York Times* bestselling author Susan Wiggs

Books by Kresley Cole

The Sutherland Series
The Captain of All Pleasures
The Price of Pleasure

The MacCarrick Brothers Series
If You Dare
If You Desire
If You Deceive

The Immortals After Dark Series
A Hunger Like No Other
No Rest for the Wicked
Wicked Deeds on a Winter's Nifght
Dark Deeds at Night's Edge
Dark Desires After Dusk
Kiss of a Demon King
Pleasure of a Dark Prince
Demon from the Dark

The Sutherland Series
Playing Easy to Get
Deep Kiss of Winter

No Rest
for the
Wicked

Kresley Cole

SIMON &
SCHUSTER

London · New York · Sydney · Toronto

A CBS COMPANY

First published in Great Britain by Simon & Schuster, 2011
A division of Simon & Schuster UK Ltd
A CBS COMPANY

3 5 7 9 10 8 6 4

Simon & Schuster UK Ltd
1st Floor
222 Gray's Inn Road
London WC1X 8HB

www.simonandschuster.co.uk

Simon & Schuster Australia
Sydney

A CIP catalogue record for this book
is available from the British Library

ISBN: 978-1-84983-419-3

Printed and bound by CPI Group (UK) Ltd, Croydon, CR0 4YY

For Bretaigne E. Black, college teammate, instigator of toga wedding showers, organizer of "wine & sign" book signings, and dear, dear friend.

Don't know what I'd do without my Bebs.

Acknowledgments

My deepest thanks go out to three amazing ladies and very talented authors: Gena Showalter for all her incredible support, Caro Carson for always being there for me in a pinch, and Barbara Ankrum for her eagle-eyed critiques and encouragement. And thank you to Richard, my wonderful husband, for confirming the times of sunrises and sunsets all over the globe and for verifying the travel and transportation logistics in this book.

No Rest
for the
Wicked

Prologue

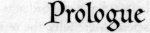

Blachmount Manor, Estonia
September 1709

Two of my brothers are dead, Sebastian Wroth thought, staring up from the floor as he fought to keep from writhing in pain. *Or half-dead.*

All he knew was that they'd returned from the battle-front . . . wrong.

Every soldier came back changed by the horrors of war—he himself had—but Sebastian's brothers were *altered.*

Nikolai, the eldest, and Murdoch, the next eldest, had finally returned home from the Estonian-Russian border. Though Sebastian could hardly believe it, they must have left behind the war that still raged between the two countries.

An angry storm boiled, lashed inland from the nearby Baltic Sea, and out from the torrents of rain, the two strode into Blachmount Manor. Their soaked hats and coats stayed on. The door remained open behind them.

They stood motionless, stunned.

Before them, spread throughout the main hall, was the carnage that used to be their family. Four sisters and their father were dying of plague. Sebastian and their youngest brother Conrad lay battered and stabbed among them. Sebastian was still conscious. Mercifully, the rest weren't, not even Conrad, though he still hissed with pain.

Nikolai had dispatched Sebastian and Conrad home to protect them mere weeks ago. Now all were dying.

The Wroths' ancestral home of Blachmount had proved too tempting a lure to marauding bands of Russian soldiers. Last night, the soldiers had attacked, seeking the rumored riches here as well as the food stores. While defending Blachmount against dozens of them, Sebastian and Conrad had been beaten and then stabbed through the gut—but not killed. Nor had the rest of the family been injured by them. Sebastian and Conrad had held the soldiers off just long enough for them to realize the home was plague-stricken.

The invaders had run, leaving their swords where they'd plunged them. . . .

As Nikolai stood over Sebastian, water dripped from his long coat and mingled with Sebastian's congealing blood on the floor. He cast Sebastian a look so raw that for a moment Sebastian thought that he was disgusted with him and Conrad for their failure—as disgusted as Sebastian himself was.

And Nikolai didn't understand the half of it.

Sebastian knew better, though, knew Nikolai would shoulder this burden as he had all others. Sebastian had always been closest to his oldest brother, and he could almost hear Nikolai's thoughts as though they were his own: *How could I expect to defend a country, when I could not protect my own flesh and blood?*

Sadly, their country of Estonia had fared no better than this family. Russian soldiers had stolen harvests in the spring, then salted and scorched the earth. No grain could be coaxed from the soil, and the countryside starved. Weak and gaunt, the people had easily succumbed when plague broke out.

After recovering from their shock, Nikolai and Murdoch drew away and conferred in harsh whispers, pointing at their sisters and father as they debated something.

They did not seem to be discussing Conrad, unconscious on the floor, or Sebastian himself. Had the younger brothers' fates already been decided?

Even in his delirium, Sebastian understood that somehow the two had been changed—changed into something his fevered mind could scarcely comprehend. Their teeth were different—their canines were longer, and the brothers seemed to bare them in fury and dread. Their eyes were fully black, yet they *glowed* in the shadowy hall.

As a boy, Sebastian had listened to his grandfather's tales of fanged devils that lived in the nearby marshes.

Vampiir.

They could disappear into thin air and reappear at will, traveling easily that way, and now, through the still-open doorway, Sebastian spied no sweat-slicked horses outside, tethered in haste.

They were baby snatchers and blood drinkers who fed on humans as if they were cattle. Or, worse, they turned humans into their kind.

Sebastian knew his brothers were now among those cursed demons—and he feared they sought to damn their entire family as well.

"*Do not do this thing,*" Sebastian whispered.

Nikolai heard him from too far across the room and strode to him. Kneeling beside him, he asked, "You know what we are now?"

Sebastian nodded weakly, staring up in disbelief at Nikolai's black irises. Between gasping breaths, he said, "And I suspect that . . . I know what you contemplate."

"We will turn you and the family as we were turned."

"I will not have this for me," Sebastian said. "I do not want it."

"You must, brother," Nikolai murmured. Were his eerie eyes glinting? "Otherwise you die tonight."

"Good," Sebastian rasped. "Life has long been wearying. And now with the girls dying—"

"We will try to turn them as well."

"You will not dare!" Sebastian roared.

Murdoch cast a look askance at Nikolai, but Nikolai shook his head. "Lift him up." He made his voice like steel, the same tone he had used as a general in the army. "He *will* drink."

Though Sebastian struggled, spitting curses, Murdoch raised him to a sitting position. A sudden rush of blood pooled from Sebastian's stomach wound. Nikolai flinched at the sight but bit his wrist open.

"Respect my will in this, Nikolai," Sebastian grated, his words desperate. He used his last reserves of strength to clench Nikolai's arm and hold his wrist away. "Do not force this on us. *Living isn't everything.*" They'd often argued this point. Nikolai had always held survival sacred; Sebastian believed that death was better than living in dishonor.

Nikolai was silent, his jet eyes flicking over Sebastian's face as he considered. Then he finally answered, "I can't . . . I *won't* watch you die." His tone was low and harsh, and he seemed barely able to maintain control of his emotions.

"You do this for yourself," Sebastian said, his voice losing power. "Not for us. You curse us to salve your conscience."

He could not let Nikolai's blood reach his lips. "No . . . damn you, *no!*"

But they pried his mouth open, dripped the hot blood inside, and forced his jaw shut until he swallowed it.

They were still holding him down when he took his last breath and his sight went dark.

And none will hear the postman's knock
Without a quickening of the heart.
For who can bear to feel himself forgotten?

—W. H. Auden

1

Castle Gornyi, Russia
Present day

For the second time in her life, Kaderin the Coldhearted hesitated to kill a vampire.

In the last instant of a silent, lethal swing, she stayed her sword an inch above the neck of her prey—because she'd found him holding his head in his hands.

She saw his big body tense. As a vampire, he could easily *trace* away, disappearing. Instead, he raised his face to gaze at her with dark gray eyes, the color of a storm about to be unleashed. Surprisingly, they were clear of the red that marked a vampire's bloodlust, which meant he had never drunk a being to death. Yet.

He beseeched with those eyes, and she realized he hungered for an end. He *wanted* the death blow she'd come to his decrepit castle to deliver.

She'd stalked him soundlessly, primed for battle with a vicious predator. Kaderin had been in Scotland with other Valkyrie when they'd received the call about a "vampire haunting a castle and terrorizing a village in Russia." She had gladly volunteered to destroy the leech. She was her

Valkyrie coven's most prolific killer, her life given over to ridding the earth of vampires.

In Scotland, before this call to Russia, she'd killed three.

So why was she hesitating now? Why was she easing her sword back? He would be merely one among thousands of her kills, his fangs collected and strung together with the others she'd taken.

The last time she'd stayed her hand had resulted in a tragedy so great her heart had been broken forever by it.

In a deep, gravelly voice, the vampire asked, "Why do you wait?" He seemed startled by the sound of his own words.

I don't know why. Unfamiliar physical sensations wracked her. Her stomach knotted. As though a band had tightened around her chest, her lungs were desperate for breath. *I can't comprehend why.*

The wind blew outside, sliding over the mountain, making this high room in the vampire's darkened lair groan. Unseen gaps in the walls allowed in the chill morning breeze. As he stood, rising to his full, towering height, her blade caught the wavering light from a cluster of candles and reflected it on him.

His grave face was lean with harsh planes, and other females would consider it handsome. His black shirt was threadbare and unbuttoned, displaying much of his chest and sculpted torso, and his worn jeans were slung low at his narrow waist. The wind tugged at the tail of his shirt and stirred his thick black hair. *Very handsome. But then, the vampires I kill often are.*

His gaze focused on the tip of her sword. Then, as if the threat of her weapon were forgotten, he studied her face, his eyes lingering on each of her features. His blatant appreciation unsettled her, and she clutched the hilt tightly, something she never did.

Honed to masterly sharpness with her diamond file, her sword cut through bone and muscle with little effort. It swung perfectly from her loose wrist as though it were an extension of her arm. She'd never needed to hold it tightly.

Take his head. One less vampire. The species checked in the tiniest way.

"What is your name?" His speech was clipped like an aristocrat's, but held a familiar accent. Estonian. Though Estonia bordered Russia to the west and its inhabitants were considered a Nordic breed of Russian, she recognized the difference, and wondered what he was doing away from his own country.

She tilted her head. "Why do you want to know?"

"I would like to know the name of the woman who will deliver me from this."

He wanted to die. After all she'd suffered from his kind, the last thing she wanted to do was oblige the vampire in any way. "You assume I'll deliver your death blow?"

"Will you not?" His lips curled at the corners, but it was a sad smile.

Another tightening on the sword. She would. Of course, she would. Killing was her only purpose in life. She didn't care if his eyes weren't red. Ultimately, he would drink to kill, and he would turn.

They always did.

He stepped around a stack of hardbound books—some of the hundreds of texts throughout the room with titles imprinted in Russian and, yes, Estonian—and leaned his massive frame against the crumbling wall. He truly wasn't going to raise a hand in defense.

"Before you do, speak again. Your voice is beautiful. As beautiful as your stunning face."

She swallowed, startled to feel her cheeks heating. "Who do you align with . . . ?" She trailed off when he closed his eyes as though listening to her were bliss. "The Forbearers?"

That got him to open his eyes. They were full of anger. "I align with no one. Especially not them."

"But you were once human, weren't you?" The Forbearers were an army, or order, of turned humans. They refused to take blood straight from the flesh because they believed that act caused bloodlust. By forbearing, they hoped to avoid becoming like crazed Horde vampires. The Valkyrie remained unoptimistic about their chances.

"Yes, but I've no interest in that order. And you? You're no human either, are you?"

She ignored his question. "Why do you linger here in this castle?" she asked. "The villagers live in terror of you."

"I won this holding on the battlefield and rightly own it, so I stay. And I've never harmed them." He turned away and murmured, "I wish that I did not frighten them."

Kaderin needed to get this killing over with. In just three days, she was to compete in the Talisman's Hie, which was basically a deadly, immortal version of *The Amazing Race*. Besides hunting vampires, the Hie was the only thing she lived for, and she needed to confirm transportation and secure supplies. And yet she found herself saying, "They told me you live here alone."

He faced her and gave a sharp nod. She sensed that he was embarrassed by this fact, as if he felt lacking that he didn't have a family here.

"How long?"

He hiked his broad shoulders, pretending nonchalance. "A few centuries."

To live solitary for all that time? "The people in the valley sent for me," she said, as if she had to explain herself. The inhabitants of the remote village belonged to the Lore—a population of immortals and "mythical" creatures kept secret from humans. Many of them still worshipped the Valkyrie and provided tributes, but that wasn't what made Kaderin travel to such an isolated place.

The chance to kill even a single vampire had drawn her. "They pleaded for me to destroy you."

"Then I await your leisure."

"Why not kill yourself, if that's what you want?" she asked.

"It's . . . complicated. But you save me from that end. I know you're a skilled warrior—"

"How do you know what I am?"

He gave a nod at her sword. "I used to be a warrior, too, and your remarkable weapon speaks much."

The one thing she felt pride in—the one thing in her life that she had left and couldn't bear to lose—and he'd noted its excellence.

He strode closer to her and lowered his voice. "Strike your blow, creature. Know that no misfortune could come to you for killing one such as me. There is no reason to wait."

As if this were a matter of conscience! It wasn't. It couldn't be. She had no conscience. No real feelings, no raw emotions. She was coldhearted. After the tragedy, she'd prayed for oblivion, prayed for the sorrow and guilt to be numbed.

Some mysterious entity had answered her and made her heart like ash. Kaderin didn't suffer from sorrow, from lust, from anger, or from joy. Nothing got in the way of her killing.

She was a perfect killer. She had been for one thousand years, half of her interminable life.

"Did you hear that?" he asked. The eyes that had been pleading for an end now narrowed. "Are you alone?"

She quirked an eyebrow. "I do not require help from others. Especially not for a single vampire," she added, her tone growing absent. Oddly, her attention had dipped to his body once more—to low on his torso, past his navel to the dusky trail of hair leading down. She imagined grazing the back of one of her sharp claws along it while his massive body clenched and shuddered in reaction.

Her thoughts were making her uneasy, making her want to wind her hair up into a knot and let the chill air cool her neck—

He cleared his throat. When she jerked her gaze to his face, he raised his eyebrows.

Caught ogling the prey! The indignity! *What is wrong with me?* She had no more sexual urges than the walking-dead vampire before her. She shook herself, forcing herself to remember the last time she'd faltered.

On a battlefield, an age ago, she had spared and released another of this ilk, a young vampire soldier who had begged for his life.

Yet he had seemed to scorn her for her very mercy. Without delay, the soldier had found her two full-blood sisters fighting in the flatlands below them. Alerted by a shriek from another Valkyrie, Kaderin had sprinted, stumbling down a hill draped with bodies, living and dead. Just as she'd reached them, he'd cut her sisters down.

The younger, Rika, had been taken off-guard, because of

Kaderin's panicked approach. The vampire had smiled when Kaderin dropped to her knees.

He'd dispatched her sisters with a brutal efficiency Kaderin had since emulated. She'd like to say she started with him, but she'd kept him alive for a time.

So, why would she repeat the same mistake? She wouldn't. She would not ignore a lesson she had paid so dearly to learn.

The sooner I get this done, the sooner I can begin preparing for the Hie.

Squaring her shoulders, she steeled herself. *It's all in the follow-through.* Kaderin could see the swing, knew the angle she would take so that his head would remain on his neck until he fell. It was cleaner that way. Which was important.

She'd packed her suitcase lightly.

2

As a young man, Sebastian Wroth had desired so many things from life, and having grown up wealthy among a large and supportive family, he had expected them as his due.

He'd wanted his own family, a home, laughter around a hearth. More dearly than all the rest, he'd longed for a wife, a woman to be his alone. He'd been ashamed to admit to this female that he'd managed none of those things.

Now all Sebastian wanted was to gaze at the fascinating creature just a little longer.

At first, he'd thought her an angel come to set him free. She looked it. Her long, curling hair was so blond it appeared almost white in the candlelight. Her eyes were fringed with thick black lashes and were dark like coffee, a striking contrast to her fair hair and wine-red lips. Her skin was flawless, light golden perfection, and her features were delicate and finely wrought.

She was so exquisite, and yet she carried a killer's weapon. Her sword was double-edged, with a *ricasso*, an unsharpened area on the blade just above the guard. A skilled user would loop a finger over the guard for better control. She confidently carried a sword not made for defense, not made for battle.

The creature carried steel forged to deliver quick, silent deaths.

Fascinating. An angel of death.

He'd considered it an undeserved blessing that hers would be the last face he would behold on this earth.

Yes, he'd thought her divine—until her smoldering gaze had strayed lower, and he'd recognized she was very much flesh and blood. He'd cursed his useless, deadened body. As a turned human, he had no respiration, no heartbeat, no sexual ability. He could not take her, even though he thought . . . he thought this beauty might actually receive him.

The loss of sexual pleasure had never bothered him before. His experience as a human had been limited—very limited—by war, by famine, by the need merely to survive, so he'd never felt that his turning had deprived him of much. Until now.

He'd never been attracted to small women, because he'd known if he did somehow manage to bed one, he'd dread hurting her. Yet with this one, the most ethereal and fragile female he'd ever seen, he found himself wondering what it would be like to carry her to his bed and gently undress her. His mind began to riot with imaginings of his big hands cupping and stroking her slight body.

His eyes dropped to her slender neck, and then to her high, full breasts pressing against her dark blouse. Now, this part of her was far from slight. He wished he could kiss her breasts, run his face against them. . . .

"Why are you looking at me like that?" she asked in a halting, baffled tone, taking a step back.

"Can I not admire you?" Amazingly, he took a step forward. Where was this coming from? He'd always been awkward and unsure around women. In the past, if he'd been caught staring like this, he'd have turned his face away, muttering apologies as he left the room. Perhaps he'd at last found freedom in imminent death.

Then again, he'd never stared, never hungered, as he did now for this slip of a woman with her lush breasts. "A dying man's last wish?"

"I know the ways a man looks at a woman." Her voice was sensual, a voice from dreams. It seemed to rub him from the inside. "You're not merely *admiring* me."

No, he was thinking at that moment that he wanted to rip open her shirt, pin her shoulders to the ground, and suck on her stiffened nipples till she came. Pin her shoulders hard and lick her—

"How dare you play with me, vampire!"

"What do you mean?" He met her gaze. Her eyes flicked over his face as though she were attempting to read his thoughts. Could she begin to guess the battle inside him? That in one instant the idea of being gentle was replaced with the impulse to cover her on the ground?

What is happening to me?

"I know you can't feel this . . . this . . ."—she made a small sound of frustration—"you can't feel what you are appearing to. It's impossible, unless—" She gasped. "Your eyes . . . they're turning black."

Black? His brothers' eyes had turned black with sharp emotion. He hadn't known his did as well. Was it because he'd never felt anything so sharply as his desire for this mysterious female?

He felt like he'd die if he didn't act on that desire—

A sudden explosion of sound made him swing his head around, his body tensing. "What was that?"

She took a quick glance around her, eyes alert. "What are you talking about?" she demanded.

"You do not hear that?" Another shaking like that, and the castle would collapse. He had to get her away, even into the morning daylight outside. The need to protect her had suddenly become critical, undeniable.

"No!" Her eyes went wide, her expression aghast. "It can't be!" She backed away from him, moving gingerly, as if he were a snake about to strike.

Another explosion. He traced to just in front of her, and her sword shot up in a blur. He snatched her wrist, but she struggled. Christ, she was strong, but he seemed to be stronger than usual himself, more powerful than he ever could have imagined. "I don't want to hurt you." He pried the weapon from her hand and tossed it to his low bed. "Do not fight me. The roof is about to fall—"

"No . . . no!" She stared at his chest—at his heart—in horror. "I am not a . . . Bride."

Bride? His jaw slackened. He remembered his brothers explaining that when he found his Bride, his eternal wife, she would *blood* him. With his blooding, his body would come back to life. He'd always believed they'd lied to dull the bitter sting of what they'd made him.

Yet it was true. The sound he'd heard was the rush of his own heart beating for the first time since he'd been turned into a vampire. He rocked on his feet as he inhaled deeply, breathing at last after three hundred years.

His heartbeat grew stronger, faster, and his sudden erection was tight and throbbing, pulsing with each beat of his heart. Pleasure seemed to course through his veins. He'd found his Bride—the one woman he was meant to be with for eternity—in this hauntingly fine creature.

And his body had awakened for her.

"You know what is happening to me?" he asked.

She swallowed, backing away farther. "You're changing." Her blond brows drew together, and in a barely audible whisper, she added, "For . . . for *me*."

"Yes. For you." He crossed to her until she stared up at him. "Forgive me. If I had known this was true, I would have searched for you. I would have found you somehow—"

"No . . ." She swayed on her feet, and he laid one palm on her slim shoulder to steady her. She flinched but allowed the touch.

He realized then that, just as he was changing, so was she. He thought he saw silver flash in her glinting eyes. A swift tear dropped down her cheek.

"Why do you cry?" Women's tears had always wrecked him as a mortal, but hers made him feel as if a thousand knives twisted inside him. When he brushed her hair back, he sucked in a ragged, unpracticed breath. Her ear was sharply pointed. Up closer, he could see the smallest fangs.

Sebastian didn't know what she was, and he didn't care. "Please do not cry."

"I never cry," she whispered. Frowning in confusion, she patted the back of her hand against her cheek and drew it down to see that it was wet from a single tear. Her lips parted, and she stared, first at the tear, and then at her sharply curling fingernails, which were more like elegant claws. Her gaze darted back to him, and she swallowed as if with fear.

"Tell me what troubles you." He had a purpose now: to protect her, to care for her, to destroy whatever threatened her. "Bid me to help you, Bride."

"Not a Bride to one of your kind. Never—"

"But you've made my heart beat."

She hissed back, "You've made me *feel*." He didn't understand the meaning of her words or her reactions during the next several minutes as he gazed down at her, greedily learning her features—the sweep of her thick lashes when she glanced down, the full red pout of her lips. Waves of emotion shimmered in her eyes and seemed to pain her. Her body shook. As abruptly as they'd started, her tears dried.

Then she smiled up at him, a heartrending curling of her lips. Her eyes were merry, darkly teasing. Nothing had ever aroused him so much as that look, and he wondered how much more he could take. But her smile faded far too soon. She shuddered violently, lowering her forehead to his chest.

Just as his aching erection was becoming impossible to deny, she lifted her face, and her expression had changed once more. A flush tinged her high cheekbones, and her lips subtly parted. Her fingers clutched at his shoulders. As she gazed at his mouth, her tongue dabbed at her bottom lip and left no question about what she was thinking of doing.

She was . . . aroused. For him. He didn't understand what was happening to her—or to himself.

His eyes widened, then narrowed, when she placed her delicate arms around his neck. *I could touch her. . . . She would accept my touch. . . .* His shaft had never been this hard. He wanted to bury it inside her so badly he'd give anything.

She tilted her head, still staring at his mouth. "I miss this . . . ," she murmured in a whiskey voice. He didn't have time to ponder her words, because she tightened her arms, bringing their bodies together. He groaned to feel her breasts pressing against him. They were so full and plump—he knew they would fill his palms perfectly.

Christ, he'd suffered centuries without contact with

others, much less touch, and now he was feeling his Bride, soft and pliant in his arms. He was afraid he was dreaming. Before he lost his nerve, his hands dropped to her waist, dragging her more firmly against him. "Tell me your name."

"My name . . . ?" she murmured absently. "My name is Kaderin."

"Kaderin," he repeated, but it didn't fit her. As he stared down into her shimmering eyes, he thought the name was too cold, too formal, for the creature in his arms. "*Katja*," he rasped, surprised to find that his thumb was slowly brushing her bottom lip. The urge to kiss her was overwhelming. "Katja, I . . ."—he began in a rough, breaking voice, and had to swallow to continue—"must . . . I must kiss you."

At his words, the dark hazel of her eyes turned completely silver. She seemed to go into a trance. He was not so far gone as not to notice this stunned reaction, but her full red lips were glistening, beckoning him.

"I used to love being kissed," she whispered in a dazed tone, her breaths growing hectic.

Could he possibly stop with only that? With an unsteady hand, he cupped the back of her head, about to draw her to him. Surely she was strong enough to take him—she was some sort of warrior and would likely be quick to check him if he hurt her.

For some reason, he sensed she wouldn't give him that teary, betrayed look women had cast him in the past if he'd accidentally stepped on their toes or collided with them coming around a street corner, that look that brought him so low.

"Vampire, please," she murmured, "make it worth it. Make it . . ."

When their lips touched, he groaned; electricity seemed to prick at his skin. He pulled back from her. "My God." Nothing had ever felt so powerful, so right, as this kiss. Her hungry expression deepened.

If it took becoming a vampire to have just this one perfect moment, would he suffer it again?

When he kissed her again, lightly at first, she moaned, "More," against his lips.

He clutched her tightly in his arms, then somehow remembered himself. *No, fool. . . .* He eased his hold.

At once, her claws bit into the backs of his arms, making him shudder. "Don't hold back. I need *more*."

She needed more, needed him to give it to her. Because she was . . . his. When this finally sank in, his shyness burned away. In the course of a heartbeat, he now had a woman of his own. He wanted to roar with triumph. The feel of her claws sinking into him—as if she feared *he* would get away—was ecstasy. *She needs me.*

"Kiss me more, vampire. If you stop, I'll kill you."

He couldn't help but grin against her lips. A female threatening him if he should *stop* kissing her?

So he did, tasting her tongue, teasing it, then claiming her mouth hotly, wetly. He savored the slow undulation of her hips against him, in time with each thrust of his tongue.

He kissed her with all the passion long denied him, with all the hope that had been wrenched from him returning. Weariness of life had just been replaced by purpose— because of her. He let her know how thankful he was . . . by kissing her until she panted and sagged against him.

Yet he was losing control. Impulses came for him to do things to her body, wicked things, and he knew that soon he would obey them. "I'll always give you more, until I die."

And now, for the first time in three hundred hellish years, Sebastian desperately wanted to live.

3

As if she'd been hurled down from a great height, all the emotions lost to Kaderin, denied to her for the last millennium, crashed into her. Fear, joy, longing, and an undeniable sexual hunger warred within her—until he stoked her lust hot enough to drown out all other feelings.

She was reeling, confused. All she knew for certain was that she needed release so badly her yearning pained her, made her whimper. And each of his fierce, possessive kisses increased her agony.

As she threaded her fingers through his thick, tousled hair, she couldn't think, couldn't begin to reason out why this was happening to her. Inexplicable wants wracked her—to lick his skin, to have his body pressing heavily on hers.

She brought her parted lips to his neck, kissing up from his collar. In turn, he thrust his erection against her, as if he couldn't help himself, then seemed to be willing himself not to do it again. But she was thrilled to find his shaft was huge and rigid, insistent against her. It made her body grow wet, wanting it.

Unable to stop herself, she flicked her tongue out to taste his skin. Sensation spiked within her, and she moaned. Had any male ever tasted so good? His taste made her body react with animal needs so strong, she twitched as she resisted them. She wanted to rip his jeans from him, take that thick shaft in both hands, and lick its length in a frenzy.

Imagining that made her roll her hips against him, and after a shuddering hesitation he met her. He hissed in a breath and rumbled foreign words in her ear. The entire castle shook—from *her* lightning, a Valkyrie's lightning produced by her emotion.

Lightning, pleasure of any kind, had been denied her for so long.

She knew this was forbidden, knew she would regret it, but at that moment, she didn't care. For some unknown reason, she'd been granted a window of opportunity with this male, enabling her to know passion once more. Just once more, that was all she wanted, before cold and nothingness crept over her again. . . .

So she took his kisses and returned them. Even as her ardor overwhelmed her, she tried to justify her actions. They wouldn't do more than this. This was forgivable. They were still clothed.

He clutched her ass, fingers splayed, holding her firmly so he could thrust. *Strong male . . . immortal male . . .*

With a body like a god's.

"Harder," she whispered, then somehow she was backed against the wall, his hand behind her head to take the impact as he pressed her into it. His entire rigid body covered hers. Good, he was getting more aggressive. *No! If he takes the reins, I'm lost . . . lost to him.*

It had been so long.

A tight and aching coil was rapturously unfurling with each of the vampire's determined shoves. "Don't stop," she pleaded between ragged breaths. For the first time in a millennium, she was going to climax.

Reading her mind, he rasped, "Can I make you . . . come like this?"

"Yes!" she cried against his mouth. "Keep going! I need you to!"

"*Need?*" He groaned as if excited by the word. "The problem is . . . I will, too." His voice rough with lust, he said, "I've got to take you, Bride."

She stiffened at his words, as if she were waking up, then turned her face away. "Wait! I can't . . . I can't do this!"

"I can give you what you need, I swear it," he grated, even as he cursed his lack of experience. He'd figure it bloody well out. "Just let me have you."

She shook her head wildly, thrashing in his arms. "Noooo!"

As a human, he would have let her go immediately. But instinct told him not to. While understanding so little about what was happening, he somehow knew it was critical to have something shared between them, even a brief morning of pleasure.

He couldn't allow this to stop—not before he'd given her release and taken his from her body as well. "Then we'll only be as before." If this was all she'd permit before she came to her senses, then he'd take what he could get.

"You don't understand—"

Shocking himself, he cut off her protest, hands cradling her face so he could take her mouth hard. She tensed, seeming merely to endure his kiss. Then, after a moment, she gave an answering moan that made him sweat with relief. Her claws were back into his shoulders. He rocked into her, and his thoughts grew murkier, replaced by urgent want.

The rougher he became, the more she gave cries into his mouth that drove him wild, urging him on. Yet even as she took his aggression with obvious pleasure, the wall was crumbling behind them.

Suddenly, she hopped up, wrapping her legs around his waist. "Ah, God, that's it, Katja." He clenched her generous, round ass in his palms, groaning at the feel. Here, too, she was in no way slight, and he loved it.

He squeezed her lush curves, kneaded her, and she panted in his ear, "Yes, yes, you're so strong."

Strong? He shuddered. That pleased her? "I've never felt anything so damned good as your body—"

His words died in his throat when she dropped lower, clutching his shoulders and hanging from her straightened arms to grind against him. She kept her silvery eyes on him, one tiny fang digging into her bottom lip as he stared down in disbelief. She was wild, making his cock twitch and pulse, nearing orgasm.

Hold on, he commanded himself. *She needs to come.*

She pulled herself up to kiss and nibble at his ear, putting her silken neck right before his mouth. *Bite her.* He licked her neck, wanting to take her there so badly. No. He couldn't do that to her.

Why not? She likely thought him a monster already—

She slapped her palm hard behind her, pushing off the wall so he went tripping back over books. Pages flew as they tumbled to the ground with her on top.

She was frantic, shed of inhibitions, grinding against his shaft while tonguing his mouth. Her ass moved so sensuously beneath his palms as she worked her body against his—never in his most fevered fantasies had he imagined this.

He no longer cared if he spilled his seed into his pants. He was going to come harder than he ever had. *Shameful, degrading.* He didn't care.

He rolled her onto her back, pinning her arms above her head, giving in to the most primal urge to rock his hips. He ached to thrust against her. He needed to master her, and from the way she reacted, with her eyelids fluttering closed as she moaned, she needed it as well.

"I didn't believe it was true," he groaned.

Her head thrashed, the blond silk of her hair filling him with her scent.

"Katja." He thrust harder and she writhed wildly beneath him. "You're *mine*."

"Yes, yes . . . you're making me . . . come." She arched her back, crying out. He wrapped his arms tightly around her torso, trapping her against his body as he bucked furiously against her.

He groaned toward the ceiling, neck tensed, as his seed began to pump from him. With each shot, he gave a brutal yell. She was still coming, her claws sunk into his back.

He gave one last violent shudder, then collapsed on her, stunned to silence by the pleasure. His breaths, so new and astounding to him, were ragged.

But when he realized what he'd just done to her, he flushed, humiliated, pushing up from her and averting his eyes.

Bride or not, she was a stranger to him, but he'd shamed himself like a green lad in front of her. Much worse, he'd used all the strength in his body to hold her down and shove against her. How could he *not* have hurt her? How could he not have bruised her perfect skin? He dreaded meeting her eyes. To see that betrayed look . . .

Yet then, she tugged him back down and turned her head slightly, seeming to nuzzle the side of his neck. She began rubbing her face against his, almost like a cat. Though she had the strangest manner of showing it, he knew she was indeed giving him affection.

Affection. Another ecstasy for him. He hadn't been touched in so long.

He rested on his elbows as she gazed up at him with her eyes soft, flickering between silver and dark hazel, her expression satisfied. Holding her face with both of his shaking hands, he brushed kisses over her eyelids, her nose. She was the loveliest creature he had ever imagined—and the most passionate—and she was his.

His voice hoarse, he said, "I have not told you my name. I am Sebastian Wroth."

Still seeming entranced, she murmured, "*Bastian,*" making him want to squeeze her.

He grinned down at her. "Only my family used to call me that. It pleases me that you would."

"Uh-hmm." She scratched his neck in languid circles.

Excitement was still drumming in him. The idea of learning everything about her filled him with anticipation, but first he had to know—"Did I . . . did I . . . hurt you?"

"I'll be sore." Her lips curled, then she rubbed her face against him once more, this time as if grateful. "But only in the most delicious places."

His cock was still semi-hard in the wet heat of his jeans, and the way she purred that one simple word, *delicious,* made it swell once more. He didn't understand how she could simply shrug off being hurt, but there was no way he'd act on the need welling once more. He fought to ignore how good she felt beneath him.

He brushed back her hair, revealing her pointed ears. The tiny fangs, the claws, the eyes . . . "Katja, what are . . ." He cleared his throat. "What *are* you?"

Her brows drew together. "I'm a—" She tensed in an instant. Her eyes cleared completely, as though she'd just woken up. All the supple muscles of her body that had gone soft and pliant after her orgasm now grew rigid.

With a sharp inhalation, she kicked him off her—hard—sending him to the opposite wall, then shot to her feet. "Ah, gods, what have I done?" she whispered, bringing a tremulous hand to her forehead. Her face was cold, but her eyes burned wild as she backed away.

He stood, hands in front of him so as not to startle her.

But then she roughly ran her sleeve over her mouth, infuriating him. He recognized her disgust, recognized the sentiment.

He'd shared it about himself ever since he'd been turned.

"We're going to forget this happened, vampire." She couldn't believe she'd just felt gratitude toward him. Because he'd given her relief from desire? What the hell had happened? Reality was seeping in, and with it came shame so hot it stung her.

"How can I possibly forget this?"

Maybe a capricious power had played with her, forcing her to do things she would never do. Or had she caught a spell? She had to leave at once. "Vow not to tell anyone, and I'll let you live for now."

"*Let* me live—?"

He didn't finish the sentence, because in the space of

three words, she'd collected her sword, then shot behind him to tuck it menacingly between his legs. She'd moved so quickly she was a blur.

"Yes, let you live," she hissed at his ear.

"You are unused to this." He traced across the room and stood, arms out, a hand on each side of the doorway. "As am I. We will find our way with this together. But you *are* my Bride."

She closed her eyes, struggling for calm. "You're not my husband. And never will be."

"This can't be random, Kaderin."

Enough. As she started for the door, she could sense apprehension building in him. They both knew the sun would protect her. All she had to do was get past him—

Suddenly, she doubled over as sorrow for Dasha and Rika ripped through her like barbed wire dragged through her veins.

"Kaderin?" He strode toward her. "Are you hurt?"

Gulping air, she shoved her hand out to stop him before he reached her, and forced herself to stand. All Valkyrie were related, but she and her two sisters had been born together. Triplets. Inseparable for one thousand years, until two had died in battle. Because of Kaderin's weakness . . .

"Kaderin, just wait—"

She charged for the door, but he traced back to it and held his ground. She feinted left and ducked right, moving so fast she knew he couldn't make out her form. As he blinked, she swooped around him, bringing the sword handle crashing back into his chest, deciding at the last minute not to crack his sternum.

He gave a bellow of fury when she barreled past him. She darted down a rotting landing, toward the three sets of winding stairs, running through massive cobwebs so thick he must have traced through them for centuries.

Half staggering, half tracing, he was right behind her as she bounded down the stairs. But she pushed a hand on the railing and vaulted over to the next flight of stairs, then once again to the ground floor.

With a hoarse yell, he leapt down behind her, lunging for her. At the last second, she shimmied out of his grasp, reaching the heavy front doors. She burst through them, wrenching them off their rusted hinges and sending splinters arcing into the air.

Even outside under the morning sun's protective watch, she didn't slow. She raced down the valley toward the village—ragged breaths, leaves crackling beneath her boots, the warmth of the light. *Don't look back.*

Tears blurred her vision as she fought not to sob. The sorrow ached as unbearably as it had when she'd collected and buried the . . . pieces of her sisters. She ran away as if to forget that last night, as if to leave that memory back at that desolate castle. *Don't look back. . . .*

After the burial, she'd torn at her hair and clawed at her skin, alternately shrieking with fury and grief and yearning for the oblivion of death herself. Exhaustion finally rendered her unconscious, and in that heavy sleep, an unknown power had communicated with her as a voice in her mind, promising surcease from the pain yet deadening all of her emotions.

Then, as now, the pain was unbearable. Just as she had before, she prayed for mercy.

But none came. Had Kaderin been forsaken? Had she angered the mysterious power? *Don't look back.* But she did.

The vampire had followed her.

4

Val Hall Manor, New Orleans,
Home of the tenth of the twelve Valkyrie covens

Sometimes Nikolai Wroth really hated his in-laws.

He exhaled wearily as he accompanied his Bride, Myst the Coveted, to the expansive front porch of her former home. They'd just made it to the front steps when the first shriek sounded.

He wasn't surprised, having already learned that his mere vampiric presence would be enough to provoke this nest of Valkyrie.

Though he was a Forbearer, he was often hated as much as Horde vampires—natural-born vampires, a faction that had warred with the Valkyrie since the first days of the Lore. In addition to killing his Bride's kind, Horde vampires often imprisoned them and fed nightly on their exquisite blood.

He understood their hatred of the Horde, and as a Forbearer, he shared it, having battled against them since he'd become a vampire. But this mattered little.

Another scream, and then more followed. Nikolai still was unused to his in-laws' shrieks. They liked to scream. Yet even if they had been silent, he would know their rage over his sensed presence, because the Valkyrie produced lightning with emotion, and right now the yard was like a minefield of exploding bolts.

The many copper rods planted all around the grounds couldn't contain such an onslaught. The ancient oaks surrounding the manor were lashed with ribbons of lightning and gave up their smoke, thicker than the fog.

Did anything smell as odd as burning moss?

He shook his head to the sky but didn't see the stars above him. No, his view was blocked by the wraiths the Valkyrie had paid to circle and guard the manor. The ghostly fiends howled their amusement down at him.

Nikolai had no patience for them. A month ago, when he'd tried to trace into Val Hall to win Myst back, they'd caught him and thrown him so far he'd entered another parish. Nothing could penetrate their guard.

With the wraiths, the lightning, the shrieks, and the smoke, it was no wonder other Lore creatures feared Val Hall almost as much as they feared the Valkyrie themselves. The fact that his beautiful wife had hailed from this place of madness always astounded him.

Tonight she had coaxed him to trace them here to ask Nïx—the oldest Valkyrie and a soothsayer—to help them find his two younger brothers. He secretly thought this a fool's errand. Nïx, or Nucking Futs Nïx as the coven called her, was rarely lucid and had a diabolical sense of humor. And Myst had been warned that Nïx was "in a pissy mood" this evening.

In fact, all the Valkyrie he'd met were . . . eccentric. Even his wife, Myst, thought in ways he didn't understand. And if Nïx was unmatched in Valkyrie madness . . . ?

But he had to try. He couldn't go on any longer wondering if Sebastian and Conrad were alive or dead. The last time he had seen his two youngest brothers, they were just about to leave Blachmount as newly turned vampires. They were both weakened and had gone half mad at the turning. Although three hundred years had passed, Nikolai did not delude himself into thinking that they had forgiven his offenses against them.

He and Myst gained entrance past the wraiths the only way possible. She offered a lock of her hair as toll, and one swooped down for it. In exchange for the wraiths' unfailing guard, the Valkyrie proffered their hair, which the wraiths wove into a braid. Once the braid attained a certain length, they could bend all living Valkyrie to their will for a short interval.

Once inside the darkened manor, they passed the ultramodern movie viewing room. The Valkyrie were obsessed with movies, indeed with anything modern and ever-changing, whether it was technology, slang, fashion, or video games.

A number had grudgingly accepted him now that he and Myst were married and because he'd helped save the life of Emmaline, a member of their coven. He'd even garnered permission—through blackmail—to enter their home at will, becoming the only vampire alive who'd seen the inside of this legendary place.

From the viewing room, they crossed to the stairs and up to the second landing. Myst had explained that Val Hall was like a violent Lore version of a sorority house, complete with catfights and clothing thefts. At least twenty Valkyrie lived here at any given time.

She stopped at a door with a sign painted to read "Nïxie's Lair, Forget the Dog, Beware of Nïx." Myst listened at the door, then knocked.

"Who is it?" came a muffled reply.

"Aren't you supposed to know that?" Myst asked, turning the knob when the door was unlocked.

They entered the room and found it darkened as well, lit only by a computer screen. Nïx stood, her expression inscrutable as she swiftly braided her long black hair. She had on jeans and a small T-shirt that read "I play with my prey."

Inside were a massive TV, hundreds of shades of nail polish, and a pinup poster of a man identified as "Jeff Probst" and labeled "The Thinking Woman's Sex Symbol." On the floor lay piles of shredded books, crashed paper airplanes, and what looked like the remains of a grandfather clock that had been torn apart in a frenzy.

Myst wasted no time. "We're searching for his brothers, Nïx, and we need your help."

Nïx snared one of the few untouched books from the floor, then sat on her bed. He caught the title—*Voodoo Lou's Office Voodoo Kit: Take Charge of Your Career . . . with Voodoo!* "And why would I assist the leech, hmmm?"

Myst's green eyes flashed with anger. She still called *other* vampires leeches and didn't care if her sisters did, but, as she'd said to Nikolai, "It's a double insult to call *you* one. If you're a leech and you like to drink from me, what does that make me? A schmuck? A suckah? Do I look like a *host* to you?"

Myst leaned back on Jeff Probst and drew a knee up. "You'll help us because I'm asking you to and you owe me for keeping a juicy secret from the coven."

Nïx made a scoffing sound as she ripped her sharp claws through the voodoo book. "What secret?" She yanked up another tome—*The Crutch of Modern Mysticism*—flexed her claws, then seemed to think better of completely mauling it, instead ripping out several pages, one with the chapter heading "Why It's Easier to Believe."

"Remember the year 1197?" Myst asked.

"B.C. or A.D.?" Nïx said in a bored tone as she began an intricate creasing of a book page. Origami? A form started to emerge.

"You know I'm only circa A.D."

"A.D. 1197?" Nïx murmured with a frown, then her face colored. Her expression turned mulish, and her fingers began flying over the paper, deftly folding. "Not sporting to bring that up. And one more time—I thought he and all of his pack mates were of age!" When her fingers stilled, she placed the perfect form on her bedside table. It resembled a dragon poised to attack. "Do I bring up *your* unpleasantries? Do I call you Mysty the Vampire Layer like the rest of the Lore does? Like the *nymphs* do?"

Myst clasped her hands to her chest. "Oh, woe, the nymphs have shunned me. I weep bitter tears." Her face hardened in an instant. "What information do you need from us to help you see something?"

With a huffish flip of her heavy braid, Nïx turned from Myst to Nikolai and asked, "Why do you want to find them?" She started another origami without looking, this one requiring four pages from the *Crutch* book.

"I want to know if they're alive or dead. To know if I can help them and bring them back home."

"Why did they leave?" The way she studied him was almost invasive. Her fingers were so fast they were nearly invisible, making the paper appear to fold of its own accord.

He put his shoulders back, hating having to be so open with her. "Sebastian was enraged that I turned him against his will. Both were furious that I tried to turn four young sisters and our elderly father when they were dying." Myst studied him, nibbling her lip, knowing how reluctant he was to speak of this. "I have no doubts that they went away only to get strong enough to come back and kill me." *Because both had tried just before they left.*

Sebastian had woken with that terrible hunger that Nikolai remembered so well. When they'd placed a tankard of blood in front of Sebastian, he couldn't drink it fast enough. But once he'd comprehended what he'd done, he'd lunged for Nikolai's throat. . . .

Nikolai had waited months at Blachmount for them to return, uncaring if either attempted it once more. Each day they didn't return made him wonder if they could fend for themselves, gathering blood each night—without drinking humans. Without killing.

Never lowering her gaze from his face, Nïx finished a twisting shark and placed it by the dragon creature. He found his eyes drawn to the shapes again and again.

"You knew they would be angry?" Nïx asked.

After a hesitation, he admitted, "I did. But I turned them anyway."

When Myst saw him exhale wearily, she began relaying to Nïx everything he'd told her of his brothers. Granted a reprieve, Nikolai yet again justified his decision to himself. That night, seeing Sebastian about to die had made Nikolai realize how much Sebastian especially had missed out on. All he'd wanted was a family and a place to live in peace. Sebastian had never had a chance to find either—he hadn't yet *lived*—and Nikolai couldn't accept that.

As a lad, Sebastian had shot to his full height of six and a half feet early, without the weight and muscle that would come a year or two later. Though he'd been rangy and awkward, Sebastian had almost fared better before his body had caught up with his height.

After that, he hadn't known what to do with his size, with his incredible strength that grew every day. He'd accidentally blackened more than one girl's eye with his elbow and actually had broken one's nose that way. He'd stepped on so many toes that the village girls joked that they wouldn't walk near him without "clogs and fortitude."

But the worst occurred when he and Murdoch had been running in the village, most likely doing some mischief of Murdoch's, and Sebastian had collided with a woman and her young daughter. He'd laid both of them flat, knocking the air from their lungs. A disturbing experience in itself, but once the woman and girl got their breaths back, they'd screamed bloody murder.

Sebastian had been appalled at himself. From the time he was a small boy, he'd always had a shy bent, and things like this made it much worse. He'd become unsure around all women, without the smooth charm of Murdoch or the indifference of Conrad.

At thirteen, Murdoch had had a devilish grin that had already earned him entrance under many women's skirts in the village. At the same age, Sebastian had been the quiet lad with a sweating fistful of crushed wildflowers that would never make it to their intended.

So he'd turned to his studies. Incredibly, even after he'd trained for war since he was old enough to hold a wooden sword, Sebastian's mind was the strongest part of his body. He'd written treatises and scientific papers, which garnered him the notice of some of the great minds of the time—

"You've seen something," Myst said, bringing Nikolai from his thoughts.

"I can tell you where Murdoch is."

"I saw him only yesterday," Nikolai grated. Murdoch lived at Mount Oblak, a castle seized from the Horde. It was the new Forbearer stronghold, so Nikolai traced there most days.

"Oh, yes. Of course," Nïx began in a sarcastic tone. "Murdoch is right where you left him."

"What's that supposed to mean?" At her blank look, he said, "About Murdoch—what did you mean?"

"Did I say something? What did I say? How am I supposed to keep track of what I said?"

He was losing patience. "Damn it, Nïx, I know you could tell us where they are."

Her eyes went wide as she breathed, "*Are you psychic, too?*"

Sometimes he really hated his in-laws.

"Nïx, I need you to help with this," he said, biting out the words. As a former general in the Estonian army, and a current one with the Forbearers, he was used to giving orders—and having them obeyed with alacrity. This . . . this *asking* for things was excruciating.

Yet now Nïx concentrated only on her craft, until she'd folded what looked like an intricate fire, gingerly placing it next to the other two. More pages ripped free, folding at an even faster rate. Nikolai found his attention riveted to the creations that she seemed compelled to make.

Moments later, she'd wrought a baying paper wolf. Four shapes placed as though for a storyboard. Myst spared them no more than a glance, but Nikolai was enthralled.

"Nïx, try harder!" Myst snapped, and Nikolai shook himself, forcing his gaze away.

"I can't see Conrad!" she snapped back, and lightning struck nearby.

"What about Sebastian?" Myst said. "Tell us anything."

"Anything? Well, what do I know?" Nïx frowned. "What do I know? Oh! I know what I know!"

Nikolai paced impatiently, gesturing with his free hand for her to continue.

She shrugged. "Right now, your brother Sebastian is bellowing at someone outside a castle, demanding that they return to him, wishing it with everything that he is." She smiled, as if pleased with herself for seeing so much, then gave a quick clap. "Oh! And his skin just caught fire!"

5

Why would she run from me?

Repeating this agonizing question over and over in his mind, Sebastian scuffed through the pouring rain and the puddles of water along the main street of the deserted village.

At sunset, just as he'd set out to search for her, the rain had begun. Even now, hours later, it still fell with a pounding force, visibly eating away at the cobblestone grout. It struck his burned face and hands, but he hardly perceived it.

What the hell had happened? He'd just been feeling the centuries-old weariness lifting, disappearing with her arrival. Now it had returned doubled.

"Don't!" he'd bellowed to her. Before he'd been forced to trace back, she'd turned to him, her eyes wide, her lips parted. She'd seen his pain, his skin beginning to burn.

Her expression had become stricken. He'd seen that look before. It was the same one soldiers had a split second after a cannon blast had landed too close—as if they simply couldn't assimilate what had just happened.

Why did she run? What did I do wrong?

He'd searched all night, scouring the empty streets and the entire valley. He'd traced to the airport, but he knew she was long gone.

As were the denizens of this village. Only a dog howled in the background. Though Sebastian had avoided humans since he'd been turned, he was fully prepared to question them now. He was desperate to. If they had information about his mysterious Bride, he'd become the thing they feared in order to get it from them.

Yet they had disappeared. Even the home of the butcher who secretly sold him blood and occasionally transacted for clothing and books was darkened and empty. Apparently, she'd warned them that he'd be searching for her with a vengeance.

Again and again, Sebastian contemplated what he knew about his mysterious Kaderin. At times he thought her too beautiful, too perfect, a vision who existed only in his fantasies. He had been alone for so long . . .

And had been mad in the past.

But if he thought he'd imagined the entire thing, he had a glaring bruise on his chest and rents in his shirt from where her claws had dug into his back and his arms. God, she was fierce, his Bride, and even now he was hard for her.

Never before had he felt such lust. No woman had ever stirred him to anything like this. Surely the desire for her was stronger because he'd abstained for so long. That had to be it. He hadn't even taken her.

Hell, he hadn't even seen her naked body or touched her skin.

He shook his head, flushing yet again at his behavior with her. He was in no way experienced, but he knew enough to know that what they'd done was . . . irregular.

In his entire life, he'd had sex fewer than half a dozen times, with just two women, if you could call it that with the second. Sebastian had never been inclined to charm ladies, but even if he hadn't been quiet and introspective, there simply hadn't been time, opportunity, or, more important, women to have.

His family's home of Blachmount had been secluded from towns and markets. Any attractive farmers' daughters within a hundred miles had been hopelessly in love with—and most likely enjoying—Sebastian's rakish brother Murdoch. Which excluded them forever from Sebastian's interest. He could never have compared with Murdoch's experience, and he'd dreaded looking down as he took a woman and knowing that she was thinking the same.

If not Murdoch, Sebastian still had to compete with two other older brothers.

Then came the war.

Sebastian's forgettable—or disastrous—experiences had not prepared him in any way for Kaderin's passion. She had been as frantic as he was. He couldn't even imagine what she would be like naked and writhing beneath him. His erection throbbed at the idea, and he cursed it.

She'd urged him on and then reveled in his strength, like some wild creature. Which reminded him that not only did he not know her full name or how to contact her—he didn't even know what her species was.

If only he understood more about this world he now inhabited, the Lore. He was as ignorant of it as he was of modern human culture.

When he had awakened from the dead all those years ago, Nikolai and Murdoch had tried to explain what they knew of the Lore, which was little—they'd only been turned recently themselves. Sebastian hadn't listened. What good would their teaching do him if he was going to walk into the sun anyway?

For all these years, he'd avoided Blachmount, instead residing in the one country where no one would have thought to look for him. What if he returned now? Could he even predict what he would do if he faced Nikolai?

From the corner of his eye, Sebastian caught sight of something. He twisted around to find his reflection in a shop window. As he stood arrested, he brought his hand up to grasp his chin.

Christ, why *wouldn't* she run?

He looked like a monster in the pouring rain. His face was sun-blistered down one side and gaunt from irregular feeding—he had never been able to make himself drink enough to sustain his weight. His hair was cut haphazardly, and his clothes were worn and threadbare.

In her eyes, Sebastian was penniless, living in a heap, without friends or relations. He'd given her no indication that he would be a worthy partner for her. In his time, a female had needed to be assured that the male she cast her lot with could provide for her. Surely something so elemental hadn't changed.

Worse than all this, he was a vampire—which she clearly detested.

He would never be able to share days outside with her. God, how he already missed the sun—now more than ever because he couldn't walk in it with her.

Vampiir. He raked his hand through his wet hair. *What kind of children would I give her? Would they drink blood?*

He'd have run from him, too.

How could he expect her not to be repulsed by what he'd become, when he himself was? He subsisted on blood. He was relegated to shadow.

"You'll never be my husband," she'd vowed.

"I'll destroy myself," he'd vowed to Nikolai the last night he'd seen him.

How could Sebastian persuade her to live with him, when for three centuries he hadn't been able to persuade himself that he deserved to live at all?

Yet even briefly, Sebastian had gotten her to kiss him and accept his unpracticed advances. With time, surely he could overcome her aversion.

Perhaps other vampires were evil—he'd never seen any besides his brothers. But he could prove to her that he was not. He could protect her and provide anything she desired.

Returning to Blachmount was no longer avoidable—all his wealth was there, buried on the grounds. Before Sebastian and Conrad had left the battlefield, Sebastian had amassed a fortune in war spoils from the Russian officers, including the castle he currently occupied.

He had half a dozen chests filled with gold coins, stamped with the imprint of some ancient god in flight. Several more chests contained jewels the officers had plundered from the east before their greedy gazes turned to neighboring Estonia.

He would force himself to drink and to buy new clothes. He'd purchase a new home for them—he'd be relieved if he never returned to that wretched castle.

When he found her again, he would appear as a man worthy of consideration as a husband. But to acquire the things necessary to do this, Sebastian would be forced to navigate the new world around him. He'd seen cars but had never driven one. He'd seen advertisements for movies but had never viewed one. Planes flew overhead, and he knew the composition of their engines from books, but he'd never traveled in one.

And he would have to walk among humans, though he'd always felt that they could look at him and suspect what he was—an abomination, trying to pass as one of them.

Or worse, he feared that he might crave drinking them. Yet, never had that happened before Kaderin's golden skin had been just before him. Could he control himself with her? Was it selfish to seek her? No, he was disciplined. He could *forbear*, as his brothers' order called it.

He wanted his Bride back, and would have her again if it killed him.

Turning away from the window, he stared out into the rain, realizing he'd been wanting her all his life. Sebastian shook his head ruefully. Even before she'd become all he had.

London, England

Everything is under control.

Kaderin's blessing was back in place, even though, to any who saw her, she appeared disoriented.

Since the time when London had been a marshy encampment beside a forgettable river, vampires had hunted in the fog here. And whenever she'd visited, she'd hunted them.

After her debacle in Russia, she'd chosen to come to this Lore-rich city because she had a private flat here that none of the Valkyrie knew about, and because it was a good base for the Hie—not because she couldn't face her coven.

Tonight was her first in the city, and she'd set out for King's Cross with one objective: to kill leeches. Beneath her trench coat, her sword and whip rested hidden. She meandered down a cobblestone back way she remembered well—

just over a century ago, two vampire brothers had nearly be-headed her on these very bricks.

Kaderin didn't despise vampires only for her sisters' sake.

Along the alley, she'd gradually begun to act as though she were lost in the dingy veil of the city, even subtly limping—signaling a predator that dinner was here for the taking.

She tried to convince herself that her excursion wasn't meant to prove anything. This wasn't an exercise to see if she still had the stones to hunt vampires. That would be too cliché, too movie-montage-worthy, as she *busted heads* and *cleaned out the streets of London*.

To kill tonight was, simply, her life as usual.

A gang of five of them materialized from thin air. "Seems my birthday came early, boys," Kaderin drawled. They were dressed like street thugs, and their glowing red eyes were spat-tered with floating black flecks. Dirty eyes. When they drank beings to death, they drank from the pit of the soul, taking all the bad, absorbing all the madness and sin into themselves.

The five surrounded her; she yanked her sword free and struck hard without delay.

A flip of her wrist claimed her first head. *Lookit*, Kaderin thought. *A vampire's head rolling across a London back alley. Business as usual. Control.*

They began tracing all around her, striking out with fists or blades. She yanked her coiled metal whip free from her belt. Titanium. With a whip, she could contain a tracing vampire. One recognized her with the first crack and escaped, fleeing the fight.

Ah, but the other three are going to roll the dice.

Her whip caught one's neck, coiling round again and again, snapping at the end.

The house always wins.

She yanked, sending him listing toward her, right into her sword's reach. As she severed his head, she kicked behind her to ward off the other two. She ducked under the bigger one's blade, and it sank into his comrade's temple.

Blood sprayed. She was in her element now. Cool dispassion. Cold killing. Her sword flew, her whip cracked—she was back to normal.

How irrational she'd been, fleeing hysterically from Russia, with all the weeping and uncontrollable shaking. How many times had she moaned, "Oh, dear Freya, what have I done?" or recalled the look on that vampire's face when he'd realized he was going to have to let her go into the sun?

She'd had an indiscretion. As Valkyrie sometimes did.

Like Myst the Coveted? Kaderin thought, delivering a killing blow to the vampire with the knife jutting from his head like a horn. When Myst had been in a Horde prison, the Forbearer rebels took the castle, and one of their generals had freed her to make love to her. Before the Valkyrie could rescue her, things had gotten out of hand in a dank cell.

Myst's status among the Lore—which she'd built over lifetimes—was ruined. She was shunned, an outcast. Even the nymphs ridiculed her. There was no ignominy worse than that—

The last one threw a hit to Kaderin's jaw that had her seeing double for a moment, but she blindly punched out and connected. Then she was back on her toes, sword gliding, thoughts whirring. As the two of them circled each other, Kaderin recalled the ultimate fall from grace. Just decades ago, a Valkyrie named Helen had had sex with a vampire, and then bore his child, Emmaline. Helen had died of sorrow—because the vampire had turned on her.

Another strike of her sword. The last one barely dodged it and cursed her.

"Goodness. I have *never* been called a bitch before." She wiped her sleeve over her face, and their eyes met.

Vampires turned. That was what they did. She hadn't missed that Sebastian had hesitated with his mouth over her neck, even giving it a slow lick. He'd contemplated it.

Yes, eventually, even Sebastian would drink a victim to death, accidentally or not. His steady, clear gray eyes would grow dirty red with bloodlust, and the Horde would claim yet another soldier. Just like the one in front of her.

The thought had her charging forward with a shriek. She dipped and rolled, planting her sword up through his chest. Shooting to her feet, she snatched it back to swing for the head with a clean slice.

Her sword didn't whistle, because air rarely perceived it in time.

Too easy, not worthy, she thought as she dropped down for his fangs. *Four. Whoop-de-fucking-do.* If they'd been fish, she'd have caught and released.

But she was back, and now her mind was clear regarding Sebastian Wroth. No longer did that vampire's loneliness cling to her like the fog crawling on this city. With this clarity, she would be back to normal for the Hie in just two days. She would not be *freaking out*, as she'd predicted on her way to London. Nor would she be so *sc-sc-screwed*, as she'd figured.

No, here she was. Cold as ice.

From King's Cross, she jogged back toward her place in Knightsbridge, her blood-soaked clothing cloaked in the night mist. Her courtyard townhouse was in the perfect location. Close enough to shopping—if Kaderin was ever moved to that—but it also backed into narrow and murky mews, which allowed her to enter the residence unseen. From the back, she bounded over her courtyard wall, let herself in, then dashed up the stairs.

Kaderin yanked off the clothes she'd filched from Myst, took an appraising glance, and tossed them onto the do-not-resuscitate laundry pile. She hopped into the shower, washing away all the blood.

As she lathered her hair, she didn't think about the vampire. At all. She ignored questions about why he'd been in that castle and what exactly had made him want to end his forlorn existence. All that information, such as where he had been a warrior, was incidental.

After she won the Hie, and when she was ready, she'd return to finish him.

In the meantime, he would be searching for her. Vampires who'd found their . . . their Brides didn't tolerate losing them. But he wouldn't be able to find her, knowing nothing but her first name. The villagers would scurry away in fear before each sunset, staying away at night until she could return—or they would face her promised wrath.

And anyone else from the Lore who could reveal that information would run from the sight of him simply because he was a vampire. He was an outsider everywhere, with everyone, whether human or Lore creature. And while she competed in the Hie, he certainly wouldn't be able to locate her. In the coming weeks, she'd never sleep in the same place twice and would be racing to the farthest reaches of the earth, obtaining prizes, jewels, and amulets.

She'd face him when she chose, and on her terms. Yes, everything was under control.

6

In the last three days, Sebastian had found it hellish to be around so many humans—a blood drinker, a predator, walking among them as if he were still one of them. Especially since women had begun gazing at him longingly, and even following him, to his consternation.

But he reminded himself what was at stake and completed task after task in anticipation of finding Kaderin, even as he had no idea how to do so. The villagers, his only lead, had disappeared, at least during the nights. Of course, she'd warned them.

After all this time away, he'd finally returned to Blachmount, and he'd been awed as ever by the old manor, even if it was as decrepit as his own holding. He'd dug up gold from his chests, then sold the coins in Saint Petersburg. Cash in hand, he'd bought clothing at the only place he knew wealthy men acquired clothing—Savile Row in London. He'd been to the port of London once when he'd been mortal and remembered it only vaguely. Yet one mental picturing of it put him there.

Money got him tailoring appointments after sunset, and each night before he set out in that city, he forced himself to buy and drink blood from the butcher.

He'd done these tasks because he wanted to become a

man she could want. But he was also desperate for anything to keep his mind occupied. At every turn, he wondered where she was at that moment and if she was safe. She'd cried that morning, had doubled over in pain.

And he couldn't find her.

Her accent had a tinge of a drawl, but that helped little in determining her place of origin. He couldn't trace to her home country to begin a search, because he didn't even know what continent she lived on. Besides, his brothers had told him that vampires could only trace to places they'd already been. If she wasn't in Europe or Russia, then he couldn't reach her.

Again and again, he'd thought, *If only I could trace directly to her.*

The idea that a vampire didn't need to know *how* to get to a destination, only to *envision* it, didn't make sense to Sebastian. He'd traced from Russia to London to buy clothing, but he couldn't imagine the exact route. If merely seeing the location was the requirement, then why couldn't *a person* be a destination?

What if there was more to tracing, and his brothers didn't understand everything about it? They had been newly turned themselves all those years ago and had admitted their ignorance about so much in the Lore.

It might be that vampires traced to individuals every day. . . .

Sebastian was unique among his family—he was the dedicated scholar, the one introspective son among four. In battle, Sebastian had used cunning as much as strength, relying on foresight as much as on past training. He was a thinker who liked to solve problems, and his father had instilled in him the belief that the mind was capable of unimaginable feats if one were strong enough to believe them possible.

And Sebastian needed to believe that tracing to her was possible. The alternative was to wait out the villagers, which was untenable.

His family had known he'd been courted by chivalric and church orders, as well as other secret sects of arcane knowledge, seeking to recruit him. What they didn't know was that he'd accepted an offer with the Eestlane Brothers of the Sword, learning about the world from isolated Blachmount, corresponding with masters of physics, astronomy, all of the sciences. Eventually, he'd even sailed the Baltic and North Seas to be knighted in London.

While his brothers had been fighting each other or chasing women, Sebastian had been studying, growing confident in his ability to learn.

It might just be that Sebastian's sacrifices then would benefit him now, as he chased the only female who'd ever mattered to him.

Filled with a burning determination, Sebastian had traced back and forth to places he only vaguely remembered from boyhood, studying the amount of effort, the amount of mental clarity, required.

He convinced himself that he just needed to see her as clearly as a location.

There was danger inherent in tracing to a place unseen. She could be under an equatorial sun at noon, and he could be too stunned to get away. She could be on a plane. If his trace was mere feet off, he could be sucked into an engine.

Hell, it would have been worth it.

*   *   *

Perhaps when Kaderin had determined that everything was under control, she might have done so too hastily.

Since that night, her blessing had been behaving like an engine in an old Karmann Ghia convertible—sometimes it slipped. There she'd be, cruising along, the same as usual, then, out of nowhere—a slip.

For instance, right now, she felt an odd, hollow kind of ache. She thought she was . . . worried. Coincidentally, Kaderin had a pressing urge to know if her niece, seventy-year-old Emmaline, the daughter of Helen, was better. The last time Kaderin had checked in with her New Orleans coven, she'd learned that Emma had been critically injured by a vampire.

She rang the manor, hoping she wouldn't get Regin the Radiant. Kaderin wasn't ready to talk to her, not yet, not so soon after her reckless morning with the vampire.

Regin's entire race had been annihilated by the Horde.

Kaderin had molded Regin into a killer like herself, training her and stoking her hatred of vampires. "Sword up! Remember your mother," she'd told the girl again and again, and all the while she was telling herself, *Remember your sisters.*

Don't be Regin . . .

Regin answered with: "Bridge. Uhura here." Kaderin sighed, then shook her head at the *Star Trek* reference. Kaderin did not appreciate *Star Trek* references.

Yet that was the thing about Regin. Aside from her boiling hatred of vampires, she was easygoing, quick to laugh, a prankster.

"Hi, Regin, it's Kaderin." She swallowed. "I'm calling to check on Emma. Is she any better?"

"Hey, Kiddy-Kad! She's totally better. She's healed already."

"Healed?" Kaderin asked in surprise. "This is great news, but how can it be? Did the witches help?"

"Actually, she's already wed that Lykae—that hateful one we wanted to neuter—two nights ago."

Had Regin just purposely glossed over that question? Kaderin wanted to know more but had always believed that in digging for secrets, she was begging Fate to somehow reveal her own. And now with her new secret? Kaderin would let Regin coast by so very easily right now.

"I can't believe she married him." The werewolf had absconded with Emmaline, taking her back to his castle in Scotland.

"I *know*. A freaking *Lykae*. It could be worse, I suppose. Could have been a leech." Though Emma was half leech herself and drank blood for sustenance, the coven didn't think of her that way whatsoever. "Nah, Emma isn't *that* big of a bonehead."

Kaderin felt a tic in her cheek, almost as if she had winced. The Valkyrie covens were at war with the vampires even now, and the Lore was hurtling toward an Accession—a war among immortals that occurred every five hundred years. During times like this, Kaderin was expected to be *ridding* vampires from the earth, not *riding* them. Did her face just get hot?

"We tried to call you," Regin said. Kaderin heard her blow a gum bubble. Like so many Valkyrie, she would chew only one specific brand, Sad Wiener Peppermint, which was beyond foul. Kaderin herself secretly preferred Happy Squirrel Citrus. "I think you left your sat phone at the Lykae's in all the confusion."

"I remember," Kaderin said, but she had to wonder if

they'd truly called her. Kaderin was an emotionless cipher, and many were uncomfortable around her—especially at celebrations.

Kaderin recognized when situations might be humorous but was never moved to laugh. She knew she loved her half-sisters but never felt the need to show affection. At a wedding, she wouldn't have even approached a smile.

She bit her lip and stared at her feet. Luckily, Kaderin couldn't perceive the sting of hurt feelings from being left out, either. No, not at all. "Well, Regin, it happens that I didn't mind ditching the phone since you'd locked the Crazy Frog ring tone into it."

"Me? Who? *Whaa?*"

"Tell Emma congratulations for me," Kaderin said. "Is Myst around?" Maybe Kaderin could uncover why Myst had been so tempted by that vampire general—without revealing that she herself had been pleasured by one.

"She's busy."

"With what? When will she be able to talk?"

"Dunno." Another gum bubble popped. "So the Hie cranks up in two days. Are you ready?"

Another change of subject?

"Everything is in preparation," Kaderin answered. All her supplies were packed and her transportation confirmed. That had proved easy enough. The Accord—a federation of twelve Valkyrie covens—had agreed that they needed the capability to move readily about the world—especially Kaderin in the upcoming Hie. So they'd established a network of helicopters and jets available on most continents.

Pilots would be on call for Kaderin in all the key capitals. As she'd specified, they would be demons, and they wouldn't ask a lot of questions.

Naturally, the Valkyrie, with their lavish sensibilities, had only the best. Any competitors in the Hie worth their salt would be taking advantage of modern modes of transportation. But not all would enjoy luxury helicopters and Learjets.

"So where's your first stop?" Regin asked.

"All the competitors have to meet at Riora's temple." The goddess Riora was the patroness of the Hie. It was her competition—she made the rules; she decided the prizes.

"Kind of like an orientation?"

"I suppose." Kaderin's first jaunt would be from the exclusive and modern jetport at the London City Airport to Riora's ancient temple, hidden in an enchanted forest. The temple had been built before humans began keeping their histories and was found only with secret coordinates.

Kaderin might as well be going back in time, and yet she'd be traveling there in an Augusta 109, the fastest and most richly appointed civilian helicopter in the world.

Regin sounded as if she were typing on a keyboard. "You know, the results of this Hie are supposed to be posted in real time to the Net. Which is convenient, since you've never sent word back to us about how you're doing—even though we got you all those carrier pigeons. By the way, I adored and named all of them, and you . . . you just *tossed* them."

"Internet results will be interesting, and the birds, though beloved, preferred to be free." Pigeon drama. Scenes like that one reminded Kaderin why she worked alone.

7

❦

At sunset, Sebastian took a shower the only way he could in his castle—with melted snow water caught in a cistern and piped freezing cold into a small tiled and drained room. After that he dressed in new clothes. He shined his sword, sheathed it with a belt at his hips, and sat on the edge of the bed, prepared to test his theory.

Everything depended on his success. *I must find her to have her.* His hand was damp around the hilt of his sword.

Then he frowned. If this could work, he didn't want to appear adversarial to her. He could just see himself materializing at a family dinner—the overgrown vampire with the very big sword. He unstrapped the belt, placed it aside, then sat once more.

This was all about sense detail. *Focus.* He concentrated on her for long moments. *Wipe everything from your mind but her. . . .*

Nothing. He lay back.

Imagine seeing her beautiful face once more. Her elfin features, the delicate chin and high cheekbones, the way she'd gazed up at him with those smoldering hazel eyes.

He slowed his breathing. *Recall how she felt beneath you.* Her body was soft, giving, a perfect fit to his.

The remembered scent of her hair and skin called him as

sharply as a cry for him would. He began tracing, feeling himself leaving the cold of his castle and moving toward warmth, having no idea what he would find.

Temple of the Goddess Riora, Codru Forest, Moldova
Day 1 of the Twelfth Talisman's Hie

The usual suspects, Kaderin thought with boredom. From her perch on a balcony rail, she surveyed the assembly gathered below her in the gallery of Riora's temple.

As with most temples, Riora's sported the obligatory marble Palladian style, with dishes of fire and candles to light it. Yet that's where the similarity ended. Tucked deep within the heart of the enchanted Codru Forest, it had lichen-covered oaks punching through the walls or lying fallen inside. Roots buckled the heavy floor. The dome was a skylight with glass cut into an intricate and patternless design.

"Order overcome, impossibility incarnate," that was Riora's motto. She was the goddess of impossibility and exalted proving possible the *im*possible. Few knew this, though, and she was coy, joking and spreading rumors. In the last fifty years, she'd come out as the goddess of bowling couture.

Kaderin waited with hundreds of other competitors, because Riora was tardy again. Nothing new there. To get her to be on time, Kaderin had been tempted at the last Hie to declare it impossible for goddesses to be punctual. But then Riora would just have declared that it was impossible for a Valkyrie to bathe in a vat of boiling oil for a decade.

To pass the time, Kaderin gazed down with disdain at the nymphs, making sure they saw her contempt. She jerked her chin up at Lucindeya, the siren who had been her closest competition at the last Hie. Lucindeya, or Cindey, was a violent, merciless rival, and so had earned Kaderin's respect. They customarily used each other to advance until it was only the two of them in the finals.

Then all bets were off.

At last count, Cindey had broken dozens of Kaderin's bones. But then, Kaderin had snapped at least twice as many of hers, cracked her brain bucket, and, rumor had it, ruptured the siren's spleen.

To the adorable-looking kobolds, a type of ground-dwelling gnome, Kaderin reached to her sword sheath at her back. She grasped the hilt, not even needing to draw it for the largest male—still standing only four feet tall—to swallow and swiftly lower his gaze. The kobolds only *appeared* wholesome and kindly—until they turned ravening.

Kaderin was one of the few beings alive who'd seen them as they really were, reptilian predators who sprang from the ground as they hunted in packs. She still did not find the term *killer gnome* hysterically funny as her sisters all did.

The crowd of entrants consisted of all makes and models in the Lore: trolls, witches, and the noble fey. Demons from many of the Demonarchies were present.

Kaderin noted the veterans who were out to win the grand prize—whatever priceless good was offered this Hie. She identified the scavengers who only wanted to snag the individual talismans allotted for each task.

And then there were the newbies. She could make them out in an instant, because they would dare to stare at her.

As a competitor—and the reigning champion for more than a millennium—Kaderin had become more high-profile in the Lore than many of her sisters. She'd garnered power and respect for her covens—and for herself. Had she been a *feeler*, she would have been prideful of her reputation. She couldn't believe she'd so easily risked it with her recent indiscretion.

Relative to her sisters, her fall from grace would be a nosedive—

Suddenly, her ears twitched. Sensing something in the shadows at the back of the balcony, she turned and spied a massive male, eyes glowing in the darkness. A Lykae? Now, that was unusual. The werewolves and the vampires never entered this contest.

The Horde vampires found it beneath them, and the mysterious Forbearers didn't know of its existence. The Lore found it both amusing and shrewd to keep those turned humans in the dark about their world.

Historically, the Lykae couldn't be troubled to care.

In the past, this set of circumstances had been fortuitous. The Lykae—for all their wild, seething good looks—were single-minded and brutal. And the vampires? With their ability to trace, they would be nigh undefeatable.

The werewolf moved from the shadows, approaching her, and she recognized him as Bowen MacRieve, best friend and cousin to Emmaline's new werewolf husband. He'd lost weight over the last millennium, but other than that, she sensed that he'd changed little—which meant he was still gorgeous.

"Kaderin." His golden eyes were vivid, his dark hair thick and long. He didn't address her as "Lady Kaderin," as the rest of the Lore did, but then, he didn't fear her.

"Bowen." She briefly inclined her head.

"I dinna see you at the wedding. Quite nice affair."

He'd been at Emma's wedding, and she'd missed it. "I'm curious about why you are here."

"I'm entering." His voice was a rumbling Scottish brogue.

Deep voices were attractive. An unbidden memory arose of the vampire's gravelly voice breaking between kisses. She shook herself. "You'll be the first Lykae to do so. Ever."

He leaned his tall frame against the wall, utterly nonchalant. He was as tall as the vampire, but rangier. Both were rugged, but Bowen probably would be considered more classically handsome.

Comparing him to the vampire? Lovely. As if Sebastian Wroth were USDA grade A?

"Are you alarmed, Valkyrie?"

"Do I look alarmed?" She always enjoyed asking that, since she knew the answer was invariably no. "Why now?" She'd seen Bowen fighting vampires on a battlefield ages ago—he'd been pitiless in the past, and she'd bet that hadn't changed, either.

He answered, "A friend told me I might have a particular interest in the prize." Yes, if possible, Bowen was more handsome, but the vampire's eyes were so very gray, so dark and compelling. If a woman got lost in eyes like Sebastian's, she'd want to please him in any way he desired. Bowen's eyes? One glimpse of them, and a woman wouldn't know whether to jump him or run from him.

Clearly, Kaderin's blessing was holding, because she didn't feel even a flutter of desire for the Lykae.

"You know what the prize is?" she asked, but Bowen wasn't listening. The witches had just arrived—one called Mariketa the Awaited and another woman Kaderin didn't know—and he was busy scowling at them. "If you're this easily distracted," Kaderin said, "I'll have no problems."

He bit out, "What are *they* doing here?"

Kaderin quirked a brow. "They're here to compete. As they do every Hie."

She knew the Lykae never purchased magicks from the House of Witches—the Lore's mystical mercenaries. Kaderin had heard a hundred discountable rumors why, and on occasion, she'd speculated at the truth. She couldn't imagine life without the convenience of spells—which could vampire-proof chains and trace-proof cages—any more than she could imagine life without showers. Both scenarios were barbaric to Kaderin.

Now, seeing Bowen's expression, Kaderin wondered if the Lykae eschewed buying spells simply because the witches creeped them out. "Do you know what the prize is?" she asked again.

"I doona ken exactly," he said, his attention locked on the two. "But I know enough to warn you that I'll kill for it." He finally faced her to say, "And I daresay killing you would jeopardize the Lykae's tenuous truce with the Valkyrie."

"So, because of Emma and Lachlain's marriage, *I* should back out? Even though this is *my* competition, and has been since you were a wittle puppy?"

He shrugged his broad shoulders. "I'd rather no' hurt you, all in all. I've never struck a female, much less done the damage I've heard this contest calls for. Damage like *you've* meted out."

"Werewolf, don't hate the player—hate the game." She turned from him, dismissing him. An early broken leg would put the dog out.

At least there wasn't a vamp—

The vampire appeared out of thin air.

Her claws scrabbled along the railing as she fought to stay upright.

8

How in the hell did he find me? She had marble under four claws from where she'd just saved herself from a fall.

He'd first appeared in the back of the gallery, and now she watched as he traced into a darkened corner. No one had noticed him yet—or they'd be scattering as if someone had pulled the fire alarm—because he was able to half-trace, barely visible and unscentable to the low creatures. She'd seen vampires who were able to do that clever trick, but they'd been much older.

Yet she'd seen him perfectly. And, great Freya, if he'd been handsome before, now the vampire was *devastating*.

Everything about him was different. He'd gained muscle in the last week, making his shoulders broader and the muscles in his arms and legs fuller. His clothing was casual but expensive, with a tailored fit that highlighted his powerful body. His thick, straight black hair was still long but trimmed.

But how in the hell did he find Riora's temple?

Her first thought was that there was a Valkyrie stoolie, feeding him information about her movements. But no, even the rogue ones she feuded with would never betray her—especially not to a vampire.

It must have been the villagers. Those little punks! Her eyes narrowed. Those little *condemned* punks.

A young winged demon unwittingly scampered past his leg, and from Sebastian's reaction, Kaderin knew he'd never seen beings like these. He was hiding his surprise well, which was a good habit to have, since the denizens here would home in on all his reactions, seeking out a weakness.

If he limped, their claws would be drawn to his leg. If he fell to his knees, their fangs would go for his jugular without thought. Such was the world of the Lore.

"Valkyrie," Bowen intoned from behind her. "I've something for you."

How dare he interrupt her staring? She turned and beheld . . . diamonds. A gorgeous diamond necklace, offered in his palm.

One of the few Valkyrie weaknesses was the fact that glittering jewels could mesmerize them. Valkyrie had inherited the need to acquire from their goddess mother Freya, and stones like these held a fatal attraction of sorts. Not just any shiny bauble—cubic zirconia wouldn't do it—but deep, vibrant diamonds.

Valkyrie trained exhaustively to be able to resist, yet Kaderin hadn't bothered in centuries. Aversion training tended to be tricky when there was no inclination to possess.

Had Kaderin been a *feeler,* she would have been spellbound by the dazzling stones, as he obviously intended. She might have been fascinated by the way the temple's fires illumined them, making them sparkle, or enthralled with the tiny pinprick spears of flame-red light. *Glint, glint, glint . . .*

She jerked her gaze up. Odd that she wasn't a feeler, and yet something very akin to fury was threading through her veins right now. "Very clever, Bowen. Yet your tricks won't work with me." But damn if they almost hadn't. *Shake it off. Don't hand this weakness to him.*

When he grinned with satisfaction, she resisted the urge to glare and made her expression blank before she turned to find the vampire again. Two of the nymphs were trailing him.

"These tricks work with other Valkyrie," Bowen said. "Do they no'?"

Without glancing away from Sebastian, she said, "Try it with Regin or Myst. Then let me know how that works out for you."

Could those nymph tramps stand any closer to Sebastian? Kaderin had never understood Myst's particular dislike of them. Now Kaderin knew Myst was right—they were a bunch of little hookers.

From behind Sebastian, one said, "I'd wear his corsage to an orgy any day," giving him the long look.

He turned, finding the nymphs in their gauzy, transparent clothing. The two didn't bother hiding their lust, and to his credit, Sebastian didn't drop his jaw the way a human male would have.

Kaderin didn't believe that, as a whole, the nymphs were more beautiful than the Valkyrie, but everything about them screamed, *Easy lay! When you don't want to work for it!* And curiously, many males found that more appealing than the Valkyrie's *Do it and die, simian.*

"Mmm, hmm, mmm," said the smaller of the two nymphs. "As good from the front as he is from the—"

"No . . ." The first paled and whispered, "He's not a demon. He's a *vampire*."

The other shook her head. "His eyes are clear. And he doesn't smell like one."

Kaderin saw Sebastian's brows draw together; no doubt he was wondering, *What do vampires smell like?*

The first screamed, "Vampire!"

When the two blended into the temple's oaks, Sebastian looked as though he'd just prevented himself from taking a step back. All around him, beings became aware of him and scattered. Most turned humans would be delirious after this show. If anything, Sebastian stood straighter and looked even more arrogant than when he'd first appeared. With narrowed eyes, he scanned the area.

She could imagine his thoughts. Yes, this situation was confounding, but he was here for a reason.

To find his Bride. Because vampires who'd found their Brides didn't tolerate losing them.

Sebastian glanced up, and found Kaderin perched on the balcony railing above.

She was here. By Christ, he'd *succeeded*.

He'd traced to her.

He almost exhaled heavily in relief, but he stifled the urge, keenly aware that all around him were beings—from nightmare and fantasy—and every eye was on him. When his relief turned to smug satisfaction over his feat, he hid his smirk.

Then he realized what she was wearing. Clad in a sinfully short skirt, a leather jacket, and sleek half-boots, she sat with one bared leg hanging down, the other stretched out in front of her. Infuriated by the display, Sebastian glowered at the males in the motley assembly.

He'd never been a jealous man before. He had never found anything he wanted solely as his own. Now jealousy ate at him, made his fangs sharpen, and made him want to bare them. She was *his*. And he didn't want to share the merest glimpse of her body.

She turned away, ignoring Sebastian, to talk to a large

male with a wild cast to his eyes—who was standing much too close to her.

Sebastian had known he would be the pursuer in this relationship, the one with the most to gain. But after the morning they'd had, he'd at least expected an acknowledgment when she saw him once more. Or even a reaction? Perhaps her lips had parted, and maybe a tinge of pink flushed along her high cheekbones.

What was she doing here with all these other beings? If he even let himself think about what he was seeing all around him, he might go mad. Again. So he tried to ignore them, and any additional appurtenances—horns, wings, multiple arms—they might possess.

Never had he felt more unsure of himself—he felt alternately like a baffled human and like a monster. He hadn't missed that those females who'd *disappeared into the trees* believed vampires were worse than demons in this world. Sebastian almost cursed Nikolai yet again for forcing him to become something reviled—even to these creatures—but reminded himself that if not for his brother, Sebastian wouldn't have lived to find Katja.

Channeling all the aristocratic arrogance that had been instilled in him from birth, he strode up the stairs toward her. "Katja," he began, and just when he thought she would completely ignore him, she finally turned. As he passed a rotting log on the stair landing, he heard a whisper from within: "*Did he just call her* Katja? *Cover the pups' eyes. This will be messy.*" A glance back found the log stuffed with troll-like creatures. He'd never even seen them.

At Sebastian's approach, the wild-eyed male she'd been speaking with sank back into the shadows.

"It's important that I speak with you," Sebastian told her.

"*He wants to talk to her,*" came another whisper from the log.

"Were you invited to this place?" Kaderin asked.

"No."

She tilted her head. "Then how did you trace to a place that's not on any known map? I know you haven't been here before."

"It wasn't that difficult," he said, for some reason deciding not to reveal his feat. "I must talk to you about what happened."

From the log: "*What happened with Lady Kaderin and a vampire? What sodding happened?*"

"Then you've wasted a trip. I've nothing to say to you."

When the man in the shadows gave him a killing look, Sebastian did bare his fangs then—it felt satisfying. He clenched his hands into fists to think that man had been sidling so close to his Bride. But who wouldn't when she was clothed in such a manner? "Why are you dressed like this?"

"*Oh, no, he didn't.*"

"*He did!*"

She quirked an eyebrow at Sebastian, then parted her red lips to give a casual hiss in the direction of the log. They fell silent instantly.

Down in the gallery, the nymphlike women smirked and whispered about Kaderin "slumming" with a vampire, "just like her sister." Kaderin's dark eyes widened as if she were amazed by their temerity. She feinted as though she was about to jump down, and they fled back into the oaks.

Sebastian's attention returned to focus on Kaderin—

There was no time even to tense for the attack.

9

Bowen lunged from the shadows, barreling into the vampire. As Kaderin watched his furious charge, she only wondered why it had taken Bowen so long to attack, since the Lykae were at war with the vampires. Maybe Sebastian's clear eyes had thrown him, or perhaps the fact that Sebastian didn't smell like blood and death had confused Bowen.

In a tangle of flying fists and claws, they both slammed into a wall, shaking the solid marble temple all around them. A crack surfaced in the dome's skylight.

Sebastian shoved Bowen off and lunged for his throat with one hand. His other was a fist shooting out. Bowen hit at the same time—they smashed each other's face.

Kaderin didn't see this winding down anytime soon. They were attractive, well-built warriors—there were worse things to watch. She settled in, expecting to observe with typical cool dispassion.

Punishing blows continued to connect from each. Sebastian was somehow holding his own with Bowen. The gallery was abuzz with surprise. True, Bowen looked as if he'd lost a stone of weight since the last time she'd seen him, but still . . .

Merely shaking off a Lykae's punch to the jaw was unheard of.

They crashed over the railing just in front of Kaderin's seat, plummeting to the ground below. Sebastian didn't trace, instead taking the impact. He was fighting a member of the most physically powerful species in the Lore, and if he didn't start sparing himself these blows, Bowen would easily kill him.

On their feet again, they circled, eyeing each other for weaknesses, striking out in intervals. Yes, Sebastian was taking the crushing blows, but he seemed to be ambidextrous, hitting as squarely with his left fist as his right, cleverly aiming and spacing his own as well.

Bowen had his deadly claws and speed, but Sebastian was skilled. Very skilled, she determined, and he wasn't even using his key advantage.

His lips were drawn back from his fangs in fury. His irises turned black, and his body tensed, seeming to grow even larger. *Immortal male . . . powerful male . . .* She caught herself leaning forward.

He was stronger than she'd ever imagined. Which meant he was more attractive than she'd ever feared.

An image flashed in her mind of his massive body covering hers that morning. How tightly his strong arms had wrapped around her as he rocked his hips into her. . . .

She shivered and stared down in puzzlement when gooseflesh rose on her arms. *That's new.*

Bowen lashed out with his flared claws. Sebastian leapt back; Bowen's claws rent through the thick marble column as easily as through talc. Sebastian's fist shot out, breaking Bowen's nose, just as Bowen slashed with his other hand.

He carved four deep furrows in Sebastian's torso. Blood poured from both warriors.

Murmurs began in the gallery:

"*They desecrate Riora's sacred temple! She will be enraged.*"

"*Oh, gods, look at the marble. We are all beyond doomed.*"

"*Somebody put a plant in front of it!*"

Kaderin sighed. And this was the world she belonged to.

Soon louder protests sounded. Riora was a diva who made Mariah Carey look meek. Taking away the competition for spite wouldn't be beyond her.

One of the new competitors asked, "But who could possibly break up a fight between a Lykae and a vampire?"

All eyes fell on Kaderin.

"The witch could do it." Kaderin's tone was studiously bored as she flicked her hand at Mariketa the Awaited. Mariketa was supposed to be one of the most powerful born into the House of Witches in generations and apparently was here to compete even though she couldn't be more than twenty-two years old or so.

Not that you could tell her age from her appearance— she wore a hood and a cloak *and* a glamour spell so thick it seemed shellacked on her. Which made Kaderin wonder what kind of visage she was hiding.

The girl answered, "I can't practice in another's temple."

Without the Hie, half of Kaderin's life's purpose would disappear. She sighed wearily, then drew her sword from the sheath at her back as she dropped down. She sauntered casually to the fight and dived down, springing up between them with her arms outstretched, her sword pressed into Bowen's chest, her claws positioned at Sebastian's throat.

Bowen snarled, pressing forward into the point. "Get the fuck out of the way, Valkyrie. Clear eyes or no', do you no' ken what he is?"

Sebastian traced out of her grasp to her side, then shoved her behind him. He kept his arm back and against her, leaving himself exposed to Bowen. She was so surprised by the gesture that she allowed it, hiding a frown behind his broad back.

But then Bowen lunged, clenching his hands around Sebastian's neck to twist his head off. Sebastian used his free arm to go for Bowen's throat, refusing to remove the arm at her side.

Which made her want to crack a grin.

A male guarding *her*. How . . . novel.

She shook herself and clutched Sebastian's protective arm to lean out from behind him. "Bowen, you're fighting in Riora's temple," she said. "If you continue this, you risk the Hie." Beneath her fingers, Sebastian's muscles were tensed from the fight, his body thrumming with power and heat. Seemingly helpless to stop herself, she inched closer to him, enjoying the hell out of his scent. Now he bent his arm back to bring her in to his body.

Why wasn't she fighting him?

"I doona understand you, Kaderin," Bowen bellowed.

She leaned to the side again. "No competition. She'll take it away."

"She would no' do that. No' over the death of a vampire."

Kaderin nodded, and strangely, Bowen's eyes went even more wide and wild, turning to the ice-blue color of his beastly form. He released Sebastian, his flattened palms shooting up. He seemed to curse himself in Gaelic.

A Lykae eager to end a fight before a kill? And while a vampire still had his throat clutched in a death grip? This was indeed a week of firsts.

"Let him go, Sebastian," Kaderin said. "You must."

"Finish this," Sebastian demanded of Bowen, biting out the words.

Bowen just wiped his face on his sleeve. "I will no'. No' now." As soon as Sebastian released him, he backed away, hands still raised.

She couldn't imagine that Bowen had ever backed down from a fight before. He was a proud alpha male, and he'd been trained from childhood to kill vampires. *How much he must want this prize.*

Bowen dropped back into the shadows, eyes glowing.

When Sebastian moved to follow him, she said, "No, you have to let him go."

Sebastian turned to her, and she had to stifle a wince at finding that he was insufferably sexy fresh from the fight. His muscled chest heaved with exertion and was marked with bravely earned injury.

Too bad he won't scar, she thought, sheathing her sword.

"You desire me to let him go?" With a brief glance down at his ghastly injuries, he said calmly, "I tend to punish slights like these." Such an understatement rumbled in his deep voice.

He'd held his own against Bowen. And had been ready for more.

Warrior. Immortal. I've never made love to an immortal.

Sebastian's gaze kept flickering over her, as though still starved for the sight of her. Without warning, he grasped her arm and traced her to the darkened balcony once more.

"Don't ever put yourself in danger like that again," he said to her.

She looked into his eyes, and the floor seemed to wobble. "Y-you traced me?" Dizziness. Her first trace. Trippy. "That wasn't very considerate."

"I should have warned you, Katja."

In another instant, the entire world seemed to go off-kilter—sights and sounds and even the beat of her heart were different. . . .

Oh, gods, Kaderin was feeling again—and there was no denying it now.

She swayed slightly, but he still held her arm. *Sc-sc-screwed.*

As though she'd been scoured clean with icy water, the blessing was . . . gone. Utterly.

She released a pent-up breath, accepting what she instinctively knew was true: it *was* Sebastian who brought out her feelings. There was no capricious power toying with her, no new spell. It was simply . . . him.

And she wanted to scream to the sky in frustration, because she didn't understand why.

The Valkyrie didn't believe in chance, in randomness. So what could it possibly mean when the pull of a vampire could ignite emotions, that had been stamped out so completely, and for so long?

As she gazed up at Sebastian, she experienced her newest emotion. *Dread.*

10

Kaderin had that bomb blast look again, and he wondered if tracing had done that to her. He mentally kicked himself for not anticipating this.

Out of the corner of his eye, Sebastian spied beings easing up the stairs to eavesdrop on them. He stepped in front of her and bared his fangs at them. They scattered.

When he turned back, she seemed to be growing less distressed.

"Kaderin, never get in the middle of a fight as you did. I had that under control."

"Did you, then?" she asked in an inscrutable tone. "He's a Lykae who had not yet unleashed the beast inside him." When his brows drew together, she said, "A Lykae, a werewolf?"

"Then what would happen? He'd become a forest wolf?"

She eyed his hand until he released her. "You wouldn't be that fortunate." Then, speaking absently as though recalling a memory, she murmured, "The Lykae call it 'letting the beast out of its cage.' He would have grown a foot taller, and his claws and fangs would have shot longer and grown razor-sharp. Wavering over him like a phantom masking his body would be the image of a brutal, towering animal." She finally glanced up. "And if you refused to trace, his beast would have been your last sight before your head was sliced from your body."

"That would remain to be seen." He narrowed his eyes. "What did you mean about a competition?"

"You don't know?" At his shrug, she said, "You'll find out soon enough." She headed back to her railing.

"He called you a Valkyrie?" he asked quickly.

She turned back, tucking her hair behind her ear. "Yeah, so?"

"Aren't Valkyrie . . . bigger?"

She gave him a look of disgust. "The *vampire* turning his nose up . . . ?"

"No, I didn't mean it like that—it's merely difficult to believe, since you're so small—".

"Small? I'm almost five and a half feet tall—a very good size for a Valkyrie." Then her expression became one of realization as she said, "I *hate* being called small."

Why couldn't he have been allotted *a fraction* of Murdoch's charm? "I want five minutes of your time."

"We both know you will never be satisfied with that. If I thought I could rid myself of you by giving you five minutes, it would be done."

"At least tell me why you abruptly ran from me. What brought about the extreme turn in you?"

"I realized with perfect clarity that I want nothing to do with you."

He lowered his voice. "I refuse to believe that after what happened between us."

She seemed to be just barely holding on to her patience. "Look, if you somehow found out who I am in order to track me here, then you must know enough to know that I kill vampires. Period. That's my job—that's my life. And *you* are a vampire. Ergo . . ."

"Yet you couldn't kill me that morning? Or even tonight upon seeing me? You've not done your job."

Her lips parted. "I *chose* to spare you—"

"Why?"

Now she seemed to grind her teeth—and to be struggling for an answer. Finally, she said, "Because I didn't think it would be sporting."

"What does that mean?"

"The vampires I kill usually disagree with my agenda." She reached the rail, sitting once more. "They tend to fight back," she added, drawing her sword from her sheath and laying it over her lap. "So, vampire, this runtling Valkyrie who sucks at her job is inviting you to go toss yourself—and declining further conversation."

"Toss?" A second later, he clenched his jaw. "I see."

From her leather jacket, she pulled out a diamond hone file and began sharpening the blade.

"Katja . . ."

She concentrated on even strokes of her file, up and back. "Kaderin."

No response. Her body seemed to go wooden, and she appeared lost in the movements.

In a flash, he realized two things. She found this task soothing, and for some reason, she needed to be doing it right at this moment. He knew she was done talking to him for now. He'd been completely shut out.

It was then that he noticed the murmurs about her in the gallery, her name in whispers. His hearing was much more acute after his blooding, and his ability to trace without fully materializing was improved as well. One thing was certain—she was their favorite subject, and he could learn much. After one more fruitless attempt to speak with her, he forced himself to leave her, tracing down behind them, listening for any information.

He heard elders in different factions explaining things to younger ones and discerned that they had gathered for a Lore scavenger hunt of sorts. All the people here were waiting to compete for some prize, as yet unrevealed.

He moved past a trio who spoke only in guttural stops, toward another two—a normal-looking father and a very demon-looking boy, already speaking about Kaderin.

"No one's ever seen her smile," the father said in a low voice, with a glance at her before his eyes darted away. Did they all fear her?

Sebastian had seen her smile—and it had hit him like a booted kick to the groin that he hadn't seen coming.

The father continued, "She's a mystery, that one. Drives males crazy."

I'll attest to that.

"Why's she called Kaderin the Coldhearted?" the demon son asked.

Is she?

"Because she is cold. Merciless. Our people have a rule about never going after the same prizes as the Valkyrie."

Fascinated all over again, Sebastian muttered, "She is truly a Valkyrie."

When their talk turned to someone named Riora, he traced to another pair—a figure in a hooded cloak and an older woman carrying a red apple. "The Valkyrie shows up, you walk the other way, Mariketa," the woman said. "Remember that always. Some say she warns once, but I'd rather not bet on it."

He couldn't see this Mariketa's face because of her hood, but her voice sounded young. "Isn't she small for a Valkyrie?" she asked.

He realized Kaderin could hear them as well when she sat up straighter. The corners of his lips curled. He loved how small she was compared to him, how fine she was, and yet he'd been unable to express that to her. She was so elegantly built but stronger than he'd ever imagined a female could be.

"They're all small and fey. It's a biological advantage," the woman explained. "You never quite believe what they can bring to a fight. Until it's quite too late."

In the past, sharpening her sword had been a kind of ritual to focus her thoughts. She'd begun now because she'd never been more confused in her life.

Why was she feeling? Why him? Why *now*?

But there was no need to panic, she assured herself yet again. The blessing *had* to come back. As it had before. Certainly, it would. If the vampire's presence acted as Kryptonite for her blessing, then she just needed to lose him.

She spied him skulking from group to group. Of course, she heard them whispering about her down in the gallery. And Sebastian was listening to it all, unnoticed. He half-traced very easily, too much so. In that state, vampires were too insubstantial to be killed.

Yes, he was learning about her, but then, no one knew enough to indicate weakness. Her history was shady. She worked to make it so. She saw him narrow his eyes to hear her called "Lady Kaderin." "Lady" was the Lore creatures' attempt at erring on the side of caution, and they were right to do so.

Then Kaderin heard this little gem from a demoness: "For some reason, Kaderin has lost a lot of her *humanity*. She's been existing on animal instinct for a while now."

She said this as if living by animal instinct were a *bad* thing. Just as Kaderin was about to drop down and go a-torturing, an elf in a robe crossed to the altar at the back of the gallery—the altar that was off-center. Kaderin recognized him as Riora's scribe, aptly named Scribe.

He scratched his head. "I say, where is everyone? My goddess will arrive shortly."

The beings went silent in anticipation. It wasn't every day that one kept company with a goddess. That mouthy demoness licked her hand and smoothed her boy's hair around his velvety new horns.

When Riora appeared, Scribe announced, "The goddess Riora." The newcomers and the less jaded immortals stared in wonderment. Scribe fell back, looking enormously proud to be a servant to such a divinity.

Riora was resplendent, as goddesses tended to be, clad in a diaphanous gold robe, cinched tight under breasts so ample that many mistook her for a fertility goddess. Her wild raven hair flowed and waved as though in a constant swirling wind, and suddenly Kaderin wished Sebastian had never seen Riora.

Feigning nonchalance, Kaderin tilted her sword and picked up his reflection. She wouldn't care if he was staring slack-jawed like most of the other males. She wouldn't at all.

Yet, in the glow of one of the most ravishing female forms in this reality, Sebastian's gaze was locked on Kaderin. She tucked her hair behind her ear, oddly flattered, then scowled at herself. Tucking her hair? That was a gesture she used to make—in antiquity—whenever she grew flustered. *Who are you these days, Kad?*

"Greetings, Lore," Riora began in her throaty voice. "Tonight commences the Talisman's Hie, a contest that has not changed since its inception. The rules remain the same and are tedious to repeat"—she waved her hand dismissively and rolled her eyes—"every . . . single . . . two hundred and fifty years. So I'll give you the lowdown.

"You go all over the world and retrieve for me the talismans, charms, amulets, jewels, and other magickal gear that I want. Some of the tasks I've chosen have multiple items available at the end, and some have just one. All are designed in order to force you beings to fight. Which is *fun*. For me. I'm told not so much for you."

She frowned, shrugged, then said, "Each item is assigned a point value based on the difficulty in reaching it and the number available. When you reach a talisman, simply hold it steady above your heart, and it will find its way to me."

She raised her pale arm, and Kaderin thought for a moment she'd snap her fingers and drop her knuckles to her hip. "It was once observed to me that this mode of teleporting is amazing," Riora mused, tapping her chin. "I do not find that so. What is amazing is that all of you actually can boast hearts of some fashion, cold though they may be." She flashed a look at Kaderin, who raised an eyebrow, then continued, "The first two competitors to reach eighty-seven points go to the finals. The reason for this number is that there's no reason. After that, it's head-to-head for one last prize."

Riora perused the crowd—doing a double take at *the vampire*—before she went on to say, "There aren't that many rules, but I'll give you the biggest three. Number one:

No outright killing of competitors until the final round. Though maiming, debilitating, and mystical or physical imprisonment are, of course, all acceptable." She nodded eagerly as she added, "And encouraged." She held up two fingers. "Number two: Only one prize per customer for each task. In other words, you can't clean out the stash and leave nothing behind for everyone else. And last: Do not commit any act that will draw human attention to the Lore. This has become more important than ever in this day and age. You will be disqualified immediately and be subject to my . . . displeasure."

Flames beside her altar flared, lighting her menacing expression. Kaderin was among the few who knew that this seeming mask, so wild and feral, was in fact Riora's true appearance.

The fires fluttered as if from a breeze, and her façade grew pleasant once more. "For each competitor, I have a scroll at the altar with my shopping list. In any given one- or two-day period *or so*, the lists will update themselves at 7:43, Riora Standard Time, which means that could be *a jot* irregular. With each update, you'll be given a new slate of tasks to choose from to be completed in a specified time frame. When the new tasks appear, the old ones are rendered worthless. Be aware, though, that some prizes and tasks will repeat, if I really want them or am amused the first time you attempt them."

One of the nymphs in the back muttered, "Nereus, for one." Nereus, the obscenely endowed sea god who took flesh in payment for his talismans, was a Hie regular.

Scribe scowled; Riora ignored them. "Now, would you like to know what you're competing for?" Everyone drew in. The temple fell silent. "The grand prize, as always, is priceless and powerful." She paused for dramatic effect, and Kaderin tilted her head, curious about what she would be dragging back to her coven this time.

She'd scored armor that couldn't be pierced and a battle ax that could kill Lore beings without having to behead them—the usual way for immortals to die. But both had been given in tribute to the Valkyrie's stalwart allies, the Furies. She'd won a choker that gave its possessor the siren's song, but that was kept by the New Zealand coven. She'd earned an armband that made its wearer feel overwhelming sexual desire. No one knew where that one was, and that made more than one Valkyrie nervous.

Riora's gaze passed over her once more. Kaderin felt the weight of the moment, pressing down on her. . . .

"This Hie, you will compete for Thrane's Key."

Kaderin's cold heart stopped.

11

At the gasps, Sebastian turned to ask what Thrane's Key was, then remembered none of these beings would speak to him.

Finally, Riora explained, "The wizard Thrane dabbled with time travel, and his key unlocks a door through time, enabling its possessor to go into the past. It is theoretically the most powerful weapon on this earth."

Sebastian was still much the human he once was, unversed in things from the Lore, but he was certain that the elemental traits of the earth were not different no matter who—or what—inhabited it. Physics was not different. Tracing, for instance, was possible by the laws of physics; time travel was not.

"How many times will the key work?" the Scottish bastard asked.

"Twice."

The gathering erupted in noise once more. Was this competition a scam of some sort? Why were they so quick to believe the female at the altar who spoke of time travel so blithely? Was this Riora truly a goddess? She seemed otherworldly, to be sure, but so did Kaderin.

He traced back toward the woman with the apple and

the girl Mariketa. The others seemed not to notice him. The Scot kept him pinned and Kaderin ignored him.

The woman murmured to Mariketa, "The Valkyrie wants the key. Badly."

Kaderin looked the same to Sebastian—her face calm, her measured strokes on her sword never varying.

"How can you tell?" Mariketa asked.

"Cold Kaderin's giving off lightning. Valkyrie produce it with strong emotion."

Was that true? He glanced up through the glass dome and saw bolts painting the sky. The morning at his castle, he'd been so absorbed with her, so focused on keeping her there, that he'd noticed little else. Now, thinking back, he recalled thunder had been rumbling on a crystal-clear morning. He stared in awe. Did he find the lightning more fascinating because it was hers?

"She will be even more vicious than before," the woman continued. "We'll stay clear of her."

He dropped his gaze to Kaderin once more. He'd experienced her violence already, but *vicious?* She could not appear less so. Her blond hair curled gently over her slim shoulders. Her fingers were fragile-looking, deft. So fair and delicate, Sebastian thought.

Yes. Fair and delicate. His eyes narrowed. Even as her file smoothed up and back over her weapon until the razor-sharp edges glinted.

The key. To go back in time.

Kaderin's sword hand shook wildly. *Keep it together!* Yes, she'd just received life-changing news, but she could never let anyone know how dearly she needed to win this prize. She needed to be *cold.*

She balled her hands into fists. Through the observatory skylight, lightning could be seen forking across the sky. Furtive glances were cast her way.

Lightning? Again?

Much was on the line. *Everything* was on the line. Her past and her future.

Her sisters' futures.

She could bring them back. All she had to do was win this competition.

As she had the last five. Most Lore beings hadn't lived long enough even to conceive of a time when Kaderin didn't win.

The thought of Dasha and Rika back with her, back within the coven, made the corners of her lips awkwardly twitch again. It was as though her face were relearning how to smile, much as it had when she'd smiled at Sebastian.

She could teach her sisters about this new age, show them the wonders of it. They could have her room at the manor—Kaderin had one of the best views of the murky bayou. She'd give them all of the few clothes and jewelry pieces she owned. Kaderin never shopped and had a habit of filching from the coven whatever clothes struck her fancy. Now she could use the money she'd saved all these years to spoil them.

To atone. For causing their deaths.

I have to stop shaking.

All she would need was once with the key. She would give the second time to the Accord—and let them decide what to do with it.

The last time she'd seen her sisters had been when she'd buried them. To have a vision to replace that horror, she would do anything, eliminate anything that got in her way.

In the past, she'd been brutal to her fellow competitors. *They've seen nothing.*

Her gaze flickered down over them, and she saw not living beings but obstacles to be removed. The vampire was an obstacle as well, confusing her and undermining her intimidation of these people, which she had always wielded like a weapon. She would strike out—but not with anger. She would unleash her chilling brand of menace.

For her sisters . . . anything.

She studied her reflection in her sword. If the vampire got in her way, she'd slice her blade through his neck. She wouldn't even wait to see his body collapse before she turned and forgot him.

I could enter.

Sebastian could give her something she wanted badly. He could win this competition, and in doing so, he could garner her affection.

In his mortal life, he'd been a knight but had no lady to offer his sword. Now he did.

"Then let it be known who's competing," said the pale, waxy-skinned man beside Riora.

All seemed to defer to Kaderin, and she stood, sheathing her sword behind her with one perfectly threaded stab. With her shoulders back and her voice ringing clearly, she said, "Kaderin the Cold of the Accord, competing for the Valkyrie and the Furiae."

Furies exist too? Is she part Fury?

When she sat, a black-haired female stood. "Competing for all Sirenae, I am Lucindeya of the Oceania Sirens."

So, sirens exist outside of myth as well. He ran his hand over the back of his neck. *Astonishing.*

From just to his right, the girl in the cloak announced, "Mariketa the Awaited, from the House of Witches."

Witches, too.

It was one thing for Sebastian to encounter the clearly "mythical" beings. His eyes grew accustomed to them soon enough. But it was somehow stranger to hear beings who looked human stand up and so easily announce that they weren't.

When he'd been out among humans, feeling that he was a predator, he might actually have been among other creatures entirely and never known it. . . .

Sebastian's adversary emerged from the shadows. "Bowen MacRieve of the Lykae Clan." He had a Scottish accent but didn't differentiate his clan as being from Scotland. *Are all werewolves Scottish?* Sebastian thought, half delirious. *Well, why the fuck not?*

Under her breath, the woman with Mariketa muttered, "Bowen? I hardly recognized him since he's lost so much weight."

He's been bloody bigger than this?

"Then we just got another contender. Gods, he's a ruthless one. Amazing. The blogs will go wild over this."

Who are the Blogs?

Sounding as if she barely moved her lips, Mariketa muttered back, "Why does he keep staring at me?" Indeed, the Scot was staring, scowl in place.

The woman shrugged, seeming stumped as well.

Demons of all shapes and sizes from monarchies of demons, or the "Demonarchies," announced their intent to compete. A female who resembled Kaderin's kind, with large luminous eyes and pointed ears, was representing the "Noble Fey and all Elvefolk." When she acknowledged

Kaderin with a dignified bow, Kaderin inclined her head graciously.

She respects that competitor?

"Any others?" Riora asked.

Silence. They all glanced around. When he stood, Kaderin's eyes widened, and she slowly shook her head at him.

"I'm Sebastian Wroth, and I enter as well."

Kaderin briefly raised her face to the glass ceiling.

Muted hisses accompanied his announcement but fell silent wherever he glowered. Clearly, being a vampire had earned him seething hatred in this realm, but it seemed it also earned him some power.

"Which faction do you represent?" Riora asked in an amused tone.

He stared at Kaderin as he spoke. "None."

"Ah, but you must to enter. A sponsorship of sorts." When he turned back to her, Riora nodded winningly and added, "Like cotillion. Or AA." Then her eyes bored into his as if she could see into his mind.

"He's a Forbearer, Riora." Kaderin stood. "A turned human. It's against the law to teach him about this world, and he will learn much in this competition."

"Is this true?" Riora asked.

"I do not align with them." Who to represent now that he'd renounced the Forbearers? That left the Horde, which was as unthinkable an option as the Forbearers.

Then . . . an idea. A gamble. He turned to Riora. "I represent you."

Riora pressed her splayed fingertips to her chest. "*Moi?*"

Murmurs erupted. The nymphlike women snickered.

Kaderin shot to her feet. "He can't represent you, Riora. *You* are not a faction."

"Why, my cold Kaderin, I think you are deeming it *impossible*."

Kaderin seemed to flinch at the word, parting her lips to argue—

"He was a knight," Riora said.

How in the hell does she know that? Suddenly, he recognized the only explanation. *Because she is a goddess.*

"He has pledged his sword to me, and I accept."

More murmurs. Kaderin looked as if she'd been slapped. She shot him a look of pure menace.

"Excellent," Riora said with a clap. "Two powerful newcomers to the games." Riora gave Kaderin a speaking glance. "Finally, we might have a real competition."

12

By entering the Hie, the vampire had just safeguarded his life from every competitor, including Kaderin, at least until the finals.

By representing Riora—a bloody brilliant move—he'd protected himself against the most egregious treacheries from all competitors.

The infuriating vampire was proving difficult to dismiss. Kaderin was beginning to really remember *infuriating*. Quite akin to *frustrating*. She had those two down.

She dropped from the rail once more, intent on reaching the altar to collect her scroll. She waded past obsequious beings, desiring to pay their respects to her, to the Accord, and to the great Freya and mighty Wóden—as if Kaderin could simply text-message two sleeping gods.

"Katja," the vampire said, cutting a path through the crowd as beings dove and cowered from him.

"That's not my name," she snapped without slowing, but he easily fell into step with her. *When did it get so hot?* She found herself knotting her hair up. "Tell me, leech. Did you enter to keep Bowen from killing you or to prevent me?"

"Leech?" He frowned, then seemed to shake off her insult. "We've established that you can't kill me."

She glared at him over her shoulder. "I ache to make those your last words."

"I am beginning to understand this." He was calm on the exterior, gentlemanly even, but she knew the ferocity that lurked within him—tonight she'd seen it. "If this contest is important to you, then let me help you. I could trace you to many of the places, and you could defeat everyone." He hesitantly reached his hand to her shoulder, but he saw that she was about to hiss, and he drew it back.

"I'm going to defeat them anyway."

"But why not take an easier path?"

"Okay, I'll play." She crossed her arms over her chest, and his gaze dipped to her cleavage. She snapped her fingers in front of his face.

When his eyes met hers, he scrubbed his hand over his mouth. "I apologize." But his expression said he found it worth it. "You were about to . . . play?"

"Have you ever been to New Orleans?"

"In the United States?" At her nod, he said, "Not yet."

"What about South America?" she asked. "Africa?"

He hesitated, then shook his head.

"Vampires can only trace to places they've already been. So, where were you planning to trace me? Around your backyard?" she asked, with a deceptively pleasant mien that faded in an instant. "Vampire, this game is for the big kids only." She glanced up at the cracked skylight to the lightening sky. Dawn would come in less than an hour. "And it's almost your beddy-bye time."

"I could travel with you, to keep you safe."

"Travel with me? Do you think I would stop and wait around every single day? To cut my time in half because *you* can't go in the sun?"

He looked as if he'd briefly forgotten a harsh reality and she'd just reminded him. "No, of course not," he said quietly. "I just wanted—"

"You're crowding me. Didn't anybody ever tell you that females don't like to be crowded? One of women's big three turnoffs. Not very sexy."

For some reason, that made him frown, and immediately back off. His voice was gruff when he asked, "What are the other two?"

"You're wearing out number one. How about working on that first?" She turned from him to get to the altar, and surprisingly, he didn't follow.

She passed Scribe, who'd begun cleaning the temple—though not so much as to effect order. He plucked a camouflaging tree limb off the damaged column. When he saw the claw marks, he scowled at nearby creatures, who studied their hooves.

She strode past him with a kindly greeting, addressing him as "Sacred Scribe," which always put him in raptures, and he stumbled on the limb, nervously stuttering a reply.

At the altar, Riora was speaking with two elves, saying something about the "real-time coverage of the competition online" and ordering them to "drive visitors to the site."

Still feeling the vampire's eyes on her, Kaderin hopped up, the only one in the Lore who would dare such a thing. She plucked a scroll from a pile of them and unrolled it. Every competitor would get the same list of tasks—and each list included the talismans or sought objects, the coordinates for finding them, and a brief description. As usual, there were about ten choices of tasks in any given round.

Once Riora was finished with her spate of PR, she said, "And how are your parents, Kaderin the Cold?"

Kaderin knew Riora was inquiring about two of her three parents. Kaderin's birth mother had been mortal. "They sleep still, Goddess," she said absently, reading. Gods derived power from how many prayers and offerings they received with each passing of the sun, hence Riora's Internet attempt to garner more. But there were so few who worshipped Freya and Wóden that the two slept to conserve their energy. "Interesting talismans this Hie," Kaderin observed.

In the past, Kaderin had always gone after the closest talismans first. Now, with more than one real contender, she would devise new strategies, shake them all up. She would go for the far-flung points and the more difficult tasks at the outset.

"I thought so," Riora said. "Pity I'll only get about half on that list. You know, because of all the accidental deaths."

Kaderin nodded in sympathy. Then her gaze landed on the option for the highest points offered in this interval: twelve points to retrieve one of three mirror amulets. The most she'd ever gone for was a prize worth fifteen points. This task wouldn't be so much about life-threatening peril but more about logistics. Whoever could arrange to get there first—won.

Though the destination fell outside the Accord's network, Kaderin had other resources, and for the first time in a Hie, she was going to ask her coven for help. *Just please don't let Regin answer when I call.* . . .

Kaderin heard helicopters outside, engines humming louder as their bows dipped to surge forward. *Strike hard, strike fast. Yes, that one.* She rolled the parchment up and dropped down.

Before she could leave, Riora asked, "You disapprove of my vampire knight?"

Kaderin faced her. "I'm well aware that you couldn't care less about my approval. Or my extreme and absolute lack thereof." Why was Riora studying her so closely? Kaderin flushed under her scrutiny. Riora had always seemed to take an unaccountable interest in Kaderin, but this was intense.

"You seem different."

'Cause I can freaking feel! "New haircut," Kaderin mumbled instead. Could Riora sense her new emotions—most particularly, her shame over her attraction to the vampire? Her gaze darted to Sebastian.

"So, the interest flows both ways, *Lady* Kaderin? How inconvenient."

"Pardon?"

Riora tilted her head and perused him. He leaned against a wall, staring at Kaderin with his arms crossed over his muscular chest above his injuries. "Of course, if one were to be interested in a vampire, that one you could almost justify."

"Riora, I never said I—"

"I'm merely saying it appears as if some gods blessed my knight in form."

Kaderin felt her expression tighten. "Did they bless your knight with a raging appetite for blood?" she snapped, shocking even herself.

"*Watch your tone, Valkyrie.*" The flames hissed and swayed. "This isn't a coffee klatch." Behind them, Scribe leapt back, swatting when his sleeve caught fire.

Kaderin ground her teeth, then said, "Yes, Riora."

She sighed. "Go." Her tone gentled. "If you win the race, you can bring back your sisters."

Kaderin's eyes narrowed. "You know about them? I've never told you of my loss."

"I already knew of you when they were killed."

"If you understand how important this is, then would the incandescent Riora like to bestow some tips on the race?"

Riora gasped, playful once more. "You treat me as if I'm a one-nine-hundred chess helpline. I feel cheapened." She regarded her nails. "I've blinded men for less." Scribe was again busy behind them, more tentatively dousing the last of the fires, but he paused to nod, as if he'd definitely seen that one happen.

"I'm sorry. I should have known," Kaderin said. "Everyone says it's *impossible* to get information out of you."

"You'd best step lightly, Valkyrie," she warned, but she was amused. She glided forward to put her arm around Kaderin, startling her. Riora's touch was warm and soft, as she shepherded her to the side. Then, in a low tone, she said, "Here's a hint. If you come across the blade of the blind mystic Honorius, know that he charmed it never to miss its target."

Before Kaderin could ask her more about this cryptic hint, Riora turned abruptly. "Oh, here comes your vampire. He can't stand it anymore."

Kaderin tried to deny that he was hers, but Riora spoke over her. "Look at him watching you so greedily! And how arrogant his stance! What thrilling hubris—and broad shoulders." She gave a growl in her throat. "Shall I stall him while you leave? It won't be a chore."

Kaderin pressed her lips in irritation, then felt ridiculous. She couldn't be jealous over a vampire. "I'd appreciate that. Though I don't think it *possible* to stall him for more than a few hours."

"Cheeky, Valkyrie," Riora said, her gaze never wavering from Sebastian. "You have a day."

*   *   *

"Vampire," Riora murmured as Sebastian strode by. "A word with you."

He impatiently turned to her but continued glancing at Kaderin as she crossed the length of the temple. She met the werewolf near the arched doorway, and they had a terse exchange.

"Relax—yes, she's getting away from you. But then, nothing has changed since five minutes ago, when she never wanted to see you again. So, who carved you up? Was it that naughty red-clawed Lykae presently threatening Kaderin?"

Sebastian was going to kill him. "We had an altercation," he said absently, beginning to stride to Kaderin. "I must go—"

Riora appeared in front of him. "How did you find this place?" she asked, her voice becoming more forceful. "I don't recall sending you an invitation, neither does Scribe here"—she snapped her fingers, and the man dropped his candle snuffer to hurry to her side—"and I'm not certain I appreciate you crashing my party."

"I traced here." He had to remember he could reach Kaderin at any time. And that he had better not anger the deity who had given him the favor of competing.

"You couldn't ever have been here."

Finally, the Lykae loped away. Kaderin gave the Scot a vulgar hand gesture behind his back, then stared in obvious bafflement at her own finger.

"I traced to Kaderin." When Sebastian saw Kaderin dig a phone from her jacket, then slip through the doorway, he turned back to Riora with his jaw clenched. "She was my destination."

Riora's lips curled as if she were delighted. Suddenly, her eyes seemed to burn. "But, vampire, that's *impossible.*"

In a distracted tone, he said, "Perhaps it was considered so before, but—"

"How did you do it?" She placed her forefinger on the altar and used it to press herself up to a sitting position at the edge.

He hurriedly explained how the variable constraints couldn't be separated. You couldn't have one possible and the other impossible when they were so similar. If it was a feat of mental dexterity and sense-memory detail, then it followed that tracing could be taken to extremes not seen before.

"Ut-ter-ly fascinating." She turned to the small man, fanning herself. "Scribe, I think I'm in love. He's like my very own foot soldier! How shall I reward him?"

Scribe said, "To tell by his grinding teeth and bulging jaw, I'd say he has only one desire at present." Sebastian saw that Scribe did not appreciate his interest in the Valkyrie.

"Oh, yes. *Kaderin.*" Riora sniffed. "I'm jealous, vampire, and let down. And later I shall cry."

Sebastian sensed power in her, fickle power, and until he knew what he was about in this world, he thought it wise to tread carefully. "I . . . meant no offense."

Scribe cleared his throat, and as if the words were tortured from him, he said, "Goddess Riora, it's incumbent upon me to tell you that your attraction to this male is quite possible. I daresay his winning over Lady Kaderin is, given her history, *im*possible."

Her eyes widened, and she nodded sagely. "Ah, you are right. *This* is why I keep you alive—"

"What about Kaderin's history?" Sebastian interrupted.

Riora squinted at him as if he were a bug she'd never seen before, actually leaning her head in closer to his face. "You spoke over me. I've conflicting impulses to boil you and coddle you."

"Goddess, I apologize," he said, but he continued undaunted. "You mentioned her history . . ."

As though the trespasses were forgotten, she whispered in a conspiratorial tone, "Vampires have behaved *very* badly toward Kaderin. And, well, you're a vampire."

His fangs sharpened at the thought of her being hurt. "What was done to her?"

She ignored his grated question, and asked one of her own. "Do you have any idea how high you reach for one such as her?"

In fact, he was well acquainted with that idea. Though Kaderin abhorred what he was, he couldn't be more pleased with her. When she'd hopped up onto this altar next to Riora, he'd seen that the goddess had nothing over his Bride.

Still, he raised his chin. "I have wealth to spoil her and strength to protect her. She could do worse for a husband."

"Arrogant vampire." She chuckled. "She's the daughter of gods."

He swallowed. *And that would be why she outshone a goddess.*

"Still feel so confident?"

He hadn't been before. Now he wondered if even the minuscule odds he'd given himself were overestimated.

She asked, "Do you plan to win the key for her?"

"Yes, exactly."

"Wouldn't want it for yourself?" she asked. "Imagine the possibilities."

"It is hard for me to believe it would work," he admitted. "Is there any proof it will?"

"No. I have no proof, at all." Riora sighed. "Just the word of Mr. Thrane."

Sebastian ran his hand over the back of his neck, but the movement made his chest muscles scream in protest. "Then can I ask why you are convinced it will work?"

"I am convinced it will work, vampire, because it's impossible for it to work!"

Just when he wondered if rational discussion with her was possible, she suggested, "You should take this day to learn about Kaderin."

This definitely struck Sebastian as a worthy plan. "I would love to, but I lack the resources to learn anything."

"Resources abound. Kaderin likes the *now*, and Valkyrie are amused with evolving human culture. Yet you do not seem to know much about this time. Read as much as you can get through today. And listen to the TV out of the corner of your ear."

"TV. I don't own one."

"I daresay Kaderin does, and I can say with certainty that she won't be at her flat today."

Trespassing in his Bride's home when she wasn't there?

"Scribe knows her address in London." A look passed between them, and Scribe's pale face seemed to darken as though flushed.

"Yes," Scribe said with a thinly veiled sneer. "If you go there, remember that Spike TV and the Playboy Channel will hip you to our times as well as anything. Start there."

Sebastian would be sure to steer clear of whatever he'd just suggested. He glanced at the door once more, though he knew Kaderin was long gone.

"Still antsy?" Riora asked. "You can trace to her at any time."

"You said there are prizes all over the world. I do not know that I can trace halfway around the earth, much less accurately to her."

She murmured, "It would seem impossible. But in the past, she's always stayed on this side of the earth at the start. Close by Europe. Low-hanging fruit. That's the way she's always worked. And since dawn's less than an hour away, you would trace to her right into the sun. . . ."

Surveying his chest, she said, "Let her go, knight. Besides, you need to heal. I fear Bowen hasn't had all his shots."

Trust a mad goddess and her vengeful scribe? Beggars couldn't be choosers. *And you don't have a friend in the world.*

"Right." Sebastian nodded firmly. "How far can she get in a day?"

13

Prize: Three mirror amulets, used as glamours,
worth twelve points each

Voila," Regin said to Kaderin, pulling down her fuzzy
purple scarf. "I *told* you I'd get you a snowcat. I *told*
you I had Russian connections. And what is that?" She
tapped her chin. "Hmmm. Oh, yes, let me look. A snowcat."

Kaderin cringed at the black-market vehicle before
them. This junker was supposed to take them to the amulets
closeted in the Transantarctic mountain range?

She had seen similar vehicles used to groom snow in the
States. And so she was aware that this one, purchased from
Regin's Russian connections, was . . . subpar.

Of course, when Kaderin had called the coven, she'd gotten none other than Regin.

Kaderin glowered at her, pulling her farther away from
the five Russian humans who'd choppered them to the

abandoned station. The ex-military crew was a small pha-lanx of a larger consortium that sold off military equipment for the Russian mob.

Regin had told them she and Kaderin were scientists; Regin sported disco swirl snow boots.

Kaderin had been forced to abandon the sleek Augusta 109 helicopter, leaving it and her pilots behind on one of the helipads of an unregistered icebreaker. Apparently, nei-ther the Augusta nor the pilots were comfortable flying in the extreme low temperatures here. The Russians' helicop-ter, the Arktika Mi-8, was—fitting, since it was a Cold War relic.

And now, this sad, sad little snowcat.

She'd known better than to let Regin assist her with this multi-leg jaunt, much less meet her. Yes, Regin did have the military contacts Kaderin had known she'd need to get south—really south. And yes, Regin had sworn she spoke Russian, which was about the only Baltic language Kaderin didn't have a handle on.

But the easiest way to get disqualified from the Hie was to draw human attention to the Lore, and Regin's utter lack of subtlety—and her glowing skin—kept Kaderin wary.

When asked why her skin was so radiant, Regin had been known to answer, "Eight glasses of water every day. Skin polish! Fateful swim in a radioactive lake. . . ."

"Regin, why is the cab *wooden*?"

She tilted her head, puzzled herself, then rallied to say, "Just on the outside. Inside? We'll be like joeys in a pouch, not that we're going to die of cold anytime soon, even if it is negative fifty right now. Hey, did I mention the bucket seats, baby? This is the Cadillac-o-Snowcats."

Regin is young, Kaderin reminded herself. *Only ten centuries old.*

"Lookit, it's not like we have much choice about the snowcat, anyway. This is as far as the crew will take us."

"I still don't see why we couldn't just fly all the way to the mountain range." Kaderin gazed longingly at the Arktika— even that tin bucket of a whirlybird was preferable. Two soldiers had anchored it down and were keeping it running—it was night in Antarctica in the middle of austral fall, and if the helicopter rotors stilled for even a few seconds, they would freeze that way.

"You will if the wind starts whipping up," Regin answered. "Freak katabatic winds aloft. I learned that word today."

Aloft or katabatic? Kaderin was tempted to ask.

"Besides, at that altitude and in this season," she continued, "the rotors would definitely freeze. And we don't have an automatic thermoelectric anti-icing system. We're all manual."

As if to illustrate "manual," two other soldiers were spraying a de-icer on the less intricate snowcat engine, a secret cocktail of calcium chloride that was stronger than any on the market, black or not. The last soldier, the leader, Ivan, was a tall blond of exceptional good looks. He took another swig from a flask of vodka that never froze, then gave a bow to Regin.

Earlier, he and Regin had been playing slap hands, gloveless, in subzero temperatures, because "it hurts worse in the cold."

Regin waved back at him, smiling sunnily even while muttering, *"Young, dumb, and hung. Where do I sign?"*

Kaderin pinched her forehead. She had finally decided to ask the coven for help and wound up with the most frat-pledge-esque of the Valkyrie—and the one she'd dreaded facing.

Regin's mother, the last survivor of a vampire attack on the Radiant Ones, had been on the verge of death when rescued by Wóden and Freya. She'd been scarred with bites until the day she died, years later. Even on her beautiful glowing face.

Regin had learned to count by them.

Kaderin began pacing. "You shouldn't have come, Regin."

"You had two prerequisites." Regin plopped down on a snowbank. "And I do believe I have Russian ex-mil contacts, and I speak the language—"

"Oh, come on! I've since learned that you do not by any stretch. You think *Dostoyevsky* is Russian for 'How's it hanging?' "

She blinked up at Kaderin as she paced by. "Then how *do* you say it?"

"I—don't—know."

"Then how do you know it's not *Dostoyevsky*? No. Really." She blew a bubble with her gum—possibly the first to do so at this location—but it flash-froze, and she had to crunch it back to gum consistency with her molars. "Obi-Wan, I was your only hope."

Regin knew Kaderin did not appreciate *Star Wars* references. "There had to be someone," Kaderin insisted.

"Would you rather Nïx had come?"

Nucking Futs Nïx. "As a matter of fact, she was on the list of prizes. Or at least, the hair of the oldest Valkyrie was."

"No wonder!" At Kaderin's raised eyebrows, Regin explained, "Right before we took off, Nïx called to tell me she went into the Circle K to get a *People* and some madman sheared off most of her hair." She added, "Nïx thinks it's 'becoming.' Kind of like an early Katie Couric or Tennille of Captain and—"

"Silence, Regin!"

"*What?*" She stomped one of her hyper–pink and purple snow boots. "What'd I *say?*"

"Myst could've come."

"I told you, she's busy."

Kaderin said, "And you never told me with what."

She hiked her shoulders and averted her eyes. "Dunno with what."

"Regin, I've told you what's at stake."

"I know. And we're totally going to win the key."

Kaderin didn't miss that Regin had slipped *we're* into that sentence. "What is taking them so long? These amulets are decade-long glamours. We're going to be overrun with trolls and killer kobolds wanting to look human."

Regin snorted, she laughed so abruptly. She bent all the way over, elbows past her knees.

"Damn you, it isn't funny."

Once her guffaws died down, Regin said, "You are the only person on earth who calls them killer kobolds. That's such a slippery slope away from killer gnome."

"Have you forgotten that they took my foot?" She'd just been frozen into her immortality—mere days earlier—otherwise, it would not have regenerated. In any case, it had hurt like hell. "And when was the last time you lost a body part?"

Regin gazed up solemnly. "I lost a finger in the Battle of Evermore."

"Oh." Kaderin frowned, then cried, " 'The Battle of Evermore' is a Led Zeppelin song!"

"Yeah. But wasn't it written about us?" Regin's eyes widened. "Hey, speaking of songs, lookit what I made for our snowcat ride." She pulled out an iPod, careful to keep it rubbed warm. "A snow-trip mix!"

Kaderin saw red and pounced on her, shoving her into the snow. She ceased when she registered that Regin was too dumbfounded to fight back. The Russians stopped what they were doing, staring, no doubt wondering why two sci-entists were wrestling in the snow.

Kaderin stood, giving Regin a hand up, and eked out an unpracticed smile for the Russians.

"Tetchy," Regin said, brushing off her clothing. "Seems somebody's shucking their cursey-wursey."

Only ten centuries old. Only ten centuries . . .

"It's not a curse. It was—it *is* a blessing." She lifted her chin, not wanting Regin to know she'd begun to feel again—and that she didn't see that woeful development ending anytime soon. If Kaderin's coven mates found out, they'd be so happy, making a huge deal out of this. Which, coincidentally, could now embarrass her. "I apologize. The stress of the Hie makes the blessing waver at times—" She broke off when a helicopter flew over, a Canadian flag on the tail. *You said we couldn't fly!*

"Wow," Regin said casually. "They must have an auto-matic thermoelectric anti-icing system."

Just as she was about to destroy Regin, Ivan called out, waving them over to the snowcat. Kaderin pointed at Regin but couldn't manage words. Regin pointed back with a wink, then turned to grab their gear, including their swords hidden in ski cases.

Shake it off. Focus.

After Ivan opened their doors and they climbed in, he pulled down his mask and leaned in close to Regin to say something very earnestly in Russian.

Regin translated. "He says if a storm blows in or if we're not back by a certain time, they'll be forced to leave us."

"How much time do we have?"

"They've got enough fuel to keep the rotors creeping for four hours." Regin tapped her chin with her gloved fingers. "Four hours or possibly forty minutes. I can't be certain, since my knowledge of Russian really does blow," she admitted baldly.

Before Kaderin could say anything, Regin raised her hand and lovingly scrunched Ivan's cheeks. She waggled his face back and forth, then pushed him back with a forefinger against his lips so she could slam the door shut.

"Hey, there's more than one amulet, right?" Regin said when they were alone. "You don't get extra credit for being there first."

Kaderin slid her sword out of the case in the backseat, readying for trouble. "No. But they could set traps."

"And how are kobolds going to chopper out here in the first place?" Regin asked. "I just can't picture the critters at the helipad, you know?"

"They can turn invisible and stow along. I unknowingly sailed one all the way to Australia in the last Hie," she said, then added, "Sadly, he had an accident and wasn't quite up for the return trip." When Ivan gave them another formal bow, Kaderin frowned. "What type of scientists did you tell them we are, anyway?"

"Glaciologists from the University of North Dakota studying a sudden massive fissure caught by satellite. I thought there was a certain irony in saying we had to act swiftly about a glacier."

"Dakotan glaciologists, huh?"

"If those guys want to believe two preternaturally foxy Valkyrie—one of whom is sporting disco snow boots—are scientists, who am I to naysay?" Regin blew a bubble, revving the engine. "Let the science commence."

Another helicopter banked over them.

14

At sunset, when Sebastian traced to find his Bride and his skin flash-froze, he realized the goddess had duped him.

He'd spent the entire day in Kaderin's townhouse, having traced from the temple to London, then hailed a cab. Just minutes before dawn, Sebastian had arrived at the address Scribe had finally surrendered, then traced inside.

In her home, after drawing all the curtains, he'd discovered he could, in fact, "listen out of the corner of his ear" to TV while he speed-read through newspapers. Yet he'd discovered nothing new about Kaderin from her Spartan, non-descript living space. If he hadn't smelled her scent on her silk pillow and finally found a collection of weapons, shields, whips, and manacles in a closet, he might have wondered if Riora and her Scribe had even given him the correct address.

And now this.

"Low-hanging fruit," Riora had said. "She'll stay close by Europe," she'd reassured Sebastian. Yet he'd appeared in the wake of an unwieldy vehicle choking out black smoke as it crawled over an icy plain.

His Bride was doubtless in that vehicle, and tracing to

her had taken him very far from "close by Europe." With fumbling fingers, he dug the scroll from his pocket, then scanned the ten choices. *Antarctica.*

He could see the tips of his fingers blackening from near instantaneous frostbite. *Bloody hell.* Fortunately, Antarctica was dark twenty-four hours a day this time of year; unfortunately, it was bloody cold. This was something for a man who'd been raised along the Baltic Sea to say. He needed coverage against the elements—more than the mere coat and gloves he'd bought last week.

In an instant, he traced to one of the clothing stores he'd purchased from, sure to appear in a dressing room—which luckily did not have another customer in it. After grabbing insulated gloves and layers of clothes to go under a heavy trench coat, he noted the name of the store to send payment to and exited the same way.

Fifteen minutes later, he was back again in the wake of the same vehicle, though it seemed he could have thrown it farther than it had traveled.

He wrapped a black wool scarf over his ears and face, then pulled out the scroll once more. Within the highest peak in the Transantarctic mountain range was a couloir, an ice tunnel. Inside the couloir were three amulets.

Kaderin was traveling to the mountain range towering over this plain, so that must be it. He traced to the highest overhang he could make out on the tallest mountain. From that vantage, he saw one even higher up and traced there.

Directly in front of him—a tunnel. He traced within it as far as he could see, reached the end of the first straightaway, turned left, and progressed to the next end. He easily covered ground this way. Yet even dressed in heavy clothing, he was still suffering from frostbite at his extremities, then healing from it in grueling intervals.

A narrow ledge marked the end of the tunnel, and atop it were the three small amulets that looked like jagged mirrors carved from ice. He grasped the one he intended for Katja, then traced back to the overhang to scan for her.

As he waited, he gazed out over the alien scene. He'd never imagined a landscape like this. During his human life, Antarctica had been a rumor, an impossibility.

Here the stars didn't glint but were motionless and dead like the static photographs he'd seen everywhere in London. The moon didn't rise and set, but in the half hour he'd been here, it had floated farther to the left over the horizon.

He wouldn't have been able to see this preternatural scene if he'd died. He wouldn't be waiting anxiously for his Bride.

What to say to her?

Suddenly, two helicopters roared overhead, circling before landing at the base of the mountain. Curious, he traced down. Two other competitors were organizing ropes to climb to the slender overhang. A plan formed. If Kaderin thought he was quiet and unassuming—well, he was most of the time—but if she thought that was *all* that he was, he was about to surprise her.

Kaderin swore imaginatively with every foot she climbed higher up the rock face, irritation running rife in her.

She mimicked Regin's voice to say, "Why, they must have a thermoelectric anti-icing system!"

Regin had never riled her like this before. Kaderin had always been one of the few older Valkyrie who could tolerate her for long periods of time. But Regin *had* to play "Radar Love" at least eight times. As if they were chugging along fast enough to merit a song like that. The Cadillac-o-Snowcats redlined at ten miles per hour.

Regin played "Low Rider" just as many times. If Kaderin heard that freaking cowbell one more time . . .

When they'd finally crawled to the base of the mountain, it had seemed there was a parking lot of choppers. But no one could climb faster than Kaderin could, including Regin, so she'd been left behind, happy to guard the snowcat and "rock out."

Kaderin had to keep telling herself that she would pass whoever had already started out. That she hadn't yet was peculiar.

She slammed one of her ice axes harder than she needed to, and it spiked through ice and met rock, sending vibrations up her aching arm and numb fingers.

Focus. She was just thirty or so feet from the highest overhang. *Get in, get out.* Vodka-laced Russians held her fate in their human hands.

But she was having to work for this one. Though she was only at about twelve thousand feet, the air at the poles was thinner, making it feel like a much higher altitude, and she carried a large, unwieldy pack of diverse gear.

Her secret for winning the Hie all these times? Well, besides merciless brutality to all competitors?

She was *always* prepared for anything—

A sudden wind howled past the mountain. *Katabatic?*

She was tossed fully horizontal, gritting her teeth, clinging to her twisting axes.

Sebastian lost his breath when the wind gusted, flinging Kaderin to her side, just below him.

He traced to her in an instant, seizing her coat, but came

back to the ledge empty-handed. He tried once more, boomeranging back with nothing.

Only on his third attempt did he snatch her back with him.

She evinced little reaction that he'd traced her—or that he was beside her on a different continent at the bottom of the world.

Her gloved hands still clutched two ice axes, and her sword was sheathed across her stuffed pack. She had wickedly sharp ice cleats attached to her boots, the front spikes jutting like a rattlesnake's fangs.

When the wind died a second later, she briefly looked heavenward. "I had that."

"Maybe." His chest was heaving, and he hadn't shaken his alarm. "Why in the hell couldn't I take you back at first?"

Catching her breath, too, she answered, "I had a good grip on my axes." She stowed them in string loops on the sides of her pack. "Understand, vampire, if I fight you, you can't trace me. I'm far too old, and too strong."

Old and strong? She could not appear less so. He was struck again by how small she was. Standing a foot shorter than he was, she seemed so fragile, and yet she was laden with that pack. She looked as if she'd fall backward under the weight, and he didn't want to let go of her. She was winded from the climb and miserable, and for what reason? None. He could have traced her to this summit in the blink of an eye.

"Why did you fight me?" he demanded. "You were about to fall."

"Only if my axes failed, and I do believe they held out, even when a hulking vampire was yanking at me." Between puffs of breath, she asked, "How'd you get here before me?" But she was already peering around him, demonstrating her true interest. "You were in the Norwegian helicopter, weren't you?"

"I've never been in a helicopter. I traced to you."

"Vampires don't have that ability."

"I do. I thought of you as my destination. It's how I found you at the Hie assembly." Without any more acknowledgment, she began to pass around him, but he stepped in her way. "If you had allowed me to help you, I could have accompanied you here. You could have pointed to the summit and I would have traced you there an instant later."

As he had done with her competitors, in exchange for information about her.

She shrugged. "I like climbing."

"Clearly. You look . . . invigorated."

At his sarcastic tone, she straightened her hat over her braids, then dropped her hands with a scowl.

He exhaled heavily. *I haven't insulted her enough in the last day?*

"Move out of the way." She sidled around him, but he blocked her once more. "I don't have time for this."

"No, I have to talk to you. Obviously, you want to win this, for whatever reason. And I want to provide for you whatever you wish for. So, desist, and let me win this for you. You know I will give you the prize at the end." *Useless though it might be.* He stifled his irritation that she believed in this so blindly.

"*Give* me?" Her eyes flashed. "The vampire will *give* me the prize?"

That was probably not an optimal way of phrasing—

"You don't even know enough to know how ridiculous I

find your words. I am proud and notoriously malicious, yet you think I'd allow you to make a gift of what I can rightly take?"

Definitely not going as he'd envisioned.

"Now, stand aside. More are ascending as we speak."

If she could be ruthless, he could as well—and he had been prepared to be. "There are no prizes left. I have the last one of the three."

Her lips parted.

"I suspected there might be problems and that I might need leverage. So I traced the siren and a ground dweller to the cavern behind us. Now there is one prize available to you—and it appears you *will* be accepting it as my gift to you."

Just then, Lucindeya the siren strolled out with her amulet, holding it above her heart. It *disappeared*. And for a moment, the area smelled of fire and damp woods.

"Thanks, vamp. Remember what I said," she purred, then cast a look of triumph at Kaderin. Lucindeya had confided to him that it would gall Kaderin to be assisted in spots of trouble. He'd assumed the siren simply didn't want a vampire helping her competition, but Lucindeya had said that she would love to see Sebastian win Kaderin, because "nothing would bring down the high and mighty Kaderin like falling for a leech."

She'd sworn to the Lore—which she and the kobold seemed to take very seriously—that the surest way to lose Kaderin would be to help her, especially in a physical contest. So when Sebastian had first discovered Kaderin climbing, he'd had to stop himself from tracing her to the top, though he was sweating with fear for her.

Then he'd seen her flung sideways like a rag doll.

Kaderin eyed the siren, then turned to him. "You'd bet-

ter hope Cindey doesn't hum you a tune unless you want to
be her lapdog."

"Please, Valkyrie," Lucindeya interrupted as she readied
for her descent, pulling gear from her pack. "As if I'd even
clear my throat to snare a vampire." She flashed a smile up
at Sebastian as she hammered her anchor and threaded line.
"No offense, vamp." And then she began rappelling down.

Once she was out of sight, Kaderin glanced past him, and
her eyes widened. Sebastian turned to spy the kobold sham-
bling down the long ice tunnel, his jaunty whistle echoing
along the couloir.

When Sebastian had asked the kobold if Kaderin was
married or had children, the kobold had revealed that as far
as anyone knew, she was single and had not "issued off-
spring." Sebastian didn't know how much credence he
could give to the kobold's words, since he'd also sworn that
Kaderin didn't eat or drink—anything.

Sebastian turned back and found Kaderin had gone perfectly still, her eyes locked on the ground dweller's every
movement as he neared. It was as if a predator had spied
prey.

Without glancing away, Kaderin said, "Do you know that
I hate kobolds almost as much as vampires? And Cindey
was my stiffest competition at the last Hie." She finally
faced Sebastian. "So if you wanted to piss me off, you've
succeeded."

"Kaderin, that was not my intention."

A branch of lightning struck in the distance across a
cloudless night. He now knew that it came from her.
"You've put me in an untenable position." Removing her
gloves, she neared until she was toe-to-toe with him. "And

do you know what else you've done?" She reached up her delicate hand and gently brushed the back of her smooth claws down the side of his face. Just as he was about to close his eyes, she continued, "You've underestimated a Valkyrie."

Like a blur, she dropped down to a crouch, one leg straight out, sweeping around to stab the kobold through the throat with her cleats. As she rocked closer to the trapped creature, her arm shot out, then she gave her leg a decisive yank back to dislodge the being.

She was on her feet again in the blink of an eye, amulet in hand. Sebastian couldn't speak. Giving him a bored look, she leisurely curled one finger around it at a time and held it over her heart. Until it was . . . gone.

The kobold lay writhing, hands clamped to its throat and gushing yellow blood.

When it continued to thrash, she exhaled impatiently—then shuffled her foot at it, brushing it over the edge to fall thousands of feet. As Sebastian stared in shock, she tilted her head. Then, as if thinking, *While I'm here . . .* , she plucked the siren's anchor out of the rock. She yanked until she'd dislodged the next one down as well, then let go. A scream carried on the wind.

Stunned by her sudden viciousness, he snapped, "I was responsible for this. Why not take the prize I hold?"

"They'd been warned." She yanked out her ice axes. "But next time, I will take yours. I promise you."

Then she simply dropped from the ledge.

He dove for her, reaching out, but she'd disappeared. He caught sight of her as she snagged a lip with her axes five hundred feet down.

Just as he traced to that ledge, she freed herself with a violent heave and plummeted once more, before catching with a jerk lower down. A roar of breath left his body, and he sagged when he saw her reach the base.

With a glare up at him, she tossed the axes and sprinted for her vehicle.

15

Kaderin groaned to see the kobold had plunged directly into the roof of the snowcat, bending it down in a V, and now lay sprawled, unconscious.

Lucindeya? Kaderin had passed her at one thousand feet, hanging on with her fingertips, cursing her in what humans assumed were dead languages. *"I didn't think you'd start this early, lightning whore! It's on!"*

"Hey!" Regin called. "What hit the roof? I don't have comp and collision on this thing. Hee-hee."

Kaderin slammed into the cab, gasping after her exertion. "Just go!" She put her hands to the window and ducked and twisted, scanning for Sebastian through the scratchy glass. It was only a matter of time.

"Um, shouldn't we get whatever is up there off the freaking roof? You know, so we'll be sveltely aerodynamic again."

"Kobold," Kaderin said dismissively, still fighting to catch her breath.

At that, Regin shoved the door open and patted around blindly on the roof. She jerked the moaning kobold off by his ankle, flinging him far.

"Put this thing in gear!" Kaderin snapped. "And get your swords ready." Regin's swords were more like refined cutlasses, worn crossed over her back in twin sheaths. They were short enough that she could use them freely in the closed cab.

Regin drew them immediately, glancing around for a foe. "What? Where's the bogey?"

"Vampire!" Kaderin gasped. "And he's right—" Kaderin jumped, startled when Sebastian appeared outside not a foot away. "Here!"

When he traced inside the snowcat compartment to sit in the backseat, Regin tensed, turning slowly. Any other creature in the Lore would have witnessed her eerie movements as she prepared to spring and would have known life was over.

Kaderin might not be allowed to kill him, but Regin would do so with glee.

Suddenly, Kaderin didn't know if she wanted to see this. After all the vampires she had killed and had seen killed, his imminent death was making her . . . nervous?

"Kad, baby," Regin began with a menacing purr, "you brought me a kill? And here I was getting light on fangs." Regin's swords shot out, positioned around his neck like they were hedge clippers. She wrenched them together.

But at the last second, he'd traced a foot over. Her swords sliced only air and each other with a pure metallic ring. He was either the fastest tracer they'd ever encountered, or he'd never been fully substantial to begin with.

"You can't kill a competitor," Sebastian said to Regin with infuriating calm.

"Not a competitor yet, leech." Regin's swords shot out once more and flew together. "I just drive the boat."

But he'd nonchalantly traced over again. "You try my patience, creature," he said to Regin, then gave Kaderin a last look. "Tonight, Katja." He disappeared.

"Damn it!" Regin snapped. Then the situation seemed to hit her. Her jaw dropped, and she swung her face to Kaderin. "*Katja?*" she cried, pointing a sword.

"Just shut up. I don't want to hear it."

"A vampire just called you a nickname! A *sexy* nickname."

Kaderin waved her hand dismissively. "He thinks I'm his . . . Bride."

Regin threaded her swords in their sheaths. "*Yeah? That so?*" she said, speaking far too loudly in the enclosed space. "Seems to be catching." She yanked the gearshift to speed them off at a loping ten miles per hour.

"Catching? What do you mean by that? Because of Helen?" Helen's transgression was seventy years ago. Would the covens never let it die? And if not, what would they do if they found out about Kaderin and Sebastian?

"Helen. Sure. Whatever," Regin muttered, surly again. "What's this leech's plan for you?" She drove like a consummate trucker, one hand at six o'clock on the large wheel, the other on the gearshift.

"He wants to help me win the Hie."

She made a sound of frustration. "Like you'd trust a leech with something this important!" Without even trying to miss, Regin ran straight through a snowdrift. "When you're barely trusting *me* to help you!" A frantically blown gum bubble. "He seemed really possessive of you already. You haven't . . . you haven't, like, lifted tail for him?"

"No! I didn't have sex with him!" she said honestly, hoping to manage a believable amount of indignation. *Thank the gods I didn't go that far. Would never. I can always deny . . .*

"What did he mean by tonight? He can't find you."

Um, actually he might be able to. "I can't imagine, Regin." *No, no way.* Tracing to a person was impossible. Vampires just didn't have that talent. And yet he'd surprised her in so many ways already. She knew he was unique. If he truly could come to her, would he tonight?

"What are you going to do in the future if you go up against him again?"

"I don't know," Kaderin admitted. "I can't kill him, because of the competition."

"Contain him, then. If he's not that old, you could still hold him with a reinforced shackle. Or throw a boulder on him. On his leg. He'd be trapped."

"Unless he took off his leg the way Emma's Lykae did to get to her."

Regin shuddered. "Eeesh, that skeeves me."

Kaderin hadn't really thought much about Lachlain's act. Now she found the idea of him willfully amputating a trapped leg to crawl through vampire catacombs to reach his mate on the surface vaguely . . . romantic? Would Sebastian do that for her?

"*Hell.*" He would.

"What's that?" Regin asked. When Kaderin just shook her head, Regin said, "I'll stay with you tonight. Maybe stick around for tomorrow's task." Regin had told Sebastian that she wasn't a competitor *yet.* Kaderin knew she needed to nip this even before Regin turned on her music. Again.

"*All . . . my . . . friends . . . know the low rider.*"

Kaderin pinched her forehead. Cowbell. How much more could she stand?

She was faced with the very harsh realization that she'd rather be accosted by the arrogant vampire—one of her immortal enemies—than stay with Regin for another twenty-four hours.

No more cowbell. "I think I can handle it."

After the unqualified failure of his first outing, Sebastian traced back to his chests to retrieve more gold—having determined that he might need to secure more money than he'd first suspected.

He had the feeling this courtship would be . . . protracted.

As he shed layers of clothes, preparing to dig, he felt the amulet in one of his pockets. With a shrug, he drew it out, then held it above his heart. His lips parted when it vanished. It bloody worked for him, too? The smell of the temple's fires flared over the Baltic brine. He'd . . . he'd simply have to think about this later.

He snatched up the shovel he'd left for the purpose, and while he dug, he wondered if he would ever be able to forget the sight of Kaderin stabbing that kindly-looking old kobold through the gullet.

As a human, Sebastian had killed and dealt viciously with his enemies. But, Christ, he wished he hadn't seen her attack—so quick and thoughtless, as if by rote.

Though he'd seen women resort to violence in wartime to protect loved ones, he'd never sensed such ferocity in a female.

He understood he couldn't compare Kaderin to the women of his time. He couldn't even compare her to *human* females. His sisters would have fainted before injuring an insect. They would have fainted at the mere *idea* of climbing a mountain. He knew this, but it didn't make seeing Kaderin's cruelty any easier.

He feared his Bride enjoyed it.

Digging down, he found nothing. Brows drawn, he drove the shovel deeper. Still nothing.

His fists clenched the handle to splinters and dust.

The chests were gone.

Kaderin slouched in her leather recliner on the jet, satisfied with her success. The chair beside her was empty as Regin lay on the floor of the plane, legs propped up on the chair arm. They'd planned to drop Kaderin at a Rio executive airport, then fly Regin home to New Orleans.

Yes, Kaderin was satisfied. No matter what had happened, she was in the lead. Or at least tied for it, with Cindey and that sodding vampire. How, on the vampire's first Hie—on his very first task—had he scored the maximum? Insufferable. At least Bowen hadn't been there, and the next-highest task had been only a nine-pointer.

"I really can stay with you, if you need me to," Regin offered for the fifth time. "We would make the most kick-ass-est team ever."

"I tried teaming up for my first Hie," Kaderin answered. "Alas, my partnership with Myst ended in a difference in opinion—one that entailed her sucker-punching me in the mouth and me tossing her by her hair. Sorry, Regin, but I'll always work alone. Besides, the amulet was a good start. Twelve points out of eighty-seven."

"What if that vamp finds you again?"

If he'd been telling her the truth on that ledge, Kaderin figured that would be happening sooner than Regin thought. "I'm sure I can figure out something to take care of him."

"When did you blood him? In Russia?" When she nodded, Regin said, "Did he trace before you could kill him?"

Her face flushed. *No, I was too busy grinding on him.* "I

didn't have my whip with me," she said, hedging while still telling the truth. She felt she might as well be wearing a scarlet letter. Or at least a T-shirt that said, "Kissed vampire. And I was digging it."

"Regin, why are you so eager to help me out? You seem very keen to get out of—and stay out of—New Orleans."

She began nervously tinkering with her iPod. "Nïx told me that . . . well, Aidan the Fierce is returning soon."

"Your berserker?"

Regin had kissed Aidan—although she shouldn't have, because her kisses were as drugging as the most powerful mystical narcotics and just as addictive. Even after that berserker had died in battle, he'd defied death to seek her again in another life.

In fact, he'd reincarnated at least three other times, yearning for Regin so badly that he was cursed to be a Version 2.0, a reincarnate, for eternity.

"He's not *my* berserker," Regin said.

"What would you call him, then?"

She shrugged.

"What would you call the fact that he perpetually finds you, remembers who he was, and then somehow gets killed fighting to win you?"

"A game we play?" Regin winced. "Did I just say that?"

Kaderin rolled her eyes. "Then shouldn't you be in New Orleans, battering up?"

Regin glanced away and softly said, "I was kind of thinking that if he didn't find me this time, he might live past thirty-five."

Kaderin didn't know what to do with this sudden seriousness from Regin, so she said, "What am I supposed to do with this, Regin?"

"You're whack, d'you know that?"

"What if Ivan the Russian was your berserker, and you just didn't know it?"

Regin studied the ceiling. "I always know him."

"Why don't you just accept him? Run into his arms?" Freya had taught the older Valkyrie that they would know their true love when he opened his arms and they realized they'd always run to get within them.

"I have my reasons." Regin put her chin up, though she was lying on the floor. "They are myriad and complex."

"Give me one."

Regin faced her. "Okay, I'll give you one, a Regin Reason Lite. With a situation like this, you have to ask yourself, is the grope worth the slap?" When Kaderin frowned, she added, "You know, is the cake worth the bake?"

"Oh. So it's not?"

"Among other things, I'm not keen on falling for a mortal and cursing every day that passes because he'll die within a blink of my life. Then to pine for him to return?" She shook her head firmly. "Not worth the bake."

"I understand. It's best to forgo a small amount of pleasure to spare yourself a lot of pain." Kaderin did understand—so why had she taken pleasure from Sebastian, knowing it would wreck her afterward?

"Exactly! It's just self-preservation. No one in the coven gets it. They only want me to live in the moment. Nïx advised me to 'find and bang my berserker.'" She exhaled wearily. "But that brings a question to mind. Are you going to get a male now that the curse is lifting? Word around the coven is that you haven't had a little some-some in a thousand years."

Kaderin saw no reason to deny it. Even before her blessing, she'd been so cautious about trusting that she'd had few lovers. "I'm not so selfless that I would give 'a little some-some' when I get nothing out of it. I don't feel desire like that." *Liar, liar, liar.*

"Maybe not in the *past*," Regin said with an exaggerated wink-wink. "So, what's your type? Or was? Do you even re-member?"

What *was* her type? Kaderin flushed, denying her first thought. "I was always defenseless in the face of swineherds."

Regin laughed, and when Kaderin chuckled slightly, she exclaimed, "This is so weird! You were all freakishly unemotional before I was even born. I've never known you any other way." Regin gave her an appraising glance and declared, "You're kinda cool when you're not mystically lobotomized."

16

❧

Sebastian's coins, his gold, all the wealth he had in the world, had disappeared.

His head shot up, fangs sharpening. *Nikolai.* It had to be. What was left of the shovel handle dropped to the ground. Clenching his bleeding fists, he traced inside Blachmount, stalking from room to room, scarcely noticing the changes throughout. Sebastian found him striding through the main hall—where Sebastian and the rest of his family had died.

Nikolai appeared stunned to see him—even before receiving the first crushing blow to his face.

"Where's my goddamned gold?" Sebastian bellowed, with another punishing hit.

"I retrieved it." Nikolai dodged—or took—the blows without striking back. "I was keeping it safe."

"You had no right! You did it so I'd be forced to confront you."

"Yes," Nikolai said simply.

Sebastian struck out again, then lunged forward to shove Nikolai into the wall, pinning him there with a forearm under his chin. All of this reminded him too much of the night he'd risen, bringing back the pain with it. "You want a confrontation? Just like before?" Nikolai had refused to fight him, just as he was doing now. That night, if Murdoch hadn't forced his hands away from Nikolai's throat, Sebastian might have killed him.

He remembered that time through a haze, remembered being alive but dead, with no heartbeat or breath, trapped in twilight. He'd been so weak, waking with a frantic thirst—one that could be quenched only by blood.

He'd been cursed, because his brother had ignored his desperate wish to die with his family. He punched the wall beside Nikolai's face. "You made me an abomination."

"I saved your life," Nikolai bit out.

"And then immediately wanted me to pledge it to your army. A mortal life of battle after battle wasn't enough—you wanted me and Conrad to fight in a never-ending war."

"It's worth fighting."

"It's not *my* war."

"Do you still hate me so violently for my deeds?" Nikolai demanded. "Is that why you've never returned here?"

Sebastian released him. "I don't hate you," he finally said, surprised to find this true. "I don't care enough about anything to hate. No longer. Three hundred years took care of that." He backed away. "I just want you to stay out of my life."

"Do you want my apology? I give it."

"I don't want your apology—because I know in the same situation, you'd do it again. . . ." Sebastian's attention was distracted when a female entered the room.

"Nikolai?" Her gaze took in Nikolai's face, then she turned to Sebastian. "Apparently, he won't hit you back, but I will."

Recognizing her features, Sebastian asked, "Valkyrie?"

"How do you know what I am?" She faced Nikolai. "His heart beats. He's blooded."

Nikolai had always been aloof and possessed of a rigid

self-control. So it was even more unexpected when he glanced from the Valkyrie back to Sebastian, and his eyes went wild. Nikolai's first hit connected before Sebastian had time to tense.

Nikolai bellowed, "Is it her? Did she make your heart beat?"

Sebastian struck back, connecting squarely with Nikolai's jaw. "No," he bit out.

Nikolai lowered his fists and backed away, inhaling deeply. "You found your Bride before you came here?"

Sebastian glowered, running his sleeve over his bleeding lip.

"I am . . . sorry. . . . I thought . . ."

"Just tell me where my gold is."

Nikolai ran his fingers through his hair. "This isn't how I've imagined this meeting would be, Sebastian. I regret hitting you. I lose my head with her. But you understand now that you've been blooded."

You don't know the half of it.

"Sebastian, this is Myst."

"We've been searching for you," she said, with the same accent as Kaderin's. Though their coloring was completely different—Myst had red hair and green eyes—their features were similar. "I've heard a lot about you."

He gave her a quick jerk of his chin in greeting, then turned to Nikolai. "My—gold."

"Very well." Though Nikolai evinced no expression on his face, Sebastian knew him well enough to discern his bitter disappointment. "If you'll follow me."

As Nikolai led him toward their father's old office, Myst followed, eyeing Sebastian warily, as if she considered herself a little guard for Nikolai. If she were half as vicious as Kaderin, she'd be tremendous at it.

The office that the three of them entered was being ren-
ovated, and shutters had been placed over every window. "I
can't believe you're restoring Blachmount," Sebastian said
in a disgusted tone.

"We plan to live here. Of course, you are always welcome
to stay here," Nikolai said, but Sebastian scowled at that.
"And you can trace to this specific room at any time if you
need shelter in a hurry," Nikolai added. "These windows
will be shuttered during the day without fail."

As if Sebastian would ever want to be here voluntarily.
"How did you find my crates?" he demanded.

"I thought I sensed you the other night out on the prop-
erty, so I scoured the grounds for some hint of you. I hadn't
been optimistic about locating you again, especially not . . .
recently." He cleared his throat, and a look passed between
him and Myst. "Discovering the shovel and freshly dug
earth was a great relief—"

"*Take me to my gold.*"

Nikolai's lips thinned, but he crossed to the back wall to
unlock a small wall safe. The bricks around it were new, as
if repaired where someone had recently yanked it from the
wall.

"How did you know what I am?" Myst asked him, drawing his attention. "Most mistake the Valkyrie for nymphs."
She shook her head, then murmured to herself, "*Hate those
little hookers.*"

"I've seen your kind before," he said.

"Where?" Nikolai asked, retrieving a case from the safe.

"Around." Sebastian's eyes narrowed when Nikolai set it
on the desk.

"I see," Nikolai said. "I've exchanged most of your gold for
cash, and it's been invested. In this briefcase, you'll find the

investment portfolios and information on your bank accounts. There is a laptop, a sat phone, a temporary Estonian identification card—though you'll need to get a photograph soon—and credit cards. You are as established as a human would be."

Sebastian was seething. Nikolai was doing what he did best, which was *whatever the hell he wanted*. "You had no right."

"I'd hoped to assist you. You couldn't have been dealt with fairly for these riches. You and Conrad are wealthy men."

"You know where Conrad is?" He'd lost track of his brother after they'd left Blachmount as vampires. If Sebastian had rapidly gone out of his head with hunger and confusion, Conrad had fared much, much worse.

Nikolai's face fell. "No. I have searched for both of you. Have you seen him recently?"

After a hesitation, Sebastian shook his head. He hadn't seen Conrad since just weeks after their turning. That last day, Conrad had spoken cryptically of things he'd left undone as a mortal, tasks he could now complete as an immortal. At dusk, he'd disappeared and never returned. "What of Murdoch?" he asked, curious to know if he'd lived or died. How many brothers did he truly have?

"I can take you to him right now. He's at the Forbearer stronghold."

Sebastian cast him a black look. "A place I will never go—even if I had any inclination to see him."

Myst walked between them to break up the tense moment. "Why are you so angered over the past? Seems you'd be grateful to Nikolai. Without his actions, you'd never have your Bride."

I don't have her now. "I wonder if that might be a blessing." He took the case and traced away.

At the edge of the Atlantic Ocean, in a secluded villa on the beach, Kaderin lay in her bed, staring at the ceiling in misery.

She needed action, but she was forced to wait for the scrolls to update. Yes, action, or she needed sleep.

Normally, she required only about four hours in a twenty-four-hour period, and she could go for days without when pressed, but she wanted to be at one hundred percent after the Antarctica trip. She was sore from her climb—and descent—and soon she would really start to rack up the injuries.

Yet she couldn't fall asleep. Her T-shirt was too confining over her breasts and driving her crazy. She loathed sleeping with anything over her torso, but tonight she had to *prepare for the possibility of company*. And even the fine bedclothes in this lavish rented residence were like burlap compared to her Pratesi sheets. Worse, the bedroom was large and echoing and dark. Too dark.

Though fearless in battle, the Valkyrie often had secret weaknesses. Lucia the Archer was terrified of missing her target, since she'd been cursed to feel indescribable pain every time she did. Nïx feared foreseeing the death of a Valkyrie so much that, to this day, she never had. Regin, always the first to run screaming a war cry into the fray, was afraid of . . . ghosts.

And Kaderin? When alone, she had once suffered from lygophobia, the fear of dark or gloomy places, even though she could see near perfectly in the dark.

By the way she was eyeing the bathroom light switch, she apparently had the fear once more. Yet another weakness from before the blessing, rearing its ugly head. She rose to flip on the light, then returned.

The sinister Valkyrie with the nightlight—that was her.

It was uncomfortably quiet here, just as it'd been at her London flat. She'd grown used to living in her coven at Val Hall, amid the reassuring shrieks of her half-sisters and the thunder rattling the manor. All night, Valkyrie pushed in and out of the groaning oak front doors.

She turned to her side in a huff, glaring at her regular bedmate—her sword. Another huff had her back to it. She was . . . lonely. She still hadn't shucked *his* loneliness from that morning in his wretched castle.

Why not just think about him? Allow herself to mull over the vampire and be done with it?

For instance, she could contemplate why he wanted to die. Had he lost a loved one? A woman? It made sense. He was in his thirties, and would likely have been wed. If Kaderin had lost a husband, she'd probably see the appeal of becoming a hermit. She might even consider dying if she thought she could rejoin the one she loved.

But if he'd been married, then why would he seem so oddly unsure about kissing her at first? Of course, it'd been a while for him, but there was something so hesitant in his demeanor.

Then he'd quickly gotten back in the saddle.

She'd found herself thinking sometimes about his consuming kisses, reliving them and that entire morning. Worse, whenever she thought about the details of what she'd done with him, she didn't feel only shame. She recalled riding his huge shaft, and an answering wetness came between her legs. Her breasts grew swollen and achy. Her claws curled to clutch him to her.

The changes, these shifts in her personality, couldn't be

explained. She believed a god or some power had blessed her with numbness. A mere spell wouldn't have lasted this long, and the Valkyrie weren't very susceptible to spells, anyway.

No, she'd been blessed by a tremendous power.

A power that could be neutralized by her attraction to a rumbling-voiced vampire?

His bottled-up ferocity had a way of calling to her own previously deadened sense of it. Perhaps that was why she was so attracted to him. Because they were alike.

But why did she have to recover desire now, when so much was on the line? *Inconvenient* did not begin to describe this timing. She turned to her back and skimmed her hands inside her shirt, but her palms felt too soft against her breasts. *His* hands had been so enticingly callused, and as hesitant in the beginning as his kisses.

Rough hands, delectably firm lips, intense eyes. Everything about him was made for decadent dreams of sex, except Kaderin didn't dream, not since the blessing.

But she did fantasize, and easily called up a memory of his muscular body. She bit her bottom lip. The truth was that there was a lot of him to like. She'd never accepted many lovers—even when she'd been a feeler—because it was hard for her to trust, and of the handful she had welcomed to her bed, she'd never had an immortal one. None had possessed even half of her strength.

The vampire was stronger than she was.

She would never sleep with him.

If he's coming, then where the hell is he?

For hours, Sebastian sifted through all the forms and paperwork in the briefcase, attempting to discern if he had wealth. But his mind was completely preoccupied.

He knew she couldn't go after another prize until the scrolls updated, so he didn't believe she'd be in danger. And yet, at sunset, he finally gave in and traced to her.

He found himself standing in a spacious bedroom, in what seemed to be a private residence. The clock said it was just after 4 A.M., which meant he was on the other side of the world. A bed sat in the center, and he traced to the foot to glance down.

His Bride was sleeping in the center of it.

Would he ever get used to tracing directly to her? The advantages of this couldn't be calculated.

His self-congratulations faded when he saw that she slept fitfully. She lay on her front, her torso bare but for her shining hair cascading down. A shirt was wadded up near her head. One slender arm stretched out to the sword that rested beside her.

A sense of unease passed over him. Did she sleep with a sword as defense against the possibility of his finding her, or was her life always as dangerous as it seemed today? If the latter, he didn't know if he could ever let her out of his sight again.

Her eyes darted behind her lids, and her pointed ear twitched as if to detect the sound of danger. Was she listening for the approaching footsteps of an enemy?

Her breaths were pants, the way young animals breathe in sleep.

Around the sword handle, her fingers curled surely, and seeing that made his chest feel tight. He could protect her if only she'd allow it.

Surprisingly, she seemed to calm in his presence, so he removed his sword belt and jacket and laid them on a nearby bench. With leisure to study her, he drank her in with his gaze. He'd never thought of a woman's back as sexy, but hers was. He wanted to clasp her slim shoulders and pull her close to kiss along the delicate indentation of her spine.

Her smooth, golden skin beckoned him. It couldn't be as soft as it looked.

She murmured something from dreams and shifted her position, turning her head to the other direction. She drew her knee up, and the sheet slid off her, exposing the small pink shorts she wore. They were pulled aside, and in the shadow he caught a stolen glimpse of her female flesh and groaned. She was blond there, too, perfect and beautiful.

Born of gods? He was confident of it.

He had to touch her there, kiss her. He'd never taken a woman with his mouth, though he'd fantasized about it often enough as a mortal man. He barely stifled a shudder of pleasure at the thought of doing it to her.

With his shaft hard as iron, he reached forward. . . .

17

No, Kaderin didn't dream, not since the blessing, so even in sleep, she was confused about why she dreamed the vampire was nudging her legs apart.

Of course, it's a dream. A wicked one. I'd never sleep through a vampire's presence.

She allowed the dream vampire to continue touching her, seduced by his ragged breaths as he skimmed his fingers up her inner thighs, his hands shaking. In her dream, they were hot, one covering her ass, the other tugging aside her loose silk shorts to bare her sex.

He hissed in a breath. Could dreams be this real? She couldn't remember! She shouldn't be feeling him leaning down, pressing his weight into the bed. To kiss her? Kiss her precisely where?

His voice a broken rasp, he said, "*I want my mouth on you . . .*"

Her eyes flashed open. She whirled to her side, slamming her free hand to the bottom of her sword hilt, flipping it up. It stabbed through the bedspread to rest under his chin. Holding it in place, she turned onto her back and shot up in bed, then gasped.

She was half-naked, still breathing heavily, dazed by her arousal—and just in front of her, the vampire's huge erection strained thick against his jeans.

She swallowed, jerking her gaze up, but regretted catching his eyes. They burned with lust, and thought seemed to flee when she looked into them. But when he tried to peer down at her uncovered breasts, she shook herself and jabbed him.

"Very well," he conceded, raising his hands. "I might deserve that for touching you while you slept, but know that in the end, I thought you had woken."

"How long were you here?" she asked, her voice high.

"Almost ten minutes."

She glanced past him and saw his sword laid across her bench, his jacket slung beside it. She just prevented her jaw from dropping. "Impossible."

"Bride, you keep saying that about things that have already occurred."

She couldn't think! No vampire had ever taken her unaware. She slept lightly, had been trained to after years of battle. Yet she was supposed to believe she'd slept—and dreamed—through a leech's fondling her?

What was it about this particular vampire? *Why can't I run this sword through him?* A tiny flex of her wrist would incapacitate him. Then an easy swing for the head.

But she couldn't because of the competition. *Yeah, right, only that rascally competition prevents me.*

There was a reason that would completely explain why she couldn't hurt him. But she refused to entertain it— couldn't. If she did, life as she knew it was over. . . .

"I will not stand here like this much longer, Katja," he said quietly. "But I will turn my back if you'd like to dress."

The gentleman vampire. His words were steady and low, but she sensed he was barely in control, as if he were actually considering just knocking her sword from her and covering her in the bed. What would she do if he did?

She wished she knew. Predictable Kaderin, steady Kaderin, was now volatile.

The way he studied her with such blatant appreciation unnerved her. In the old country, during a storm, the sea grew violently colored, slashed through with shadows, streaming with black like coal.

That was the color of his eyes glowing in the darkness. A storm over water.

An inane thought arose. *I always fancied storms.*

She inwardly shook herself. Every second with the vampire, who was possibly the most sexually attractive male she had ever encountered, she played with fire. And not just with *his* wants, but with her own new feelings—pleasure at the rumble of his voice, excitement at his looks of longing, satisfaction that she wasn't alone in the room anymore.

For an eternity, she'd watched everyone around her act as slaves to emotion, behaving unreasonably, irrationally. Now she was one among them, and she was unpracticed. Adrift.

"I'll dress." She lowered her sword and stood, snagging her shirt and shimmying past him. He must have caught a glimpse of her breasts—he didn't bother to stifle his groan. As she crossed to her bag, she could feel his gaze on her ass.

As soon as she'd been old enough to leave Valhalla as a new immortal, she'd noted that men found her backside arousing. Now, she traipsed, exaggerating the sway of her hips. He'd gotten her hot. *Turnabout's a bitch.*

He rasped a curse in Estonian, and she immediately knew he wasn't aware that she understood the language. For some reason, she believed he would never speak like that around her.

"Katja," he said from behind her, "what would it take to get you back in that bed with me?"

Katja! Over her shoulder, she said, "That's not my name, and nothing you have." To arbitrarily change a name that had been honored and revered for twenty centuries—the nerve! To punish him, she bent over straight-legged when she laid her sword over her suitcase and dug out a cami bra to go under her shirt. When she rose and peeked over her shoulder, he was scrubbing his hand over his mouth, looking dazed.

Which was rewarding. Though, again, he appeared for all the world as if he were about to toss her over his shoulder and trace her to his lair.

What would it be like to be taken by a male like Sebastian? The idea of truly being at the mercy of a dominant male with only one thing on his mind was . . . titillating.

Even as it would never happen. With her back to him, she dragged on her clothes. "You need to understand that I will *never* sleep with someone like you." She turned in time to see his eyes darken at that.

"Someone like me?" He was seething with tension.

Had her words hit an unknown chink in his armor? "I kill vampires—I don't screw them."

"Would you sleep with me if I weren't a vampire?" This question, this subject—if she could want him—was very important to the vampire indeed.

She tilted her head, exaggerating a measuring look over him. He seemed to stop breathing. *How to answer?* Admit aloud her shameful desire for a vampire, or possibly crush his ego? Why should she care about the latter?

Because I wasn't born a cruel person.

"Do you find anything attractive about me?" He was very

arrogant when he asked, but his voice was gruff, and she sensed his uncertainty. In a flash, she knew some woman had gotten hold of him and damage had been done.

And he'd just revealed a weakness to her.

He took a hesitant step forward. He'd also done that at the castle and the temple, restraining himself when he so obviously wanted to get closer.

The vampire was a markedly physical being, even if he didn't seem to recognize it. Those two other times, he'd seemed to unconsciously position himself in ways that were less threatening to her, forcing himself to appear standoff-ish. When he was calm, he held his body very still. No gestures with his long, muscular arms or pacing in great strides. Just stillness.

When not calm—like when attacked by a werewolf—he moved with unfathomable speed and aggression.

He'd probably intimidated the hell out of women in his time. Men didn't often come six and a half feet tall and so generously built back then. He needn't have bothered trying to appear non-threatening to her. The pleasure she garnered from ogling his massive body was probably the reason he was still here—and not bleeding.

"What does it matter if I find anything attractive about you?" she finally asked. "You think me too small."

"No," he said quickly, then exhaled. "I had just heard tales that the Valkyrie were large warriors, akin to Amazons."

"Naturally, those would be the tales. If you're the sole survivor of an army attacked by us, are you going to say we had our asses handed to us by petite, nubile females, or by she-monsters who can bench Buicks?"

She knew her speech was fast and peppered with slang,

but after a moment, he followed the gist of what she'd said and grinned.

Gods, she didn't need to be reminded of that grin, the one he'd sported while still gently thrusting atop her, after he'd just made her have an orgasm for the first time in ten centuries.

"That makes sense." He grew serious, and quietly said, "You must know I find you perfectly made." He looked away. "You're the most beautiful thing I've ever beheld. That is what I wanted to tell you at Riora's temple."

Her heart sped up so rapidly, she was sure he would notice.

He turned back to her. "But you haven't answered my question."

"It's hard to see past the vampirism," she said honestly.

"I wish to God I wasn't one."

She tapped her cheek. "Hmmm. If you didn't want to be a vampire, perhaps you shouldn't have drunk a vampire's blood when you were on the verge of dying."

In an inscrutable tone, he said, "The turning was done against my will. I was injured and too weak to fight hard enough."

He'd fought it? "Who did it?"

"My . . . brothers."

This is interesting. "Are they still alive?"

"I know two are. One is missing." He clenched his jaw, seeming to rein in his temper. "I . . . I do not want to speak of this."

She shrugged as if she couldn't care less, though she *was* curious, then crossed over to his sword, unsheathing it. A battle sword. The rosewood handle had scales carved into it and was long, so he could wield it with both hands. The one-edged blade was wide and unyielding. It would have cut through chain mail—or a man's middle—in a single blow.

"You brought this here?" She faced him. "Did you think to subdue me?"

"I thought to protect you, if the need arose."

She was impressed with its weight, with the obvious care he'd taken with it. "It's nice, I suppose. For a beginner."

"Beginner? I painted that sword red for years—until the night I died."

He was an Estonian living in Russia, he had "nobleman" written all over him, and he'd said he'd been in that castle for centuries. Which meant he had to have fought in the Great Northern War between Russia and the neighboring Nordic countries. That had been a gruesome one. Starvation and plague had decimated populations, though she suspected the male in front of her had died in battle.

He said, "You know enough about swords to see that it is a fine one."

She sheathed it and laid it back down. "I prefer light and quick, but with your hulking build, your fighting style would have to rely on brute strength."

"Hulking? It's not a bad thing to have power behind a sword," he said in a defensive tone.

"No, but power can never beat speed."

"I disagree."

"I've lived for many years," she said. "My existence is a testament to speed."

"Then you have not faced a worthy hulking brute."

She stifled a grin and said, "Silly vampire, I would *spank* you if we fought. And no offense, but didn't you die by the sword?"

"I did. Yet you profess to fight by the sword. *No offense*, but you couldn't swing a death blow against one of your oldest enemies."

"I might have chosen not to kill you, but right now, the thought of maiming you for a few days sounds very appetizing. Maybe pluck an organ from you, make you regrow it. That one never gets old." It did, actually. She'd done it to a leech before—repeatedly, even after she'd tired of it.

"How am I expected to believe that, Katja? I think you don't wish to injure me at all. I don't think you can."

She sauntered up to him. "Vampire." Her hand shot forward to the crotch of his pants and very firmly clutched his sack, her foreclaw slicing his jeans behind it. His eyes widened, and his feet shuffled to a wider stance that would keep his body from falling over. "I could geld you with one flick of my claws"—she tugged down, making him groan in pleasure and pain—"and I'd purr while doing it."

18

He suddenly felt the smooth pad of her forefinger *in* his jeans. At the shock of her cool skin against his, he jerked, but she held him in place with a sure grip. She grasped him, and her forefinger stroked. He found his hands on her shoulders, rubbing up to her neck and back.

Even as he relished his first real touch in ages, he thought, *She cut through my jeans that easily?* Yes, with one flick. Surely she wouldn't cut him.

"You need to leave, vampire. Or I'll make that gravelly voice of yours considerably higher."

"Do it, then." He still hadn't even recovered from seeing her breasts for the first time. Or her bending over. Christ almighty, that had taken his every ounce of control not to seize her hips and fall into her. And now this? "Do it, or get used to having me around."

"What makes you think you get to decide the either/or? I might throw a new variable into the mix." The little witch continued stroking that forefinger, sending waves of pleasure through him. His mind blanked, just as she'd intended.

When she removed her hand completely, he shook his head hard. "We're at an impasse. I won't leave, and you don't wish me to stay. So, I have a proposition."

She yawned. "Enthrall me."

"You believe I'm a beginner with my sword? Then let us have a contest to see who's the best swordsman. The first to three points of superficial contact wins. If I win, I want your time until dawn to ask you questions—and have them answered honestly."

"It's against the law to tell one of your kind about the Lore."

"You don't strike me as very law-abiding."

"I am. When I make the laws."

That interested him. Exactly how much power did she wield? Was every creature in this world afraid of her?

"And when I win?" she asked.

"I'll leave you to sweet dreams with your sword for the night."

"The words *candy* and *baby* spring to mind . . . but you've got a deal." She tossed him his sword, then collected her own, letting her loose wrist circle it silently through the air. "When I win, you will leave immediately."

He freed his as well. "I doubt—"

She charged, striking with a blinding speed. He barely got his sword up in time. She parried again, and metal clanged as he did his damnedest to block her without hurting her. Her sword wasn't optimal for hand-to-hand battle. It had no knuckle bow to guard her fingers. If he slipped, she'd lose her fingers.

He had a good block and counter to her parry, but if she turned the wrong way . . . *Can't risk it—*

Her sword pressed into his chest. "Point," she said, her voice laced with smugness.

His lips nearly curled. They resumed. She was astoundingly good. Her eyes revealed nothing. She telegraphed no move, gave him no hint of weakness. He'd never imagined a female could keep him on his toes.

And he found himself enjoying the hell out of it, found himself enjoying pride in her skill. "You must have trained for years."

"You have *no idea*," she drawled.

Suddenly, she was no longer in front of him. But her sword was. In the blink of an eye, her sword was snatched behind him and planted into the skin over the base of his spine.

Sweet Christ . . . she moved faster than gravity.

From behind him, she whispered, *"That's called speed, vampire. Beginning to see the appeal?"*

Blood dripped. He gritted his teeth. "A blow to the back, Kaderin?" He was disappointed in her. He'd thought they had found some common ground. Even before he'd been knighted, *living by the sword* had always meant more to him than merely *fighting with a sword*. "Not very honorable of you."

When she faced him once more, he realized he could no longer treat this with anything but deadly earnest. He had to earn her respect and was learning that she wouldn't appreciate the qualities he'd always thought women valued. Courtesy, for instance, had garnered him nothing at the assembly or at the bottom of the world.

"Honor gets you killed," she said. They circled each other, her bare feet silent on the tiled floor. Her silk shorts kept fluttering, giving him tantalizing glimpses. Fighting her was the last thing he wanted to be doing with her. "I've found honor and survival to be mutually exclusive in the Lore."

"You are jaded. Too much so for someone so young."

This seemed to amuse her. "And do you think me young?"

He was centuries old, and before he'd met her, he'd often felt ancient. Her youthful energy and looks made him doubt she was a day over twenty-five. Or she had been before she became immortal. "I know you've competed in at least one Hie before, so you have to be older than two hundred and fifty years. But I doubt much more."

"What if I told you I'm very old indeed?" she asked. "Would it hinder your attraction to know that *stars* look different now from how they did when I was a girl?"

Her voice was lulling, and he found himself relaxing his guard and puzzling over her words—

She parried once more, flying to get to his back. He barely twisted around with his sword in time.

"I'm no match for your speed, unless I trace," he began, "which has always seemed cowardly to me. But since you don't see a problem with such tactics—" He traced behind her in an instant and swatted the broad side of his sword against her ass. "Point. And I believe I just *spanked* you as well."

You don't have to taunt her. Her shoulders stiffened just as weird lightning lit the sky outside and killed the shadows in the room. That same electricity he'd felt when he'd kissed her crackled in the air. Thunder rattled the glass doors. *Valkyrie give off lightning with sharp emotion.*

"Tracing." She pivoted slowly. "Thank you for reminding me of what you are."

It was as if some dam had burst. Her sword cut through the air like its own entity, reflecting light from bolts outside. She held the hilt so loosely, so confidently, and he found himself enthralled with her movements—to his detriment.

Yet her skills and technique could be beaten by focused power, and finally he began using his strength over hers. If he connected cleanly with her sword, then he followed through with all the power in his body, making her weapon quake and waver in her hands, jarring her with each brutal strike.

He feinted, catching her off-guard, just long enough to deliver a particularly punishing blow against her sword. He'd thought to send it flying, ending this, but amazingly, she somehow held on to it. Her body staggered as though she'd taken the hit to herself. She fell to a knee. Lightning exploded outside.

His chest seemed to clench. "Damn it, you weren't supposed to be able to hold that." A lifetime spent trying to avoid hurting women, and now he'd struck out at her as if she were a man?

"I don't plan to lose." She looked up at him through loosened curls. Her eyes were silver. "Can't exactly win without it, now, can I?"

But her faltering was just enough for him to trace to her. He forced himself to drive his advantage. He tapped his flat sword at her shoulder. "Point."

Her breaths were ragged. "This isn't yet finished."

"I didn't mean to hurt you."

"Only hurts for a moment." Her nonchalance disappeared when she sprang from the ground, charging once more. Their swords clashed again and again, mimicking the lightning outside. Her eyes began glowing in the scant intervals of darkness.

Then she pulled back, lowering her sword. Her brows were drawn as if in pain, and she was panting. The bolts quickened outside. In a pleading tone, she cried, "Ah, gods, Bastian, do you want me to beg you for it?"

He drew his head back in astonishment. Had he missed signals? Was she going to accept him? Her uncanny eyes called to him even as thunder exploded ominously.

Already thinking about where he would taste her first, he lunged for her—

Her blade planted just above his heart, and her eyes went dark and cold in an instant. "Point." She jabbed the tip and twisted, tearing his flesh with a menacing sneer. "I win, leech."

At the sight of his blood slipping down the center of her sword, he imagined all the others who'd bled on her blade, all the others who'd fallen for her beauty and trickery. How many had thought they were about to have her just before their lives ended? A sudden violent mix of thwarted lust and rage like none he'd ever experienced overwhelmed him.

He growled with fury, tossing his sword away as he traced behind her. He yanked her to him, his arms capturing hers against her body. She gasped, but when he pressed an open-mouthed kiss to her neck, she didn't immediately fight him, seeming to await his next move.

Good. He wanted her to surrender to him—in all ways, not just in this contest. She was close enough to feel his cock straining against her, and he wanted her to feel it. He wanted her pinned beneath him in bed, mastered by him. At the idea, he thrust uncontrollably against her soft ass. She sucked in a breath and seemed to flex her body into his. Emboldened, he brushed the backs of his fingers over her nipples. She shivered.

The storm whipped up outside, seeming to goad him. His hands caressed up from her flat belly, sliding under her bra and shirt, lifting them above her breasts. She sucked in a breath but didn't stop him. He sensed she was curious about what he would do. So was he.

He gently cupped her full breasts in his palms, groaning with pleasure. Her breathing quickened when he thumbed the peaks. She had luscious nipples, small and deep pink, begging to be suckled. He rolled and pinched them again and again, until they were so hard he imagined they ached. He saw her fingers go limp, and her sword clattered to the ground.

That was his permission. He kissed her neck, thrusting slowly against her. He wanted to do to her what her touch had done to him—stripped him down until there was no thought, only the need to have her. He wanted to make her shiver more, to wring moans from her lips.

When she raised her hands behind her to thread her fingers through his hair, he closed his eyes in bliss, groaning, kissing, kneading.

She froze just as a sudden jolt of ecstasy shot through him so much sharper than before—as if fire coursed through every vein in his body.

Her blood had touched his tongue.

"Bastian? Did you . . . bite me?"

Can't deny it. He was shuddering, and his eyes were rolling back in his head as he squeezed her. He'd accidentally grazed her neck in his frenzy, taking the merest drop.

She shoved his hands away from her, yanking her clothes in place and struggling to be freed. He finally managed, "I didn't intend to. I didn't plan to—"

When he released her, she turned, casting him the

expression he'd hoped never to see again. Seeing that betrayed look in her silver eyes was worse than he could ever have imagined.

Her hurt was swiftly overcome by fury. "You had no right!" The doors at the balcony flew open as the spray of ocean and rain punched inside. With the wind tugging at her long hair, she screamed, "You've stolen more than my blood!"

She sank down, snatching her sword, then charged him, slashing. He traced to his sword to block her. She feinted a forward parry, then twisted to swing backhanded at his torso, putting all her strength into the blow. He traced back at the last second, or she'd have cut through him.

"*I'm sorry*," he rasped, leaving her.

Back at his castle, he sank into the bed, staring at the ceiling. He'd taken her blood, the smallest drop, and the taste of her had pleasured him so profoundly he knew he was changed forever.

He'd rather not know exactly what he could never have again.

Kaderin was right—it was more than just blood. But why did she think it so? What more had he stolen?

It had been an accident, but how many times could he continue to use that as an excuse? Intent, or lack of it, rarely erased the offense, anyway. This he knew.

He'd taken straight from the flesh. A true vampire. He remembered Murdoch had told him, "There are dangerous side effects to drinking from a source. You could turn evil."

"And then I might be in danger of losing my soul?" Sebastian had sneered.

He could no longer be a Forbearer, should he have chosen that road for himself. . . .

Hours passed as he analyzed this eve. He recalled every word, every look, struggling to make sense of what had happened.

When he finally fell into a deadened sleep, Sebastian dreamed of a foreign land, inundated with rain.

The sun shone through the deluge, that bright intense light found in the northern lands. Kaderin was there, blinking against the rain. He saw it all as though through her eyes, and he knew it was very long ago.

She and others of her kind were trying to sleep on the bare ground on a hill. Only on an incline would the mud and water run down and not soak them any more than need be. They wore armor, breastplates of gold that were dented.

Kaderin's beaten armor cut into her ribs if she slept on her back and the undersides of her breasts if she slept on her sides. Ants crawled underneath the metal, stinging relentlessly, and sand trapped inside abraded her skin like sandpaper. She tried to ignore the discomfort—her cadre had not slept in seven days, and they needed the sun as their sentinel against the vampires they battled each night.

When she switched positions from her back to her side, the mud sucked down, making it difficult to move. "I vow to the gods," Kaderin said in a foreign tongue, tugging on her armor, "if we live through this, I will never sleep so confined again."

He should not understand her language, what sounded like a mix of old Norse and old English, but he did.

"Save your vows, *Kader-ie*," said a grinning young woman beside her who resembled Kaderin. "We all know we're not living through this one." Several around her chuckled. Kaderin laughed, too—because it was likely true.

And what else could one do with the knowledge of imminent death?

The dream changed to the actual battle they'd awaited. Sebastian had been in numerous battles, but he had never seen anything as grisly as this. In a night bright with lightning, metal rang against metal. Shrieks and thunder were deafening. All around Kaderin, vampires slashed at and beheaded Valkyrie who looked no older than girls.

Kaderin fought three at one time and couldn't break free, even when just beside her, a vampire lifted a Valkyrie's small body and brought it crashing down over his knee to break her back. Kaderin was close enough to hear the bones cracking but couldn't get to her.

From the corner of her eye, she saw the vampire's head drop to the girl's neck, then twist like a beast's as he pulled free the front of her throat. Just as Kaderin's sword sliced through one of her opponents, the crouching vampire lifted his head and smiled at Kaderin with flesh still in his mouth and blood spilling from his lips. . . .

Sebastian woke in a rush. He gazed around the room, confused to find he wasn't on that field of battle. The dream had been that lifelike. He'd heard her heart thundering in her ears, and experienced her rage as distinctly as he'd felt the hot blood from a vampire's severed jugular spraying her. It had gotten in her eyes and marred her vision.

How could he dream these things with such clarity? What if this had really happened to her? He recalled her comment from earlier in the night: "You've stolen more than my blood!" This must be what she meant. The dreams were real. He didn't understand how it could be possible, but he'd experienced . . . *her memories.*

Her lack of humanity, and her "history" with vampires,

which Riora had mentioned, had just become clearer. Because somehow he could see it. He raked his fingers through his hair. The armor and weapons of that battle had been from antiquity. "What if I told you I was very old indeed?" she'd asked.

She must be well over a thousand years old.

And Sebastian feared her life had been a series of battles like in the dream. Why would she ever give him a chance if she believed he would turn into one of those fiends?

After tasting her blood, would he?

19

The vampire stayed away for two days, then returned every night thereafter.

For the last week, he would trace to Kaderin, assisting her in whatever task she'd committed to, or taking a chair in whatever hotel room she'd stayed in for the night. If she went out into the sun or traveled by plane, he would vanish, spending the day who knew where or how.

Though she'd railed at him, ignored him, been caustic to him, nothing could prevent him from returning again and again—and there was nothing she could do about it.

But she had to admit she was less stressed that she would die when he was around. She had a massive warrior shadowing her each night, ensuring that nothing assailed her.

In their first conflict with multiple combatants, she'd drawn her sword and strategically put her back to the wall. In the second conflict, she'd unconsciously backed to him—and he was quick to point that out as they fought side by side.

Arrogant leech.

Whenever he was near, she studied him, trying to uncover some hint that he regarded her differently after tasting her blood. Kaderin knew what happened when a vampire drank straight from the flesh. Her blood could possibly give Sebastian her memories. It might make him want to attack others for more.

The brief sympathy she'd felt that night when she'd learned that he'd been forced to become a vampire had evaporated when he'd taken her blood. Did she think it had been by accident? Yes, but that didn't change the fact that it had happened. Did she believe she was partly responsible? Yes, she'd allowed him to kiss her neck, and castigated herself for that daily.

Yet that didn't mean she should continue to be around him when his mere presence made her unthinking, restless, even occasionally . . . wanton.

So far her game hadn't been too affected. They'd each already earned forty points, fairly easily, but then they had not encountered Bowen—who might frown on their growing tally.

In fact, she'd heard from Regin that the Lykae had taken out most of the competitors who'd gone up against him. In just one task, two of the demons, the young witch, and the elven hunters had all gone missing, rumored to be imprisoned somehow.

Bowen hadn't been disqualified, so they couldn't be dead, but the competition was lost for them.

Kaderin also had heard that Mariketa had managed to fling off a curse at Bowen—one of the worst for an immortal. If true, then Bowen would cease regenerating from injuries.

Kaderin knew she'd face Bowen soon enough, and when she did, she would strike first. For now, she needed to stay focused. She simply couldn't get used to Sebastian's care of her, couldn't get used to his watching over her as she slept.

One night, she'd awakened, blinking up at him. "Why do you keep coming back just to sit beside my bed?"

Seeming surprised by the question, he'd answered in a gravelly voice, "This is . . . satisfying. To me. I find it deeply so."

Before she'd turned onto her other side, she'd studied his face, trying to understand him, but only became convinced she never would.

Then, last night, she'd had yet another nightmare. She seemed to be plagued with them, as if compensating for her eternity of dreamless nights.

She definitely could not get used to his enfolding her in his warm, strong arms to soothe her, rubbing her back, rumbling, "*Shh, Katja,*" against her hair.

Though Kaderin didn't yet know this, Sebastian had basically moved into her London residence, since she never traveled there, preferring to sleep on her plane or in hotels.

Showering in her flat was more convenient and had other advantages, such as the water not being melted snow. Sebastian enjoyed sleeping in her bed, imagining her there with him.

Not far down the street, there was a bookstore and a butcher, and both stayed open after dark. Not to mention that the flat had a refrigerator—which was convenience itself—and remote controls. Beautiful things. He was really enjoying this new time now that he was immersed in it. Even the Lore in general was growing on him—because it was her world.

Each sunset, he traced to her. A couple of nights, he'd found her asleep with her sword. As ever, she would sleep fitfully, as though in pain. Other nights, he caught her nearing some prize. If she ran into difficulty, he would swoop one up for her, then go back and take one for himself, just so another couldn't have it.

He would be patient. This union was supposed to be for eternity—it followed that their courtship would be extended. He wasn't a patient man, but he could do whatever it took to get what he wanted.

Wondering what he would find tonight, he traced to her, arriving in yet another hotel room. But she wasn't in the bed, nor did he hear her in the shower.

The room's balcony doors were opened, overlooking a valley lit by a half-moon. He crossed to them and found her unconscious. She was lying on her front, one arm stretched out for her sword, which was covered in mud and blood. He lifted her gingerly, but she moaned in pain. He realized with a surge of fury that she'd just made it inside.

Damn it, what is it about this prize? Why would she continue to risk herself like this? He'd asked her repeatedly, sure to voice his opinion of the key. "Why do you want it so badly?" he'd asked. "The key won't do as it's purported. So is it just winning the competition? For ego or for posterity?"

"Posterity?" she'd answered with a quirked brow. "Do you mean in the progeny sense or notoriety after death? Because neither is forthcoming."

Now he flinched, wishing he could take the pain for her. When he wet a washcloth and wiped her down, she moaned again. Dark, mottled bruises marred her skin all over. Gritting his teeth with anger, he dressed her in his shirt and put her to bed, sitting beside her in the room's one chair.

He found himself feeling as if they were married already. He didn't know if this was a symptom of the blooding, but he found himself thinking of her as a wife—one who despised him, wouldn't share his bed, and, worse, wouldn't allow him to protect her.

And he continued dreaming about her each night, staggeringly vivid dreams.

In many dreams, Kaderin spoke in an old language he had no knowledge of, yet he understood her. He heard her thoughts, felt her fears. Once he'd dreamed she was on a battlefield, absently marking the severed heads of vampires she'd killed, carving an X with her sword as she sought her next fight. He now knew she was marking them to come back for their fangs later.

The more of her memories he garnered about the Horde, the more he instinctively knew he would never join their number. Since he'd taken Kaderin's blood from her body, he'd never experienced even the slightest urge to drink another. He'd been around humans since then and hadn't even thought about it.

Near dawn, when he saw she was sleeping soundly, he finally nodded off, swiftly becoming immersed in a scene from her past.

He could tell from Kaderin's clothing that it was in the early nineteen hundreds. She was hastening after a raven-haired female named Furie—their half-Valkyrie, half-Fury queen. Furie was setting off to battle the Horde's king, because a Valkyrie soothsayer named Nïx had told her it was her destiny.

"Nïx told me you intend to fight Demestriu," Kaderin said from behind her. "But all she knows is that you're not coming back. I want to go with you and make sure that you do."

Furie turned. Overall, she resembled Kaderin's kind—delicately built with feylike features—but Furie had more prominent fangs and claws. Her eyes were striking but odd, with dark rings around irises of a vivid purplish color. She could not have passed as a human as Kaderin could. "You can't feel, child," Furie intoned. "How will you help me?"

Can't feel? Yes—he'd dreamed Kaderin experiencing a deep, wrenching sorrow, but it hadn't lasted long. One morning she woke . . . changed.

"It makes me cold," Kaderin said calmly. "It makes me good."

Something like affection might have glimmered in Furie's uncanny eyes. Then she said, "I'm fated to go alone."

"Change fate." Kaderin knew Furie would consider her words blasphemous. The Valkyrie didn't believe in chance. For them, everything happened for a reason.

"Have you lost your beliefs along with your emotions?" Furie's anger was building. Kaderin could sense it like animals sense storms, but it didn't deter her. "Only a coward would try to escape her fate. Remember that, Kaderin." She continued on.

"No, I'm going with you," Kaderin insisted, hurrying to her side.

Furie turned and tilted her head sharply. "To keep you here"—she snatched Kaderin's wrist, twisting her arm back behind her—"and to ensure you always remember what I said . . ." With one brutal yank she snapped Kaderin's arm—her sword arm—then released her.

Kaderin stumbled back to face her, but the heel of Furie's palm slammed into her upper chest. Something else snapped. Kaderin flew a dozen feet back, the force rendering her unconscious before she hit the ground.

He never got a chance to see how hurt she'd been, or how she'd recovered, because another scene arose.

Kaderin's boots clicked as she sprinted down foggy back alleys. The rookeries she passed were filled with Lore beings, their deadened eyes staring out of the mist. It was London in the eighteen hundreds.

Her sword was strapped securely over her shoulder, and her thin shackles were tucked into her belt at her back. She was tracking two vampires, brothers, and her ears twitched when she sensed them. She drew her sword, but they were fast as they suddenly traced around her. One delivered a crushing blow to her head from behind, the other dealt a hit to her temple that nearly blacked her vision completely. A trap.

They let her stumble away for a goddamned block. Playing with her.

Tired. I just want to sit, she kept thinking in a daze. *Just for a second.* She finally collapsed, falling to her back.

The vampires returned, one holding her down, the other raising his sword above her neck. And she felt not even a trickle of fear. As they bent over her, their eyes became more apparent to her dimmed vision. Red, dirty eyes, staring down at her. No, she didn't feel fear, no revulsion—just *nothing*.

Another vampire materialized, likely wanting to see the momentous kill. The brothers' attention was drawn away for an instant. It was all she needed. Earlier, she'd fallen back onto the shackles. Without warning, she whipped them out and cuffed their wrists together. They struggled to break free, but somehow the metal held even with their obvious strength. They tried to trace in different directions and couldn't.

As she rose, the third vampire fled. She tilted her head at the two, and murmured, *"I told you I'd kill you,"* then let instinct take over—

He bolted awake at the sound of her shrieking, the loudest he'd ever heard, and clamped his hands over his ears. When the windows began to crack, he lunged for her and forced his hand over her mouth. Her fingers shot out, claws bared to snatch at his heart, but he caught her wrists in his free hand.

She was staring at him but seemed unseeing, her pale face lit by a series of lightning strikes just outside. He pulled her into his arms until she finally stopped fighting. But then she began softly weeping. His whole hand pressed the side of her head to his chest.

As he sat back in the chair with her in his lap, his dreams came over him in a rush. For ages in the past, Kaderin hadn't *felt?*

And now she clearly did.

No wonder she'd been so confused the morning they'd met. He didn't understand how this could have happened to her, but he'd experienced her lack of emotions. He couldn't imagine how difficult it would be to recover them.

"You've made me feel," she'd hissed at him that first morning.

Could I really have had something to do with this?

Her shoulders shook, and his shirt grew wet with tears, and it was killing him. "*Brave girl,*" he murmured against her hair. "You are safe." No wonder she was vicious. She'd had to be to survive. "It doesn't have to be like that anymore." Eventually her breaths grew quick and light as they did when she slept.

He'd begun to recognize that although she was perfect on the surface, his Bride was wounded, scarred inside, and now he knew why.

And he'd seen only a few nights in her life.

He knew she feared at every hour that he would become

like those who had toyed with her in a filthy back alley and had savaged her army of young Valkyrie. She dreaded seeing his eyes turn red.

When she clutched his shirt in her panting sleep and nuzzled his chest, realization hit him sharply. Staring out over her head to the valley below, he suddenly knew that he was meant to be here at this very moment, to comfort her, to protect her.

All the choices he'd made to direct his life—and all the choices that had been taken from him—had conspired to bring her to him. His seemingly endless years at the castle, though he'd been alone and weary, had been a worthy sacrifice to ultimately have her.

Sebastian was meant to call her his own. The good and the bad. She'd been made for him, and he for her.

Tomorrow, Sebastian would face Nikolai again. He could no longer deny that Nikolai's decision for him had been a fated one.

20

Cave of the Basilisks, Las Quijadas, Argentina
Day 10

*Prize: Two eggs of the Basilisk,
each worth thirteen points*

The crackle of flexing scales and the sibilance of a forked tongue sounded behind Kaderin, echoing throughout the cavern system.

With her sword sheathed at her back, she sprinted, her night vision taking her from one underground chamber to the next. She'd covered every inch of this hive of tunnels dug through solid rock in antiquity.

Yet she'd been unable to pinpoint the exact position of the three beasts she'd heard stirring down here. Nor had she been able to find either of the eggs, or an alternative exit.

Each tunnel had a high-ceilinged chamber at its terminus. In the chambers were the old nests of a basilisk, a giant scaled dragon with dripping fangs the size of her forearms and a lethal tail, corded with muscle.

She had checked every nest for eggs but found none.

There was another cavern system in the mountain a ravine over—the prizes must be in that one. The only things she'd found here were the ancient remains of female human sacrifices, and more recent ones from archeologists of the ill-fated variety.

The name of the area, Las Quijades, meant "the maxillary bones." Many thought the region was named after the bandits that used to run rife through these valleys, who gnawed on cow jawbones. Or they assumed the name referred to the abundant dinosaur fossils discovered here.

Neither was correct. The basilisk young killed by ripping the jaws from the heads of those human sacrifices.

The archeologists who dug here didn't understand that not all the dinosaurs were embedded in rock yet. They would explore, deeper and deeper, and then a team would be eaten, and the government would say they were lost in a flash flood—

No more scales flexing. Silence. In the lull, Kaderin's ears twitched, detecting footsteps—running, with a quick footfall but heavy in weight. *Bowen*. It had to be.

She'd known they would have a confrontation and had suspected the high point value of this task might attract him. But she'd been greedy for those points as well, and there *were* two eggs. Ah, but just to make things more interesting, Cindey was on her way here as well. Kaderin had spied her renting a Jeep in San Luis, the closest town, just before she herself had set out.

A sudden quake of the entire tunnel. A basilisk was angered and ready to kill, signaling its fury by swatting its massive tail against the tunnel walls. Each hit sent boulders tumbling, forcing Kaderin to run around them, leaping and dodging, shuffling her feet through the ancient bones.

Though basilisks were fearsome, they moved slowly in their hive, and she knew she could kill one, possibly two, at a time. But she didn't want to—she had an affinity for monsters.

Kaderin herself was a bedtime warning to low-creature young in the Lore: "Eat your grubs, or Kaderin the Cold will sneak under your bed to steal your head."

Turning back for the entrance, she sprinted past walls with ghostly cave paintings until she reached the three-way junction at the entryway. The sun was shining a welcome, illuminating a different type of cave painting there. Before being sealed in, each sacrificial victim had been given a reed filled with a type of paint. She would place her hand against the wall, blowing the paint around it, leaving the outline. The handprint was the only monument she ever received. There were thousands of them—

Kaderin caught sight of Bowen across from her.

A face-off. Time seemed to slow. He'd taken out half of the competitors, and all of the strongest ones except for Lucindeya and Kaderin and Sebastian. She knew he sought to remedy this with her right now.

His eyes glowed in the dark—just as hers did—and his expression was full of menace. A jagged cut marred his face and showed no sign of regeneration. Exhaustion seemed to weigh on his shoulders. The witch's curse. It was true.

Her head jerked to the right—the direction of her only escape.

When he began sprinting to the entrance, she recognized immediately what he intended—imprisoning her just like the others. She dug her toes into the gravel, shooting forward into a focused charge.

She was fast for a Valkyrie, but even cursed, he beat her

there. In the sun once more, he glanced up. She'd be able to escape before he could bring down the rocks, she'd be able to—

Casting her a cruel smirk, he dug into his jeans pocket. Dread settled over her. He slid out that diamond necklace. She hadn't bothered to train against this. . . .

It glittered in the desert sun, radiating sharp blue and white points of light. *I revealed my weakness, handed it to him.* Entrancing light, seemingly endless.

He tossed it in her direction. *Just to touch it . . .* When it was still in the air, her gaze locked on it, following it down until it landed at her feet on the loose gravel. She froze, transfixed, dropping to her knees as though praying to the stunning necklace. Something so fine couldn't be left in the dirt. Not this. She scooped it up with both hands, running her thumbs lovingly over the stones.

She could hear Bowen straining outside, cursing in Gaelic, could hear his claws scraping down boulders to dislodge them. But she couldn't pull her eyes away.

Not until the cave went dark in a series of deafening booms, and the glittering ceased.

That morning, Sebastian had left Kaderin sleeping peacefully. Then, as usual, he'd traced to her flat to shower and drink.

As he dressed, he'd reflected that he'd made no discernible progress with Kaderin over the last week. If for no other reason, he needed to go to Blachmount because he was ignoring a resource he badly needed—his brother was wed to a Valkyrie. One who was blood-related to Kaderin. Which meant information there for the taking.

Once he'd forced blood down, he traced to Nikolai's

shuttered office, finding him perusing papers. Though usually so reserved, Nikolai didn't bother hiding his pleasure at Sebastian's arrival. He quickly stood and said, "Sit. Please."

Sebastian took the seat he indicated, but being back here again made his shoulders knot with tension.

"We've heard you entered the Hie," Nikolai said, taking his own seat once more. "The first vampire ever to do so. We were quite astonished."

Sebastian shrugged.

"Myst goes on the computer each day and checks the results. She has a half-sister in the competition. Is she your Bride?"

"Yes," he admitted. "Kaderin."

"Myst has told me Kaderin is—how did she put it?— 'gorgeous to a near freakish degree.' And a stalwart fighter." His tone hopeful, Nikolai asked, "Do you love her?"

"No. But I recognize that she is mine. And that I am meant to protect her."

"It's enough. More will come with time," Nikolai said. "We've wondered what made you decide to represent Riora."

Sebastian shrugged. "I align with no one, and she demanded that. It was a gamble."

"You could have said the Forbearers or King Kristoff."

Sebastian felt his expression tighten. *King Kristoff.* Sebastian had never been able to understand how Nikolai could have died at the hands of Russians, then, on the same blood-wetted battlefield, sworn allegiance to Kristoff—who was a *Russian*, vampire or not.

"It was only an observation. The invitation to join us is

always open." Nikolai added, "Every single time I kill a red-eyed vampire, I am glad that I did."

"You've encountered them?" Sebastian asked.

"I've warred against them. We are gaining momentum." Nikolai steepled his fingers. "Sebastian, I've always respected your intelligence. We would welcome your counsel gladly. After the Hie, naturally."

After experiencing Kaderin's dreams, fighting against the Horde began to have distinct appeal, but Sebastian planned to take Kaderin somewhere away from constant war and death. The last thousand years of her life might have been hellish, but he'd be damned if he'd allow the next thousand to be. He said simply, "Don't plan on my participation."

Nikolai nodded, but Sebastian knew this was far from over. "About this competition, and the rumored prize," Nikolai began. "Have you thought about using it to save our family?"

Of course, Sebastian had. Even after all this time, the guilt was unrelenting. When called to protect his family, he'd failed—*five successive times*. "I don't believe it will work," Sebastian said. But if it would, if he could somehow undo the past . . .

It wasn't reasonable to blame himself, it wasn't logical, but he couldn't seem to stop. Conrad had felt the same—before he'd lost his mind, at least.

The aristocracy of Sebastian's culture was raised to revere the military and to fight. Yet fate had given him an invisible enemy bent on wiping out his family, for which there was no defense, no battle. He'd had to sit, watching impotently, as everything he loved died.

Sebastian had been a favorite big brother to four younger sisters. He'd been nearly old enough to be their father and was essentially more of one than their own preoccupied father. With each of their little crises, they'd run to Sebastian. He'd plucked splinters and dried tears. He'd taught them science and astronomy.

When they fell sick and their young minds had comprehended they might actually be dying, they'd looked to him to fix it.

And seemed bewildered when he couldn't. As if, instead, he *wouldn't*.

"You can't go into the past to change the future," Sebastian said absently. "Not without creating chaos." Part of him had wanted to believe in the key even though it flew in the face of reason, and even though the goddess had no evidence that time travel was possible.

But if Sebastian allowed himself to believe he could get his family back and then had his hopes disappointed . . . He didn't think he could take losing them twice. To this day, he couldn't bear to remember the night they'd died. Seeing the despair in their eyes, and then, when he and Conrad had fallen, to hear their faint, terrified cries.

Both he and Conrad had wanted to die that night with their family. The country was in shambles, wracked by plague and famine. They were done. They'd fought, they'd done their best. They should have been allowed to die.

And their sisters? They'd been as delicate and fair as the four older brothers were dark and fierce and would have starved before they voluntarily tasted blood. They couldn't even have contemplated it. "Why did you try to turn the girls?" Sebastian asked. He had no anger in his tone, but now that he was steady and rational, he wanted to hear Nikolai's reasoning. He wanted—for the first time—to understand it.

"I had to," Nikolai bit out, averting his gaze, but not before Sebastian saw his eyes had wavered black. "The thought of them dying so young tormented me."

"They might have been frozen into perpetual childhood, never to see the sun again."

Nikolai faced him. "We do not know that they wouldn't have aged to adulthood, as natural-born immortals do. It was possible."

"And our father?" Sebastian asked. Their father had been longing to reunite with his wife from the day she'd died in childbirth eleven years prior.

Nikolai's expression grew weary. "I've never been noble like you, Sebastian. Survival and living are what I revere. They might have lived—to me, the rest is incidental. And after all this time, I see we still disagree on that subject."

Sebastian stood to leave. "We do."

Nikolai stood as well. "Think about the order, Sebastian."

Sebastian supposed he should get this out of the way. "I can't join your order." He shrugged nonchalantly. "I didn't quite forbear, as it were. I've tasted blood from the flesh."

21

With the blessing gone, Kaderin had been helpless to move, to attack Bowen, to flee, only wanting to behold the stones and faceted lights. Even now, as she petted them, her heart ached to see them shining again.

The basilisks' hissing, wet roars made her shake herself. The beasts were miles down, far away from the bright entrance, but clambering toward it now. They'd be in no hurry, though, likely thinking that Kaderin was a sealed-in sacrifice.

With a shuddering exhalation, she forced herself to toss the necklace away, then rose and surveyed her predicament. The bastard had done a fine job of barricading the entrance.

Even with her strength, she couldn't budge the boulders. She ran into them, tackling them, shoving her shoulder against them. Nothing. She couldn't use her sword. It was not thick and weighty like Sebastian's. She'd have to dig.

She figured she'd lose her claws with every four inches she dug into the rock. She would grow them back within a few hours. The top boulder's diameter was at least sixty inches.

Ergo . . . let's do the math . . . I'm screwed.

Worse, the chamber's darkness had begun weighing heavily on her—the way one felt when saddled with a ponderous hex. She gave a bitter laugh. She was now officially a vicious Valkyrie assassin—who was scared of the dark.

The wraiths had never creeped her out, she found the basilisks kind of endearing, and she could be thrown into a cage with a thousand contagious ghouls and not blink an eye—as long as the cage wasn't gloomy and oppressive.

If she had action, she could ignore her fear, but simply sitting here with nothing to do but contemplate it . . .

She had two alternatives. She could wait for the vampire, hoping he ignored her last irate demand that he leave her alone. But even if he did come to the rescue, he wouldn't be able to trace her where she needed to go—which was mere feet beyond these boulders. She'd wager that Sebastian hadn't previously visited any Argentinean cave entrances.

Besides, how long could she wait for him to save her? Sooner or later, the basilisks would make their way to the surface.

Her second alternative was to begin digging. *These rocks are the only thing standing between me and that prize.* She dropped to her knees once more and stabbed her claws into the rock. Two inches down, she lost her first, then another. Damn it, this was futile. A wasted effort in a dark, foul place. She was about to lose those thirteen points.

The rock dust made her eyes water. Yes, the rock dust made her tear up—

"Well, well," a rumbling voice said from behind her. "I'll wager you are happy to see me right now."

Sebastian. Kaderin whirled around. Though the space was pitch black, she knew he could see perfectly, because he was studying her expression. Then his gaze fell to her claws before she eased them behind her back. There was no hiding that she was shaken.

"Clawing free, Kaderin?" He strode to her, and helped her to her feet. "How long have you been trapped in here?"

She brushed her knees off. "A couple of hours."

"How did this happen?"

"Bowen pulled down the rocks when I was inside."

"MacRieve?" Sebastian clenched his fists. "I will kill him for this."

She shrugged. "Promise? Because that would eliminate two competitors."

"Is he still near?" Sebastian narrowed his eyes, clearly hoping he could face him now.

She shook her head. "He'll have collected his egg and be long gone. He's done what he set out to do with me, and he's already removed several of the demons and all of the fey from the competition completely. Anyone who faced him is out."

"How?"

"All we know is that he's trapped them somewhere."

"What about the young witch?" Sebastian asked. "Surely MacRieve wouldn't have hurt the girl."

"He got Mariketa as well, but she managed to curse him first," Kaderin said. "He seems to be weakening and not regenerating from injuries." She jerked her chin in Sebastian's direction. "Bowen will come after you next. As of yesterday, I was tied for the lead with him—"

"As expected—"

"And also tied with *you*. He'll attempt to take us out one by one."

"I look forward to facing him. I'll relish killing him for trapping you here."

Her answer was another shrug. Sebastian fell silent, and

she knew he was waiting for her to ask him to trace her out. She drew in the gravel with the toe of her boot.

"Damn it, ask me to take you from here," he grated.

"No."

"You'd rather rot in here?"

"I was making progress," she said.

"Obstinate female. Is it impossible to admit you're relieved I'm here? That I could save your hide right now?"

"No," she said simply. And she didn't elaborate, making him look like he wanted to throttle her.

She had to assume Bowen had collected his prize in the next ravine over, but Cindey could still be beaten. *If* Kaderin got out of here soon.

"Very well, I'll leave you to your progress." He turned to trace, and she hurried forward, touching his arm.

"Look, I don't want to be traced to your backyard. The prize must be in the next cavern system over, and it's just across a ravine." She crossed to the rocks, and pushed with frustration. "I need to be directly on the other side of these, and I know you can't trace there."

"Because you assume I haven't been there before?"

She piped her lip and blew a curl out of her eyes. "Do you often visit Las Quijadas, Sebastian?" At his blank look, she added, "Argentina."

"No, I can't trace there. But . . ." He studied the boulders, then pushed against one until it began to move.

When she gasped, he stopped. "Seems I could free you, after all."

She gave him a tentative touch on his chest. "What would it take to get you to finish moving those?"

"What are you offering?" he asked, his voice rougher.

"Money? Would you take money to push these free?"

"I've plenty of my own. More than enough for both of us."

She scowled at that. "What do you want, then?"

"I want"—he ran his hand over his face—"to . . . touch you. Not here, but tonight—"

"Not going to happen." She crossed her arms over her chest, and his gaze landed on her damp cleavage. As he had that night on the coast, he looked like he was considering throwing her over his shoulder and tracing her back to his bed. "I do so wish my breasts would stop staring at your eyes."

His head jerked up, and he had to clear his throat to rasp, "Kiss me. Kiss me, and I'll free you."

"The last time that happened you *bit* me, and you could do it again." Kissing Sebastian always seemed to lead to more. Last time, it had led to his taking her blood.

And possibly her memories.

"I never bit you. I grazed your skin. Accidentally."

"Then tell me you haven't contemplated doing it again."

"I"—he exhaled heavily—"cannot. The pleasure was too intense to ignore."

She was shocked by his honesty and didn't bother disguising that fact. "Then I'm betting in the same situation it would happen again."

"I would vow not to."

"Unless, of course, it happened"—she curled her fingers into air quotes—"*accidentally*. Since I can eventually dig my way free, that kiss doesn't seem worth the risk."

He nodded, resigned. "Very well. We can sit here till we fossilize. I can be as stubborn as you, Bride."

"So, you're to wait this out with me?" she asked. "Won't *you* have a problem with losing the prize?"

"I have no interest in winning this competition."

"I knew you entered just so I couldn't kill you."

"You couldn't kill me before I entered. Do you not wonder why you've destroyed so many of my kind before me and then were unable to swing your sword to my neck?"

"I don't know why that happened," she admitted. "But I've stopped questioning it."

"Why won't you let me win this competition for you? That was the only reason I entered."

"There's no one you would want to save from the past, no loved one?" she asked, noting that a shadow passed over his eyes. *Who had he lost?* "A deceased wife, perhaps?"

"You are well aware that I don't believe this key will work."

He hadn't answered her question. *He's been married?* "Why are you so certain?"

"Time travel is impossible," he answered in a tone that held zero doubt.

And the wife? "I bet you believed vampirism was impossible, too, till you woke with a marked hankering for blood."

"No, my culture was superstitious to the core. Even with my science background, belief came to me more easily than I would have thought. Besides, it isn't impossible according to the laws of nature."

And what about the wife?

"Anyway, I was never married."

She marveled that he hadn't been—and that she was somehow pleased by this fact. "At your age?" she asked, taking a seat. "You must have been thirty."

"Thirty-one. But I'd lived on a battlefront since I was nineteen. There was no way for me to have a woman for my own."

"But now you feel you're ready?"

As if giving her a vow, he met her eyes when he rumbled the word: "Yes." Her toes curled in her climbing shoes.

"And what about you, Kaderin? Will you finally tell me why you are bent on winning this?" He looked away when he asked, "Do you seek to retrieve a husband?"

When she didn't answer, he turned back.

After a moment, she grudgingly shook her head. "I was never wed." She would never tell him her real motivation—there was no reason to, even if she had the inclination—but she also wouldn't let him think she fought this hard for a lost husband or lover. "My covens and the Furies have done me a great honor in choosing me for this contest. I won't fail them." She shrugged and added honestly, "And I simply want to defeat everyone."

"So, all of this is about pride and ego?"

She made her tone bored when she asked, "Aren't those good enough reasons?"

"I don't believe so. There's more to life than winning this competition."

"I agree. There's also killing vampires. Those two things give my life purpose."

He said nothing in response to her comment, just gave her an inscrutable look. She knew he disapproved of her priorities and the way she lived her life, but at that look, she began to suspect he also felt sorry for her. She tilted her head. "Tell me, then, how would you envision our lives together?"

"We could see the world. Rebuild the castle, start a family."

A *family?* If she and Sebastian had children, they could be like her little half-vampire niece, Emmaline. Kaderin inwardly shook herself. "I live in New Orleans, I compete, and

I kill vampires. You'd expect me to give up everything?" She drew her knees to her chest. "You want me to act like women you've known and it will never happen."

"No, I truly do *not* want you to act like women I've known," he said, so vehemently she was taken aback. "And I have no preference for where we would live. I'd go wherever you would be happy. Killing vampires? Fine. The Hie? Also acceptable—if I'm there with you."

"Acceptable." *Is he joking?* "The more I get to know you, the more I realize your being a vampire is only *part* of why I'm indifferent to you."

Acceptable? As soon as he'd said it, even before her eyes flashed, he'd known that perhaps that wasn't the best word to use with a daughter of gods. A *fifth* of *any* of his brothers' charm.

"Then lay out the other reasons you're indifferent," he said.

"Talking to you is like talking to a human."

He snapped, "I wish I *were* still a human—"

"But you're not. You're an enemy to my kind."

"I've told you, not by choice. Or by deed."

"It disgusts me that you drink blood. You live a parasitic existence."

It had always disgusted him as well. The only time it hadn't had been his one hot, rich taste of her. Now he found himself defending the vile act. "I get blood from a butcher. How is this different from humans getting meat from the same? Besides, what living thing isn't a parasite?"

"Me."

"Do you eat meat? Drink wine?"

"No, and no. I ingest nothing."

"How is that possible?" he asked, incredulous, though the kobold had said as much that night at the Pole.

"Just the way I was engineered," she answered in a tone that made it clear she'd say no more on the subject.

Damn it, he'd have to return to Blachmount and ask Nikolai about this. "Engineered? As in *designed?*"

She narrowed her eyes. "Don't I look as if I could have been designed? Do you look at me and think, *obviously an accident of nature?*"

"No," he said, realizing he'd insulted her once more. "Not at all. I just—"

"Our kinds are going to war. Did you know that? A war like you've never imagined—"

"Yes, the Accession," he said in a dismissive tone.

"It's hardly something to wave away."

"My brother told me you would bring this up as an obstacle between us. He's assured me the Forbearers will ally with the Valkyrie." When she began to argue, he cut her off. "Whether the Valkyrie want them or not."

She pressed her lips together. "You seem quite iron-willed," she finally said. "Why not use that will to rid yourself of this compulsion for your puny, undesigned Bride?"

"Why would I put time and effort into attempting to forget you when I could spend that same time and effort to win you?"

"Because winning me is impossible. The other option may not be."

"I have to try." There was no way to rethink this. "I want you. In my life."

She tapped her chin. "And by 'in my life,' you clearly mean 'in my bed.' "

"I won't deny that I want both." He'd had a taste of her

passion, and he wouldn't rest until he'd claimed her. "I constantly think about what it would be like to take you."

Pink flushed across her cheeks, and she nibbled her bottom lip. That habit of hers never failed to charm him. "But you don't love me any more than I love you."

"No, I don't," he admitted. She fascinated him, frustrated him. And every hour since she'd blooded him, he needed her, but even he understood that it wasn't love.

She rolled her eyes. "A hint, Sebastian? If you're courting a woman, you could pause a nanosecond before declaring that you *don't* love her. Maybe act as though you'd considered the possibility. Or you could lie. Or you could gloss over it by predicting that you will in the future."

"I won't lie to you. And about love? Unions have been built on far less than we have between us. We'd have passion. Attraction. Respect."

"You flatter yourself," she said, examining her broken claws.

"And one thing I can promise you. The next thousand years of your life will be nothing like the last. Not while I live."

Her gaze shot up. "What does that mean?" she asked in a measured tone.

"I know about your . . . blessing. You didn't feel emotion for a millennium."

At his words, her face paled. "Do you know why it happened?"

Had her voice quavered? "No. Nor how it came about. Only that you woke one morning, and there was just . . . nothing."

She gave him a sharp glare. "Don't you dare say it like that! As if I were lacking."

"Kaderin, not to be able to feel *is* to lack."

"You assume it's necessary to feel to get by? Or that I would want to, anyway?"

"No, I—"

"You know from my blood, right?" When he nodded, she said, "Because you *stole* my blood, you have my memories. Lovely. How much have you seen?"

"I've seen old battles, and hunts, and random flashes of conversation—like Riora telling you about a blind mystic's blade." He had seen her attacked by dozens of kobolds, barely defeating them, then peering down to find her leg from midcalf down was gone. No wonder she'd taken out the kobold in Antarctica. *And I'd traced it to her prize.*

"Now do you understand why I was incensed? You can know my secret thoughts. And deeds. Have you seen me with other men?"

"No, and my brother has told me that I won't, because you are my Bride," he said.

"Have you seen why my emotions have returned?"

He ran his fingers through his hair. "I believe I had something to do with it. You said as much that first morning."

"I spoke rashly." At his look, she added. "It was coincidental."

"Perhaps I could believe the timing coincidental had you not been my Bride."

"So you figure I awakened you physically and you awakened me emotionally?" she asked in a scoffing tone. "Tea for two?"

"Yes. Precisely."

"Even if that were true, it doesn't mean we have a future together. I'm not what you need and will only make you miserable. This I can promise you. Besides, if I accepted you as mine, my family would ostracize me. I'd be shunned."

"Myst the Coveted doesn't seem to concern herself with that."

Kaderin tilted her head, then grew very still. "What are you talking about?"

"My brother's wife, Myst."

She shot to her feet. "Myst may have the morals of an alley cat, but even she wouldn't dare marry a leech."

"You do not know about this?" He frowned. "They've been wed for some time."

Kaderin was going to kick Regin's glowing ass so hard. . . .

Myst had married . . . a vampire! Kaderin put her forehead in between her thumb and forefinger. "Your brother—he's the Forbearer general who freed her from the Horde prison. Wroth. Nikolai Wroth." *I knew she wasn't over him!*

"Yes. You've met him?" Sebastian asked.

"I've heard of him." And now that everything was becoming clearer, she realized she'd heard of Sebastian as well. The four Estonian brothers. Warlords so fierce and unyielding as humans they'd even drawn Lore attention.

They'd been fierce and unyielding—defending their people.

He studied her expression. "I wonder if this news helps my cause or hurts it?"

"I . . . I don't know . . . anything." Not anymore. So Forbearers were fair game? No, Dasha and Rika would never stand for her accepting a vampire.

"Then just tell me one thing, Kaderin. Do you ever think about me when I am away?"

Lie to him. Could she have an affair? Of the most illicit kind? Just to enjoy his responsive body for one night?

Myst had freaking married one! And Myst was a pagan like her! Kaderin doubted very seriously that General Nikolai Wroth had agreed to wed in accordance with orthodox paganism.

A bond like marriage was a huge deal for Valkyrie and for immortals in general. *Until death do us part* took on a whole new meaning when both parties could potentially live forever.

No, Kaderin couldn't have an affair. Not when she was Sebastian's Bride. Because he would never accept only that and she could never give him more. "Think about you? Sebastian, I'm a busy person. I don't spend a lot of time with introspection. How about I leave that up to you?"

"What does that mean?"

"Seems like all you did for three centuries was *think*."

He was furious, as she'd planned. "You know nothing—"

A roar sounded to their left, shaking the cave. And then, from their right, another one answered. Somewhere even farther in the distance, a third called.

They were nearing, gathering.

Here.

22

Kaderin leapt forward, tackling him into the dirt.

A quick kiss, seal the deal. Get him to move the rocks.
She grabbed his stunned face, then pressed her lips to him.

Quick. To get what she wanted. *Stop lingering!* "There. I kissed you," she said, sounding breathless. "Now, move the damned rocks—"

His hands landed heavily on her ass, forcing her against his already hard shaft. When she couldn't prevent a moan, he took one hand and clutched her nape, pulling her down. He took her mouth with his own, slipping his tongue between her lips, sweeping it against hers.

The hand on her ass moved between her legs, cupping her firmly. She gave a startled cry against his lips, and before she could stop herself, her knee shot up to allow him more access.

He groaned, rubbing and kneading her there with his big palm, his mouth slanting against hers over and over. His kiss was desperate, a *night before the gallows* kiss.

They were rolling in the dirt in the face of attack, both of them sweating, his sword hilt poking her hip bone, and she couldn't get enough of his taste.

He flipped her over, just as he had that morning in his castle. She wanted it as much now as she had then. "You drive me mad, Katja," he rasped. "I can think of nothing but you."

He rolled to his side, hand pinning hers above her head. He bent down to place an open-mouthed kiss on her collarbone. As his other hand dipped toward the waist of her pants, he said at her ear, "Tell me you think about me."

She might have murmured that she did think about him while he was inching that shaking hand down her belly. Was he shaking in anticipation of touching her flesh? He began pulling loose the tie on her pants, and she yanked her hands free—but not to stop him. No, she was letting him.

Only fair, she thought deliriously, *since I'm stuffing my hand into his pants*. With her first touch of him, she moaned. He threw his head back and yelled out, bucking into her fist. So hot, so smooth and hard. She thumbed the slit in a wet circle.

When he faced her again, his eyes were black with want.

"We've got to stop this," she whispered, even as she moved her fist on him. "These beasts . . ."

"Are suitably terrifying. Doubtless." He pressed a brief, hot kiss to her mouth, then met her eyes again. "Appreciate it if you'd keep . . . *stroking*."

She did. Her hand seemed magnetized to his shaft, loving when it pulsed and jerked in her palm. But even as he seemed to be losing control, he took his time with her, teasing her belly, then lower to her sex. She wanted passion, swift relief, but she got the impression that this was very important for him—that he wanted to savor every second.

Just as he was about to work his hand into her panties, he froze, palm resting low on her belly. She shimmied up to get his hand lower.

"Still," he murmured. He shook his head hard, as if clearing it. She arched her back and looked behind her.

Fifty yards away, slitted eyes the size of footballs glowed green in the dark.

He exhaled. "I've seen better timing."

"You have such a gift for understatement." Whose amused tone was that? She was in a sweltering cavern with vicious dragons about to be breathing down on them and a vampire's big fingers inches from being worked inside her. "And you don't seem *suitably terrified*."

Her fight to keep from grinning ended when he said, "I'm sorry, Bride. I have to trace you from here."

She snatched her hand from his pants and his from hers, then rolled away.

"I can fight them while you push the rocks." Back on her feet, she retied her pants, then unsheathed her sword.

The largest basilisk edged closer, no doubt thinking them trapped. Basilisks had a waddling gait that was completely misleading—a biological advantage that served to make prey docile. The tunnel wasn't wide enough for more than one to pass, but when they got into the chamber, they could charge them at once.

Sebastian stood as well. "That is not how this will work."

"I freaking kissed you! If I get into trouble, then you can trace me, but just try the rocks. Or you break our deal."

"For another kiss, then. Later. We need to finish what we've started here—"

"*You're curb-boosting me?*"

He clearly didn't understand the term. "You want out, then you'll agree to get to somewhere dark within an hour after you get that prize."

Who was this new ruthless vampire? "Fine." *Very uncool.*

"You have a deal." *I'm lying like a rug.* "Now, get your ass in gear and push."

With another shake of his head, he rose, surveyed the basilisk's unhurried but steady progression, then set to the rocks.

She should have been readying for a battle, scouting the lead basilisk's crimson scales for weaknesses. And yet all her desire-saturated mind could think about was how utterly delicious the muscles of his back looked, bulging with strain, threatening to rip through his shirt. She wanted to squeeze them, scratch them, lick them.

She should be worrying about the siren, about the contest, *or, hey, how about the dragons?*

The beast slowly pressed down on them, and she could make out a second's eyes peeking out just behind it. As soon as the rocks went, they'd spring in attack.

She kept jerking glances over her shoulder. Regin had asked her what her type was. As he turned to push with his back, displaying chiseled abs beneath his sweat-soaked shirt, Kaderin admitted it to herself.

She apparently fancied black-haired, grave-eyed vampires of the excruciatingly gorgeous type. With scars and rough hands. She bit her bottom lip. And if she continued staring at his powerful, sculpted body, she was in danger of spontaneous orgasm.

"Bride, I never thought I'd ever say this to you, but you must *focus.*"

The way she was staring at him, little fang pressing against her plump bottom lip, eyes flashing silver, was making him crazed.

"O-of course." She faced forward. "I've got this one

down." One last glance over at him, and she muttered a curse. "Lookit, the instant the rocks go, these three will attack. Fast. You've got to trace immediately."

"They look slow."

Without turning, she said, "They want to look slow. You trace, and I'll dive out, okay?"

"Will they chase you outside?"

"They won't be able to see in the sun very well."

"The rocks are about to go," he grated. "Get back—"

Sunlight shot in like a beam. Luckily, it was late in the day. He lunged back, leaving her room to leap for the hole. She shimmied out. But the basilisks charged with phenomenal speed, all three reaching the chamber and leaping with claws bared.

The largest crashed through all the rocks after her. Dust and rubble exploded into the air. Sebastian couldn't see her, only heard snapping jaws, then spied her as she ducked. Jaws slammed shut just over her head.

Sebastian dove for her into the sun, swallowing a bellow of pain, snatching her ankle. Just as he was tracing them, she kicked him in the face and scrambled away.

Before he could stop, he disappeared without her, then sent himself right back into the fray. Even half-tracing, he could barely see in the light. His skin burned as though splashed with acid.

The basilisk had disappeared? Kaderin was on her tiptoes at the very edge of the cliff, arching her back to keep from falling. Before he could get to her, she'd righted herself, skipping along the edge. She'd tricked it into falling?

The smallest one and the other were venturing out, blinking and hissing at the light. He dodged swiping claws to trace back into the dark at the other end of the cavern, then yelled for them.

When they sprang back inside the tunnel, he dropped onto his back beneath the larger one and thrust his sword up at its belly. A death blow, planted between scales as big as plates. Gutted. He yanked the blade back, rolling out of the way.

With a wet roar, it pitched backward onto the small one, trapping it. Sebastian shot to his feet, tracing to the last basilisk. As it scrambled to get free, claws frantically digging into the ground in front of it, Sebastian raised his sword over its neck.

It froze, then slowly turned its head to blink slitted eyes up at him. There was fear there.

Kaderin probably would have killed it already—and would likely see him as weak if he didn't.

"Oh, *bloody hell*," he muttered, leaving it behind and tracing for her.

Damn it, he would *not* return later and free it.

Then, into the sun once more, swinging his head back and forth to find her as his skin threatened to catch fire. The pain was grueling. Out of the corner of his eye, he spotted a cave above the ravine. He traced in, doing his best to half-appear.

Even though he watched from the edge of the cave, the sun still reflected off the sand and rock, killing Sebastian's already damaged eyes, but he could tolerate it for a minute, maybe two, in this form.

He spied the largest basilisk twitching at the bottom of the ravine, with its head exploded against a rock. Kaderin was still on that ledge. Just as Sebastian was about to bellow at her in fury for kicking him, her gaze locked onto something in the ravine. Her face grew cold. A *predator*. That's all his mind could come up with to describe her.

Kaderin began pumping her arms for speed, sprinting until she became a blur. Blinking against the light, he didn't quite believe his eyes when she dove into the same ravine as the dragon.

He traced down, scouting another overhang, just in time. In front of him, twenty feet away, the siren gave a cry of surprise—just before Kaderin landed on her back, audibly knocking her breath free of her lungs. Kaderin had her knees dug into Lucindeya's shoulder blades, an arm tightening around her neck.

Just when he'd decided to brave the sun and trace Kaderin from there, Lucindeya jabbed up with an elbow. Somehow, Kaderin ducked around and missed it. She eluded any defensive move the siren had. She needed no help.

All around Kaderin, heat boiled up from the rocks. As he watched her through the haze, he realized he was awed by her, by the power in her graceful body.

And even by her sheer viciousness.

Kaderin yanked the siren up by the hair, swinging her around by it, gaining momentum until no part of the woman touched the ground. Kaderin finally released her grip as though with a bola, her fingers splayed.

The cliff face crumbled under the blow of Lucindeya's crashing body, rocks plummeting onto her back. Kaderin didn't wait to watch her being completely buried, but jerked her head up to the next mountain. She ran, leaping at the rock face, digging her claws in for a good start, scrabbling up to a high cave.

That cave at the top—that darkened cave—must hold
the prize. And Sebastian could beat her to it. He pressed his
sleeve against his cut lip, tasting his blood from where she'd
kicked him.

Kaderin would be meeting him after all.

And the terms of the deal had just changed.

23

Kaderin staggered into the cave, panting with exertion from the climb. When her vision adjusted, she found the vampire casually tossing the prize up from his palm.

The eggshell had pale striations of color twining around the width and was so fragile it was transparent.

"Now we're going to do things my way, Kaderin."

Her eyes followed it as he tossed it up and down. "Just give me the damn thing."

"You never intended to meet with me." He looked infuriated with her. The sun had blistered his forearms and one side of his face. "And you kicked me." A trail of blood had eased down from the corner of his bottom lip.

"I kicked you in reflex." That was true. The basilisk had just burst through the rocks as if they were packing-peanut fillers and was on her heels. "For future reference, don't grab my ankle from behind when I'm being chased by things with long, prehensile tongues."

No matter what had happened between her and Sebastian, she wouldn't have tried to knock him out. Not to be a dragon's dinner or to burn in the sun any longer, although . . . "In any event, you deserved to be booted. You changed the terms of our deal when I was under duress! Not very gentlemanly."

"I feel less and less like a gentleman with you." The very delicate egg was flipping end over end in his palm.

"You could break that." She could scarcely breathe. "It's the last one." She was easing closer, tilting her head, studying for a way to seize it.

Something dangerous flashed in his expression. "Do you think to take it from me?" He *dared* her to.

She froze, having no wish to tangle with a vampire while keeping the egg whole. "But you have to hurry," she said desperately. "When Cindey gets here, she'll sing, and then you'll give it to her."

"I don't believe she'll be moving for some time after what you did to her."

"She's immortal. She'll shake it off. And she's hurt me far worse in the past. But she could reach us very soon. One pure note out of her pipes, and you'll be her slave forever." At that thought, Kaderin inexplicably craved kicking her again. Or a really well-placed bitch-slap. At her larynx.

"If you believe that, then you won't mind striking yet another bargain to get this prize."

"I've told you I will never sleep with you." A bead of sweat trickled down her neck, then between her breasts. His gray eyes followed it greedily, then flickered with black. Storm over water. She shivered in the heat.

Even though his face was burned on one side and his hands as well, she was attracted to him and still aroused from earlier. Coldhearted? Once. Hot-blooded? He made her so. He alone could. And not just with sexual passion.

She'd enjoyed kicking Cindey's ass, and for some reason, she'd enjoyed that he'd seen her doing it.

"I want to spend a night with you, touching you," he said, his voice low. "That is all. However and wherever I choose."

She raised her brows. "So it'll be all about me? You say that now, but I know you think to seduce me to do more."

"No, I won't expect you to touch me whatsoever. I won't expect sex."

"The altruistic vampire. And you're just going to be doing these things to me and not reacting?"

He ran his free hand over his mouth. "No, I believe I will be reacting quite a bit. Let me worry about my reactions. You have my word. No more. No less."

She tilted her head. "And then I get the prize?"

"When I'm done with what I plan."

She didn't like how his words shot a spike of desire through her. "You might break the egg. Give it to me first."

"Not likely. I'll keep it safe, and you know you'll get it after. Unlike you, I keep my word."

"You won't go dental on me?" At his nonplussed look, she said, "No biting. Or I swear to the gods, I will bite you back, and you won't like it."

This seemed to amuse him for some reason. "No biting. I vow it, though I've always suspected you capable of checking me like that."

How could she do this? How could she *not*? For the prize, she could.

For her curiosity, she . . . must.

What would it be like to be a slave to his touch for one whole night? When she acknowledged her answer to herself, she glanced away and muttered, "I'm flying across the Atlantic tonight." She flushed, already imagining him in that lavish stateroom bed on the jet with her. "You could accompany me."

He was doing that hesitant-stepping-forward thing again. "You want me to go on your plane with you?"

"If you want to take your payment in the next twenty-four hours."

He crossed to her until they were toe-to-toe. "Why not let me trace you back across the Atlantic?"

"You can only go to places you've been before, and I'm betting you've never been where I'm going," she answered, gazing up at him. "Besides, I take flying time to rest."

She swallowed nervously when he rasped, "I wouldn't count on resting this evening."

Hours later Kaderin paced in the main cabin of the jet, furious over more things than she could process.

The first: Because of the Lykae's stunt, she was being forced into this situation with Sebastian. And she'd left the diamonds. Silly Valkyrie.

The second: Two of her half-sisters, her coven mates, had been wed, and she'd heard of it after the fact. *They are so not getting gifts from me.* Were her sisters that averse to her presence at weddings? *Am I that dismal?*

The third: As if she weren't already nervous about Sebastian coming over, now she kept thinking about his past. As in all wars, the Valkyrie had had a correspondent in the field covering the Northern War, and they'd learned that the Wroth brothers were brutal warlords known for their skill and ferocity. The brothers had bought their people a decade of freedom against a force much greater in number.

No wonder Sebastian had known how to fight so well.

The eldest—Myst's *husband*—was the most well known, but Kaderin had definitely heard of Sebastian as well. He'd been a master strategist, a harsh commanding officer, and a ruthless warrior.

She'd seen that authoritative officer side of him today, had heard it in the tone of his voice. And the way he'd eyed that trickling bead of sweat, his eyes so intent, let her know he was going to be ruthless with her tonight.

He'd be arriving within hours, but that fact hadn't sunk in until she'd told the pilots to delay their takeoff from San Luis until twenty minutes past sunset—and not to disturb her for any reason during this trip. . . .

All of this was Bowen's fault. What in the hell was he even doing competing and why was he so determined to win? He was as unwavering as *she* was. A sinking suspicion came, and she rang Emma's sat phone, hoping to catch her in Scotland.

"Kaderin! It's so good to hear from you!" Emma said, sounding delighted. "Regin told me you were feeling again. Congratulations, Kiddy-Kad! That must be *so* cool, I've got so much I want to ask you about that, and, oh, oh, did they tell you—get this—I got married!"

"I heard, sweet. Congratulations. Emma, I'd love to talk to you about all that, but first, tell me, do you know of a Lykae named Bowen?"

"Sure," Emma said, then asked, "Why do you want to know?"

"You're not following the Hie online?" Yes, they were honeymooners, but still . . .

Show Kaderin some love.

Kaderin had her answer when she heard the sounds of teeth snapping and fabric being ripped. Emma cried, "Lachlain! Oh! I'm running out of clothes!"

"*Buy—more,*" came a muffled growl.

Kaderin assured herself she was not jealous that Emma was seventy years old and already had found a gorgeous, mondo-rich king. Oh, and one who had proven he would die for her and was at this moment ripping off her clothes with his fangs. Emma was everything that was sweet and lovely, and after her trials—and near death—she deserved her new life as Lachlain's queen.

Still, Kaderin sighed, unable to help feeling very old and very alone. Then she recalled that she wouldn't be alone for long. She had a man coming over this very night . . . to do things to her. She shivered, then shook herself. "Emma, about Bowen . . ."

"Oh, Bowe. Sure, I know him. Know he's supercali hot." A male sound of displeasure had her covering the phone and saying, "Not as hot as you are!"

So Emma's new werewolf husband was the jealous type? Kaderin rolled her eyes.

"Yeah, Bowe's got that tortured, brooding thing going on. He lost his mate in the eighteen hundreds, and he's done nothing but search for a way to reunite with her ever since."

The breath left Kaderin's body, and she sank onto the bed.

"Kaderin, I-I kind of have to go. Can you call me later?"

"Sure, Emma. Have fun," she said absently, then hung up. *At least now I know what I'm truly up against.* In Bowen's mind, this win equaled the life of his mate. But how would he know to enter? Who was the friend he'd referred to who'd alerted him to the contest?

Her dismay rapidly turning to ire, Kaderin dialed the coven, calling for Nïx.

For once, Kaderin found it fortunate when Regin answered. She wasted no time on pleasantries. "Any reason you didn't tell me Myst married a general in the Forbearer army, more specifically a vampire?"

"Lookit, I didn't want to distract you from your job," Regin said. "This Hie is your Big Thing. And I know when I first found out, I was seriously, fucking, shrieking distracted. I mean, I knew you would never get freaked out—well, at least, you wouldn't used to—but I thought it would be prudent to just hold off a few days. It was my idea, not Myst's."

"This connection might have been nice to know in certain situations, Regin. For instance, that vampire in Antarctica that you almost killed is now our brother-in-law!"

"No way! Nikolai Wroth's brother?" A pause. "But does that matter? Can't we still kill him? I wouldn't have told anyone if you wouldn't have. What happens in the South Pole, stays in the—"

"Regin, if you keep something like this from me again, I will annihilate you. You know I'm stronger than you are."

"Ah, but I'm *wily*."

Kaderin exhaled. "How can Myst be certain he won't turn?"

"I'm not exactly speaking to her."

"Then just let me talk to Nïx."

A second later, Nïx said in a jovial tone, "Kiddy-Kad!"

"Nïx, why is it that Bowen MacRieve—a Lykae who lost his mate—would know to enter this competition to retrieve her? Let me add that I know Bowen attended Emma's wedding, as did you—a soothsayer."

"Um, I dunno. Dumb luck?" Nïx said. Kaderin could just see Nïx twirling her silky black hair, trying to appear innocent. Which reminded Kaderin . . . sometimes tasks repeated.

"Cut off all your hair," she said, her tone seething. "Then shear it every day thereafter until I tell you to stop."

"Go from Katie to Sinead? Well, I *am* sassy enough to pull it off—"

"Just do it!"

"Angry, Kaderin? How unlike you."

"I'm livid, as you well know. Nïx, why would you do this to me? Why tell Bowen about this? You had to know he will fight to the death to bring back that mate."

"Oh, yes, especially since she died fleeing him! It's been killing him slowly, making him crazed. He hardly eats or sleeps and hasn't glanced at another female since then."

Kaderin put her forehead between her thumb and forefinger. "He'll be unstoppable. They *live* for nothing else."

"More unstoppable than a guilt-ridden two-thousand-year-old Valkyrie who, incidentally, keeps winning these things? I was thinking it'd be a wash."

She exhaled, striving for calm. "Since you gave him information, now help me. Why am I feeling now?"

"Because it's time for you to."

"Oh, since you explained it that way." Kaderin rolled her eyes. "Will I win the Hie?"

"Lemme check." She hummed, and Kaderin could almost see her peering at the ceiling in concentration—

The phone dropped.

A chill crept up Kaderin's spine just before Nïx's screams erupted.

"Nïx!" Kaderin snapped. "Nïx, what's going on?"

A minute later, Regin had the phone. "What the hell did you say to her?" In the background, thunder boomed in a deafening succession like cannon blasts. Nïx sobbed hysterically.

"I just asked her if I'll win the Hie! Why? What's happening?"

"I don't know—I've never seen her like this! She's white as a ghost and mumbling incoherently." To Nïx, Regin said, "Calm down, sweet. What's upset you?"

Kaderin heard Nïx's voice, heard her desperate ramblings, but couldn't make out the actual words. "What is she saying?" Kaderin demanded.

"Oh, Kad," Regin whispered, all her temper gone. "She said . . ." Regin swallowed audibly. "She said that . . . in the competition, before the next full moon . . . you're going to . . . die."

Die? Kaderin frowned in confusion, wringing her hands around the phone. *How should one respond to that? I can't imagine.* Her inane reply: "Oh."

Regin, fired up once more, said, "Get out of the competition now!"

"You know that won't help," Kaderin murmured. "When your number's up, it's up."

"Yeah, but you can still freaking *duck*."

"Regin, how can you say something like that?" Kaderin demanded, even knowing she herself had once said much the same. The memory of Furie lashing out at her was as clear as if it happened yesterday. For her own heedless words, Kaderin had had her arm broken and her skull and sternum fractured.

"Where are you right now? We'll come get you, guard you in the coven."

"Nïx could be mistaken," Kaderin offered, surprised to find her eyes had watered in a rush. "Or she read the premonition wrong." But she said that only for Regin's benefit. Kaderin knew Nïx was never wrong. And she'd *never* seen the death of a Valkyrie before.

"Nïx is presently rolling on the floor. *Something* is happening."

"Oh." *How brave Furie had been to go meet her destiny, how stoic.*

Kaderin could aspire to that.

"Damn it, Kad, tell us where you are!"

"Regin, only cowards don't meet their fate. If I'm to die in this competition, then that's the hand I was dealt. I'll play it out."

"You're talking crazy. You shouldn't be alone right now, not with this news."

She tilted her head, staring out the window. "I . . . won't be." Because dusk was in a couple of hours. "I'll be fine, Regin. I'll check in later," she added, then hung up, turning off the ringer.

Kaderin knew that in the days leading up to the full moon, her coven would fight to find her, calling incessantly, trying to track her movements through her phone and credit-card use, as well as through the Accord's network. But Kaderin knew all the tricks, and if she didn't want to be found, then she wouldn't be.

She shook. The sun continued to set, and she had a vampire coming over.

24

D id you dress for me?" Sebastian visibly swallowed when
  Kaderin stood at his arrival.

He'd been doing that tentative-step thing as he entered,
but after his gaze raked her from head to toe, he strode forward as though pushed. There was no mistaking his appreciation of her tight black sweater, short skirt, and strappy
heels.

She was glad when his avid gaze strayed again to her
breasts, or he might have seen her dropped jaw.

The vampire was undeniably *hot*.

He was so tall that the highest point of the plane's seven-
foot ceiling barely cleared his height. He wore dark jeans
that highlighted his narrow hips and a dark shirt that
molded to his muscles. Everything was tasteful and seriously
expensive. His face was completely healed, and his longish
black hair was damp at his collar from a recent shower.

Sexy. He has too much of a biological advantage. What female could be expected to turn *him* away when he wanted
to be inside her?

When he met her eyes again, he had such a ravenous
look that she grew flustered, feeling a blush creeping over
her cheekbones. *Blushing. Now the vampire has me blushing.*
"This is how I usually dress." *After nervously trying on thirty*

combinations of clothing. "That is, when I'm not fighting, running, or climbing."

He reached forward to brush his hand at her nape. "Or diving from cliffs to tackle unwitting sirens," he said with a half grin.

So, he was going to be charming tonight? Little did he know that she was a-sure-thing. He didn't have to unleash an arsenal of devastating good looks and that quiet, unstudied charm.

She was his tonight.

Before he'd arrived, she had been miserable. She'd felt so alone and so, well, doomed. After much soul searching, Kaderin had made a decision.

In the young, immortal words of Regin: *Fuck it.* If she was going to die, Kaderin was going to have one night of passion before her dirt nap. And she couldn't think of anyone she wanted to be with more than him—for this one night.

She'd told him this was how she usually dressed, and that was true, but she didn't want him to suspect that she'd tried on everything in her bag twice. She'd stared in the mirror, considering her appearance for the first time in ages, wondering what he would find attractive about her—or was it merely the blooding that made him fancy her? She'd been so anxious about being intimate with a man after so long, she could scarcely close the tiny fastenings on her heels.

Sad but true, she was grateful to him for his company. If he weren't here, she would have done nothing but mull her death, but now he was with her, and there was something in his eyes, something a bit *alarming* that thrilled her.

She bit her bottom lip. Call her Betty Fucking Crocker, because the cake was so going to be worth the bake.

"You look beautiful." Such simple words, but the way he said them, his eyes so compelling, gave her shivers.

She glanced down at herself and back up. "Not too small?"

That gorgeous grin again. Gazing at his chiseled, masculine face changing expressions was a decadent pleasure. "I love how you are made. Even as I'd worried about hurting you when I touched you." Listening to the low timbre of his voice was just as blissful. She knew she shouldn't enjoy these things so much, and yet she couldn't help it.

"Hurting me?" She gave a light laugh. "Losing limbs hurts. Boiling oil hurts. Whatever you can dish out, I can take—if I wish to."

He closed in, all hot, massive male, towering over her. Gods, he smelled good.

"And do you wish to, Kaderin?"

Yes! She wanted him to kiss her, to lick her body. Him, a vampire. When she nodded breathlessly, his hand cupped her face, drawing her in so he could take her lips.

His kiss was gentle at first—though she could tell he struggled to make it so. Then he groaned, and it turned desperate, that gallows kiss. Tonight she shared the sentiment completely.

The lights blinked twice, and she finally forced herself to break away. "We're about to take off. It's, uh, customary to sit."

He dropped into the closest seat, seizing her waist, then dragged her across his lap. When he settled her ass over his rampant erection, he hissed in a breath, and she gasped, reminded of his size.

In an awkward attempt at conversation, she asked, "H-have you ever been on a plane before?"

"No." He brushed her hair from her neck to press a sizzling kiss to the bared skin. "And I doubt that I'll remember much of flying this time."

When he nuzzled her neck, she stiffened and pulled away. "No biting?"

"No, I promise," he said. "I am sorry it happened that night."

As her uncontrollable emotions continued to do, unbidden words bubbled up from nowhere. "Sebastian, no matter what happens in the future, I want you to know that I'm . . ." She glanced down and murmured, "I'm glad you're here now."

But he curled his finger under her chin and caught her eyes. He looked *proud* of her. "Thank you for telling me this."

"I just felt I should."

"These feelings are confusing, are they not? Mine are, too. But we'll muddle our way through."

She wouldn't be around long enough to. . . .

With that thought in her mind, she turned to straddle him. Her hands trembled as she cradled his face. She leaned in to press her lips against the corner of his mouth, his cheek, and lower to his neck, then returned to brush her lips fully against his. As before, the mere contact of his lips with hers made her breathy and abandoned. She tilted her head to deepen the kiss, setting in to him, licking his lips, his tongue.

She drew back to work her sweater up and off, then reached back and unsnapped her lacy bra. When she faced him again, his gaze was rapt on her bared breasts, his jaw slackened.

Today in the cave, she'd determined that he hadn't

wanted to rush their encounter. Now, she again had the idea that he wanted to take this slowly, and judging from his reaction, he thought she'd just skipped a step.

"I . . . Katja . . ." He swallowed, seeming to memorize the sight. As if he believed he'd never see something like this again?

The awful truth was that she enjoyed him gaping at her breasts, enjoyed his pained expression when her nipples hardened right in front of his eyes.

"So lovely," he said, his voice rumbling in that sexy way, shooting heat through her that centered between her legs. Gods, she'd missed this.

He placed his hands flat on her back and pulled her forward to lightly lick one of her nipples. She moaned at that small contact even before he took it between his lips. Groaning around the peak, tongue flicking, he sucked hard until it throbbed. He released her only to repeat the attentions to her other breast, then he stopped to gaze again. She had the crazy idea that he wanted to see what he'd wrought with his lips.

But his breaths were heating the wet peaks, making her ache. "Please, Bastian," she murmured. If he was going to touch her, he needed to do it *now*.

He moved her until she lay across his lap, her neck against his arm. "Spread your legs," he rasped, pressing them open until her skirt rode up enough to reveal her panties. He grazed the backs of his fingers up her inner thigh.

With his eyes heavy-lidded, he pulled her panties aside with one hand, reaching his other hand around her waist and down to begin stroking her. He bit out a foreign curse at how wet she was. "For me," he said, his voice hoarse. It wasn't a question, but she got the sense that he wanted her to assure him.

"For you," she whispered, making him shudder.

"That pleases me. You should be, since I'm hard for you constantly." He rubbed her wetness around, making her gasp, seeming fascinated with how slick she'd grown. When he slipped his finger into her, he groaned from low in his throat, and she writhed, feeling his shaft pulse beneath her.

"I'm going to kiss you here"—he rocked his hand upward, delving deeper, as his thumb slowly stroked her clitoris—"all night."

She cried out. She'd always found that act intensely erotic, and now the wicked thought of a vampire doing it to her made her squirm.

Who was this domineering, sinfully sexy man? He'd seemed cautious, even tentative, in the beginning. But not now.

Never had a takeoff felt so good. "Bastian, I need—"

"You want me to kiss you, Katja?"

"Yes!" She rolled her hips to work his finger in and out, and he groaned against her damp nipple.

He continued this agonizing play until they leveled off and the lights in the cabin dimmed to darkness except for the light over the table opposite them. He lifted her and gently placed her on the table, pressing her back.

His hands skimmed up under her skirt until he could hook his fingers around her panties. She shimmied to help him as he tugged them off.

He pushed her skirt to her waist, then sat before her in the plush seat, in the dark while she was lying back in the light. He placed his palms on her legs and gently spread them. When she was bared to him, he rasped, "*You're beau-*

tiful," making her sex clench. She whimpered as he continued to stare.

She'd never been looked at like this, never felt so exposed and vulnerable. And yet she trusted him with her body. At last, he pressed his lips to her thigh, kissing higher with wet licks until she was shivering, threading her fingers in his thick hair.

She sighed, drawing up her knees and letting her legs fall open for him to do as he would.

25

◈

Her inner thighs were like silk. Nothing could be so soft. Sebastian already felt as though he'd explode, and he hadn't even tasted her.

He wanted to savor the experience, but he'd waited too long for this fantasy. After the cave, he'd paced in her townhouse with nervousness for hours. He'd known what he was going to do to her tonight—what he'd thought about again and again. But could he please her? Would she be able to tell he'd never done this before?

Now that he was certain he was about to have it, he was desperate for his first taste of her.

He gave a last kiss on her thigh, and then, with a growl, he found her wetness. Mouth open, he rubbed his tongue at her center, in a long, slow lick. As she cried out, his body shuddered with pleasure, his cock jerking in his pants. "You're like honey."

Wet, slick, luscious. For more than three hundred years, he'd waited for this.

And she was so fucking worth it.

Encouraged by her cry, he licked more deeply and felt her growing wetter against his tongue. She moaned, and her arms fell overhead. He'd never imagined her sex could be so hot, the flesh so giving. *I will never get enough of this. Never.*

If it took becoming a vampire to have this one night with her, would he suffer the turning again?

In the space of one of his new heartbeats.

When he lashed a hard stroke of his tongue against her swollen little clitoris, she sucked in a breath and arched her back sharply. How had he ever thought he could handle his own reaction? It was everything he could do not to yank out his shaft and impale her exactly where his tongue was dipping right at that moment.

But then, there was no way he would forgo this pleasure now. He had waited for so long and already he was in love with the act. Her sexy heels were digging into his back, urging him on like spurs.

She leaned up on her elbows to watch him, biting her bottom lip, panting, sending a shock of lust through him. She touched her own breasts, strumming her nipples as if for him. How did she know he was enthralled with her pink nipples and plump, soft breasts? For her to play with them . . . ?

"Bastian!" she cried. "I'm so close. . . ."

No, not yet! Shouldn't have taken her with my fingers. She'd have lasted longer. I could have had my mouth on her longer. But she threw back her head, arching with her nipples tight and pointing, and he couldn't stop himself from licking her madly.

She moaned as she began coming, and his eyes closed with pleasure, as it went on and on. Her lithe body shuddered against him and her cries filled his ears.

Once she'd finished, she pushed at his head to close her knees, when all he wanted to do was taste her orgasm. No, damn it, he was going to have more of this. Had to. "I'm not done yet," he growled, not recognizing his own voice.

Her eyes widened when he scooped her up and carried her to the bed in the back, tossing her down. The room had a panorama of small windows, and all around her, he could see lightning striking in the background. Sebastian was in a plane—actually flying—and he could not give a damn.

When he moved her bodily so he could lie between her legs, she said, "Bastian, I-I can't . . . not so soon."

She pushed at him when he spread her legs wide once more, but he yanked her arms to her sides and clutched her wrists, capturing her in place.

"*Spread your legs,*" he ordered in a tone that dared her to deny him.

She did with a whimper, knowing what was to come. He set back in, more aggressive, emboldened at how he'd made her come already, at how she'd given off lightning. He'd worried that he would be awful at this, that she would yawn with boredom. But she'd made it so easy with her moans and cries, letting him know exactly how she liked to be kissed.

When he decided to try suckling her clitoris, she moaned with abandon, head thrashing on the pillow, making him grind his cock into the mattress in agony. Her legs fell wide again in total surrender, and light exploded outside; the plane shook as she rolled her hips to his waiting tongue.

"Yes . . . yes . . . yes," she cried, panting, writhing. She screamed—loudly—when she came, and though he held her wrists, her claws dug down and shredded the sheets.

He devoured her until he'd wrung every last whimper from her. Then he kissed her silky thighs where he'd squeezed too hard, wanting to soothe her even as he ached.

"Bastian?" she murmured.

He finally pulled himself away and rose to sit back on his haunches, not bothering to hide his amazement. She appeared to share the feeling. "Well"—she had to swallow before continuing—"you're, uh, certainly no slouch in that department."

Sebastian was proud and relieved. Very relieved. But now he would have to leave her. He had a cock full of seed that would not be denied. And he'd promised her he'd do no more than touch her. Even in the unlikely event that she wanted to make love to him, he didn't want her to *in exchange* for anything—

"Bastian," she purred. "I want to touch you."

He shook his head. "I told you I wouldn't." But when she reached out her soft palm, his hips shot forward, seemingly of their own accord, to place his cock at her disposal.

By the time he'd gathered the will to think about denying her, she'd already undone his jeans.

In a throaty whisper, she asked, "Do you think I could let *that* go unrewarded?"

Kaderin grasped his shaft, pulling it free. Her eyes widened at her first sight.

Gods, he was glorious. The crown was glistening, the shaft so thick as it pulsed and throbbed in her palm.

She glanced up to find his face flushed as he looked down to where she held him. When she caught his darkened eyes, she realized he wanted her to like what they were doing, that he wanted her to find him attractive.

"I love the way you feel," she murmured as she circled her fingers around him, squeezing him firmly in her fist until he groaned low. "I couldn't stop touching you even if I tried."

Pulling on him, she eased him down to where he rested over her on his hands and knees. Then, stroking his length, she touched the head to her breast. He began shuddering, his legs shaking. She rubbed it against the flesh, even around one of her nipples. With her other hand, she cupped his heavy sack, kneading.

She saw him clench his jaw and sensed he was just preventing himself from thrusting into her palm to end this. "*Katja* . . . I'm about to . . . come."

"Yes!" She stroked him harder, faster.

He bit out, "Like this—?"

She pressed the head directly to her aching nipple.

"*Ah, God*—" The words ended with a brutal yell as he ejaculated against her. She pumped her fist, shivering at the first contact. The room lit with lightning once more.

When she'd stroked him spent, he looked as if he could scarcely believe what he'd done. "I didn't expect . . . I didn't plan for this."

She bit her bottom lip. "I know."

Without another word, he pushed up, tucking his shaft back into his jeans, looking angry with himself. He rose to go to the luxurious bathroom, then returned with a plush towel, wetted on the end. When he sat beside her, he clearly wondered what the protocol was. He held up the towel with raised eyebrows, and she nodded, stifling a smile.

He reached out to clean her breasts with languid strokes, staring avidly. He exhaled a long breath and muttered, "I can't believe I did this."

Each of his light strokes relaxed her even more, and she gave him a lazy grin, no doubt surprising him. Hey, what could she say? She'd needed him for tonight, and he'd satisfied her thoroughly. Even if they hadn't made love.

Kaderin found it sexy as hell that he wasn't too suave and overly practiced in bed, the way she'd heard immortal men could be—nor was he jaded. He didn't try to hide how much pleasure he was feeling, or check his words, or downplay how much he ached.

She sighed, every muscle in her body relaxed. "Bastian, I thought tonight was wonderful."

"*You* did?" He'd just come across her breasts, watching as it happened as though out of his body. That was something he'd thought he'd go his whole life without experiencing. And though he found it hard to believe, she looked as if she couldn't be happier with him.

He shook his head again to clear it, then rose to toss the towel into the bathroom. When he returned, he leaned against the bedroom doorway and gazed down at her. She'd turned onto her side, and seemed half-asleep, but she raised her head to give him a drowsy smile. And something felt as though it shifted in his chest, twisting . . . aching.

Her sleek skirt was bunched at her waist, and her wisp of underwear had snagged on the fastening of her shoe. Seeing her like this, so soft and relaxed, made his chest hurt again. Frowning, he rubbed the palm of his hand hard against it.

When she murmured his name and rounded her back as if coaxing him to lie behind her, his eyes widened. He returned at once, sitting beside her. Yes, he would sleep with her. He yanked off his boots and pulled his shirt over his head, then reached up and closed all of the curtains.

He knew she would set out as soon as they landed—but for now, he planned to enjoy every aspect of being with his woman, including undressing her for bed.

He tugged the underwear free, removed her shoes, then

unzipped and removed her skirt. When he lay behind her, pulling the blanket over them, he could have sworn she mumbled something about a cake.

After drawing her into his arms, he buried his face in her hair and squeezed her. He'd gone from famine to feast—no middle ground. He'd gone from having no one to call his own to having a fantasy here in his arms.

He could win her. He *would* win her after tonight. He'd known he would be a good husband, a good father, but he'd wondered if he could satisfy her in bed. Now he felt confident he could, since she wasn't shy about what pleased her. *God, how she lets me know.* He grinned against her, well aware that they slept on shredded sheets.

She sighed, flexing against him. Then as if she caught herself doing something she oughtn't, she tensed. "Tonight changes nothing, vampire."

"*Tell yourself that, Valkyrie*"—he brushed her hair aside, kissing her neck and making her shiver—"*as much as you like.*"

26

❧❧

"Good morning, Katja."

She mumbled something in answer. When he'd woken, she was draped over his chest, half on him, panting with sleep. He grinned, savoring the feeling. She would deny it, but his Bride liked sleeping with him. He could get used to this ultimate luxury—blond curls spilling over his chest and warm woman in his arms, his for the taking. Was she, after last night?

She'd given him the most pleasure he'd ever experienced, and she'd also given him a teasing hint of what more he could find with her. He squeezed her even closer. When she said something he didn't catch, he let up. "Sorry."

She sounded half-asleep when she asked, "Why're you always worried 'bout crushing me?"

He stared at the ceiling. "My size has not put me in good stead with women." What a vast understatement.

"Did last night," she murmured, with a yawn against him. "Your size was a panty remover."

Panty remover? He drew her up by the shoulders, and she blinked at him sleepily like a kitten peeled off a couch.

"*Whaa?*" she muttered. "That in good enough stead?"

He chuckled, settling her back, using his whole hand to

cup her face against him. How could a few well-placed words begin undoing centuries of doubt—?

She shot up in bed, eyes wide. "We've landed?"

"About an hour ago. I turned the Do Not Disturb key, and the pilots left."

"What time is it?" She sprang from the bed. Naked. She dashed to the bathroom, started the shower, then flashed by on her way to the closet for clothes. *So very naked.*

He glanced at the bedside clock. "It's six-forty here." Where exactly was *here?* All he knew was that the pinpricks of sun coming through the shades were bright.

"I've got a car coming at seven!"

He sat back with his arms behind his head and knew his grin was one of pure masculine satisfaction. He'd never seen a woman get dressed before. He never wanted to miss it again.

This was what he'd imagined having a wife would be like. Seeing her dressing, enjoying tantalizing views of her beautiful body. But with her, the reality was so much better.

He hadn't, for instance, envisioned his wife's complete lack of modesty or wicked bed play. He hadn't imagined that her stunning eyes could burn with such absolute purpose and drive—or go silvery with desire.

She caught her ankle in the strap of her bag and stumbled forward, righting herself with a kind of preternatural grace. When she bit out a curse, he chuckled again.

She peered around the bathroom door and quirked an eyebrow until he raised his hands in surrender.

Soon he was treated to the light scents of her shampoo and soap that would be mixed with her own luscious scent. When he imagined her working soap over her sleek body, he shot to his feet. Not wasting a second, he stripped off his jeans and traced into the shower.

She cried out with a start, glanced down at his erection, then back up with her face flushed. Regrettably, she was already rinsed clean, and before he could touch her, she hopped out. She secured a towel around her torso and twisted one up around her hair, then dashed from the steamy room. He heard cabinets slamming in the bedroom as she hurried.

He didn't understand this obsessive need of hers to win. "Why are you so rabid about this prize?" he called out from under the water. "I've told you a hundred times before, the key will not work." He found an unopened bar of soap that didn't smell feminine and tore open the monogrammed seal.

She entered again, still in her towel, and squeezed toothpaste onto her pink toothbrush. She answered while brushing. "Ill ew." *Will to.*

Just as she finished brushing and exited, he finished showering, then grabbed the last towel.

On her way past the bathroom door once more, she tossed his jeans at him. He dried off, stabbed his legs in, and entered the hall—plowing right into her.

He should have known, in such a small area. *Careless. . . .*

His hand shot out to catch her, but she easily checked her fall with one light step back. Her hands flew to his chest, then relaxed to rest there, rubbing a few remaining drops of water. She didn't give him that hurt look. No, she tilted her head and studied his chest, her tiny fang pressing against her bottom lip, her eyes growing silver.

Just as he was about to pick her up on the way back to the bed, she shimmied by, then hastened down the hall, hips gently swaying under her towel. *Perfect for me.* Suddenly, he was completely respectful of fate, since it had had blooded him with exactly the right female.

When she was out of his sight, the silky underthings in her opened clothes bag caught his attention. Kneeling down to root through them, he picked out a scant black bra and matching panties that resembled no more than artfully arranged strings. He stood and clenched them in his fists, groaning to recall tugging her silk panties aside the night before. He'd shuddered to find them so very wet. . . .

She appeared, one hand on her hip, the other raised for her underwear. He reluctantly handed it over. When she turned and began dressing under the towel, he said, "I know a bit about the subject of time travel. And I know this key can't work. Have you ever studied the laws of general relativity?" he asked slowly, not imagining why she would have. His head tilted with each word, gaze locked on the edge of the fluttering towel. He needn't have bothered angling for a peek. She dropped the towel as soon as her underwear was on—in other words, when the string was in place.

He hissed in a breath. Again, his feet shuffled to keep himself from falling over. *That ass is going to be the death of me.*

"I know a bit about the subject myself," she said over her shoulder as she donned her bra. "And since the mid-twentieth century, it's been widely accepted among physicists that the possibility of time travel can be reconciled within the laws of general relativity."

His brows drew together. Perhaps he shouldn't have spoken to her so slowly. But then her words sank in. General relativity was only one argument against time travel. "Even if that were so, time travel is not compatible with the law of conservation of energy. You cannot remove matter and energy from one sphere without creating a vacuum. Nor can you take it and force it into another sphere."

Mercifully, she shimmied into her low-slung pants, though she had to bend over briefly, with her breasts threatening to spill out. Half dressed, she began combing out her long, wet hair. He sat back against the headboard once more and savored every sight.

"True. But only if you believe that all matter and energy are interconnected on a global scale," she said.

Could she be any sexier than at this moment, brushing her hair, discussing one of his favorite subjects? Somehow he managed to speak. "It must be. In a closed system, all is integrated."

Twisting the mass of curls into a knot on her head, she bared that graceful neck he couldn't seem to keep his lips from. "The earth isn't a closed system," she said with absolute authority. "There are bridges to other dimensions, even other populations like the Lore. I've been to some."

What? he thought dumbly. Christ, he believed her about this. Though it went against everything he'd learned.

And just like that, one of the foundational beliefs of his life collapsed while a slip of a female traipsed by in a silken black bra.

Shaken, he redoubled his efforts to concentrate. He wanted to convince her of this. And to be honest, he wanted to impress her. "And what about the Grandfather Paradox? What happens when a time traveler has a quantum-mechanical intrusion with his past self or his ancestors?"

"What if he kills his own grandfather? Well, if one believes tachyons—"

"*You know what a tachyon is?*" he nearly shouted.

She hooked her shirt at her thumbs, readying it to pull on. While she was under the tight fabric, he heard her say, "Subatomic particle. Travels faster than the speed of light." He had closed his jaw by the time she'd drawn it on all the way.

"How do you understand these things?" And how could this blooding be so precise?

"My dad was a god, and they tend to be quick like that. I inherited."

"Of course." He didn't like to be reminded of this. Riora had asked him, "Do you have any idea how high you reach for one such as her?" *Yes, Riora. Yes, I do.* Every day, he had a better idea, and it was killing him. He shook himself. "Tachyons are hypothetical. Their existence would threaten laws of science—"

"Like radioactivity did?" she asked in a mild tone, glancing up from lacing her boots to cast him a too-pleasant smile.

He exhaled a long breath. She was referring to a time in the early nineteen hundreds when physicists couldn't account for the phenomenon of radioactivity. They had to remain confused, embattled, until the theory of quantum mechanics was proposed.

"Clever analogy," he said, beyond impressed. Had she convinced him? No, there were dozens of other arguments to prove one couldn't go back into the past to change the future. But never had he been so glad to agree to disagree; he'd die if he didn't kiss her.

27

❧❧

Sebastian lunged for her, grabbing her upper arms and tumbling with her back onto the bed.

"What are you doing?" Kaderin demanded, but couldn't manage to sound angry enough—not when she'd been willing him to do this ever since she'd touched his gorgeous, still dampened chest.

After last night, she knew all of him was gorgeous.

She hadn't missed his heated looks while she dressed, but apparently talk about science had pushed him to the boiling point—she could feel his thick erection pressing into her. Science. She should have suspected—she'd seen all those texts in his castle, and they weren't exactly beach reads.

He sat up over her, pinning her arms above her head. In the cave, and even last night, he'd demonstrated his strength. Now, with her arms pinned, she again imagined him taking her—hard, with that rugged, flexing body. . . .

She frowned. This morning, he'd told her, "My size has not put me in good stead with women." She believed this was one of his understatements, and suspected a woman— or women—had hurt him. So why did she now feel an overwhelming urge to claw the silly bitch's eyes out?

"Kiss me, Katja." His face was so handsome, rested. He seemed on the verge of grinning. *Irresistible.*

"Why would I want to do that?" she asked in a breathy voice.

"You like kissing me, Valkyrie." He sounded proud.

Oh, Freya, she did.

And then he did grin. "Christ, I enjoy being with you." A heart-stopping curving of his lips, showing his even white teeth and scarcely visible fangs against his forever tanned skin. *Don't look at him*. She was being charmed, warming so much to him, and she cast about for things to hate. *He drinks blood. He drinks blood. He bites!*

"You *have* to like being with me," she reminded him. "I'm your Bride."

He released her wrists and sat up. "Of course, it's mystical compulsion that's making me so attracted to you. Not the fact that you just gave me a good look at how your mind works and I admired what I saw. And it couldn't be because last night you gave me the most sexual pleasure I've ever had."

She studied his earnest expression. "Was it really?"

"Before last night and that first morning with you? By miles," he admitted quietly. She believed him, though she couldn't understand it. They hadn't even had sex. Surely he'd had women fawning over him, wanting to please him in any way. Yes, he seemed shy at times, but he'd also been a sexy, intelligent aristocrat and then a master soldier.

If she'd met him when he was still a shy mortal, she'd have cornered him in a hay barn and had her wicked way with him.

"What about you, Katja?" His voice went deeper. "Tell me I pleasured you well last night."

So much for shy. Now *she* was the one blushing and averting her face.

"Kiss me, or tell me. One of the two to get me to let you go."

She made a sound of frustration. "You know you did—you were there. We almost crashed the plane with lightning!"

He leaned down and rumbled against her neck, "What a way to go."

"Why would you ask me that?"

He drew back. "Because my plan is to make you need me for this. If you feel lust"—he pressed a kiss against her collarbone—"I want you automatically to seek me to ease it."

He was so arrogant and yet unsure, forthright but furtive. And gods help her, the contradictions fascinated her. "And what about you?" she asked.

He grazed the backs of his fingers along her cheek. "You know I'll never want another."

"*Why . . . why did you want to die?*" She didn't know where the question came from, but suddenly she burned to know the answer. *Why had he been alone?*

"I . . . didn't necessarily want to die. I just didn't see the point in living." At her frown, he added, "I will explain this to you. One day. But I still don't know how I feel about that situation."

She looked away. "It's fine. You don't have to."

He pressed his hand against her cheek, tenderly, coaxing her to face him again. "I will tell you. In time. Anything you wish. I want there to be no secrets between us, because I'm going to . . . marry you."

"What? *Whoa!*" She scrambled away from him, real fear coursing through her. This was exactly why the night before shouldn't have happened. Or even this morning when they'd been getting ready together. They'd been behaving just like a married couple readying for the office, one of those couples who pass a mug of coffee and a bagel between them. Well, except that she and Sebastian didn't eat or have an office.

But she hadn't seen the topic of marriage coming up—not so soon. *Panic. No more playing with the vampire.* "You can't marry me! I'm . . . I'm a pagan!" she babbled.

This was all insanity, anyway.

I'm going to die. And if I don't die, then I'll succeed in retrieving my sisters—

A sudden realization robbed her of breath.

If she saved them, she would change history. And Kaderin would never even know Sebastian.

"And I was Catholic," he said slowly, brows drawn in confusion. "I still want to marry you."

Stumbling from the bed, she swooped up her things, stuffing items into a bag. Was she shaking? "Look, Sebastian, am I attracted to you? Yep, you got me. I'm not going to lie. Last night was . . . enjoyable. I'm glad it happened. But that doesn't mean that it will happen again. Much less that I will wed you."

"What could make it so that you would?"

"My absolute belief that I would want to spend eternity with you. Immortals really have to be careful with this, you understand, and you and I have never even had a civil conversation before today. And honestly, I don't trust you, and I can't turn off a lifetime of beliefs in the course of two weeks."

"Why not just try life with me?"

"Because unturned vampires are like nuclear bombs. The bomb itself is not a bad thing. The damage it's capable of is the bad thing. In any event, you still don't want one in your backyard."

"Give me a chance to prove you wrong."

"Sebastian, have you ever *seen* a turned vampire? If you had, you would know why I would do just about anything not to wake up to one at sunset because you went out and got frisky."

"I would never be unfaithful to you," he said, then felt compelled to tell her, "And I have seen them. Through your dreams."

She clearly didn't like to be reminded of that and looked as if she barely held on to her patience.

"And not all vampires turn. My brother didn't and he drinks from the flesh."

Her eyes widened. "That's *right*. Tapping Myst, is he, then? So much for coven secrets."

"He would never betray her." For all of Nikolai's faults, he was as loyal as men came.

"Even if you would never turn, if I accepted you, and we were together, there are only two possible outcomes for our future. One, I leave behind my family. Or two, they kill you. Period. That is our future."

"But my brother and Myst—"

"Will be running for their lives when our queen returns."

"Furie?"

"Let me guess. You've seen her, too?"

"I have." He felt his face grow cold. "She broke your goddamned arm."

"So, you've seen that she's a fearsome being."

"I don't fear her, and I would always protect you."

"You should fear her," Kaderin said, exasperated. "All vampires should. The Horde captured her and chained her to the bottom of the ocean for the last fifty years. For fifty years she's drowned repeatedly, every few minutes, only to have her immortality revive her, and no one could find her. But now we're getting close, and when she rises, she won't differentiate between the two armies of vampires. There'll be no reasoning with her. Because she wasn't exactly level-headed *before dying the last four million plus times*."

"We'll deal with that when the time comes."

"Just stop. Do you want to know what the second of the three major turnoffs is? It's pressure. I don't respond well to pressure." She snatched up her bag and tossed the strap over her shoulder.

"Wait, before you go." He traced to her flat, carefully collected the egg from the drawer he'd stowed it in, then traced back. "Here."

"Of course." She tucked her hair behind her ear, then reached for it. "I was just about to ask for this."

"No, you weren't," he said, and somehow knew he was right.

"Was too." She held the egg up, and when it disappeared, the scents from far away came once more. "I was, because I was curious if you had killed the other two basilisks or not."

Can't lie. Even though he knew she'd view him as weak. He ran his palm over the back of his neck and averted his face. "I had to kill one of them. I decided . . . not to with the smallest basilisk."

Of all the reactions he might have expected, her sound of frustration and her forefinger pointed at him weren't among them.

"Of course, you did," she said in a disgusted tone. "Stay, leave, do as you will, but I've work to do."

He was growing angry. Mercy had its place. "Would you prefer that I had killed them both?"

Forefinger still out like a sword, she sputtered, "No! But

you just *had* to turn out to be all noble and . . . and under-standing. And you are such a . . . a . . . vampire!" She frowned, then seemed to seize on a thought. "And you could have told me who you are!"

Where in the hell had that come from? "I told you my name that first morning."

"But you didn't tell me *who* you were!"

He drew back his head, utterly baffled, as she stormed from the room into the sunlit main cabin.

She was leaving, and he couldn't go with her, even though everything in him wanted to. And because of the sun, he couldn't even watch her walk away.

When she was gone, he felt as if he were missing some part of himself. Something intrinsic and critical.

He felt caged, frustrated. He punched the wall of the plane, breaking an interior panel. *Goddamn it, I want to follow where she goes.*

Gobi Desert, Africa
Day 11

Prize: A collection of water from the Fountain of Youth, infinite in number, worth seven points

Twenty miles she'd covered before finding the oasis with the Fountain of Youth. She'd scooped up its magical waters in an empty, dented Aquafina bottle and raised it over her heart in offering.

Everyone in the Lore knew that the Fountain moved from desert to desert all over the world. It was not, for instance, located in the swamps of the panhandle of Florida.

Conquistadors and their madcap ideas. How her sisters had chortled at the time.

Today she was allowing herself a more leisurely pace back, listening to Regin's iPod, which she'd left on the plane for Kaderin. The trek across the sand was uncomfortable enough without running. The sun scorched the desert like those food-heating lamps, keeping the area at a constant one hundred thirty degrees Fahrenheit. It seemed as if the sand were in its death throes, hissing at the sun.

Still, all in all, it was a good day. She was, for example, still alive.

She'd called Nïx back this morning from the car as she'd set out, hoping to catch her in a calmer frame of mind and confirm what she'd said. But, as was often the case, Nïx hadn't been lucid. She'd spoken frantically about "paper animal shapes all in a row" and "crass how-to books about the Lore." Nïx seemed to have no memory of her prediction. Kaderin provided the obligatory comments: "Is that so?" "How nice." "Sweet, let me talk to whoever is closest to you."

Even with this premonition hanging over her, Kaderin couldn't be depressed. Last night, she'd slept so perfectly, so soundly in Sebastian's warm arms, without a single nightmare. Not to mention the fact that she'd been thoroughly pleasured by him.

Besides, what else could one do with the knowledge of imminent death?

Yes, pleasured by a vampire. A gentleman warrior vampire who'd demonstrated enough strength to snap her foes like twigs and the ferocity on tap to unleash hell on them. And yet he possessed the understanding to spare a young dragon.

She'd left him miserable over the sheer fact that they

would be parted. And probably still scratching his head at her inane babbling. Which satisfied her.

As she crested another dune, she wondered if it was possible that she was falling for Sebastian. If so, the timing was pitiful. Finally to find a man she could potentially care for, and she could never have a future with him.

If she didn't die, and if she saved her sisters, she would change history—her history. She would never have been withering away in her cold, emotionless existence and never would have readily traveled to an obscure Russian castle to kill a single vampire. And somehow she knew she never would meet him in any reality, not before he finally died in whatever way.

One could go crazy trying to figure it all out.

So she wouldn't try. Instead she'd replay scenes from the night before—

Suddenly, she had the vaguest sense of his traced presence behind her. A second later: "*Bloody hell.*" Then he was gone.

He never saw her grin.

28

❦

Medellin, Colombia
Day 17

Prize: One golden and opal ring, first forged in
Mesopotamia, worth twelve points

Tonight, Kaderin's task was to get close enough to Rodrigo Gamboa, a Colombian drug lord guarded more closely than royalty, to acquire a ring, which never truly belonged to him.

Gamboa was notoriously cautious, and was rumored to have Lore blood in him. He moved most nights, and his compound was unassailable, so Kaderin was attending the grand opening of Descanso—Gamboa's newest club and money-laundry machine—which meant it was a rare event that would pin him down to one location.

Yet, unlike with Lore functions, Lady Kaderin was having to wait to get in—at the back of the line.

The difficulty in this task lay in the fact that the club would be full of humans. One had to get to him *and* avoid making a scene to alert humans to the Lore, or else be disqualified.

She'd have to make Gamboa behave rashly, persuade him to accompany her from the club, then take the ring from him when they were alone in the car. If she tried to nab the prize in public and then had to fight her way out, she'd definitely reveal she wasn't your average club kid. Her damned ears and the fact that she could toss cars always gave her away.

So tonight she planned to make nice with a boy.

Gone were her climbing shoes and heavy pack. Her sword was beneath the bed back at her hotel. Now she had tools of a different nature.

Get close to a man, quietly. She was a woman. *One plus one equals two.*

The upside of this task? She could bet that Bowen wouldn't be here.

But first she'd have to get in the club.

Wait! Was that Cindey in the line, way up front? Oh, no, she was not ahead of Kaderin. This was intolerable, and yet Kaderin couldn't just jog up there and drag Cindey out by her neck. As if she felt Kaderin's glare, Cindey leaned out from the line and gave her an arrogant wave.

Mustn't attack the siren . . . mustn't attack—

Suddenly Kaderin's jimmied untraceable sat phone rang. She slipped it from her little purse, and saw Myst's number on the i.d. "Why, Myst, how've you been?" she snapped in greeting. "Seems I owe you felicitations since you married your warlord."

Myst exhaled. "That wasn't my idea to keep you in the dark. But I also didn't think it would hurt anything to delay telling you for a couple of weeks. Especially since Nikolai and I eloped."

"Oh. Pagan ceremony?"

"Civil."

"Cool, I guess."

"So, you're Sebastian's Bride." When she didn't deny it, Myst asked, "What is going on with you and him?"

Kaderin stood on her toes to see ahead in the line. "I have no idea." Since the desert, she'd only met up with him for a couple of nights. She was zigzagging all over the world, and he'd caught her in the sun twice more. When they were together, he was reserved with her, standoffish even, which didn't surprise her after her harried reaction to the idea of marrying him.

What was taking this line so long? She'd kind of hoped to get in and out of this task. She suspected that if Sebastian did happen to show up, he might frown on her flirting—and on her clothing ensemble. Still, risking Sebastian's anger was better than a date with a very pesky werewolf.

"Sebastian's visiting with Nikolai right now. And from what I've been able to overhear of their conversations in the last couple of days, Sebastian has your memories," Myst said. "Are you letting him drink you?"

"Oh, for Freya's sake, you have got to be kidding me!" Kaderin cried, then glanced around, but no one in front of her in line was listening—and there was no one behind her. In a lower tone, Kaderin admitted, "He got dental with me. Accidentally."

"Look, Kad, I am ecstatic with Nikolai, but I realize this doesn't mean that all Valkyrie will be happy with all vampires. And I'm not sure . . . I don't know that Sebastian's head is in the right place with you. Especially with what you're trying to do. He doesn't really get it that you have to do anything to save your loved ones. He's a death-before-dishonor kind of guy."

"I've been getting an idea."

"It will kill Nikolai to see his brother suffer, but I can't let you make a mistake. I wouldn't let down my guard with him, not yet," Myst said. "And then, of course, there's the issue of Furie—"

"You know what, Myst?" Kaderin interrupted. "I can't even talk about this right now. You want to do me a favor? Keep Sebastian away from me tonight."

"How am I supposed to do that?" Myst cried. "The only thing he's interested in is hearing more about you."

"So, tell him things. Just not about the blessing. And not anything about Dasha and Rika."

"Is there anything else about you to tell?"

"Humorous, Myst."

"You asked for it, Kaderin the *Kind Hearted*," Myst said, referring to Kaderin's embarrassing former nickname. "Way to take my advice about not letting down your guard," she added.

As soon as they hung up and she stowed her phone in her purse, a burly bouncer scouted the line and spotted her. Oddly, he seemed to ogle the area of her pointed ears, hidden under her hair, instead of her short skirt.

But then he let her out of the velvet rope corral to go inside.

When she passed Cindey, Kaderin winced as if in sympathy. "Appears that the retro-hooker look wasn't making the cut tonight, Cin."

When Sebastian finally left Nikolai and a suspiciously chatty Myst back at Blachmount and traced to Kaderin, he found himself inside a nightclub like nothing he'd ever seen before. This had to be the task in Colombia. The one he'd hoped she wouldn't select.

Lights like lasers shot to the rounded ceiling in bizarre rapid patterns. Half-clad dancers in cages dangled high above the dance floor.

The cages reminded him of his last dream.

In it, Kaderin had strolled to an imprisoned man. He was young, his body beaten and broken. Without raising his head, he gritted out the words, *"Kill me."*

She smiled. "Of course, leech." Her voice was sugary. "In a few more months."

He sounded as if he began weeping.

"Then I might let you escape into the sun," Kaderin continued. "Your organs will liquefy inside you well before you die, pooling beneath your skin. But by that time, you'll crawl desperately for the light, I promise you. . . ."

Again, she'd felt nothing. No sympathy, no remorse, no hate, even.

Ever since he'd awakened, Sebastian had been filled with a marked disgust he couldn't shake. He'd visited Nikolai to ask him about these dreams, and Nikolai had warned him not to take her memories out of context. But how could Sebastian misunderstand that scene? It couldn't have been clearer.

He understood her cruelty, but that didn't mean it was easily witnessed—

Sebastian did a double take when he spied Kaderin, because he hardly recognized her.

Her eyes were kohled a deep blue, and her plump lips glistened. Her shirt was low-cut, deliberately displaying the lace of her bra. And her skirt was so short he could see her taut, lithe thighs almost up to the cleft of her ass when she slid into a booth with a group of people. Her black boots came to her knees and had wicked heels.

Even though he was furious with her for being here at all, much less dressed like this, the sight of her had his shaft rock-hard in an instant. He made a decision then—one night, he would be inside her when she wore those boots.

To all appearances, she was smiling and enjoying herself, but there was a hardness about her. The way she'd dressed left no doubt about how she planned to acquire the stone from the Colombian. No wonder Myst had been so willing to talk.

When he could drag his gaze away from Kaderin, he saw that all around her, men stared at her face or leered at her body. Sebastian's fists clenched. *Who to kill first—*

"Might as well sit," said a voice behind him. He whirled around and found the two nymphs. "Kaderin's going to be busy awhile."

He turned back in time to see a man slide in next to her and drape his arm around her shoulders. His hand almost brushed over her breast, and for the first time in his life, Sebastian *needed* to kill.

The first nymph sidled up to Sebastian. "We could pass the time. Vampire, forget about the Valkyrie. You're forbidden fruit to us as well, if that's your attraction to her."

Sebastian scarcely heard them over the pounding in his ears. "Is that the Colombian she's with?" he grated.

"That's him."

The bastard leaned over her and put his hand high on Kaderin's thigh, fingers teasing close to the hem of her skirt.

Rage exploded within Sebastian. This had to be a symptom of the blooding. He'd never felt such fury. Never.

He touches what's mine.

29

Sebastian was striding toward her, eyes black with rage, forcing people to scurry out of the way. Kaderin jumped up, excusing herself to rush behind the dance floor before he made a scene.

When he caught up with her, he clenched her arm and dragged her to a shadowy spot near the back wall. "By Christ, what are you doing?" His voice was seething. "You allowed him to touch you!"

"What are *you* doing?" she cried. She'd known if he did show up here, he wouldn't be pleased, but she'd also thought she'd get a chance to explain, instead of being manhandled. He acted as if he'd caught her in bed with a hockey team.

At first she was bewildered by his crazed expression and palpable fury. But when he tried to trace her from here and almost succeeded, her own ire flared. "Let go of me!" She flung his hand off her arm. "So help me, if that Colombian leaves without me—"

"*You plan to leave with him?*" he roared, clutching her shoulders, attempting to trace her once more. When she fought him, he scanned the building for a private spot, then dragged her into a small boothlike room with two seats and a telephone on a shelf. He slammed the door behind them, but the low thrumming beat of the music still vibrated the walls.

"How can you think to go with him tonight?"

"What I do is none of your business," she said, gritting the words through clenched teeth.

"Goddamn it, it is! His hands were all over you—and you *let* him touch you?"

"If I answer you, I'm acknowledging that you have a right to know. You don't."

"I will get the ring from the Colombian," he said quickly. "Trace beside him, take it, and trace away."

"It's forbidden. Do you know what every myth is?" When he didn't answer, she said, "A glaring example of when some Lore creature got careless. Each myth equals failure. Riora won't just disqualify you for a stunt like that—she will *punish* you."

"So, that's it, then? You've told me you're going home with another man? And I've already seen him touching you." He looked like he wanted to throttle her.

When she put her chin in the air, his eyes narrowed. "You may have your feelings back, but you're still a cold woman, Kaderin. Heartless." He clutched her nape, dragging her close. For some reason, they were both breathing heavily, audible even over the pulsing music. Before she could resist, he'd lifted her to rest on the shelf, then shoved up her skirt. He groaned to find nothing under it, then stiffened, his face becoming a mask of rage.

"Did you come here to fuck him?" With both of his hands grasping her head, he shoved his lips to her hair. "Do you want to see me snap? To kill? Why would you think I would let the mortal live if he took you?"

"Sebastian, just wait—"

He gave her a hard, punishing kiss as he pressed his palms against her thighs. Her body was tensed, but then, slowly, she began to respond to him—against her will, against reason.

Her breaths were quick. "Don't do this."

Though he was shaking with rage and lust, his fingers were gentle when he skimmed them up her thigh.

"Do you want my touch, Kaderin? Do you want to feel?"

This shouldn't happen—not now, not here. Hell, not at all. Even as she commanded herself to remember the task, she found herself responding.

Fury burned in him and his fangs sharpened with the undeniable need to mark her, to claim her as his in some way. The blooding was working on him once more.

His fangs ached to pierce her neck, and he knew he couldn't resist for much longer, knew that soon he would take her flesh savagely.

Why should he resist? *If she wants to leave with another man, she'll carry my mark. . . .*

He kissed up from her delicate collarbone, lips easing higher as his hands did on her thighs. He nuzzled her, fondling her sex, teasing her wetness again and again. When he pressed his finger inside her, she cried out, hands gripping his shoulders, clutching as her claws sank into his skin. He thrust a second into her, and she rolled her hips into his hand, fucking his fingers.

No more—he couldn't take this any longer.

He sank his fangs into her neck in a frenzied bite, almost coming instantly from the unbelievable pleasure. He was lost in the warmth of her blood, in the richness that was unique to her taste. He was lost in how tight her flesh was around his aching fangs—until he felt her body tensing around his fingers in a sudden orgasm.

From his bite.

He barely remembered to put his hand over her mouth, muffling her screams.

Her sex continued to tighten around his fingers so furiously he snarled against her skin, sucking her hard. The feel of drinking her was perfect. As if instinct was rewarding him for doing something that was unavoidable anyway.

But he stopped himself from drinking too deeply. Later, when he had her in his bed, he was going to take his release from her body while he drank her blood.

He slowly withdrew his fangs, licking the marks on her neck as he removed his fingers. When she shuddered as if with loss, he realized the bite he'd despised had made her his—even if only for a moment.

Eyes wide, lips parted, she brushed his mark with her fingertips. He'd shocked her. Good.

Then she seemed to wake up, drawing back from him. She hurriedly pulled her hair around to cover her neck, then yanked her skirt down.

When she gazed up at him, her eyes passed over his face as if she'd never seen him before. Her expression told him she was disgusted with what she found. "I don't care if you'll turn or not. You had no right to take my blood."

"Ah, Kaderin, you didn't seem to mind."

"*Thank you,*" she murmured.

He scowled. "For what?"

Her tone was quiet, grave. "For making this so easy. For making me see that there is nothing about you to tempt me to accept a vampire."

"You wanted to know why I desired to die?" he grated.

"Because I saw myself as you see me. You hate me for reasons I can't control. Reasons I'd hated myself for. But now, seeing your reaction to me makes it clear I was wrong. At least, you've saved me from my own self-loathing." After tonight, he would no longer be ashamed to walk down the street. He refused to look at himself the way she saw him.

"Do you think this is only about your thirst for blood? Give me one reason that I should choose you over every other man I've met in millennia and every one I'll meet in the eternity to come? You can't." She caught his eyes. "It's more than your being a vampire."

This struck home. Why would she see him any differently than other women had throughout his mortal life?

Because she was his Bride, he would be seduced into wanting her again and again, seeing things in her that didn't exist. Then her true nature would betray his hopes like this in an endless cycle.

He could not win her.

I'll be fighting with her for eternity. That's what faced him. The thought exhausted him.

"I'm weary of this. Of you." He put his hand above her against the wall, leaning over her. "You're right. About everything. There's no reason for you to accept me. And you were right in saying that I've been compelled to want you simply because you're my Bride. My desire for you has been forced on me. I've had no choice in the matter."

"You act as if I gave you reason to think differently," she said. "I told you all along that you shouldn't bother with me."

He clutched the back of her neck, forcing her face up to him. "You also told me on more than one occasion that you never wanted to see me again. I'll oblige you. I was the first vampire to trace to a person—and I'll be the first to forsake my Bride." Human females had begun gazing at him with open yearning, a marked contrast to the revulsion currently obvious on his Bride's face. He would take one of them. Or several.

He gave her a harsh, scalding kiss. "I will forget you, if I have to fuck a thousand women to do it." When he released her, there was nothing in her expression, infuriating him even more. "Perhaps I'll start with a female in the Lore."

Did he imagine the flicker of silver in her eyes? "Have fun with that."

"If you leave with the human, I won't leave alone, either."

As Kaderin marched back to the booth, she pulled her collar higher, feeling Sebastian's eyes on her. He'd bitten her. Not by accident. Not gently. Worse, in her position, she hadn't exactly been able to disguise her intense reaction to it.

Sebastian had bitten her.

And she'd *delighted* in it, coming with an intensity that staggered her.

She hated him for that. For her entire long life, she'd gone without being bitten, and he'd taken her neck in a phone booth in a sordid bar. She was disgusted with the situation and with her wanton response to him. She was sick of the entire night and eager to end it.

When she reached Gamboa's table, she found Cindey had taken her place beside him.

And that wouldn't do.

"You." She pointed at Gamboa. She knew that because of Sebastian's touch, her voice was husky, her hair tousled, and her nipples hard beneath the thin material of her blouse.

Gamboa stared, seeming dazed, then shrugged from

Cindey's arm as he stood. Cindey shot her a bitter look, recognized defeat, and drained her drink.

When Gamboa crossed to Kaderin as though spellbound, she murmured to him, "Take me somewhere private."

His jaw slackened. "Of . . . course." He hastily drew away to order his car brought round, and Kaderin took the chance to murmur to Cindey as she passed, "Why didn't you just sing?"

"Five hundred men in here would hear my song," she impatiently answered. "Besides, I'd prefer not to have the head of the most powerful drug cartel in the world violently captivated with me for the rest of his life. But I really hope it works out for you two kids."

Right after she whirled away, Gamboa joined Kaderin again. As they walked out, she saw Sebastian leaning over one of the nymphs, his eyes black. He cast the Colombian a killing look, then stared Kaderin down. The nymph gave Kaderin a triumphant smile and clutched Sebastian's arm.

If Sebastian was trying to make her jealous . . . he'd succeeded. Was he still hard after their encounter? What would he do to the nymph when he was heated with Kaderin's blood and aroused from her body? Trace the tramp somewhere and begin forsaking Kaderin?

When Gamboa put his hand on her lower back, she turned from Sebastian, forcing herself to look straight ahead. She didn't glance back even when she slid into Gamboa's plush limo and they started away.

Inside, her emotions simmered. Gamboa was talking to her in a low-toned, accented voice, but she wasn't hearing a word.

Sebastian's bite still throbs. . . .

She faced Gamboa, interrupting him to say, "Give me your opal ring, or I'll kill you."

He only smiled, even white teeth standing out against his tanned face. "Only the opal, *mi cariña?*" He glanced at a huge diamond ring he also wore, but she didn't follow his gaze. "You won't even look at the diamond?" he asked.

She raised an eyebrow. *He already knows.* "And why do you want me to?"

"Just to see if the rumors are true."

Kaderin exhaled. "You know what I am?"

He nodded. "My mother was a demon. I know all about the Lore."

"If you knew, then why did you let me go on?" she asked in an exasperated tone.

"Because I was curious why the opening of my club was filled with Lore beings."

"It's the Hie. The ring's a prize—a high-value prize. There were competitors and probably a score of local spectators."

He twisted the opal ring on his finger. "I've dreamed of seeing a Valkyrie all my life. This stone was predicted to bring one of your kind to it."

She didn't doubt that. Yet another example of the hand of fate at work. "Here. Behold the Valkyrie." She held out her palm. "The opal."

"It won't be that simple."

"Didn't figure you'd be the one drug dealer with a heart of gold."

"Why should I give it to you," he asked in a reasonable tone, "for nothing in return?"

A sudden thought arose. "It's not *me* you want. You just want a night with a Valkyrie, right?"

His eyes seemed to darken. "That's always been my fantasy."

"Then I will send another Valkyrie down here. One who's single." *I'm not?* "Her name is Regin the Radiant. She's a wild child. She glows. More important, she's a-sure-thing."

"How can I trust that you'll actually do this? Send her, and I'll give her the ring."

"I have to have that ring—now. And I'll vow to the Lore that she'll be here," she said, then amended that by saying, "Actually, I can't really vow that she'll sleep with you. And I would *not* recommend kissing her. But other than that, she's a party girl."

When he actually seemed to be considering the trade, she hid her surprise and said, "Just take the deal, Gamboa. I don't want to break your heart, or maul it, or pummel it tonight."

After a hesitation, he said, "How can I contact this Regin?"

Remembering that Regin had locked the Crazy Frog ring tone into Kaderin's favorite phone, she said, "How about I give you her private cell phone number?" *Turnabout's a bitch, Regin.*

He promptly handed her a card, and on the back she scratched down the area code and Regin's number—aptly, it was eight, six, seven, five, three, oh, nine. When Kaderin gave it to him, he removed the ring. He leaned closer, brushing her skin as he handed it to her. The touch did nothing for her, though he obviously thought it would. He should think that. Any woman would consider him sexy, and yet Kaderin felt no spark, no attraction.

"Tell the driver to stop the car at the next light."

"I'd give you the diamond as well if you'd stay tonight, *cariña*."

She should stay with him tonight. Sebastian was probably giving a nymph one of his fierce, heated kisses right now.

Instead, Kaderin murmured, "This sees me content."

Why not take the hot half-demon to bed? Because she wanted to go to her room. And cry.

30

Sebastian had hardly slept or drunk since the night in Colombia. For the last week, he'd struggled to get Kaderin out of his mind.

Nothing worked.

He was becoming obsessed with her. He gave a bitter laugh. *Becoming?* He was already obsessed with her.

Even after everything, he still wanted her.

Kaderin had gone to that club dressed for seduction, had fucked that male all night for all he knew—but at every opportunity, she'd told Sebastian she would never sleep with him.

For all his intentions, Sebastian hadn't touched another female, couldn't even imagine taking a woman who wasn't her. With that bite, he might have felt as though he were claiming her, but she'd claimed him as well. There was no way he was living his life without having it again.

No, he'd decided he'd settle for none but her. He needed to touch the body she withheld from him. He needed to hurt her as she'd hurt him.

She'd convinced him that her aversion to him wasn't merely because he was a vampire. And how could he not believe that, when he'd fared no better as a human?

Goddamn it, what is it about me?

That night all those years ago with the frigid widow had shaken him, crushed his already battered confidence. And even now it affected him. He hadn't been able to penetrate her. He was large, and she'd been completely cold. There'd been no arousal. No wonder—she wouldn't let him touch her body, not even her breasts. Just lifted her skirt in the bed without touching him, either.

She'd hissed in pain with each try, then finally beat against his back, screaming, "Enough, you bumbling oaf!"

He'd been twenty-three and bewildered by her sudden disgust. "Then . . . why?"

Every word enunciated, she'd said, "*I lost a wager.* . . ."

Now, Kaderin, the woman he wanted more than he'd ever wanted anything, desired him just as little.

Without fail, he'd been kind to women. He'd shown them respect and courtesy. Without fail, he'd never had success with them.

When he found Kaderin next, he would steal the prize she sought. Then he'd strike another bargain with her—this time for another pleasure denied him as a mortal, one he'd fantasized about for so long.

He didn't recognize himself in the mirror. His face was pale and gaunt, his eyes constantly black.

He was becoming as ruthless as she was. Gone were the impulses to tenderness, the feeling of being charmed when she tucked her hair behind her pointed ear or blushed along her cheekbones.

Maybe when all was said and done and he'd turned as vicious as she was, he'd be a fitting mate for her.

Battambang Province, Cambodia
Day 24

**Prize: The Box of the Nagas, one ancient wooden box
carved with the heads of five Nagas,
worth thirteen points**

In the darkened night, through pounding rain, Kaderin spied an odd treeless field. In this region, the sweeping jungle tumbled over everything stationary, from car chassis to carved temple, but not here. No homes were built in the field. Only piles of rusted junk littered it.

At the edge, a sign stood planted at an angle, with creeping vines weighing it down. She tugged the vines from it and found the square metal of the sign had been cut into an hourglass shape, most likely so the locals wouldn't use it for roofing material.

Emblazoned across the front was a skull-and-crossbones warning.

So this would be it—a boundary minefield clotted with explosives.

And somewhere in the center was buried a wooden box carved with Nagas, serpent gods. Inside that was a sapphire the size of her palm.

Riora didn't seek the sapphire; she wanted that box.

With the steady rain—May equaled monsoon season—the field was more of a morass, with soupy mud and splashing puddles. Kaderin exhaled. Mines *hurt*, but she needed some high-dollar points. She, the Lykae, and the siren continued to be neck-and-neck. There was only one prize here, and she had to have it.

At the edge, she swallowed. *Easy to lose a foot here.* She'd lost a foot before, and she had to say she'd enjoyed cheerier scenarios.

She flexed her fingers, then got to work, scanning for something heavy to toss into the quagmire. If she was quick, she could detonate quite a few—

Her ear twitched. Over the strengthening rain, she barely heard the stealthy movements of a predator. *No . . . not the . . .*

Son of a bitch. There was Bowen, and just to his right, the sodding siren.

The three grasped the situation at the same time. All dashed heedlessly past the warning sign, sprinting out into the muddy space. The Lykae was fast and ran as though crazed. He let his beast out of its cage, turning in the midst of the field, his body becoming bigger, fangs lengthening. His normally short, dark claws shot longer and grew stronger. When he glanced back to snarl at Kaderin, she saw his amber eyes had turned ice blue.

Though Kaderin was fast and Cindey was strong over the slogging terrain, they shouldn't be able to keep up with him as they were. He'd smoked her in the cave. The witch must really have cursed him.

Kaderin ran in his path, exactly where mud flew up in intervals, letting him take the risk. Cindey began gunning to pass Kaderin on the right.

An idea arose. Kaderin pumped her arms, darting forward. "Cindey!" she called. "The right leg!"

She nodded. A breath later, they both dove for him, tackling him into the mucky ground. He twisted around, white fangs bared, snapping at Cindey, who jammed her elbow into his throat. He slashed out at Kaderin with his deadly claws, but she sprang back. They whistled by just millimeters from her face. If Mariketa hadn't weakened him, they'd both be dead.

As the two wrestled to hold him, inflicting injuries to down the large male, he fought like the animal he was. The three covered a large area, yet they hadn't triggered a mine—there had to be one close by. "Kick, you idiot!" Kaderin screamed to Cindey.

They dodged claws, booting his chest to send him rolling over and over far back. All three heard the distinct metallic *click*. He had time only to grit his teeth.

Light flashed. Kaderin yanked the siren in front of herself for cover. Bowen flew in a hail of red mud fifty feet away, but the explosion caught them as well, catapulting them back.

When it ceased raining clumps of earth, Kaderin shoved Cindey off her. Moaning, Cindey staggered to her feet, holding her sensitive ears, blown from the percussion. She had blood splattered all over her, running down her bared arms and neck through runnels of mud.

As Kaderin scrambled to her feet, she saw Bowen, who had a short bar of shrapnel jutting out from his ribs. Claws digging into the ground, he rose to his hands and knees, then unsteadily to his feet. He must know that if he removed the metal, the blood loss would put him out of this.

Kaderin took inventory, assessing her own injuries. Apparently, she'd caught a good bounce for once, just a few scratches.

Incredibly, Bowen loped ahead, dripping blood, turning back toward the explosion. She yanked her head around, perceived a kind of fluorescence in one of the puddles. The explosion must have unearthed the box. She surged forward, darting through the mud, uncaring of the mines. She gained on Bowen.

The bar was skewered completely through him. His jostling run was no doubt agony, but he was still going. Soon they were side by side. There, glowing before them, was a wooden case, smaller than a cigar box. It was sealed and bobbing like flotsam.

Kaderin dove for it, just as Bowen did. Sliding through the mud, they collided, butting heads so hard her vision briefly blurred. The box went sloshing back.

His ice-blue eyes showed a complete loss of reason. His voice was guttural and breaking. "You're about to wish I could kill you."

They both dove forward once more, grappling for the prize. As it bobbed down, they rooted blindly for it, uncaring if they were about to have their hands and faces blown off. They each snagged it with one hand. She hissed, snapping her teeth, reaching over her shoulder for her sword just as he raised a hand spiked with those deadly claws—

Sebastian appeared, seizing the box from both of them.

Kaderin blinked up at Sebastian through the rain. Time seemed to stand still.

She was transfixed, awed, by the savagery in his jet eyes, the harsh lines of his face, his coal-black hair whipping over his chin.

Suddenly, she was desperate to be the female a male like that would always come for. Ached to be her.

He stood with one foot in front of the other. She understood why immediately—he was standing on a mine. Judging by the menacing look on his face, this was on purpose. He held out his hand. "*Come to me.*" She lunged for him just as Bowen did. Sebastian snatched her away and traced them to the edge of the field.

The mine exploded. Sebastian pushed her back behind him, much as he had that night at Riora's assembly.

When the air cleared, she edged beside him and saw Bowen shuddering, lying on his front where he'd landed. Blood ran freely from his mouth. He mumbled what sounded like a woman's name. Of course, his mate's name.

He seemed to sense they were still there, and raised his face. She hissed in a breath at the sight. One eye was gone, and the left side of his forehead and temple had been burned away. But his wasted body and dazed mind were still desperate for the prize, for the mate he'd lost as she'd fled him so many years ago. Somehow he was digging those claws into the ground to drag himself forward.

"Trace me, Sebastian," she whispered. He did nothing. "He'll hit another mine if we stay."

"Exactly." Sebastian's eyes were dark as the night and chilling. "He deserves it for what he did to you."

Bowen was crawling toward them, and Cindey was walking in circles, blood pouring from her ears, mumbling something . . . something about a baby, and Kaderin couldn't watch any longer. In the past, she'd have looked on with satisfaction as her competitors suffered.

But she was different now. Or, more accurately, she was as she used to be from the very beginning.

"*Please, Bastian,*" she cried, turning to grab his shirt with both hands. He tensed with surprise, studying her face. Whatever he saw in her expression had him wrapping her tightly in his arms and tracing her away.

Bowen's anguished roars echoed in her ears long after they'd disappeared.

31

Back in her flat, she shivered in her wet clothes. The storm seemed to have followed them to London and raged outside. Dusk had just settled over the city. It was six hours earlier here than in Cambodia, which meant the night had started over for her. For them.

Without a word, he tucked the box into his jacket pocket, then took her hand, leading her to her bathroom. He turned on the shower, then began to unbutton her shirt.

His eyes were as wild as that Lykae's had been. "Do you want that box, Kaderin?"

She nodded, still out of breath.

He pushed her shirt past her shoulders, then pulled it down her arms, freeing it. "You have to pay for it." He unclasped the fastening at the front of her soaked-through bra, then it, too, fell to the ground. At the sight of her breasts, he inhaled deeply but didn't touch her, only continued to undress her. She had to hold on to his shoulders as he unzipped her pants and dragged them and her panties from her.

When she stood before him, completely unclothed, she asked in a bewildered tone, "What do you want?" She was still dazed—not only by the violence of the night, but by that look of his in the rain. She shivered to recall it.

"Wash off the mud, and come to the bedroom," he ordered, his voice rough.

She stared at the door for long moments after he left. Then she noticed, in *her* bathroom, all of *his* things. Razor, toothbrush, soap. The bastard had moved in? Her attention had been focused on him when they first arrived, but now she could recall seeing books and newspapers lying scattered throughout the flat. A pair of boots had been kicked off at the door. "The bloody squatter," she muttered as she stepped under the water.

As she scrubbed away at the mud covering her, she wondered what he would demand. She was infuriated, but at the same time, she was burning with curiosity.

Would he try to drink her again? Or make love to her? Or both? She hated that imagining *either* made her aroused.

But even though she truly yearned to make love to the man she'd seen in the storm and confusion tonight, she wouldn't be coerced into it.

After washing her hair, she dried off and shrugged into a pink silk robe. When she returned to the bedroom, stepping around *his* things, he stood.

He'd removed his wet jacket and shirt. His chest was still damp, the muscles tense. His eyes were black once more. "Come here," he said, and she could barely make her feet move.

Worrying her bottom lip, she crossed to him. When she stood in front of him, he wasted no time, palming the curves of her ass under her robe, making her gasp.

Then he languidly kissed her neck with slow licks, before dipping to her breasts. When he sucked her nipple through the silk, she moaned, and her knees went weak. But he held her firmly.

"Bastian," she breathed. "I want to tell you something." Would he believe she never intended to go to bed with Gamboa?

He drew away. "The time for talking is over. Now, do you want your trinket or not?"

"I won't make love to you," she told him.

His lips curled into a cruel smirk. "You assume that I *want* to make love to you?"

She blinked up at him, clearly surprised by his words. "What if I told you that I want you to give me the prize? As a gift to your Bride? You offered once."

"We're past that. I'm not a gentleman anymore. I'm not even a human. And you're no lady."

When he pressed down on her shoulders, there was no mistaking what he desired. She stiffened, but he said, "Oh, no, you want your prize, then you'll do as I wish."

She went to her knees before him. "Couldn't get a nymph to do this?"

"Why would I settle for a nymph when I have a Valkyrie at my bidding?"

"And *this* is what you want?" she asked, gazing up at him.

"Yes," he rasped, one hand on her head, the other clutching her nape. He wanted her before him like this, to be forced to look up at him and acknowledge that he was in control. He could master her if he chose. He wanted her to taste him, to show him this pleasure.

No, not like this.

Where did that thought come from? When he was so goddamned close to finally knowing what this was like?

He ground his teeth, not even able to imagine what her mouth closing over his shaft would feel like. But doubt nagged him. Lust warred with an indistinct warning deep inside him.

The way she turned to me tonight . . .

He choked out, "Stop." He clutched her shoulders. "Get off your knees. I don't want you to do this." He yanked her to her feet, then strode away. "This would make you a whore. I can't do that."

"How is it different from the basilisk's egg?" she asked, her tone rising with anger.

"Then I sought only to touch you."

Her eyes flashed silver. "Why do you even care if this would brand me a whore?"

"Do you know what this is like? I know you care nothing for me, but I feel as if we're wed. For you to have gone to another man . . . and let him touch you . . ." He ran his hand over his face, his arousal waning quickly. "Forget it." He tossed the box onto the bed and turned away. "You can have it."

"Payment on the pillow? But, Sebastian, I didn't *earn* it." Before he could trace, she said, "By the way, you arrogant ass . . ."

She sauntered to his back, trailing a finger over his shoulders, which tensed from the light touch. Lowering her voice to a breathy tone, she said, "You've just sacrificed the chance to experience how an immortal female *worships* a male with her mouth."

Her finger skimmed to his front as she walked around to face him. She stood on her toes, and at his ear, she murmured, "I would have given you the hottest, wettest kiss you've ever received. I would have spent ages taking you with my tongue."

Sudden sweat beaded on his forehead.

"But now, I've only to thank you for saving me all those *hours*."

He shuddered, then strode away from her with a grated sound of frustration. "Do you think this was easy to give up when it would be from you?" He felt crazed with lust. Curiosity goaded him. He threw his hands up, pacing in long strides. "Seeing you on your knees when I've never had—"

"Had what?" When he said nothing, just stilled and ran his hand over the back of his neck, she asked softly, "You've never had that?"

Sebastian looked away sharply, unwilling to admit it to her, and unable to deny it.

He isn't denying it? Kaderin's lips parted. *He's never experienced that?*

The idea shocked her. Then it *stirred* her, making shivers dance up her spine.

I could be his first.

She could admit that her anger had come partly from thwarted desire. When the wet material of his pants had hugged his thick shaft in front of her, she'd grown weak with humiliation and heat because she'd wanted to taste him. Now that arousal roared to life once more.

To be a male's first at anything? She tilted her head at him. "Have you . . . imagined me doing it to you?"

He scowled as if her question was absurd.

"I see." He seemed volatile, seething inside. She felt as if she'd cornered a wounded bear and needed to move gingerly. "Why would you give away the opportunity?"

He snapped, "Because it's not over with us!"

She drew back her head. "Even after Colombia?"

He crossed to her. "Tonight, at the minefield, you were *different*. It's . . . just not over."

At his words, a well of emotion swept her up. Desire, yes, but now she could admit there was much more. Sebastian had wanted to be cruel to her—clearly had needed to be.

Yet he couldn't.

Even when he craved this pleasure so badly, he couldn't force her to do it.

Suddenly, tenderness for him threatened to overwhelm her. So much so that the thought of him yearning all these years for something he'd never experienced made her ache as well. She found it unbearable to think of him wondering what it would be like with her.

She'd desired the merciless man she'd gazed up at in the rain, but she also hungered for the man here before her now with vulnerability in his eyes. "What if I wanted to do it?" She nibbled her bottom lip. "Would you still like me to?"

She saw him go hard as steel again. "I . . . only . . . only if you wanted to."

Oh, she did. She lifted her hand to stroke his face tenderly. He closed his eyes briefly at her touch. *And I'm going to make it so damn good.* If he'd waited his entire life for it, she'd guarantee it would be worth the wait.

And, of course, she had to live up to her careless bragging. *"Worship," Kaderin? Well, actually* . . . She recalled a scene she'd inadvertently witnessed long ago. She'd crept into a dark warlock's harem to free a witch who'd found good favor with the Valkyrie. The Valkyrie weren't susceptible to spells, but this warlock had been powerful and Kaderin had been alone. She'd found a hiding place to stay until everyone went to sleep.

She'd ultimately waited till dawn. Because one of his

concubines had pleasured him for hour after hour in a most *original* manner.

Kaderin had filed the idea away, thinking, *One day, if I find those desires again, I'd really like to try this.*

That time was now. She wanted to give Sebastian an experience to remember—for eternity. An immortal version of what he'd fantasized about. "I *do* want to, Bastian." Now she laced her arms around his neck. "But I have conditions."

A hint of a wounded half-grin. "You always have conditions."

"I think you can live with these."

Ten minutes later, Sebastian found himself chained to Kaderin's bed.

He should have seen that wicked glint in her eyes and traced the other way.

But she'd been giving him soft kisses with those ruby lips as she'd smoothed her palms over his chest and torso. When she'd asked him to give her five minutes to get ready, he'd obliged and left the bedroom. He'd been kicking off his boots when she'd come to take his hand, stroking it sensuously with her thumb. She'd tucked her hair behind her ear, smiling at him over her shoulder as she led him to her bed.

Did he ask what she'd done in her room? Hell, no. At that point, and after that bewitching smile, if she'd murmured, "I'm leading you into the fiery depths of hell," he'd have followed dumbly.

Then they'd lain on the bed, slowly kissing again. The way she would give soft moans into his mouth maddened him. When she lapped her tongue against his, he couldn't stop imagining how it would feel on his cock. . . .

Then he'd suddenly found one wrist shackled to a chain she'd stretched under her bed. "What the bloody hell—?"

"Bastian, it's a condition of this deal."

Warnings had arisen. *This is not wise.* They'd just been fighting. They'd resolved nothing between them. But he knew he could break free if need be. He could trace free. *Why would she want this?*

Then she'd smiled once more, that seductive curl of her lips, and he could no longer think of anything but sliding his shaft between them. He let her chain the other wrist.

When he was secured, she'd surveyed him with eyes gone silver and licked her lips.

And one second ago, he'd watched in astonishment as she clawed his pants off, leaving him without a thread on.

"I imagined this that first morning with you," she said, pressing her lips to his torso. Her damp hair grazed over his skin, making him shudder with pleasure. "Imagined ripping off your pants to get my mouth on your shaft."

He groaned in disbelief, wondering if he'd die of ecstasy when he felt her warm breaths going lower. If this was a dream, he'd be damned if he would wake. After nuzzling the trail of hair leading down from his navel, she glanced up. "Are you ready?"

"Christ, yes, I've *been* ready—"

The first touch of her hot little tongue, running across the head of his shaft, stopped his breath.

"*Ah, God,*" he finally managed. When the slit grew moist, she dipped her tongue down and gave it a dabbing lick.

His eyes rolled back in his head.

Then came the long, slow slide of her wet lips. He arched his back. When she flicked her tongue while he was in her mouth, the pleasure was so intense he yelled out. With effort, he raised his head to witness it—he had to see this—breaths going ragged at the sight of her taking him in.

He wanted to brush her hair aside to see better, but the chains prevented him. He could have broken them easily, but she'd deemed the chains a condition. He'd never jeopardize this.

As if she'd read his mind, she smoothed her hair over one shoulder, giving him an unimpeded view.

He hissed in a breath when she caressed her face against the length, lovingly, as she had that first morning against his cheek. "What do you think?"

"Can't seem to," he said, choking out the words. She smiled.

Completely uninhibited, she continued her ministrations, making it impossible to hold out much longer. Her mouth was so hot and wet, he wanted it to go on forever, but he felt his sack tightening. "*About to come. . . .*" Just when he was about to go over the edge, she released him from her mouth, as he'd expected. He didn't dare think she'd take all of him.

"No, Bastian, you're really not."

32

❦

Brows drawn together, Sebastian grated, "Think I'd know this."

She squeezed the head of his erection in her fist, preventing him from ejaculating, then hid her surprise. *It worked!*

His shaft was swollen with seed, the pressure visibly paining him. They both stared at it, before meeting eyes.

She saw the exact moment realization hit him. "You can't mean to . . ."

When she nodded, he yanked on the chains, seeming incredulous that they were holding him.

"The chains have been mystically reinforced," she explained with a leisurely lick. "Not even an immortal as strong as you can break them, and you can't trace from them, either."

He still tried to. "Let me free," he growled. "Is this some kind of revenge?" His naked body was wracked with tension, every muscle bulging as he fought the chains. His arms grew even more huge with effort.

"Not revenge, Bastian." Once his seed descended again, and he wasn't in immediate danger of release, she removed her robe. His struggles eased as his lips parted. She leaned over, breasts close to his mouth, to prop up his head with a pillow. With his gaze riveted to her body, his battle to be free subsided. When she straddled him, he stilled completely, as if he'd forgotten to resist.

"*Closer*," he commanded.

She moved in, holding her breasts to his mouth, one, then the other. He sucked her nipples hard, groaning around each, hands clenching in the manacles.

When she pulled away, he bit out curses—until she moved down his body to take him with her mouth once more. She relished the taste of his flesh, loved how responsive he was, how disbelieving when she licked the base and down to his heavy sack.

"*These things you do to me . . . my God, I didn't know . . .*"

She couldn't take all of his prodigious length, so she used her hand as well, stroking the base.

"Katja, I'm about—"

She gripped him hard, preventing him again, and he yelled out in agony. He dug his heels into the bed to thrust, to shake her hand loose, desperate to lose his seed in any way. Never had she seen anything so erotic as his body twisting in the chains.

But she held firm, and soon he grew drugged with lust, nearly insensible. His chest was slicked with sweat, and his entire body quaked with the need for release. He reverted to his native language, and the things he told her made it clear he didn't think she could understand him. However, she spoke Estonian fluently.

Oh. Had she forgotten to tell him?

He rasped that she was his *kena*, his *darling*, that she was so precious to him. He admitted he hadn't been able to tell her that, no matter how badly he'd needed to.

He would die if he knew I can understand him.

He told her he wanted her with him, *only* him, after this

night. Just as he'd been loyal to her and would ever be. *For always*. . . .

Sebastian hadn't had another that night in Colombia? Emotion trilled through her, making her toes curl, and she became hungrier for him—if possible—and aroused to the point of agony.

Her fingers longed to trail down to her sex for what would be an instant release. *Loyal for always?* She shivered, kissing him lovingly now, breathing hot and fast. She couldn't stop a moan—

Immediately, he lifted his head, shaking it hard, as if to clear a haze. "*Let me free.*"

What had brought about this abrupt change? "Bastian, this time I promise you can—"

"Let me free, or I *will* find a way out of these chains." His demeanor was becoming alarming. His eyes were narrowed and black.

Seeing that he was serious, she leaned up. "Why? Didn't you like what I was doing?"

He yanked on the chains, straining, as her eyes went wide.

She wasn't at all certain she wanted to release the vampire she'd just been sexually tormenting. While she was naked and needing. And not when his eyes promised retaliation. "Wh-what do you want to do?" Good money said, *To turn the tables*.

If she unlocked those shackles, he'd take her this very night.

Now she felt like *he* was skipping a step.

She hadn't been prepared to have sex with him yet. *Yet?* Oh, gods. As if it had been a foregone conclusion. She'd only slept with men she'd trusted, and for all of Sebastian's considerable charms, she did not trust him.

He strained against the bonds even harder than before, but no vampire could break through those—he'd only hurt himself.

Suddenly, she became very conscious of how much larger he was than she. His cut muscles that usually thrilled her now made her swallow with alarm. His shaft, which she'd always found so big and wondrous, daunted her.

Everything added up to make her want to run, but when a trickle of blood slid from his wrist, she cried, "Wait!" and dove forward for the key. With trembling hands, she unlocked him—

In an instant, he tossed her onto her back, looming over her, and began palming and fondling her between her thighs. He groaned to the ceiling to find her so wet.

"Bastian! What're you doing?"

He faced her. "*It's time.*" His voice was unrecognizable.

"Wh-whoa, what time? Why now?"

"You're denying us for no reason . . . you want me, too." His whole hand covered her sex possessively, rubbing. "Tell me you don't need me inside you, and I'll stop." With his other hand, he grasped her breast, brushing his thumb over her jutting nipple. "Tell me."

She glanced away, gritting her teeth. Finally, between panting breaths, she said, "If we do this, Sebastian, there's no making love. There's no *claiming* me, like I'm lost luggage. This isn't a promise of any kind. Just meaningless sex." Surely he'd balk at that?

Instead, he grated, "Agreed."

"Wh-what? You're agreeing to meaningless sex?"

"Any kind with you, Bride." The dark look he gave her made her shiver, even before he growled, "I'm *due*."

"So you think you're just going to take the reins?" *If he does, I'm lost.*

In answer, Sebastian knelt between her legs, shoving them apart with his knees.

Kaderin was so beautiful, her breasts lush beneath his hands, her nipples stiff against his palms. Her sex was visibly wet, waiting to be filled, and his cock throbbed to be buried inside it.

"Sebastian, we can't just do this! I'm not ready—" Her words died in her throat when he slipped his finger inside her.

"You feel ready." He pressed a second finger in.

When her knees fell wide in surrender, he knew he was about to have her, at last, and nothing would stop him. Not after what she'd just been doing to him—and to herself. His Bride desired him, had moaned around his shaft as she licked it desperately. Her kiss had maddened him, but the idea of her aching for what he could give her was too much to take.

He didn't want to hurt her, though, and he knew he'd never been this hard. He could hold on a little longer and make sure her body was ready for him.

His fingers thrust in and out, slowly, as he played with her nipples, and soon she was as frenzied as he was. "Bastian," she cried. "I'm ready!"

When she tried to draw him down to her, claws biting into his shoulders, he caught her wrists above her head with one hand.

She went wild. Cries burst from her as she arched her back sharply. He'd known taking her would be furious. . . .

With his other hand, he grasped his shaft to guide it in. When the tip met her heat, he bit out an agonized curse, and ran the head up and down her slick sex.

"Please . . ."

He worked just the head in, and groaned in anguish. The urge to buck between her legs or fall into her was overwhelming. He choked out the words, "You're so tight." As tight as he suspected a virgin would be.

She was panting, her soft breasts pressed against his chest as she rolled her hips on his cock head to work more of it inside her. He had to release her wrists so he could clamp his hands on her hips and pin her down to the mattress.

He was desperate for release, for *her* release. He would follow her if it killed him. As he drove his length into her, inch by inch, he gritted his teeth. When he flexed his hips, plunging deeper, she cried out, and he froze. "Ah, God, I've hurt you."

As soon as he'd said it, he *felt* the real reason she'd cried out, and threw his head back at the shock of pleasure. She was coming—her sex contracting frantically around his shaft, gripping it like a hot fist, her body demanding what he had to give it.

Her orgasm continued on and on, pulling him deeper inside her. *He'd never imagined . . .*

After that, there was no denying her wet, hungry sheath. Unable to stop himself, he sank into her as far as he could go, grinding against her, yelling out, about to lose his seed right then.

He'd never known . . .

Her head thrashed on the pillow, and her sleek body twisted beneath him. Her legs tightened around his waist, locking his cock deep as she writhed, as untamed as he'd known she would be.

The pressure . . . her tight heat.

No fighting this. Pinning her down hard, he bucked uncontrollably. He gave a brutal yell as his seed came. He groaned out with each shot, over and over, relentless, as she delivered the most violent pleasure he'd ever imagined.

33

❧

Kaderin strode down the street, barely after dawn, having just left the beautiful passed-out vampire—and the box—behind.

She'd vacillated for an hour about whether to claim the points or not. In the end she couldn't do it, though she'd gotten as far as lifting the box to just below her heart. She supposed that part of her anatomy had been as affected as all the rest of her after last night.

Although she needed to get to the jetport to be ready for the next update of the scroll, she kept hesitating, distracted, replaying scenes from last night.

After he'd reached his end, he had continued to thrust so gently, rocking over her in the dark, brushing his lips over her face. She'd known he wanted to have her again, but he'd been very pale. When his body had begun shaking, she'd suspected he hadn't been drinking regularly. He had finally rolled over to his back, drawing her to his chest with the crook of his arm.

Now that she and Sebastian had made love, everything felt different to her. This morning, she was seeing things in ways she couldn't remember. Spring always imbued London with miraculous colors and scents, but she couldn't recall the last time she'd noticed.

She'd watched this city grow from a soggy camp to a grand metropolis. The thought made her pause. She was *old*. And last night also had brought into glaring relief how dissatisfied she was with her life overall. Of course, she missed her sisters, but she fully expected to retrieve them, even if she died.

Kaderin believed that sacrifice could bring them back. How many fables—which were ninety-nine percent true— told of a warrior given a chance to make up for a grievous lack of judgment? Atonement had to be Kaderin's ultimate fate. If she was to die, surely it wouldn't be for nothing? Sacrifice could restore her sisters to life, and as far as destinies went, she was honored by hers.

And besides, did she want to live forever? She *had*!

Before last night, she couldn't bestir herself truly to dread her upcoming death. Now, she wondered if it would be painful, and if Sebastian would be near.

She'd called Nïx on her jimmied non-traceable phone to get a premonition-of-doom update. She had imagined what she would say: "Hey, Nïxie! Uh, I remember you telling me that I, uh, was going to die and all that." Nervous laugh. "Well, did you see anything about a remarkably virile and sexy vampire coming with me for moral support?" But it had been late at night in New Orleans, and Nïx had most likely been out roaming the streets. Without answers, Kaderin could only speculate.

There were only so many ways a Valkyrie could die— beheading, sorrow, immolation, or some kind of mystical assassination. Beheading seemed likeliest.

A violent death. Kaderin had contemplated cheerier scenarios. . . .

As she smelled the cherry blossoms, she thought of the violence *she* had meted out over her long life, culminating in the minefield carnage last night. She recalled Bowen yearning for his lost mate, half of his head blown off and still crawling for the box. She thought Cindey had mumbled something about a baby.

Kaderin's eyes watered, and she stumbled into someone on the street. When she glanced up again, there right before her was a butcher shop.

She bit her bottom lip, recalling Sebastian's pale face. Did she dare take him blood? She looked around guiltily, as if others could hear her thoughts.

This was a step she'd never even contemplated. She wasn't merely *not* going to kill the vampire, nor was she simply *allowing* him to live. She was considering making a vampire more comfortable after the cataclysmic sex they'd just had. She gave an amazed chuckle. *How far the mighty have fallen.*

Kaderin found herself entering the shop, swept up in the foreign smell of meat. She asked for her order, and without a raised brow—this was London, after all—she received a plastic container in a brown paper bag. She fished for sterling and pence from her jacket pocket, then hurried from the shop with her purchase.

Here she was late for the airport, and all she could think about was that she'd left him hungry. This was so . . . so domestic, and it was utterly exciting for her. As it had been with him on the plane that morning while they were dressing. *Just before he told me he was going to marry me.*

Back at the flat, she noticed she kind of liked seeing his things with hers. Gone was the irritation at the fact that he'd simply moved in with her. Now she suddenly wanted their belongings to be *together*. She wanted their things *intermingled*.

She stowed the blood in the refrigerator and was immediately glad she'd brought it, because, though he seemed to have moved in, he had none on tap.

After making her way to the bedroom, she crossed to the bed. She brushed his hair from his forehead and pulled the cover over him. *Tenderness. I like this feeling. Quickly becoming one of my favorites.* Before she left the room again, she secured a blanket over the drapes as an additional safeguard against the sun.

Take away the fact that he was a vampire. Could she ever have a life with him? She overlooked Emma's vampirism and loved her.

But it didn't matter if Kaderin could accept him. Her sisters wouldn't be able to—even if she somehow would meet Sebastian in the changed reality, which she knew was impossible, even if she lived.

If she lived, she'd have saved Dasha and Rika. Saving their lives would change history. . . .

She'd thought about carrying a letter back for herself when she retrieved her sisters. But she knew how these conundrums typically worked. If she wrote a letter, telling herself to go to the Russian castle and fall for a sad-eyed, achingly gorgeous vampire, her past self wouldn't even recognize her changed handwriting. She'd think it was a trick by vampires, and she'd go there to kill him. Or someone in her coven would find the letter and go with the same intent.

And yet, even knowing how unattainable a future was with him, before she left once more, she jotted a quick note *for him*.

And mentally tallied one for herself: *Idiot, sucker, fool. Mysty the Vampire Layer? She's got nothing on me.*

*   *   *

She wasn't in the bed with him when he awoke that afternoon.

Sebastian sat up, wanting to find her, but instantly fell back, arms and legs deadened with fatigue and splayed across the bed.

Staring at the ceiling, he tried to sort through what had happened.

He'd spoken in Estonian and *she'd responded in kind*. He grated a curse. The things he'd said . . . He groaned, throwing an arm over his face.

But he'd been out of his mind. And what man wouldn't be while experiencing the act for the first time—and in such a manner? Much less knowing she was enjoying it.

And then . . . *sinking inside her*.

The most incredible experience in his entire life.

He ran his fingers through his hair as reality set in. With Kaderin, he might never experience any of it again. He wanted a loyal bond between the two of them; she'd already left without a word. This was only physical for her, like the quick release she'd craved in the cave, when he'd wanted to touch her for hours. His heart sank as he realized nothing had changed between them, just as she'd warned him before he'd taken her. And the last time they'd spoken of the future, he'd vowed that he wouldn't be in hers—

He glanced up, spying a note on the bedside table. He snatched it like a drowning man cast a lifeline.

There's blood in the refrigerator. Will be in sun today, so call me when you wake up—I put my number in your phone.
  xoxo Kaderin.

His jaw slackened. Though the letter was short, he found himself rereading it. It was like a note a wife would leave for her husband, and so he couldn't wrap his mind around it. They'd resolved nothing last night and still had the same angers between them.

Is she playing with me? Is this some sort of cruel jest? Do I have a phone?

Confounded, he scuffed naked into the kitchen to the refrigerator, taking a deep breath as he grasped the handle. There, the only thing inside—a plain paper bag.

She'd brought him blood. *Why would she do this? Is it poisoned?* He took the bag out and tossed it onto the counter, but as he turned, he saw the box from the minefield. She'd left it.

He shut the refrigerator door and repeatedly knocked his head against it.

Congo River Basin, Democratic Republic of Congo Day 25

Prize: One jade jaguar pentacle, altar tool for demonolatry, worth thirteen points

When Sebastian traced to her and found himself in a sweltering brush, he recognized which prize Kaderin had chosen.

She had navigated the jungle—the equatorial jungle—from the low lying riverside to these highlands of the Virunga Massif. Nearby was a pounding waterfall, and beside it lay an ancient grave. The prize was buried there in the rich, dark earth.

Though the canopy was dense, he was still burning,

avoiding shafts of light as though they were spears raining down. But it didn't matter, he had to do anything possible to help her . . . since she'd given up the box.

He carried it in his jacket pocket and ran his finger over it, wishing the prize weren't expired.

Was he pleased that she didn't want that between them? Without question. But now, all he could think about was the incredible number of points she'd sacrificed toward a win that she'd obviously kill for.

Where the hell is she? He couldn't spy her out through the thick growth and the waterfall's mist, but he couldn't remain much longer—

A branch cracked behind him. He whirled around—to catch the flat of a shovel with his face.

The metal clanged against his skull, reverberating . . . until . . . blackness.

When he awoke, he was being dragged. *The Scot? His face is wasted. Too weak to trace. Try again.* Blackness wavered once more.

"To some of us, leech, this is no' a game," MacRieve said. *Sound of waterfall nearing. Steam thickening. Can't trace.* "No' merely a way to impress a Valkyrie, so that she might deign to fuck you."

Dragged to the edge.

"For your stunt at the minefield, you're going for a swim, and your wee Valkyrie is going for a dive."

How high is the drop? Won't matter. The sun . . .

"I doona think you'll die, no matter how much you might want to."

MacRieve punted him in the ribs, sending him flying over the edge.

34

❧

**Tortuguerro Beach, Costa Rica
Day 27**

*Prize: A tear of Amphitrite, preserved into a bead,
worth eleven points*

Walking a bit bowlegged there, siren?" Kaderin asked lightly, though she was seething at this visible reminder that Cindey had obviously screwed the very endowed Nereus when that option had returned on the scrolls. She and Cindey were now almost tied. "Nereus must be slumming."

"Speaking of slumming, where's your vampire?" Cindey asked. "The nymphs said they heard him forsake you. I didn't think that was even possible."

"Do I look like I care?" She'd always enjoyed asking that question, since she knew the answer was invariably no—

"Yes, Kaderin, you do." Cindey sounded amazed by this fact.

Kaderin casually hissed at her, hoping to cover her dismay, because it was true that she'd been vampire-free for forty-eight hours. Sebastian hadn't called, he hadn't traced to her, and she felt like a nailed-and-bailed idiot.

Good money said she'd . . . *come on too strong?*

Yes, he'd said things, expressed sentiments and promises when she'd been kissing him. But how much weight could she put on those words? He'd been out of his mind with pleasure.

How could she *not* be his favorite girl at the time?

And really, what had they settled? Other than that the interlude was most definitely, unequivocally supposed to be meaningless sex? And exactly why had she been so adamant about that?

She had absolutely refused to call Myst to ask about Sebastian. That stance had lasted about six hours before she broke down. But Myst and Nikolai hadn't seen him or heard from him at all in two days.

Third major turnoff? Not calling. Especially after a gymnastic round of immortal sex.

Giving in to her insecurities in this new situation was better than the alternative: acknowledging that he would be here—unless he was injured. Or worse.

She figured that since her emotions were still so changeable, she might as well try them all on like new coats. And she liked the look and feel of angry and indignant so much better than worried and fearful.

None of this mattered. Once she went back for her sisters, none of this would have been. She had to remember that.

Since the morning she'd left him the letter—and left her prize behind—she'd competed at three tasks. At each one, she'd had the misfortune of meeting up with Lucindeya and Bowen.

Bowen remained gruesomely injured from the minefield, showing no regeneration whatsoever. He was still missing an eye and the skin over half his forehead. Blood had been seeping from the wound at his side, soaking his cambric shirt. The young witch's curse was not to be shaken.

Kaderin almost felt sorry for him—the way she'd feel sorry for a mindless wolf caught in the teeth of a spring trap. She'd freed them before, and they always appeared bewildered, eyes wild, having no idea why they'd been chosen to feel such pain or how to end it.

Bowen reminded her of exactly that. But, in the end, the wolves always snarled and snapped, and though he was cursed, Bowen was still a force to be reckoned with in the competition.

She'd slogged through a quicksand jungle to retrieve a jade pentacle. She'd thought she was so fast and had believed she had a chance against Bowen because he was still injured. But he'd flown over the untamed terrain as if renewed. He'd dusted her to that prize, leaving her panting and robbed of points.

He'd scrutinized her, even took a menacing step toward her. Then, as if he'd made a weighty decision, he'd turned from her.

In Egypt, Kaderin had answered a riddle of staggering complexity that left the Sphinx—and the Lykae and the siren—wondering how she'd done it. Secretly, she'd wondered herself. She'd earned the single golden scarab for ten points and had narrowed the gap on Bowen and taken a slim lead over Cindey.

But just last night in China, Bowen had been the first to the sole Urn of the Eight Immortals, leaving her and Cindey completely out for all the effort to get there. He'd reached his eighty-seven points, securing his spot in the finals.

Kaderin had seventy-four points. Cindey had seventy-two.

It hadn't escaped Kaderin's notice that she was thirteen points shy of the finals—*the exact value of the prize she'd relinquished.*

Today, the instructions were to swim out ten miles until a whirlpool portal appeared and brought them down to the prize—Amphitrite's tear, a bead said to heal any wound.

As twilight crept closer, competitors continued to line the beach. These entrants would be new ones—the veterans would have taken one look at this task, an eleven-pointer, and known some catch awaited them. Kaderin's first clue what that catch might be occurred when she'd spied cows' heads bobbing in the water just off the shore.

And that was before she even saw the first fin.

With a quick jog down the beach, she found a rivulet flowing steadily into the ocean, carrying the heads. Far upriver, a meatpacking plant must be churning out the refuse.

"Sharks!" Cindey cried when Kaderin returned. "Bloody sharks." She faced Kaderin. "You going in?"

"Might. You?"

"If you do, I won't have much choice, will I?" Cindey snapped.

The Lore beings and low creatures had taken great pains to get here, lured by the idea of a healing agent, and likely were wondering why the older ones weren't getting into the water. Then they spotted the fins, too. Not one of them talked of swimming. But Kaderin was in a desperate position.

She'd given up that damn box. *Silly, silly Valkyrie.*

"Screw this," she muttered, yanking off her sword.

"*Kaderin's going to do it!*" someone whispered. Others pointed.

Shrugging from her pack and jacket, she collected her sword, slinging the strap over her shoulder. She backed down the strand of beach and took off in a sprint, diving at the last possible moment, gaining yards out into the sea.

With smooth, even strokes, she swam freely through the sharks. *This isn't so bad.* Ten miles was nothing. If she wasn't bleeding or thrashing about, she should be fine—

An aggressive bump nearly knocked the breath from her. *Ignore it. Swim.*

Another purposeful knock.

In seconds, the sea was teeming with them, making it impossible to swim without hitting one with each kick. She knew no one had ever seen or documented anything like this. The meatpacking plant was, in essence, running a shark farm on the side.

Her sword would be useless in the water.

One shark was worse than the others, the bull of them all, giving her yet another violent shove—

Teeth sank into her thigh. She shrieked with pain, shoving her fingers at the flesh around the rows of teeth, prying the jaws apart.

She was fighting for her life now. With sodding sharks.

There came a brief thought that surely Sebastian would trace to her again and might find her remains—if there were any.

Kaderin had believed she'd die a violent death, but she'd be damned if she'd be food. She dove down, slashing out with her claws, biting them just as they sought to bite her. Outrage filled her, and red covered her vision.

She sank her claws into the bull's fin, yanked herself into it and bit down as hard as she could. Blood darkened the water, red bubbles and streams everywhere. Impossibly, more sharks came. She spit, then bit again.

I might actually die here. An immortal could die from a shark attack, if the head was severed from the neck.

Another swipe of her claws connected down the sleek side of the bull, but she couldn't fight them all off.

She swam down, determined to hide in a reef. She could hold her breath for extended periods of time.

And she couldn't die of drowning. *Just ask Furie.*

Before she could escape, the bull latched on to her leg, thrashing as it propelled her back into the fray.

Frantic slashing. Pain. When she clawed against the grain, the sharkskin abraded her fingers, tore at her claws. Twisting bodies, the *power* in them . . .

She kicked up to the surface, gasping air to return—

One seized her other leg above the knee, forcing her down in erratic yanks. The water swallowed her scream.

35

Sebastian jerked awake, then immediately collapsed back, wincing at the pain thundering through his head.

He cracked open his eyes to a starry nighttime sky. A warm breeze brushed over him as he lay unmoving on a stony riverbed. He eased up once more, struggling to determine where he was, squinting as memories from the jungle bombarded him.

That fucking wolf had tossed him into a raging river. Each time Sebastian had been dragged under was salvation from the sun, even as he sucked water into his lungs. After what seemed like days, the water had finally calmed. With his skin burning in the light, and his blood from a head injury gushing into his eye, he'd been sure he would die.

But he'd hauled himself to the shore—because he hungered for his future, with Kaderin in it. Before he'd passed out, he'd made it into the brush until only his legs were exposed. For the rest of the day, he'd burned, too weak even to move to avoid the pain.

How long had he been out? The entire day? He was thirsty, exhausted—

MacRieve threatened Kaderin. He bolted to his feet, tracing to her. When the dizziness hit from standing and he

rocked on his feet, he was already on a tropical beach somewhere just at sunset.

Which meant he was now on the other side of the world.
Again.

Dozens of competitors from the Lore gazed breathlessly
out at the sea. Sebastian followed their attention, and spied
a churning in a darker ring of water. Shark fins sliced
through the water, then slipped back down.

Something was dying out there, and no one bothered to
lend a—

A hand shot through the surface.

His stomach clenched. *Kaderin.*

An instant trace. Under the murky water with her. Impossible to see. Blood—hers—and tissue, pieces of shark
thick in the water. He struck out, fighting past the coil of
sharks to reach for her shoulders.

Missed her. One had her leg, twisting her from Sebastian's grasp, yanking down in a frenzy.

Sebastian fought with all the strength he had. He hit and
connected, slicing his hands on teeth, ignoring his own
wounds, clearing a way to her.

His hand closed in a fist over her upper arm. . . .

Fucking got her.

He traced back to the beach, tumbling to the ground,
twisting her atop him so he didn't crush her.

She wasn't breathing. He jerked up, flipping her to her
side. She coughed, choking up water. He rubbed her back as
she spit into the sand. When she'd caught her breath, he
took her in his arms, rocking with her.

What if I didn't wake when I did?

She'd be . . . dead. He shuddered. They couldn't be parted
again.

Even if he had to lock her away.

When he gently held her by the shoulders so he could see her eyes, she muttered, "You look white as a ghost."

"You were seconds away from being eaten alive!" he roared, his gut-wrenching fear for her turning to fury in an instant. "Or drowning."

"I did drown." She frowned dazedly. "Twice, I think."

"*This displeases me*. What if I hadn't gotten here in time? What if I hadn't been around to save your life?"

"Don't you get it?" she snapped. "For more than a millennium, I have won this contest handily. Then you come along, forcing me to alter my strategy." She sucked in a breath to continue. "And to take risks that I wouldn't have had to before. I wouldn't have been moved to this desperate an act if I hadn't given up the box."

"I didn't want you to give it up."

She eyed him. "Yes, Sebastian. You did."

"Not if this was the alternative." His voice was hoarse. "Do you know what it was like seeing you in the middle of that? To watch you going down before I could even react? I was watching you . . . die." He smoothed back wet, sandy hair from her cheek. "What will make you desist from this?"

"Nothing," she said, her expression obstinate. "Nothing on this earth will prevent me from winning the prize."

"Maybe your death would."

"It's been a long time coming."

In a seething voice, he said, "Bride, you have a bit of shark on your chin."

She wiped it off with the back of her arm, her mien defiant.

"*You bit them?*"

"They bit me first! And I didn't have much of a choice."

"You saw there were sharks, and you didn't think to wait for me?"

"When you haven't called? Wanna know the third major turnoff? Men who don't call after hitting it."

Hitting it?

Her ire was clearly building. "I wasn't going to wait for you when you've been a no-show for two days. Last time we really talked, I recall you informing me that you were going to forsake me. The first vampire to renounce his Bride. Blah, bluh, blah."

"You must have known that I would come for you—Wait, you said *two* days?"

"Like I care, Sebastian, if you lost track of time—"

"I was in a jungle, slowly burning to death. Or I'd have been here."

"Wh-what did you say?"

"I traced there to help you that morning. But the Scot slammed a shovel across my face, then tossed me in the river." He narrowed his eyes. "Did he hurt you?"

"No. But he did seem to make a decision about me."

"I thought I'd only been out for a day. You've been out here for two days without me?" He squeezed her hands.

"Ow!"

He peered down in horror to see he'd hurt her hands worse. They met eyes before they both lowered their gazes to her legs. Her pants were sliced through, her skin bitten and bloodied. She was injured worse than he'd ever seen. The sand around her was dark. It was blood . . . everywhere.

"My God, why didn't you say something?" he roared, furious again.

"Oh, pardon me for bleeding," she muttered when she

saw his eyes glued to her legs. "Don't want to whet your appetite."

"You can be so coarse sometimes, wife."

"Not your sodding wife."

"*Yet.*" Against her weak struggles, he scooped her up against his chest and pulled her tightly to him. In a gentler tone, he said, "I'll bring you home, and we'll bandage you."

The other Lore beings stopped in mid-stride to stare at the Valkyrie being held by a vampire. Cindey gaped at them in astonishment.

Kaderin didn't seem to care. She glanced at him and back at the horizon, biting her bottom lip, brows drawn. "The prize . . ."

Even after what she'd been through, her mind had seized again on the prize. He curled his finger under her chin, turning her to face him. Her eyes were luminous in her elfin face as she stared up at him. He wanted to give her anything she desired.

And he couldn't.

"Katja, I cannot retrieve it for you. I would. But I cannot see the destination."

"You figured out how to find me."

"If you can help me determine how to find a moving, living whirlpool and have it open for me, I will risk the sharks."

Her eyelids were getting heavy, and alarm rioted within him.

"I'm sorry, *kena*. I'll find another way." He traced her back to the flat, setting her on the bed. In a businesslike manner, he slipped her shirt off and set about cleaning and bandaging her hands and arms. But he was sweating, dreading hurting her any worse than she was.

When he ripped the remains of her pants from her, they both grew quiet at the damage. "Can you . . . you will not die from this?" he asked, his voice hoarse.

"No, not at all," she said in a sleepy tone. "Which is why I need you to trace me back to the beach at once."

Her words were ridiculous in the face of her injuries. "What truly drives you to do this? Why won't you tell me?"

She studied his face, gazing up into his eyes, as if searching his soul.

"You can trust me," he said.

She looked like she *wanted* to trust him, but couldn't will herself to. "I've known you less than a month, but I've . . . I've learned harsh lessons over the last two thousand years."

"I know. I've seen them in my dreams." He could admit to himself that in her place, he'd have a hard time trusting a vampire, too. But Sebastian knew his word was good—he just needed to persuade her. "I vow I will never be like those red-eyed fiends. There's no reason not to tell me."

"There's also no reason *to* tell you," she countered.

"I could help you."

"Won't you anyway?" she asked.

He scowled. "Of course. But there's got to be something that would make you trust me."

"Yes, my absolute belief that you would never use my trust against me."

"You know I would never hurt you!"

"I didn't say hurt me. I said use it against me." Her eyelids were getting heavy. "You do so love your leverage, vampire."

When she was safe with him, bandaged and sleeping soundly, he showered, his worry and fury finally beginning to dim. But he also became filled with a new resolve. He knew she couldn't die. But she could fucking *hurt*. And he was done allowing her to get strangled and stabbed and beaten each night. He wouldn't have it anymore.

After dressing, he slipped away, returning to the beach to see if he could do anything to help her finish this infernal competition. After her two days of competing without Sebastian, she was thirteen points away from the finals.

The exact number of points she'd sacrificed for him.

He still couldn't believe she'd given up that box. He'd checked his pockets for it but he'd lost it. Which was understandable, considering his fall and then his crawl across the riverbank.

At the beach, he spied an opportunity, and acted on it. If he couldn't remove the prize from the competition, he could remove the competition from the prize. He returned to Kaderin within fifteen minutes, shaking snow out of his hair.

When he joined her in bed, she nestled into the pillow and murmured, *"You smell nice."*

He carefully tucked her against him, reminded that she fit him so perfectly.

Her breaths grew light and quick, but they always did when she slept. She twitched and gave a soft moan. He petted her hair, soothing her.

When he finally slept, he dreamed her memories again. It was expected now. Yet these weren't memories from antiquity. Kaderin was clutching the phone with both hands, eyes watering, as one of her half-sisters delivered a death sentence.

36

Kaderin opened her eyes, confused to find herself still snuggled in *her* sheets that hinted at *his* sexy scent.

He sat on the edge of the bed, head in his hands, much as he had the first time she'd found him. She knew he'd gone from sorrow to elation that morning. She also knew that since then, he'd been disillusioned by her and hurt.

"How long have I been out?" she asked, her voice scratchy.

"Two days."

"*What?*" she shrieked, shooting upright.

He caught her shoulder when she swayed. "Easy, *kena*. You were injured worse than either of us thought. You lost a lot of blood. Let me check your bandages." He unwrapped her leg. "My God, you heal fast." By now, the gashes on her legs resembled old scars—pink and raised but seeming to fade right before their eyes.

"It's lost," she said, the words breaking. "Over." A tear slipped down her cheek, and she angrily swiped it away.

"Katja, it is not."

"With me out of the picture, Cindey has had all the time in the world. She could've gotten a stick of dynamite and stunned the sharks, or used diving equipment—"

He reached forward to tuck a curl behind her ear. "I don't believe there is much diving equipment in Siberia."

"Siberia?"

"I couldn't get the prize for you. But I could incapacitate your only real competition. I traced the siren to an abandoned coal mine in the Russian north."

Hope shot through her, warm and good. Had he protected her position in the contest? "Sh-she didn't sing to you?"

"Yes, she warbled frantically. But I remain immune." His eyes were intense, mesmerizing, as he brushed the backs of his fingers across her cheek. "It seems I am completely taken."

Emotion made her breathless and shaky. Before she could stop herself, she blurted, "I never intended to sleep with the Colombian."

Pain flashed in his eyes before he dropped his hand and stood. "It doesn't matter. You don't have to say that now."

"Okay."

He stabbed his fingers through his hair. "Damn it, you are supposed to insist and then explain anyway."

"Oh. Well, the truth is that I never planned to sleep with anyone that night."

"And your lack of underwear?" he asked with a scowl.

"Was the front line. I've found a well-timed glimpse can make men lose good judgment." She added, "You really need to rent *Basic Instinct*."

"Then how did you get the stone?"

"Gamboa had always wanted to be with a Valkyrie. So, I promised him a date with Regin—the one who tried to decapitate you in Antarctica—in exchange for the ring. And for the record, I chose that task for only one reason—the same reason Cindey did. Because we knew Bowen wouldn't."

"That is . . . good to know." Another one of his under-statements. The relief he felt was evident on his face.

"Now that I'm back in it, I need to leave quickly," she said. "Cindey is clever." Kaderin wanted to cement her place in the finals. Bowen had earned his spot—she accepted that, but he was weakening, and with the siren out of it, Kaderin could win.

"Lucindeya's not going anywhere," Sebastian said. "She must climb out of a jagged frozen pit with slippery sheer-rock faces five hundred feet high, then walk two hundred miles through waist-deep snow to the nearest town. She was dressed for the equator and seemed to be limping, walking strangely."

Kaderin tried to stifle a laugh. And failed. She startled him and herself.

"That's the first time I've ever heard you laugh." He grinned. "What? What's so amusing?"

"Walking funny, huh? That's because she did truly earn Nereus's prize."

"You mean she—?" When Kaderin nodded, he gave a chuckle and stroked his hand up and down her arm. She'd noticed he couldn't seem to stop touching her. "Do you want me to check and see if she's still there?"

She bit her lip and nodded. He disappeared, then re-turned seconds later, shaking snow from his head like a bear.

"Well?"

His face was perfectly deadpan as he said, "I fear Lu-cindeya and I are no longer friends."

She laughed again, and he grinned as if just enjoying the sight.

"I want to close this out," she finally said. "To go and get the next prize. Where's the scroll?"

He pulled it from his jacket pocket. "But, Kaderin, understand that we're doing this together." She parted her lips to argue, but he spoke over her in that officer tone. "I will not allow you to get hurt again."

She studied his face, and at length, she sighed. "Okay. We'll work together on the next one."

With a sharp nod, he joined her in bed, and they read the script together.

"Not the first one." At his questioning glance, she explained, "She's a succubus." Then Kaderin clucked her tongue. "Nereus is on here *again?* Three scrolls in a row. He must be hard up spawning. Poor siren."

"What about that one?" Sebastian asked about the third.

"Only if you like spiders the size of monster-trucks. Now, where's the highest point value?" She scanned the list, then frowned. "The Box of the Nagas again? Why does this say it's on a riverbank in the Congo Basin?"

"Because that's exactly where it is. I'd had it in my jacket that day."

She dropped the scroll and grabbed his hands. "Sebastian, it's worth thirteen points. That would get me to the finals! Can we—"

"I'll go there directly." He disappeared. Five minutes later, he returned.

With the box.

Her lips parted. "You really were there the morning after."

He drew his head back as if he wondered how she could doubt him. "Nothing else could have kept me from you."

Not only had he protected her spot in the Hie, he was giving her the finals, offering her the prize freely.

Their eyes met, and time seemed to stretch out. *Momentous.* He was offering her the chance to win her sisters back. And inadvertently ensuring she would never know him in the future.

She trembled as she accepted it, not knowing how to feel about the fact that she'd hesitated to reach for it. When she held the box above her heart and it disappeared, they checked the scroll. The script was fading, and in its place, the finalists were announced.

When she saw her name, her eyes watered and she murmured, *"No one has ever given me anything so dear."*

When Kaderin began running a bath, Sebastian decided to call Nikolai and ask him about his latest dream. He picked up her phone and studied it, about to make his first call— but she leapt forward.

"You don't want to use that one!" She handed him another phone that seemed to have been pried open and now had tape in places. "My coven will track where I am . . . and I'd rather not see them tonight." She smiled tightly, then dialed the number for him and connected the call. "And please don't tell your brother where we are, either. He'll likely inform Myst."

Sebastian raised his eyebrows, but nodded. Just when she'd walked out, Nikolai answered. Without preamble, Sebastian said, "I need to know anything you can tell me about a Valkyrie soothsayer. I think her name is Nïx."

"I've met her. She's the oldest Valkyrie, and definitely a soothsayer, though she prefers to be called 'predeterminationally abled.'" Sebastian could almost hear Nikolai shaking his head. "But, yes, I went to see her a few weeks ago to ask about you and Conrad."

"Does anything she foresees actually come true?"

"Well, we can determine this exactly," Nikolai said. "A few weeks ago, were you running from a castle into the morning sun, yelling for someone to come back to you? And then your skin caught fire?"

"My God," Sebastian bit out. "She foresaw Kaderin's death."

"How do you know this?" Nikolai asked. "It's usually impossible for her. That's the one thing she can't—or won't—see."

"I took Kaderin's memory of their conversation. She was badly shaken—and you must understand, few things leave that female shaken."

Nikolai added, "It might mean nothing, but Nïx also constructed these odd paper shapes while I was asking about you. There was a dragon, a wolf, a shark, and fire."

Sebastian swallowed. "We've faced all of those. Each one but for the fire."

"This would explain the uproar around Val Hall. Myst is secretive about coven business, but I've gathered that they are searching for Kaderin."

"No wonder she doesn't want them to know where she is." Sebastian ran an unsteady hand over his face. "Nïx predicted Kaderin's death before the next full moon. When is the next full moon?"

Nikolai's voice was grave. "Tonight."

Once she got out of the bath and threw on a robe, she found Sebastian sitting on the couch. He seemed in such deep thought, she almost felt awkward interrupting him. Kaderin shook it off. The scroll could update at any minute. She longed to experience him one more time, before she forgot him—

She hissed in a breath. *Well, that pang freaking hurt.*

"Bastian?"

Though she'd only been away from him for fifteen minutes, he stared at her as if he were seeing a ghost. Then without a word, he stood and crossed to her. He curled his finger under her chin and treated her to a kiss that was at once tender and passionate, making her melt.

When he drew back, she gazed up and found his eyes flickering over her, searching, she knew, for any hint of how he could bring her more pleasure. All he wanted was her happiness. She understood now. He would never turn—never change. She had, though.

She was falling for a vampire.

Looping her arms around his neck, she murmured, "I want you to make love to me." She'd clearly shocked him. "I want there to be *more* between us."

"Why now?" He had to clear his throat to continue. "What makes you say this tonight? Is it gratitude because of the box?"

She caught his eyes. "No. It's because you're not what I feared you'd be. And I finally see that you never will be. You're different."

He exhaled a breath. "What am I, then?"

Tonight, you were a hero. "You're a good man. You're good to me." She leaned up to whisper in his ear, "Bastian, I want to be good to you, too."

He shuddered, pulling her close against him, molding her body against his. The merest brush of his lips against hers built into a slanting feast.

She was lost in the sensation—

Did he just trace me?

Cold metal clenched her wrist. Her eyes widened when

she found herself in her bed. She fought him, but he forced her other wrist up to be chained as well.

"What in the hell are you doing?" she cried.

"I'm making sure you can't leave."

"Sebastian, you're alarming me, and I don't understand why. I was going to make love to you—"

"One last toss before you die?" he bit out.

She glanced away and exhaled. "How did you find out about the premonition?"

"Dreamed it. Why didn't you tell me you were fated to die in this competition before the full moon? Tonight?"

"Damn you, let me free! Nïx's prediction could be wrong—"

"Though she never is," he said.

"She hasn't been in the past," Kaderin said. "Besides, whether she is or isn't is incidental. If I don't win that prize, I'll be dead in a month anyway."

"What does that mean?"

"I *have* to be there tonight." Her chained arm seemed to ache where Furie had broken it so long ago. "It's my destiny to go, and I'll meet it head on."

"It's your destiny to die. And I won't allow that. You will stay here, and I will win the competition for you."

"How, Sebastian? I'm the finalist! I have to be there."

"I will go to Riora. And ask her to let me compete in your stead."

"Even if you can take my place, how will you get to the prize before Bowen does? Unless you've figured out a way for vampires to trace directly to map coordinates, you can only trace to me or to places you've already been. Odds are, you won't have been there."

"Nikolai has offered to secure transportation, a plane—"

"Look, let's compromise," she said hastily, seeing how unyielding he was. "You could help me. We could work together."

He picked up the scroll. She could tell it had updated, because his expression grew menacing. "Work together by going to the pit of the Fyre Serpénte tonight?" He gave a bitter laugh, then shoved the script at her face. "You will never go to a place known in the Lore as 'where immortals go to die' on the night you're fated to die!"

She memorized the coordinates before he took it away. "This isn't your call to make!" Kaderin had never doubted that her sacrifice could bring her sisters back, and he wanted to rob her of that. If she could save them and end this guilt . . . then she *longed* to die for it. "You're ignoring my wishes and my beliefs as though they were insane. It's galling to someone like me."

"Because they are insane! Goddamn it, tell me why you want this so badly!"

"Fine. Let me go, and I will. You asked me what you could do to make me trust you, and this is your chance. This is the test. Free me, and I'll tell you everything. No secrets between us. We'll work as a team."

He stabbed his fingers through his thick hair. "No. I can't let you go. Nïx predicted we'd face a fire, and she predicted that you would die. You know where the task is. Do you wish to die? If you go tonight, it's suicide—"

"*You* are going to talk to me about suicide? Oh, that's rich!"

"I had nothing to live for. But now *we both do!*" He knelt on the bed and clutched her nape. "I won't let you die!"

"Damn you!" she cried. "Sometimes living isn't everything!"

Her words made his lips part. "No. I used to believe that." He stood unsteadily. "Now I know I was wrong." Before he traced away, he rasped, "If you love something, you protect it ruthlessly. No matter what occurs."

After he'd gone, she lay for some time, sorting through what had just happened. He'd chained her down, intending to prevent her from bravely meeting her fate.

She'd meant what she said. If he'd freed her, she would have told him everything. She would have joined him. But she wouldn't trust his judgment when he refused to afford her the same faith.

Too bad whatever plane Sebastian was heading for could never get to those coordinates faster than the Augusta 109 helicopter she had on call.

And too bad the chains were only protected against vampires. She popped them open with ease.

37

❦

Yélsérk, Hungary, the pit of the Fyre Serpénte
Day 30

Prize: The Sworne Blade of Honorius, to win

I need your help," Sebastian had said to Nikolai after
learning that tonight was the full moon. That was all it
had taken to arrange every step of transportation.

"I can go with you," Nikolai had offered. "Myst is at Val
Hall today." His tone grew low. "They couldn't find
Kaderin, and they all are . . . gathering."

"You need to be there if Myst returns. Besides, it's just
me against the Scot and he's weakened. I can handle
this."

Just after Sebastian had chained Kaderin up, he'd traced
to Riora's temple. She was surprisingly indifferent about
Sebastian competing in Kaderin's stead. In fact, she was
more put out that he would no longer be her knight, and
hers alone. But she'd agreed.

When he'd traced back to London, a car had been waiting outside the flat to take him to a private airport. Then

there was a jet to Hungary. It was still dark when Sebastian landed a mere two and a half hours later. . . .

The truck that would take him to the pit had just arrived, earlier than scheduled, so Sebastian decided to take five minutes to check on Kaderin. He would reassure her that Riora had agreed to him competing—and convince her that he could do this.

He traced to London. To find the bed was empty and the chains broken. She was gone. . . .

When he traced directly to her, he appeared at the edge of a chamber of fire.

The cavern that housed it was as large as an auditorium, and in the center was a roiling pit of lava. Fire wisped into the air, dissipating into black smoke. Rocks crumbled down the sides into the lava, bubbling up smaller and smaller until they disappeared.

Where in the hell is she?

Stretched above the pit was a metal cable as thin as filament that was embedded into a sheer rock face. He couldn't see where it would lead—

Kaderin appeared from the other side of the chamber, wasting no time, hopping up to the side of the pit, testing the cable with a pointed toe. When she saw him nearing, her eyes narrowed with fury. "Get the hell away from me! Enough! I *need* this, Bastian. I have to have it."

Palms raised, he said slowly, "Let me get it for you."

"I've won the Hie five times before. I can do this!" She hurried onto the wire—it burned her shoes.

"Goddamn it, I'll trace you."

"To where?" she said over her shoulder. "The rock's solid. It may be that you have to walk the cable to spy out another entrance below or scan for it in the ceiling." She paused and quirked an eyebrow. "Walking this won't be a problem."

He traced to her, determined to take her from this place, but she dodged him, sending him back to the same spot empty-handed.

"Bloody stop it!" she shrieked, charging farther out on the wire. "I can walk this blind! On my hands!" In an instant, he traced once more, but again she ducked, eluding him.

A lash of fire whipped up just behind her. Even with her speed, she scarcely escaped it—and him, as he traced once more. No key was this valuable—not worth the life of an immortal.

Something bubbled up from the lava beneath her.

A true monster, a being of fire shaped like a giant snake. The Fyre Serpénte. The main part of its body lay beneath the surface of the lava, its tail and head rising above. The lash of fire actually had been part of its long tail, and it struck again just as Sebastian traced.

Kaderin twisted and lunged forward. Untouched.

He yelled, "*Stay fucking still!*"

But the fire wanted its due.

When it roared spitting balls of flame, it rocked the entire cavern. Boulders toppled over, plummeting everywhere. Fighting to reach her, Sebastian dodged and traced, but the ceiling rained them. One dropped onto his right arm, crushing it almost all the way up to his shoulder; he bellowed with pain and fury. She was barely staying balanced in the shaking chamber—

A boulder hit the center of the cable, and it snapped with a deafening twang. She dove backward, twisting in the air for the swinging line. He couldn't see from where he was . . . had no idea if she caught it.

He traced. Nothing. Body straining with effort. He was trapped, but almost close enough to reach the side of the pit. He lunged forward, tearing sinew and skin. Another frantic lunge, with a good, rewarding rip.

He finally reached it, and was able to see down. She had a hold on the cable with both hands and was deftly climbing up. With a groan of relief, he wound it around his left wrist for a better grip.

"Hold on, Katja! I've got you—"

The serpent slithered its tail up around her leg. She bit back a scream as the fire hissed against her skin, branding it. The thing was dragging her down.

Trapped as he was, he couldn't use his legs to pull. Couldn't put his back into the effort.

Her sweating body writhed in pain. She still clung to the filament, now red with blood from her ruined palms slipping down.

If he could just lose his arm, he might have a chance. . . .

As he wrenched back with the cable and away from the boulder, he saw her studying the situation, her gaze darting over his trapped arm, then down at the fire. When she turned back, her eyes were glinting. She swallowed, gazing up at him.

A calm seemed to wash over her.

His gut tightened with dread. She couldn't be considering . . . He tore every muscle in his body to wrest her from its grip, bellowing with the effort.

"Bastian." He heard her perfectly over the wails of the serpent, the bubbling, popping lava, and his own heart thundering.

"*No . . . no!*" he roared. "Don't you even think it, god-damn you—"

"I'm going to let go now," she murmured. Her eyes were clear, lucid.

"Just give me fucking time! The prediction doesn't have to be!" He somehow pulled harder, snatching the cable up with his left arm and then catching it lower down, but the serpent hissed and seized her higher on her torso. Kaderin gritted her teeth against the pain.

Can't beat it like this. In a frenzy, he lunged sideways, fighting to separate his arm from his body.

"I know where the blade is," Kaderin said. "Below the cable bolt on that wall. Fifteen feet down, forty degrees to the left." Tears tracked from her eyes. "There's a cave under an overhang—I could only see it from here."

"Don't do this! Ah, God, *please!* . . . *Don't*—"

"Come back for me. *So I can go back for them.*"

Eyes riveted to his, she let go. The serpent snatched her down.

The fire consumed her.

38

The lights of Val Hall flared sharply, then guttered out. Lightning slashed the sky, and thunder rattled the darkened manor so hard the old house groaned violently. Myst dropped to her knees just as Nïx's eyes went wild and her hands fisted in her hair. Emma wept.

When Regin shrieked, the windows burst, spewing shards, until even the wraiths fled. As though a bomb had hit, glass shattered in a radius outward from the manor, again and again, in successive waves for miles.

The Lore creatures in the city and swamps trembled in fear and knew of only one thing that could provoke the Valkyrie like this.

They'd felt the death of one of their own.

Dead. Sebastian knew she was dead, felt it in his entire body.

He loved her. Not compulsion. Love so strong it humbled him.

He stared down into the pit long after. How long could an immortal live in that flame? How much pain did she suffer?

What did she mean, "go back for them?"

A sudden dream washed over him. Kaderin was sprinting

down a hill that was covered in bodies. He heard her ragged breaths and the warning shrieks from other Valkyrie. He experienced her roiling panic.

She fought past vampires, with dirty red eyes and grotesque snarls, desperate to get to . . . her sisters.

Sebastian was still caught by his trapped arm—the one he hadn't been able to sever in time—but he fell to his knees just as Kaderin had done on that battlefield all those ages ago when she witnessed her blood sisters being butchered. The shock was like a physical strike, leveling her. She heard her sisters' heads hit the stony ground. She saw the vampire—the one she'd just *spared*—dealing the blows. . . .

When she shrieked, it was so loud her own ears bled. The young vampire Sebastian had seen her torturing in the dream had beheaded her sisters. Now that he'd felt her rage, her loss and guilt, he wished she'd shown even less mercy, wished he could have joined her in her retribution.

"So I can go back for them," she'd told him. Them. Triplets. Her blood sisters. She had lost them both in the space of minutes. That's what this entire ordeal had been about. Not mercenary, not ego. She wanted her family back. *My God, she has trusted me with all their lives*. She trusted that he could win the prize for her.

And that the key could work.

Sebastian had never dared to believe that one could go back in time. Now that belief was the only thing he had. He had to get her back. He could win this cursed thing and go back for her. Just as she'd planned.

She'd just died.

She'd just fucking *died*.

He couldn't see the cave she'd spoken of, but he'd trace blind into the rock if he had to. *Need to lose the arm first.*

Just as he decided to use his teeth, he heard footsteps.

MacRieve appeared. He studied the scene, his wasted face darkening. "What's happened here?"

Only then did Sebastian notice how much blood he'd lost from his arm. He suspected the brachial artery had been cut. Once the pressure of the boulder was removed, he'd lose more in a rush. Black spots already clouded his eyes. Did he have enough blood to lose his arm completely?

The Lykae could move the boulder. "A quake. Rocks," Sebastian told him, not daring to utter that Kaderin was gone, even if he hadn't been set on using the Lykae.

"Where's the Valkyrie?" the Lykae asked. "She ought to be here—not you."

"I'm here in her stead."

MacRieve began scanning farther into the chamber.

"You can't reach the prize," Sebastian told him. "It's across the lava, and the cable snapped."

As Sebastian had expected, he surveyed the pit, then said, "I could free you to trace me across. Then . . . an open contest to take it."

Don't look too eager. "I could double-cross you."

MacRieve narrowed his one eye. "No' if I've got a hold of your good arm."

Sebastian forced himself to hesitate, then said, "Do it."

The Scot crossed to the boulder and shoved at it, seeming confounded when it didn't immediately go. He muttered something that sounded like "*Bloody, goddamned witches.*" Putting his back into it, he asked, "Where exactly are you tracing us?"

Sebastian explained, "Below the cable, there's a lava tube, a cave."

"I doona see anything," he gritted out.

"It's there. You want the prize? Then you're just going to have to trust a vampire—"

The boulder toppled over, and MacRieve grabbed his left arm. Sebastian gaped at what remained of his right arm.

"That's got tae hurt." MacRieve sneered.

"Have you looked in the mirror lately?" Sebastian snapped.

"Aye." He hauled Sebastian to his feet. "And I plan to kill you for that. After this competition. Right now, I doona have all day."

Sebastian just prevented himself from rocking on his feet. His sight was blurred. He struggled to focus on the spot she'd described. *Stay sane. Fuck, did she mean forty degrees to my left?*

MacRieve jostled him. "Are you even going to be able to do this—"

Sebastian traced. . . .

Sweltering heat, steam, smoke. Solid ground beneath them. *Made it.* Flames with no seeming source burned erratically, but Sebastian couldn't see the blade.

Suddenly, the Scot dropped his hold on Sebastian, sprinting deeper into the cave, but Sebastian traced blindly ahead. There, on a waist-high column of rock, lay the blade, gleaming in the light of more fires and wet with steam.

Sebastian got there first, snatched it with his good hand, tensed to trace—

Like a shot, MacRieve lashed a whip, coiling the length around Sebastian's wrist. He yanked down, preventing him from tracing. "I'll be taking that now."

The bastard only had one whip. Sebastian simply transferred the blade to his right hand to raise it. But that ruined arm hung lifeless.

"Canna quite make it to your heart, then?"

Sebastian bared his fangs savagely. "I'll gut you before you get this."

"That equals the life of my mate."

"I've the same on my mind," Sebastian bit out.

"The Valkyrie died?"

Sebastian shook his head. "Not for long."

Bowen must have seen something in his expression. He had the advantage, and yet he offered, "We could share it, vampire. The key works twice."

Blood everywhere. Weak. Kaderin had asked something of him. Finally given him a chance to help her . . . "I need both of those times for her." *Can't raise my right arm over my heart. My left arm is trapped.* But the blade had powers MacRieve likely didn't know of.

According to Riora, it never missed.

The knife he held was nowhere near the Lykae's whip hand, but Sebastian concentrated on his intention to cut him at the wrist and made the merest motion toward the end, all he could manage with that wasted arm.

Suddenly, his arm shot up. The blade rose as if of its own accord and flashed reflected firelight as it struck.

Blood spurted. The Scot's severed hand dropped. Freed from the whip, Sebastian traced the distance across the pit.

"I will fucking kill you for this, vampire," the Lykae bellowed with rage. "I will eat your goddamned heart!"

Sebastian steeled himself for the jaunt to Riora's temple.

But he couldn't leave. Leaving made Kaderin's death real. *Stay sane. This key has to work.*

From the now unseen cave: "*Mark me. So help me God, I will hunt you and the Valkyrie over the earth—*"

Sebastian disappeared to the sound of the Lykae's roar—not of pain but of loss.

When Sebastian returned to the temple, Riora greeted him once again with Scribe in tow. "You have won, Sebastian. The first vampire to do so. Congratulations."

"This is for her. Always for her." His body wouldn't stop shuddering.

"Then sign the book of winners, and take your prize."

When Scribe handed him the book, he actually looked as though he respected Sebastian.

Kaderin's dead. Sign the book. Stay sane.

He saw his Bride's proud signature on every line above his own, so far back the lettering had changed. Over time, her handwriting had become harder, more angular. *Stay sane.* He signed his name with his left hand in shaking letters, stamping the page in blood.

Riora handed him a metallic key. He gripped it so hard it dug into his palm. "Tell me this works."

"It works, Sebastian. Though you may end up cursing it."

"How can you say that?"

"You know why Kaderin sought the key?" Riora asked.

He nodded slowly. "She wants her sisters back."

"If you give her the second turn of the key, she will return for her sisters and never see their deaths. She will be spared one thousand years of guilt and nothingness and instead enjoy contentment with her family."

"I want this!"

"Yet in this case, Kaderin will never be driven to journey out of her way to kill you. She will have her sisters"— Riora's eyes bored into his much as they had that first night—"but *you* will not have *her*."

He'd experienced Kaderin's memories of their deaths, of collecting her sisters from the battlefield. Burying their heads, their bodies, then clawing at her hair and skin.

If he could save her from that . . . to spare her a millennium of guilt?

As a mortal, he'd been a knight with no one to whom to pledge his sword. He'd claimed Kaderin for his own, and that meant protecting all she held dear. He lowered his head. "*She will have her sisters*." The flames flared as if to punctuate his words.

"Very well. The key unlocks a door for approximately ten minutes. It allows you to go back and to be in the same time as a previous self."

"How will the key know where to open?"

"In the end, the key is a facilitator," she explained. "You hold a tool of unspeakable power, Sebastian. Hold it out in your palm, and it will know what you must have and act to that end. But I warn you, if you get stuck in the past when the door closes, one version of you will fade, ceasing to be."

He saw Scribe in the background, his pale, waxen face showing his sorrow. He gave Sebastian a nod of encouragement.

Riora murmured, "Bring her forward, vampire."

He gave her a pained bow. "Goddess."

39

Kaderin made her way through the darkened tunnel. She knew she was close to the Fyre Serpénte's chamber, could hear the echoing space just ahead. She also knew that if Bowen wasn't already here, he'd be right behind her.

As would Sebastian.

Her ear twitched at a sound like a sucked-in breath. Not Bowen? She whirled around, and her eyes narrowed with fury. *Sebastian.* "Get the hell away from me! Enough! I *need* this, Bastian. I have to have it."

She trailed off at her first close look at him. His arm was shattered, his face blistered on one side. His shirt had been white but was now slashed and wet with crimson. Her lips parted. What could have happened to him since he'd left her in chains?

Recalling that hardened her resolve. She was so close. She didn't have time to ask. If he'd had his way, she'd still be fettered to a bed.

But, gods, had she ever seen a being in such turmoil? His eyes were fully black and seemed to glint with moisture. His hands shook. Blood dripped freely, though he seemed unaware of it.

"*I thought you were gone,*" he rasped. "Kaderin, we have to leave this place."

"What are you talking about?"

"Take my hand." He stretched out his left hand, palm up.

"Go to hell," she snapped. "Conveniently, it's located just up the tunnel."

He rocked on his feet, and his head lolled forward. He was fighting to stay conscious?

As if fearing he soon wouldn't be able to, he snatched her wrist—and traced her before she could resist. He took her away from the prize, to Riora's temple.

Kaderin shrieked in fury, the sound echoing throughout. The dome skylight began to crack, the thick sound ominous, like a fracture splintering out over a frozen pond.

Sebastian cupped her face with one hand. "No, Katja. Ah, God, let me see you."

"Have you lost your mind?" she cried, shoving him away. "How could you do this? I have to get back! Bowen was right behind me—"

"Must tell you something." He shook his head. His face was so pale.

"There's no time!"

"The key has been won—"

"Bowen!" Lightning fired all around them. Tears filled her eyes. "He took it? No . . . no!" she screamed, exploding the skylight.

With his good hand, Sebastian yanked her close, hunching over her, covering her with his body. As the glass rained down, he murmured against her hair, "*We won it*."

Her breaths were ragged. "I-I don't understand," she finally said once the glass had fallen.

"Katja, you . . . died."

She pulled back. Tears streamed down her face. "What did you say?"

"You died. Fifteen minutes after the moment from which I just took you." At her dumbstruck expression, he bit out an explanation detailing the scene, the difficulties, the incredible power of the fire. He explained her choice.

She swayed, and he caught her with his good hand. "I asked you to come back for me? I told you about my sisters?"

"Yes. I had no idea this was what you sought. Why didn't you tell me before?"

"I would have tonight! And before that, I just . . . couldn't." She bit her lip. "I let go?" When he nodded, she said, "I must have recognized something. Seen something that made me trust you completely." Her brows drew together. "Bastian, I didn't just trust you with my life." She caught his eyes. "I trusted you with my sisters' lives as well."

He said quietly, "I was humbled by it."

Riora suddenly appeared, perched on the edge of her altar, with a visibly emotional Scribe following, stepping on snapping glass.

"I had an interesting conversation with my champion," Riora began. "And he proved possible yet another impossibility. I alerted the vampire to the fact that once you got your hot little hands on the key, he would lose you forever. History would be changed. The future would buckle and grind to fit the past. You would never have found him, because you wouldn't have suffered the death of your sisters. And a vampire chose to relinquish his Bride rather than have her suffer that horror and guilt. To spare you pain, he chose to give you the key, even believing he would lose you forever."

"Is this true?" Kaderin asked Sebastian with a catch in her voice. "Y-you would do that?"

In answer, he rasped, *"Want you happy."*

Her tears ran freely.

"Why these tears, Katja?" he asked. "You will have your family back, I swear it. Do not cry."

"What's on your mind, Valkyrie?" Riora said from behind them. "Don't make me go digging for it."

On her mind? Good question. There were too many thoughts to sort through. And too many feelings. Her heart felt rent in two, choosing between her family and the vampire she was falling for.

Did she love him? She thought she might, but how did one know? Most didn't trust their own feelings anyway, much less if they were unpracticed for so long.

But Kaderin had always trusted her instinct.

She could now accept that *instinct* had commanded her right from the start not to hurt him, all the way back to that first morning. "I can't *not* know him, Riora."

"What are you saying?" he asked, seeming not to breathe.

"I don't want to have to choose."

He dragged her against his chest with his good arm, resting his chin on her head again. "For my part, if I could know for a day that I'd won you, it would be worth it."

"But you wouldn't remember winning me," she said against him.

"Wait." He set her away to give her that half-grin. "Katja, my arm is broken."

"I know!" Kaderin cried, her voice breaking. "Why do you sound so bloody delighted about that?"

"It should have been healed," Sebastian said. "I was never struck with a boulder until the serpent woke. Your crossing the cable woke it, and when you didn't cross . . ."

She sucked in a breath, and her eyes widened.

"Very good, vampire," Riora said. "Kaderin told you time travel would work. And you told her you can't go to the past to change the future. You were both right."

"I don't understand how this is possible," Kaderin said. "He changed the past. The present should be different. And you said he had to choose—"

"Ah, I . . . told a *little* lie. I wanted to see if it was possible for a vampire to surrender his fated Bride." She inclined her head at them. "And thank you both for your cooperation. Now. *Truthfully*. You can't go back and then change the future."

Sebastian's expression grew dark. "Riora, that's exactly on our agenda right now."

"Scribe! Ribbon! Shears!" In the blink of an eye, a scarlet ribbon was rolled out over the altar, stark against the marble. Scribe laid scissors into her outstretched palm. "This ribbon is time, from past to present."

She leaned down to the end of the ribbon representing the past and cut a sliver a few inches up. "I've gone back and extracted something from time, but the rest of the ribbon remains wholly unchanged. Vampire, you were absolutely right—to a point. You unquestionably cannot go back in time to change the future. That way lies madness." She frowned at Kaderin. "Really, Valkyrie, you should give him more credit. He *is* a scholar." She shrugged and continued, "But magic allows us to go back and nab a few things now and again. A mystical parlor trick."

"I won't forget him?" Kaderin couldn't stop shaking.

"No, not at all. But when you use the key, do not attempt to get clever with it. Time is living and fluid but refuses to allow the past to be. Thrane's genius was that he discovered doors to the past could be opened, but time would shut them immediately to prevent instability and chaos. So he created a key that would open millions of doors at the same time. Keeps a body busy closing all of them. The hope is that your door is the last to get shut down, because if you get locked out, you will fade."

Riora tilted her head at Kaderin, then turned that sharp, cutting stare on Sebastian. "Look at Kaderin's relief, vampire. For some reason, your pull on her was stronger than a blessing bestowed by a goddess"—she stretched her fingers out, examining her nails—"of no mean power."

"Blessing?" Sebastian asked. "*The* blessing?"

"*You?*" Kaderin whispered. "It was you?"

"Yes." Riora studied her. "That's why I was perplexed that your attraction to a vampire could neutralize it."

"Why?" Kaderin demanded. "Why did you do it?"

"You blamed yourself for your sisters' deaths, and yet you were too strong to die. Your sorrow was debilitating the Valkyrie covens."

"Why numb everything? I haven't felt joy, humor, love."

Riora delicately coughed, clearing her throat. "That was a bit unintentional." She turned to Sebastian. "You, and you alone, have freed her to feel. And it is time she should."

"This explains much," Sebastian said, then rocked on his feet.

"We've got to get you bandaged up." Kaderin leaned into him to help him stand, alarmed at how pale his face had grown. How much blood had he lost?

"Kaderin, he's bleeding all over my temple," Riora said. "And by the way, Valkyrie, you owe me for a skylight." Riora turned from her. "Scribe? Where are you? Scribe!" And then they were gone.

"Are you going to be able to trace us?" Kaderin asked.

"Of course," he grated, but he was barely able to get them back to her flat.

Stubborn vampire. He's been hiding how weak he is.

In the bedroom, his legs gave out. When she helped him to the bed, he fell back but clenched her wrist. "You're not going without me."

"Your sword arm is injured. You won't be able to defend yourself in a battle."

Sebastian said, "You've waited a thousand years, you can wait two more days."

She shook her head. "I'd be taking you into a war where you are the enemy."

"I'll take that chance, Katja. Do not do anything until I heal."

She hesitated, then said, "I won't go until you're healed."

He nodded, then passed out immediately.

She meant what she'd said. There was no way he could accompany her. A vampire on a battlefield with an army of Valkyrie? Not going to happen. Her own sisters would likely try to kill him.

But she was not leaving him when he needed her. For the last two nights, when not chaining her up, he'd been a hero to her. He'd salvaged the competition for her, given her the finals, and then won the key. Not to mention that he'd saved her life.

And then, when faced with the choice of her happiness over his own, he'd chosen hers.

At every turn, he made her feel protected, cherished. And she would respond in kind.

Her relief when she'd found out she wouldn't forget him was staggering. What did that say? What did it mean that she was as delighted about that fact as she was to be going back for her sisters?

Before she used the key, Kaderin would contact the coven and let them know she was okay, though she was sure they'd already felt her return. She would see Sebastian mended, giving him as much blood as he could drink.

She'd waited a thousand years. Two or three days wouldn't matter in the great scheme of things, would it?

Sebastian woke feeling *incredible*.

A warm, sleeping Valkyrie was draped over his chest, and he clutched her to him, amazed by all that had occurred. Memories trickled in from that hellish haze after he'd lost her, but he pushed them away.

Because he'd gotten her back.

All that mattered was that he had Kaderin safe with him. He'd gotten her back.

When she didn't wake, he slipped from the bed to go shower and to examine his arm. He stood, waiting for the black dots to cloud his vision but saw none. The bones in his upper arm and elbow felt as though they had already started to knit, and he could tell the shredded skin and muscles were connected, at least. He might not even need the sling she'd fashioned for his arm.

When he returned, showered and dressed, she was awake.

"I'm going to be healed by tomorrow," he told her. "We can go for them at sunset."

"Sebastian, once we get close enough to my sisters, they could kill you themselves." She looked away. "They would not hesitate as I did."

"I'm going with you. There's no question of it. What if you don't make the door? Then I definitely will lose you."

"Even if we wait for you to heal, you can't defend your-self without risking one of my kind."

He drew his head back. "I would never hurt them."

"I know that," she said quickly, "but they'll want you dead."

"I'm going, Katja. It must be so."

She studied his face for a long moment, then exhaled with a subtle nod. She turned her back to him, drawing her hair over one shoulder, baring her beautiful neck. "Then you have to be strong."

He swallowed tightly. "You're inviting me to drink you?"

She said over her shoulder, "You have been for a day."

And I've missed it? He joined her in the bed, turning her to face him. "No wonder I feel so damned good."

She glanced up from under a blond curl, and said in a throaty voice, "*How* good?"

He stilled. "Remarkably." Even with his body so beaten, his cock swelled in anticipation. "Tremendously."

"We'd have to be creative," she said, with her eyes al-ready flashing silver. "So we don't hurt your arm." Her idea of creative was to strip off his shirt that she'd slept in, then lay back at the foot of the high bed, positioned for him with her shining hair spread out, and her nipples already hard.

"I like creative," he rasped, ripping off his own clothes. His hands itched to touch her in a million different ways and places. He wanted to kiss her for hours.

"This should work, don't you think?" she asked. "Are you sure you're ready?" The look he gave her made her say, "Okay, okay! Just checking—"

Her words died in her throat when he crouched down and eased her legs open. He loved kissing her between her thighs and would take any opportunity to taste her. She cried out at the first touch of his tongue to her wet flesh, and moaned when he languidly suckled her.

"Bastian, please," she finally whimpered. "I need to feel you inside me."

He pressed a kiss to her thigh. When he stood, her knees fell even wider apart in blatant invitation. For him. This was still so new to him—to have this beauty asking him to be inside her was still unbelievable.

He gripped his shaft and positioned himself at her entrance, then reached forward to cover her breasts with his palms. She arched, pushing into his hands until he squeezed and groaned at the feel of her soft flesh.

As the head of his cock pressed deeper, filling her, she moaned with each inch. When she took him as far as she could, his knees went weak, but from pleasure.

With her legs locked around his waist, she undulated her hips, slowly at first, but soon she was so frantic he thought he might come just from her working her sex on his shaft. "More, Bastian!"

I'll always give you more, he remembered vowing that first day. *Until I die*. He had to hold on. . . .

He leaned down and licked her stiff nipples, one and then the other, but when she threaded her fingers in his hair and arched her back, it made him want to come even more.

He rose, about to pull out and take her with his mouth again. But she grasped two of his fingers and softly sucked the tips into her mouth, wetting them. She placed them against her clitoris, showing him exactly what she desired.

Shuddering, he strained every muscle in his body not to spill that instant. When he stroked her there, lightly pinching, she went wild, twisting and writhing on the bed.

"Drink, Bastian," she said between panting breaths. "I need you to."

Need me to drink? He never thought he'd hear those words, and his fangs ached in response.

Still thrusting, he clutched her slim shoulders, brushing his lips against her neck. When he pierced her skin and sucked, she cried out, and his eyes rolled back in his head. He growled against her flesh when her body tensed in a shuddering orgasm.

He withdrew his fangs, throwing his head back. Her blood raced through him, burning and pulsing, making him mad with lust. Her sex squeezed him, demanding, hungry. A haze seemed to cover his vision. He felt as if something inside him had been unleashed, and knew he'd need to take her hard.

When he pulled out and turned her around, she gasped in surprise and shivered. Clasping her to him with a hand over her front and the other cupping her sex, he pulled her bodily back, then bent her over the bed, her breasts pressing into the mattress. Readying. Positioning her.

He clenched her hips, pinning her in place to receive him as he eased his shaft back inside her. He withdrew slowly, then returned in agonizing strokes, soon finding a driving rhythm that made her moan.

"Harder. Please!" When he heard the thunder drumming outside, he plunged fully into her.

Building, faster, until he was slamming into her, his skin slapping hers, using his whole body to take her. He couldn't believe he'd bent her over the bed like this. Couldn't believe each time with her was more pleasurable than the last.

The headboard was banging against the wall, and still she demanded more.

With a brutal yell, he gave it to her. He held nothing back, fucking her with all his strength as her cries grew louder.

When he reared back, he could see her face turned to the side, her lips parted, her eyes silver. Her arms were stretched out, tensed in front of her. "*Bastian,*" she cried softly, stunned as well. Her reactions and the lightning outside were his permission.

"I'm going to be inside you all night. Drink you all night."

"Yes!" she cried. "Anything, Bastian. . . ."

Anything. No constraints. Utter freedom. He gave himself up to it. Years of doubt evaporated. The past grew dim against a future with her. "You need this?" he grated.

"Yes!"

"You need me?"

"Oh, yes, yes!" She stretched her arm back, offering her wrist to drink from as he continued to buck against her. When he pierced her flesh again, she instantly came with an anguished cry. He could no longer resist the pressure welling inside him, so he took as he gave, drawing her blood from her body as he emptied his seed hotly into it.

Once he could come no more, he stretched over her, still thrusting slowly.

His breaths ragged, he rasped at her ear, "*You're mine now, Katja. And I will never let you go.*"

40

The first Lore battle Sebastian would ever experience would be a clash that had occurred a millennium in the past, and was one of the most notoriously brutal ever seen.

Tonight he and Kaderin would retrieve her sisters, fully expecting to land in the middle of that war.

They'd strategized about where to use the key, deciding on the flat, mainly because the coven would try to kill him at Val Hall. She wasn't too keen on being in the city, though, in case the two didn't "travel forward well."

Kaderin was nervous about seeing them after so long and had endeavored for an hour to find clothing that didn't look too modern. As he'd waited, he'd sat back against the headboard, watching her dress, thinking over the last two days while his arm had healed.

"We're going to need more time," she'd told him after the first night.

He'd grinned. "I trust my nurse."

During that time, when he hadn't been inside her, they'd talked about everything. She'd told him what her sisters had been like, and he'd revealed what had happened with his family. He felt he could tell her anything, and that she had completely opened up to him as well.

He was learning all about her—and learning how satisfying it was simply to live with her. At his leisure, he got to kiss her ears just to make them twitch. He could study her delicate hands for what seemed like hours, enclosing them completely with his own and running the pads of his fingers over them. He got to watch her sleep—that is, when he wasn't exhausted beside her. His Bride was as insatiable as *he* was.

She was abandoned, free with her body, and gave him anything he wanted, anything he'd ever fantasized about. When he'd admitted how little experience he had, she'd seemed determined to give him everything he'd missed.

In the end, their time together confirmed what he'd known from the beginning. He never wanted to part from her.

The only obstacle to his happiness was the knowledge that the key did, in fact, work.

Of course, he was relieved that Kaderin would have her sisters, but he couldn't help thinking about what it would have been like to go back for his own family and see them once more. Maybe if he had done things differently, he and Kaderin both could have had the opportunity. . . .

"Are you ready?" she asked, finally dressed in jeans and a longer jacket, with her sword strapped over her shoulder.

He nodded and rose to collect his own sword. When he crossed to her, she held up the key with raised eyebrows. "You sure you want to go? It's going to be intense."

He put his shoulders back. "I was on a battlefront for a decade, remember?" He tucked her braid behind her ear.

She didn't look convinced. "Don't trace in front of my sisters, please. And try not to open your mouth much." When he raised his brows, she said, "Your fangs. I don't want them to see your fangs. They really will try to kill you."

"You're beautiful when you're nervous." He gave her a brief, deep kiss.

In a breathy voice, she said, "You've got your sword ready?"

His lips curled into a grin.

"Just . . . just don't get killed, Bastian." She swallowed. "Okay?"

He took her free hand, pressed his lips to her palm. "I'll endeavor not to."

As he'd done before, she offered up the key. A portal opened. They met eyes, then stepped through, hand in hand.

Into hell.

As though in a quaking black dome, thunder like cannon fire shook the earth. He'd seen it in her dreams, but nothing could prepare him for the reality. Lightning slashed across the sky. All around them, Valkyrie shrieked and pried heads from vampires. Vampires ripped the throats out of any they could overpower.

He'd never seen a Horde vampire in person. They were worse than her dreams. Red-eyed, insane.

"I see them!" she yelled, starting for them in the valley below.

But he was aching to save a Valkyrie from a vampire twice her size who had beaten her down. Kaderin must have seen the look in his eyes. "I know, Bastian! But it won't change a single thing—except that you can die. Or we won't make it back to the door with them both."

He nodded. "I'm right behind you." He still traced and beheaded the vampire from behind. Kaderin frowned at him, but he knew she wasn't displeased. Then they hurried to the flatlands where her two sisters clashed with vampires, battling with long swords, blood splashing up their legs.

When Kaderin stopped and stared at them, swallowing, Sebastian recognized that they were similar versions of her, though one was taller and one shorter. And their coloring was different. One had reddish blond hair, while the other's was darker brown.

Kaderin's eyes were glinting, her breaths shallow. He curled his fingers under her chin, coaxing her to face him. "Let's get them back."

Kaderin nodded, caressing the side of her cheek against his fingers. Then she turned to them and called in their mother's tongue, "Rika, Dasha, come!"

They both looked to her, then back at the fray. "We cannot leave!"

"Come *now!*"

Rika's eyes widened at her command, and Dasha's narrowed, but they did hurry to her. Kaderin had to remember that she had been sweet to them, gentle with them—

Just before they reached each other, a vampire charged toward Kaderin. Sebastian met him, striking viciously, clearing the way for them.

When Kaderin stood before her sisters, at last, she couldn't find her voice. With a trembling hand, she reached out to cup Dasha's stubborn chin, then brush Rika's glossy dark hair from her eyes. "I-I missed you two so much," she finally managed to say as her tears began to fall.

"Missed us?" Dasha said. "When did you dress differently—and so *strangely*? And who's that male?"

"There's no time for that, Dash." Kaderin forced herself to be blunt. "The two of you die in this battle. In ten minutes, a vampire takes your heads. And it is my fault."

Dasha opened her mouth to interrupt her, but Kaderin

raised her hand. "We must make this fast. I live one thousand years in the future now, and I'm taking you forward to my time tonight. And I'm so sorry, but you're going to lose those years. Forever."

Without blinking an eye, ever-practical Dasha said, "Seems to me that they will be lost as well if we are dead."

Rika put her hands on her knees, bending over and coughing blood. "Kader-ie, I don't understand." She'd already been hurt worse than Kaderin had ever known. "How is this possible?"

"You know extraordinary things happen in the Lore—we've seen them before. We've experienced much stranger than this," Kaderin said. "You're just going to have to trust me now because if we don't get through a certain door, very quickly, I could cease to be."

"If we leave the battle, how could we show our faces again?" Dasha asked. "We'd be known as cowards. *You* could think us cowards."

"No," Kaderin said. "You would be remembered as dying valiantly in battle."

"No one would curse our names?" Dasha asked.

"Never, I vow it."

Dasha turned her attention to Sebastian. "And the man?"

"His name is Sebastian. I . . . I love him."

The sisters both tilted their heads, watching him fighting as bodies were piling up around him. He was outright glorious, powerful, everything any of them had ever dreamed of in a male.

And they had no idea they were ogling a vampire.

Dasha whistled. "There is much to love, sister."

Rika coughed more blood. "He is beautiful, Kader-ie."

She leaned on her sword, the ultimate sign of weakness—something one simply did not do if one could possibly prevent it. "Then take us forward. Another adventure."

Dasha remained unconvinced. "There's no peace in the future, is there? We still fight vampires?"

"Yes, there are still bad vampires to fight."

"*Bad* vampires? As if there exist good ones? How strangely you speak."

Rika stumbled. "I'm dizzy. Call for your man."

Kaderin dropped her sword and scooped her up. "Just a bit longer, sweet."

When all around Sebastian lay an assortment of dead vampires, he spotted the past Kaderin fighting.

And stared transfixed.

She wore a golden breastplate and carried her sword and a whip. Though injured, she continued to fight savagely, shrieking her fury and orders over the deafening thunder.

Pointing her sword, she directed bowswomen with their flaming arrows and witches with their spells, as they hurtled their strikes in bright trails at the enemy.

She had blood running from her temple and the corner of her lips, and her blond hair was braided for battle. Her eyes were silver. She was absently marking the vampires she'd killed.

He was awed. . . .

A massive vampire with a battle ax traced behind her. She hadn't sensed him in the melee. Sebastian tensed to trace—

"Bastian, no!" Kaderin screamed over the clamor from behind him. He turned, saw her handing the wounded sister into the other's arms. Kaderin ran for him. "I'll kill you!"

He finally let her lead him away, though it went against everything inside him to leave *her* here.

When they met the sisters at the doorway, Kaderin said, "And believe it or not, I get out of that scrape. He ended up wearing that ax as a hat all night."

Sebastian yanked her to him and kissed her, pride filling him. "You were magnificent."

"Were?"

"Are. Always will be."

"Bastian, we're going back." She gave him a watery grin.

They'd saved them. He had them all here and felt twenty feet tall.

Yet then he spied her sword glinting twenty feet away. "Your sword? I can get it—"

"Leave it, Bastian. It's not important anymore! We have to go!"

No, she loved that sword. He traced to it, snatched it up, and traced back to them.

The injured sister weakly screamed, "Vampyre!"

A blade slipped between his ribs.

41

─────❧❧❧❧─────

"Told you they'd try to kill you," Kaderin whispered with a quirked eyebrow. She'd begun rolling a bandage around Sebastian's torso, now that Rika had been tended to.

He rubbed his hand over the back of his neck as Dasha burned holes with her eyes. "I believe Dasha wishes she'd sunk the blade instead of Rika," he muttered. "And twisted it."

Kaderin knew she needed to separate Dasha and Sebastian, but she didn't want to let either of them out of her sight. Even as she bandaged him, she couldn't help glancing at her sisters—Rika lying pale on the couch, Dasha beginning to pace—as if they'd disappear.

Sebastian stroked her shoulder. "They're back with you," he murmured. "They're not going anywhere."

"I know. It's just so strange."

Rika and Dasha began speaking in a mixture of old tongues.

"What are they saying?" Sebastian asked.

"They think you have some kind of dark magic to make me want you. That undoubtedly I'm in thrall to you." Once Kaderin finished up with his bandage, she rose and said, "I'll just go put Rika in bed and talk with them in the back for a bit." *And explain again that all of us would be dead if not for him.*

She didn't miss that his eyes darkened. He thought she was already drawing away.

Perhaps that was the only thing she *could* do at this time.

She lifted Rika and motioned for Dasha to follow. Dasha did so—after casting Sebastian a savage look.

In the bedroom, Kaderin laid Rika in bed while Dasha resumed pacing. "You *knew* he was a vampire. And you still fell in love with him? He's fine, to be sure," Dasha added, moving from one foreign electronic object to another, tilting her head as she lifted a clock and then a stereo speaker. "But you risk his turning."

Kaderin sat on the bed beside Rika. "Myst's husband hasn't turned. It's only when a vampire kills as he drinks. So if he drinks an immortal who can't die like that, he'll be immune—"

Her expression aghast, Dasha snapped, "You are not saying that you and Myst offer yourselves up as food."

Kaderin bit her lip. "When you put it like that, it sounds worse—"

"How else can it be put?"

Rika coughed, a rattling, ugly sound. Then, in a faint voice, she asked, "Does he actually live with you here?"

When Kaderin nodded, Dasha said, "You pluck us out of a war with vampires, then expect us to live with one?"

Kaderin exhaled, not even bothering to explain the difference between Sebastian and other vampires again. How could they believe that so readily when it had taken Kaderin weeks to see it?

Dasha lifted a hair dryer and peered down the barrel. "And what in the hell is this?"

"It dries hair." Kaderin reached forward and flipped on the switch. Dasha gasped as she aimed it at herself, then at Rika in the bed, giving Rika a look that could only be described as indicating, "*Holy shit!*"

When Kaderin pried it from her hands and turned it off, Dasha went straight for the closet, commenting on the clothes and tossing items over her shoulder into a pile to be investigated later. "What happened to the vampire who killed us?" she asked over her shoulder.

In a toneless voice, Kaderin said, "I tortured him until he begged for the sun, and six months later, I gave him his wish."

Dasha stopped and turned, brows drawn, as Rika murmured, "*You* did that, Kader-ie?"

"I didn't take losing you two lightly." *And I won't take having you back with me for granted.*

Sebastian had known it was coming, of course. He'd known she would take her sisters and leave him.

"I need time. With them," Kaderin had told him the day after they'd brought the two forward. He'd dreaded it but wasn't surprised. "I've taken them to this future, and they are confused by everything. I have to concentrate on acclimating them. They are my responsibility now more than ever."

He'd been tempted simply to tell her no, and could almost convince himself that part of her had wanted him to do so as well. But she hadn't wanted to choose between him and her family, and he wouldn't put her in that position. Besides, he didn't feel it was merely an excuse—her sisters truly did need extensive help.

He'd thought *he'd* been behind the times.

Naturally, this future shocked them at every turn, but Sebastian had learned that their first instinct in confusing situations was to resort to violence. Kaderin was right to want to shelter them back among her coven in the Valkyrie's remote manor.

Plus, the two hated being anywhere near him. The mere sight of him tracing put Dasha into a rage and made Rika grow silent and grave—which was almost worse. They were constantly wary and wouldn't let down their guard when he was near, not even Rika, though she needed to sleep to heal.

So Kaderin had shepherded them back to the coven. Once she'd gone, he could do nothing but wait as each day he grew stronger in body but weaker in spirit.

"Does she ever ask about me?" he'd asked Myst after a week had passed.

"She's been busy, Sebastian," Myst had assured him. "Her sisters' English is what you might call 'olde,' and they continue to try to slay anything unfamiliar. Kaderin will come around once they're set."

Kaderin never asked about him. Never called for him. It was as if she were willing herself to forget him. Her sisters were likely reminding her of the strife with vampires, convincing her of her folly for being with him.

"Buy an estate near her coven," Nikolai had advised. "It will be a positive gesture to her and might occupy your mind."

"Do I have enough money to buy an estate? And to live comfortably, if I'm careful?"

"You had Byzantium gold among your riches," Nikolai had answered. "A chest of it."

"What does that mean?"

"That means you are obscenely rich. And Murdoch picked the investments. He has a knack."

Sebastian turned so that Nikolai couldn't see him flush. Both brothers had helped him, expecting nothing in return.

"Is Murdoch still living at the Forbearer castle?" He would go to his brother and thank him to his face.

Nikolai nodded. "Just yesterday, he uncovered some promising leads on Conrad and is impatient to follow them all, but he'll return to the castle each dawn. When you're settled with Kaderin, you can take her there to meet him if you like."

Sebastian looked forward not only to seeing Murdoch again, but also to joining in the hunt for Conrad. He wondered if Kaderin would search with him.

Sometimes Sebastian traced to her at Val Hall. From outside the wraiths' reach, he could see her through the windows as she danced with her sisters, throwing her head back with laughter, or played video games, with her face a mask of concentration. One night, he'd watched the three of them sitting on the roof, relaxed, shoulder to shoulder. When Kaderin had pointed out a star, the smallest one had laid her head on Kaderin's shoulder.

How different the stars must look to them now.

How could he compete with them for her love?

Kaderin's sisters were learning the times with her as their guide, but Kaderin was relearning life as well.

She'd found she could tear up at sad made-for-television movies and that she loved braiding Nïx's hair, now that it had regrown in mere weeks. She'd learned that Regin's antics could make her stomach hurt from laughing.

Regin delighted in making fun of Dasha and Rika's old English, though the two were learning the modern version with an astounding speed. "Their 'ye olde brew pub' style of talking creeps me out," Regin had said. "All that *thou*-ing and *thee*-ing like they're actors from a Shakespeare festival and won't go out of character." She'd drawn Kaderin aside. "I swear to the gods, Rika said 't'asn't.' What is that? No. Really."

When Kaderin had asked Regin if she was okay about her involvement with Sebastian, she'd answered, "If by 'okay' you mean 'homicidal,' then yes, absolutely." Then she'd added in a mutter, "Your leech gave us two new Valkyrie and brought you back from the dead. Because of his brother, Emmaline lives. If there existed a turn-off-millennia-of-hate switch, I might . . . squint at it." They'd left it at that.

The only thing that hindered Kaderin's happiness was missing Sebastian.

She knew he was watching the manor right now, looking out for her. He loved her. But this was a difficult time for her sisters, and with each of their missteps and confusion, Kaderin's guilt returned.

Still, Kaderin had begun waiting for the right time to tell them all of her decision. Until then, everyone needed to be understanding of them after all they'd been through.

Dasha and Rika needed to be treated with kid gloves and eased into this time.

"*Selfish girl,*" Myst snapped, shoving Dasha against the wall by her neck, holding her there. "You can't comprehend what Kaderin's gone through for so long. She deserves this happiness. You have no idea how much. And yet you both still sneer at the idea of her with a vampire."

Rika kicked Myst behind her knee, making her stumble and release Dasha.

Rubbing her neck, Dasha said, "It is easy for you to accept Kaderin with a vampire, since you have one as *your* man."

"It doesn't matter if it's easy or not," Myst said. "You simply have to accept it—for her. She has happiness within her grasp with a strong, honorable warrior who adores her, and you are standing in their way."

"Myst, we believe even *we* might come to tolerate her decision," Dasha said. "But you forget, we were on a battlefield with Furie less than two weeks ago. Her nature isn't dim in our minds, as it is in yours. When Furie is found, do you think she would possibly let either of your husbands live?"

Rika added, "Would Kaderin run with this man? Become a fugitive? We would never see her again."

Myst shook her head, though she had the same fears. "Let Kaderin determine this. Let her and Sebastian decide if they'll take that risk." She regarded both sisters. "Kaderin and Sebastian can't live without each other. Mark my words, both merely bide their time."

42

"If Kaderin didn't send for me herself," Sebastian said at the entrance to Val Hall, "then I don't want to be here." Lightning clattered constantly. Smoke and fog inundated the grounds. The old manor was imposing, sepulchral.

"You aren't curious about what you've been called here for?" Nikolai asked. "Even Myst has no idea what this is about."

"All I know is, *she* didn't send for me." Sebastian scowled up at the ghostly specters guarding the house, and Nikolai slapped his back in sympathy.

"They will not hurt you unless you try to get in without payment or permission."

"I'm not concerned with them." At Nikolai's questioning look, Sebastian shrugged. "After the things I saw in the Hie?"

"That's right, Nïx's origami storyboard. I need to ask her about that."

Sebastian said, "I was just thinking that if this is where Kaderin calls home, she will not like the estate I just purchased."

"You gave Myst carte blanche to pick it out—a bold and reckless move, but one I feel will serve you well with your Bride."

"Kaderin asked for time." Even missing her as he did, he still felt her request was reasonable. He expected eternity with her. Two weeks was nothing. "I am intruding on her and her sisters."

Just as he was about to trace, Nikolai grabbed his arm. "How long will you wait?"

"Until she calls for me."

"I don't think it would help your cause if you shun an invitation to their coven. It's, uh, very rare." Nikolai held up a lock of red hair Myst had given him in advance. A wraith swooped down, and their way was cleared.

Reluctantly, he followed Nikolai. Inside, Sebastian heard her voice in a nearby room.

"Now, this spear is a weapon of apocalyptic power," Kaderin was explaining. "You must use it wisely, Dash. To abuse it will bring ruin to our people."

"Let me see that," Dasha said.

"No! Push the red button on the *right*," Kaderin said. "Your *other* right, Dash!"

Video games. He grinned, even as he was saddened. He missed her too much—his chest was besieged with a constant ache, and now he understood what it was.

When he and Nikolai stood at the door, Nikolai gave him an encouraging slap on the back that would have felled lesser men, then traced away.

Sebastian saw her shoulders stiffen. "Bastian?" she murmured. Lightning struck just outside.

Kaderin heard his voice, his sure footsteps. *He's come for me*.

Her mind seemed to go blank. The yearning she'd felt for so long turned to excitement, excitement to urgency.

She'd been waiting for the right time to tell her sisters

she wanted to spend the rest of her life with him. That time was now.

If she wasn't touching him in seconds, she'd go mad.

She scrambled to her feet. She knew her sisters were eyeing her strangely, knew that what she was feeling was undisguised. Right then, she didn't care. She turned and ran for him. *Bastian!* Standing at the door, so tall and proud.

When he saw her, his lips parted, then he absently palmed the center of his chest.

As she hadn't slowed, he opened his arms—she knew what this meant—but she didn't hesitate to run into them, leaping up and latching onto him. They would have gone reeling if he weren't so strong.

The Valkyrie who'd flown down the stairs at the marked lightning saw her. All around them, she heard gasps. One muttered, "*She ran to his arms. I saw it.*"

"Bastian, I missed you!" Kaderin whispered.

"God, I missed you, too," he murmured, clutching her. She felt him stiffen, and knew Rika and Dasha had appeared behind her. He released her with obvious reluctance, but once on her feet, she only turned, keeping his front to her back.

Just when she thought there'd be a confrontation, Rika said, "Kader-ie, we have a thing we wish to tell thee—" She winced. "I mean *you*."

"What is it?" Kaderin asked, pulling Sebastian's arm around her. He tightened it immediately.

"We invited him," Dasha said.

Rika added, "And now we can see that it was a wise decision."

"What do you mean?" Kaderin asked, her voice unsteady.

Dasha answered, "You spent too many years blaming

yourself for our deaths and too much time without happiness. It must stop. It is time for you to be content."

"You deserve it more than anyone," said shy Rika. She approached Kaderin and Sebastian and addressed him. "We hate that vampire for what he did to Kader-ie, and to us." She frowned at that, then said, "But you are not that vampire. If you love Kad—"

"I do," he quickly said.

She squeezed his arm.

Dasha muttered, "Then be wed with our blessings."

"Rika? Dash?" Kaderin said in a breathless voice. "Are you in earnest?"

"Kader-ie, you need him. Even if we didn't support this, you'd go to him eventually. We understand that."

Kaderin turned to him, gazing up and nibbling her bottom lip. "Yes, I would have."

"You would?" he rasped, his eyes so dark.

"Of course, Bastian." She glanced over her shoulder and said to her sisters, "Thank you. I-I don't know what to say."

"Begone," Dasha said with a scowl. "This does not mean we wish to see you two in the agonies of love, or biting, or whatever it shall be. Rika and I have video battles to master and a driving lesson with Regin and Nïx when they return with Sad Wiener gum from the pack-a-sack."

When Rika grinned and nodded, Kaderin stood on tiptoes to whisper at his ear, *"Will you take me somewhere so I can kiss you?"*

He shuddered as he traced.

"Where are we?" she asked, not wanting to take her eyes from him even to glance around.

"Our new estate," he said, studying her reaction, so clearly wanting her to like it. "Close to Val Hall," he added, leaning down to brush his lips over her ear, his breaths warm and already quickened with need.

She didn't have to see it to know she would like it. Sebastian was here, and that was all she needed to know. "Oh, Bastian," she sighed, eyelids fluttering closed as she ran her fingers through his thick hair, "I think it's the best house I've ever been in. I'm sure."

After making love in the living room, in the dining room, on the stairs, and over a bench on the stair landing, they'd finally made it to the bedroom. Just as they'd settled under the rich damask covers, a telephone rang from across the room. Sebastian tensed at the sound, and Kaderin peeked out, frowning. Who could have gotten the number already?

His low growl when she strode naked to the phone made getting out of the bed worth it.

When she answered, Emma said, "Kaderin, is that you?" Her voice was panicked. "Myst told me I could get you here. Have you guys seen Bowen?"

"Since when, sweet?"

"Since he went to some fire snake thingy in the Hie."

Oh, crap. Kaderin sidled back to the bed. "Bastian, after you and Bowen had your . . . disagreement, what exactly happened?" That whole time was a haze for Kaderin. Everything paled next to Sebastian's sacrifice for her and her family. And she didn't relish thinking about the fact that she'd . . . died, boiling in lava. Kaderin had contemplated cheerier scenarios.

"The Lykae vowed, convincingly, that he'd kill me and you after he hunted us to the ends of the earth," Sebastian answered. "And also that he would 'eat my goddamned heart.'" He shrugged. "I left him there in that cave—on the other side of the lava pit. I figured there would be a way out of the back."

Kaderin hesitated, then told Emma, "He could possibly still be trapped behind a pit of boiling lava, guarded by a fire serpent."

Emma cried, "For two weeks? Can you please go get him? He's my husband's cousin and best friend!"

"Are we using your tranq gun or ours?" Kaderin asked. "Emma, he'll be in a killing rage after losing his mate—again."

"I know, but I'm just worried he might . . . he might take the opportunity to . . . you know."

"Okay, okay," Kaderin said, then turned to Sebastian. "Can we go get Bowen sometime tonight? She's worried he'll dive in after the loss."

"Which would be tragic." When Emma heard him and screeched, he grudgingly said, "No, he won't do that. He'll need to kill me first. Trust me, I know this." He exhaled. "We'll get him." He seized Kaderin around her waist and dragged her back under the covers with him. "After."

"After," Kaderin agreed eagerly. She told Emma, "We'll retrieve him at sunset. If he's still there. I'll let you know." She hung up and absently laid the phone on the bedside table, but turned when she brushed paper.

"What is it?" he asked.

"A note." It was folded in three and had a crimson wax seal stamped with a flourishing *R*. "From Riora?"

He peered over Kaderin's shoulder as she opened the letter. "Do we really want to read this?"

She shrugged helplessly. They both read:

It is perfectly impossible for you two to be excessively ecstatic together.

*Nor is it possible for both of you to have families made
whole.*

See you at the next Hie,
Riora, goddess of all and sundry soccer anthems

A key clanged out of the letter's bottom fold. Kaderin could
hear his heart speed up when he recognized it.

Another chance at the past. For Sebastian.

"Will it"—his voice dropped lower—"could it work?"

She faced him and nodded. "Yes, I believe so. You fascinated Riora. She would want to reward you."

He swallowed. "I won't do this lightly. I must talk with
Nikolai and Murdoch and, I hope, Conrad. We will decide
together how and when this will occur and prepare for it."

As Kaderin gingerly set the key and note aside, he asked,
"Would you be comfortable with this? With my family coming forward?"

"Like you were with mine? Of course! I'll support you in
anything you want to do. And I daresay your sisters will be
easier than Dash and Rika. They probably won't slay every
toaster they encounter."

The corners of his lips curled. "This is too incredible. I
can scarcely believe it."

"Just wait until you see them for the first time. It's a
pretty big shock."

He raised his hand to cradle her face. "My sisters would
like you."

She smiled back. "They *will* like me. And I them.
Though I think you should marry me first. So we're re-
spectable."

"I didn't believe this day could get better."

When he drew her under him, resting his hips between

her thighs, she gazed into his gray eyes, the color of enduring summer storms. "I love you, Bastian."

"I'll never tire of hearing that." He nuzzled her ear and rasped against it, "Maybe one day you'll come to love me as much as I do you."

She frowned and pushed up on his shoulders so they were facing each other. "I happen to adore you, vampire." Her hands laced around his neck, and she twined her fingers in his hair. "No, I'm absolutely certain I love you *more*."

He grinned down at her, that half-grin that made her heart twist, then slowly rocked forward to fill her. "*Tell yourself that, Valkyrie.*" He leaned down to catch her gasp with his lips. "*As much as you like.*"

From the Book of Lore

The Lore

"... and those sentient creatures that are not human shall be united in one stratum, coexisting with, yet secret from, man's."

The Valkyrie

"When a maiden warrior screams for courage as she dies in battle, Wóden and Freya heed her call. The two gods give up lightning to strike her, rescuing her to their hall, and preserving her courage forever in the form of the maiden's immortal Valkyrie daughter."

- Take sustenance from the electrical energy of the earth, sharing it in one collective power, and give it back with their emotions in the form of lightning.
- Possess preternatural strength and speed.
- Without training, they can be mesmerized by shining objects and jewels.
- Also called *Swan Maidens*, *Shield Maidens*.
- Enemies of the Horde.

The Vampires

- Two warring factions, the Vampire Horde and the Forbearer Army.

- Each vampire seeks his *Bride*, his eternal wife, and walks as the living dead until he finds her.
- A Bride will render his body fully alive, giving him breath and making his heart beat, a process known as *blooding*.
- *Tracing* is teleporting, the vampires' means of travel. A vampire can only trace to destinations he's been to before.

The Horde

"In the first chaos of the Lore, a brotherhood of vampires dominated, by relying on their cold nature, worship of logic, and absence of mercy. They sprang from the harsh steppes of Dacia and migrated to Russia, though some say a secret enclave, the Daci, live in Dacia still."

- Distinguished by their red eyes, a side effect of drinking victims to death.
- Enemies of most factions in the Lore.

The Forbearers

". . . his crown stolen, Kristoff, the rightful Horde king, stalked the battlefields of antiquity seeking the strongest, most valiant human warriors as they died, earning him the name of Gravewalker. He offered eternal life in exchange for eternal fealty to him and his growing army."

- An army of vampires consisting of turned humans, who do not drink blood directly from the flesh.
- Kristoff was raised as a human and then lived among them. He and his army know little of the Lore.
- Enemies of the Horde.

The Lykae Clan

"A proud, strapping warrior of the Keltoi People (or Hidden People, later known as Celts) was taken in his prime by a maddened wolf. The warrior rose from the dead, now an immortal, with the spirit of the beast latent within him. He displayed the wolf's traits: the need for touch, an intense loyalty to its kind, an animal craving for the delights of the flesh. Sometimes the beast rises . . ."

- Also called *werewolves, war-wolds.*
- Enemies of the Horde.

The Furiae

"If you do evil, beg for punishment—before they come . . ."

- Ruthless she-warriors bent on delivering justice to evil men when they escape it elsewhere.
- Led by Alecta the Unyielding One.
- Also called *Furies, Erinyes.*

The Berserkers

"A berserker's lonely life is filled with naught but battle rage and bloodlust . . ."

- A cadre of mortal warriors who swore allegiance to Wóden, known for their merciless brutality.
- One of the few human orders to be recognized and accepted by the Lore.
- Able to conjure the spirit of the bear, and channel its ferocity.

The Sirenae

"Near the sea's edge, beware the siren's song . . ."

- A female species of immortals, they can permanently mesmerize and enslave males who hear their singing.
- Derive power from the sea and can't be away from it for more than one cycle of the moon.

The Wraiths

". . . their origin unknown, their presence chilling."

- Spectral, howling beings. Undefeatable and, for the most part, uncontrollable.
- Also called *the Ancient Scourge*.

The Demonarchies

"The demons are as varied as the bands of man . . ."

- A collection of demon dynasties.
- Some kingdoms ally with the Horde.

The House of Witches

". . . immortal possessors of magickal talents, practitioners of good and evil."

- Mystical mercenaries who sell their spells.

The Kobolds

"When eyes are on them, winsome they seem. Eyes away, and you can't imagine what they become."

- Gnomelike creatures that dwell in mines. The name of the capricious and dangerous mined element cobalt is derived from this species.

The Ghouls
"Even immortals beware its bite . . ."

- Humans turned savage monsters, with glowing green skin, yellow eyes, and contagious bites and scratches.
- Their imperative is to increase their number by contagion.
- They're said to travel in *troops*.

The Turning
"Only through death can one become an 'other.'"

- Some beings, like the Lykae, vampires, and ghouls, can turn humans or even other Lore creatures into their kind through differing means, but the catalyst for change is always death, and success is not guaranteed.

The Talisman's Hie
"A treacherous and grueling scavenger hunt for magickal talismans, amulets, and other mystical riches over the entire world."

- Held every two hundred fifty years.
- Hosted by Riora, the goddess of impossibility.
- Won the last five times by the Valkyrie Kaderin the Cold Hearted.

The Accession

"And a time shall pass that all immortal beings in the Lore, from the strongest Valkyrie, vampire, and Lykae factions, to the phantoms, shifters, fairies, sirens . . . must fight and destroy each other."

- A kind of mystical checks-and-balances system for an ever-growing population of immortals.
- Occurs every five hundred years. Or right now . . .

Wicked Deeds on a Winter's Night

Kresley Cole

Turn the page for a preview of
Wicked Deeds on a Winter's Night. . . .

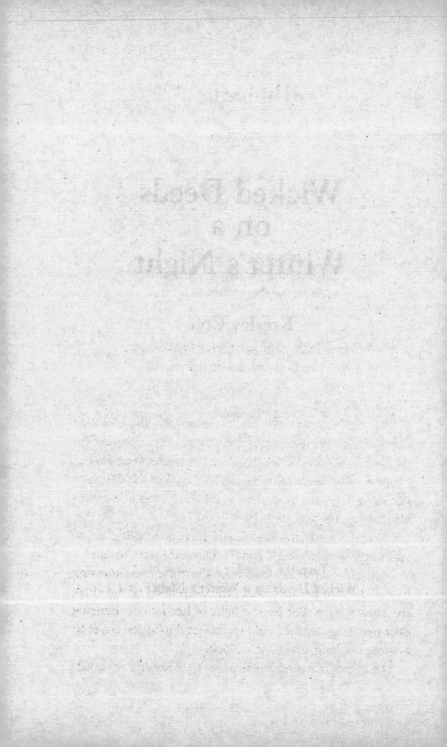

Prologue

❧

Six weeks ago . . .
Tomb of the Incubi, Guatemala
Day 3 of the Talisman's Hie

Prize: Four gold sacrificial headdresses,
each worth seven points

Stalking me, Mr. MacRieve?" Mariketa the Awaited asked the Lykae behind her without turning around. In the dark of a corridor leading to a burial chamber, Bowen MacRieve had been following her silently. But she'd *felt* him staring at her—just as she had at the Talisman's Hie assembly three nights ago.

"No' likely, witch." How could such a rumbling Scots' burr sound so menacing? "I only stalk what I want to catch."

Mari did turn to cast him a look at that, even knowing he couldn't see her face under the deep hood of the cloak she always wore. But by the light of her lantern hanging over her shoulder, she could see his, and used the cover to disguise her long, appreciative look.

She inwardly sighed. Lykae males were notoriously good-looking, and the few she'd seen had lived up to their reputation, but this one was heart-poundingly sexy.

He had black hair, stick straight and thick, reaching to the collar of his obviously expensive shirt. His body—which she'd found herself thinking about frequently over the past three days—was sublime. He stood a good bit over six feet tall, and though the corridor was wide enough for two normal people to pass, his broad shoulders and big rangy build filled the space.

But even with all his many attractions, his eyes were what made him so unique. They were the color of rich, warm amber, and yet there was a kind of sinister light to them, which she liked.

She was a little sinister, too.

"Look your fill?" he asked, his tone scathing. Yes, he was sexy, but, unfortunately, his dislike of witches was well known.

"I'm done with you," she answered, and meant it. She didn't have time to pine after brusque werewolf warriors if she planned to be the first of her kind ever to win the Hie. With an inward shrug, she continued on toward yet another burial chamber. This was the tenth she'd investigated over the hours she and several other competitors had spent deep inside this never-ending tomb.

She might have surprised him with her curt dismissal because a moment passed before he followed her. The only sounds in the echoing space were the heavy footfalls that he no longer bothered to muffle. The silence between them was grueling.

"Who opened this tomb?" he finally asked, trailing far too closely behind her.

"The three elven hunters and a couple of rage demons." Those two factions were expected to be among the top competitors in the Hie. The hunters, two males and a female, were deadly archers with lightning speed, and the male demons were physically powerful—second in strength only to the Lykae.

The stone portcullis sealing the tomb had weighed tons, and opening it had taken all of them cooperating—with the two demons lifting it and the hunters shoving a massive boulder under it to prop it open.

"And they just let you walk in after their effort?"

She stopped and faced him again. "What should they have done, Mr. MacRieve?" The others had not only allowed her to enter. Though she barely knew any of them, they had wanted to work together since there were four prizes. So they'd all split up to cover the dozens of chambers in this tomb and vowed to the Lore to alert the others of a find.

MacRieve's smile was a cruel twist of his lips. "I know exactly what I would have done."

Without hesitation, she said, "I know exactly how I would have retaliated." He seemed surprised that she didn't fear him, but the truth was that she didn't spook easily, and she was well aware of how vicious the Hie competitors could be as they raced around the world for prizes. Though killing was against the rules—at least until the final round—any other trickery or violence was encouraged.

This ruthlessness of the Hie was why *she* had been sent by the House of Witches to compete, even though she was only twenty-three—and even though she hailed from the shady New Orleans coven, the slacker Animal House of witches.

But Mari was not above trickery, and unlike many witches, she would not hesitate to use magick to harm another if they deserved it—and if she could manage it with her volatile powers.

MacRieve closed in until all six and a half feet of seething werewolf male loomed over her. He was at least a foot taller than she was and hundreds of times stronger, but she forced herself to stand her ground.

"Watch your step, little witch. You doona wish to anger one such as me."

The grand prize for the Hie was Thrane's Key, which allowed its possessor to go back in time. For a tool like that, she knew he was ready to take her out of the contest. So she had to convince him that it was impossible for him to do so.

"Likewise, you shouldn't anger me." Her voice was steady as she looked up at him. "Remember that I could turn your blood to acid as an afterthought," she said, baldly lying.

"Aye, I've heard rumors of your power." He narrowed his eyes. "Curious, though, that you dinna open the tomb with one flick of your finger."

Yes, she could have lifted the portcullis—with concentration, luck, and the absence of a hangover. Oh, and if she were in mortal danger.

Unfortunately, her magick was adrenaline-based, making it as great as it was uncontrollable.

"You think I should use magick like mine to open a tomb?" Mari scoffed. *Mistress of bluffing, working it here*. "That'd be like calling you in to lift a feather."

He tilted his head, sizing her up. After what seemed like an hour, he began walking again.

Mari gave an inward sigh of relief. If anyone in the Lore found out how vulnerable she really was, she'd be doomed. She knew this, but no matter how hard she worked, whenever she manifested and unleashed significant power, things ended up *exploding*.

As her befuddled mentor Aelianna explained, "Horses have powerful legs—but that doesn't mean they're talented ballerinas." Aelianna trained with Mari daily to control the destructive nature of her spells because she believed the subtle magicks invoked the most fear in their enemies.

And the House of Witches brokered in fear.

Plus it was difficult to get insurance when Mari kept blowing up the witches' houses. . . .

The corridor finally ended at a broad, high wall, covered in carvings of ghoulish faces and animals. She lifted her lantern high and the reliefs seemed to move in shadow. They'd apparently been put there to guard a small tunnel opening near the floor, which itself was made out like a gaping mouth with fangs dropping down.

She waved the Lykae forward. "Age before beauty, Mr. MacRieve." She sized him up again, then studied the small opening, which couldn't be more than three feet square. "If you think you can fit."

He stood motionless, clearly not about to be directed. "Only humans call me Mr. MacRieve."

She shrugged. "I'm not a human." Her mother was a fey druidess, and her late father had been a warlock of questionable repute. So Mari was a fey witch or a "weylock," as her buddies teased. "So would you like me to call you Bowen, Bowen?"

He ignored her comment. "You in the tunnel first."

"Don't you think it'd be unbecoming for me to be on my hands and knees in front of you? Besides, you don't need my lantern to see in the dark, and if you go first, you'll be sure to lose me and get to the prize first."

"I doona like anything, or anyone, at my back." He crossed his arms over his chest and leaned a shoulder against a snarling visage on the stone wall. She'd never seen a Lykae turn into its towering werewolf form, but knew from those who had that it could be as frightening as any monster, real or imagined. "And you'll have your cloak on," he continued, "so I will no' be able to see anything about you that might be . . . unbecoming."

"Twisting my words? I'll have you know that I am criminally cute—"

"Then why hide behind a cloak?"

"I'm not *hiding*." In fact, that was precisely what she was doing. "And I like to wear it." She *hated* it.

Even before her birth, she'd been predicted to be the Awaited One, the most powerful born to the House of Witches in centuries—but four years ago, it was also predicted that a male from the Lore would recognize her as his own and claim her. He would lock her away, guarding her with a ferocity that no magicks could defeat, thus robbing the House of her powers.

Ever since the prediction, she'd been forced to cover herself every single time she set foot outside of her home. Needless to say, the robust dating life of her late teens had taken a hit.

She sported the cloak, and as a backup she also hid behind a magickal glamour that disguised her looks, the tone of her voice, and her scent. If a male like Bowen did see her, he would perceive a brunette with blue eyes—when in fact she was a redhead with gray eyes—and he would have difficulty recalling anything that *was* the same, like her features, her figure, or the length of her hair. The glamour was so second-nature that she hardly thought about it anymore.

Even with all these precautions, it followed that unattached males in the Lore were to be avoided at all costs. Yet Mari had heard at the assembly—a gossip fest if she'd ever seen one—that Bowen had already found his mate and lost her more than a century ago.

Mari had felt sympathy for him. A Lykae's entire existence centered on his mate, and in his long immortal life, he would only get one—just one chance in an eternity to find happiness. It could be argued that Bowen was actually safe for her to be around since she wasn't his mate. Though "safe" was *not* how she'd describe him otherwise.

When she saw he wasn't budging, she muttered, "Fine. Beauty before age." She unlooped her lantern strap and climbed in. The space was tighter than she'd imagined, but she didn't have time to rethink her decision because he climbed in directly after her. Resigned, she exhaled and held the lantern up to light her way.

The stone was cool and moist and she was glad for her cloak—until she caught her knee on it and the tie around her neck yanked her head down. When it happened again, she shimmied, working the material back so that it flowed behind her as she made progress forward. *There. Better.*

Five seconds later: "MacRieve, you're on my cloak. Let up—"

Before she could even react, he reached between her knees and then up against her chest to slice the tie at her neck with one claw. Her eyes went wide and she dropped her light to grab fistfuls of cloth, but he jerked the cloak out of her grasp.

"Give it back!"

"It was slowing you—and therefore me—down."

She gritted her teeth, struggling to control her temper. "If *you* had gone first—"

"I dinna. If you want it, why no' use magick to take it from me?"

Did he suspect how volatile her power was? Was he sussing out her weaknesses? "You really do not want me to do that."

"You really must no' want your cloak back. Come then, witchling, just take it from me."

Glamour or not, she had grown used to the physical security of the garment. And when she realized she wasn't getting it back from him without magick, Mari just stifled the urge to rub her bared arms. Suddenly she became very aware of how high her hiking shorts were on her thighs and how her tank top was riding up, about to reveal the mark on her lower back.

She steeled herself and made her tone nonchalant. "Keep the cloak." Though she knew he was ogling her, she forced herself to put one knee in front of the other. "It'll be worth money one day."

After a few moments, he said, "Doona fret, witch. You're no' so unbecoming from my angle. Bit scrawny where it counts, but no' *too* bad."

Yep, ogling. Many adjectives could be used to describe her ass, but scrawny was not among them. *He's just making these comments and brushing up against you to unnerve you.* Knowing that didn't make his efforts less effective! "Scrawny where it counts, MacRieve? Funny, I'd heard the same about you."

He gave a kind of humorless half-chuckle and finally followed. "No' likely. Maybe you're just too young to have heard the rumors about Lykae males. Tender young ears and such."

No, she'd heard. And over the last couple of days, she had wondered about that rumor and if it applied to him.

How long was this damned tunnel—

"*Still, lass,*" he grated. Her eyes widened again when she felt his hot palm lying flat against the back of her thigh. "There's a scorpion tangled up in all that hair of yours."

"Get your hand off of me, MacRieve! You think I can't see what you're doing? I've been scanning every inch of this tunnel—I would have seen a scorpion." When she started again, he squeezed her leg. His thumb claw pressed against her skin, high on her inner thigh, sending an unexpected shot of pleasure through her. She had to stifle a shiver.

It was only after she felt a whisper of touch over her hair that she got her wits again. "Like I'm supposed to believe there's a scorpion and it just happens to be in the tunnel we're crawling in and then in my hair? Any other B movie props you'd like to reference? Is there a mummy's hand tangled up in there? I'm really surprised you didn't go with 'classic tarantula.'"

His arm shot out between her legs—again—jostling against the front of her body as he tossed something in front of her. Something with *mass*. She held her lantern farther forward—

The sight of a scorpion as big as her hand had her scrambling back . . . wedging herself firmly against MacRieve—in a very awkward position to be in with anyone, but especially with a werewolf.

He stiffened all around her. Every inch of him. She felt his arms bulging over her shoulders and his chiseled abs taut over her back.

His growing erection strained thick against her backside. *So the rumors about werewolf males are true*, she thought dazedly. *Exhibit* A.

"*Move forward*," he grated. He was breathing heavily right over her ear.

"No way. Kind of between a scorpion and a hard place here." She bit her lip, wishing one of her friends had heard her say that.

He eased back from her. "I killed the scorpion," he said between breaths. "You can pass, just doona let it touch you."

"Why do you care?" She frowned to find herself feeling chilled without him over her.

"Doona. A sting will slow you down. And I'm behind you, remember?"

"Like I'm going to forget that anytime soon." Then his callous words sank in. "Hey, werewolf, aren't you supposed to gnaw on your prey or play with it with shuffling paws or something? Want me to save it for you?"

"I could put it back where I found it, witch."

"I could turn you into a toad." Maybe an exploded toad.

Without warning, he fingered the small, black tattoo on her lower back. "What does this script mean?"

She did gasp then, as much from the shock of his touch there as from her visceral reaction to it. She wanted to arch up to his hand and couldn't understand why. She snapped, "*Are you done groping me?*"

"Canna say. Tell me what the marking means."

Mari had no idea. She'd had it ever since she could remember. All she knew was that her mother used to write out that mysterious lettering in all of her correspondence. Or at least, her mother had before she'd abandoned Mari in New Orleans to go on her two-hundred-year-long druid sabbatical—

He tapped her there, impatiently awaiting an answer.

"It means *drunk and lost a bet*. Now, keep your hands to yourself unless you want to be an amphibian." When the opening appeared ahead, she crawled heedlessly for it and scrambled out with her lantern swinging wildly. She'd taken only three steps into the new chamber before he caught her wrist, spinning her around.

As his gaze raked over her, he reached forward and pulled a lock of her long hair over her shoulder. He seemed unaware that he was slowly rubbing his thumb over the curl. "No' a damn thing's wrong with you," he murmured. "But you look a little fey. Explains the name."

"How can I resist these suave compliments?" He was right about the name though. Many of the fey had names beginning in Mari or Kari.

She gave his light hold on her hair a pointed look, and he dropped it like it was hot, then scowled at her as if she were to blame.

"Right now you're working your spells, are you no'?" He actually leaned in to *scent* her.

"No, not at all. *Believe me*, you'd know."

As if he hadn't heard her, he continued, "Aye, you are." His expression was growing more savage by the second. "Just as you were born to do."

But for some reason, she wasn't afraid. She was . . . excited. As much as she could ever remember being. He must have seen something in her eyes that he didn't like, because he abruptly turned from her.

As he surveyed their surroundings, she studied him. That night at the assembly, he'd fought a vampire in a bloody, violent brawl, and never had Mari seen anything so beautiful as the way he'd moved. The fight had been broken up, but Mari could have watched him for hours—

When MacRieve visibly tensed, she followed his gaze. There, toward the back wall, was a sarcophagus, the first she'd seen.

They both raced forward, colliding right before it.

With a growl he grabbed her arms to toss her away, his gaze already back on the crypt, but then he did a double take, frowning at her. He faced her fully as his grip eased on her. "You actually think to play with me?" His hands skimmed down her arms, then rested on her hips.

She exhaled a shaky breath. "Why do you assume I'm working spells?" She might have the requisite adrenaline flowing, but doubted she could focus it. Especially since she could feel the heat of his rough hands through the material of her shorts.

"For one hundred and eighty years I've no' touched another." He leaned in closer to her. "Have never even given a woman a second look. And it was *easy* to do so. But now I canna seem to keep my hands off a slip of a *witch*," he rasped at her ear. "A witch who has me feeling like I'll die if I doona find out what it'd be like to kiss her." He drew back, his face a mask of rage. "*O' course it's a goddamned spell.*"

He wanted to kiss her? Why now? He'd been faithful to his dead mate all this time? The idea softened something inside her—even as alarm trickled in.

What if she *was* working a spell? Aelianna had once advised Mari to be careful what she wished for. When Mari had nodded at the old truism, Aelianna had added, "No. Really. Be careful. We don't know the extent of your powers, and many witches can effect their desires with a mere thought."

Did Mari want to kiss Bowen MacRieve so badly that she was enthralling him?

When he lifted her onto the sarcophagus and wedged his hips between her legs, she suspected she might be. She swallowed. "I take it you plan to find out what it'd be like?"

The battle raging inside him was clear on his face. "*Stop this, Mariketa.*" The way he rasped her name with his accent made her melt. He removed his hands from her, but when he rested them on each side of her hips, his claws dug into the stone. "Can you no' ken why I'm in this contest? I seek *her* again and wish to be true."

He wanted his mate back. Of course. He wanted to use Thrane's Key to go back in time and prevent her death. Mari suddenly resented the woman who'd engendered such loyalty in this warrior for so many years. "I'm not . . . or I don't mean to be doing anything . . . to you," Mari whispered, but the way she was reacting to his scent, his mesmerizing eyes, and his hard body between her legs belied the words.

There was an aura about him that was staggering to her, making it difficult to think. It wasn't mere male heat and sensuality. It was raw sexuality, animalistic in its intensity— and she was starving for it.

Ah, gods, she *did* want him to kiss her. Wanted it with everything that she was, and willed him to do so.

He cupped her nape hard, staring down at her. He seemed desperate to recognize something in her, and when he clearly didn't find it, his hand on her began to shake. "Damn you, witch, *I doona want another.*"

She suddenly knew two things: He was about to kiss her so fiercely she would never be the same again.

And he would hate himself for it afterward and despise her forever. . . .

SIMON &
SCHUSTER

Kresley Cole

Dreams of a Dark Warrior

A millennium ago, northman Aidan the Fierce lost his heart
to the Valkyrie Regin the Radiant, but he was murdered
before they could wed. Since then, he has been reborn again
and again into different bodies, with no memory of the past,
only an endless yearning . . .

This time Aidan has returned as the brutal Declan Chase, a
human soldier bent on exterminating all immortals –
including Regin, the newest captive in his supernatural
prison.

To save herself, can Regin rekindle the memories of the
passion they shared, knowing that history willrepeat itself,
and he'll be lost to her once more?

ISBN 978-1-84983-038-6
PRICE £6.99